I0695157

THE LACQUERED TALISMAN

紅漆護符

THE GREAT MING HOUSE OF ZHU

VOLUME ONE

Laurie Dennis

The Lacquered Talisman

By Laurie Dennis

ISBN-13: 978-988-8552-46-7

This book has been reset in 10pt Book Antiqua. Spellings and punctuations are left as in the original edition.

FICTION / Historical

EB123

Published by Earnshaw Books Ltd. (Hong Kong)

This book is dedicated to my mother,
Martha Harris,
who traveled with me to Ming sites in China,
read and commented on all my drafts, and
ceaselessly infused me with Marthamism
(the highest form of optimism) about my
ability to tell Zhu Yuanzhang's story.

A Note on Chinese Romanization

THIS BOOK uses the Hanyu Pinyin romanization system for transliterating Chinese characters, with the exception of the word "Yangtze," which has a standardized spelling in English (in pinyin it would be "Yangzi"). This system means that readers will encounter Daoist monks (as opposed to Taoist), and Chan Buddhism (as opposed to Zen, a Japanese spelling of the same Chinese character). However, romanization is problematic for the pinyin spelling of "doufu" (known as "tofu" in Japanese), so I use the English term "bean curd." I could not avoid the pinyin spelling of "Song" for the character used as the name of a key Chinese dynasty, the surname of Chancellor Song Lian, and for Song Mountain in Henan Province – those unfamiliar with the Chinese language will have to try to look past the musical meaning of this word in English, and use a long Chinese "oh" sound when "Song" appears in the text as a proper noun.

I have devised English names for a few key locales: Ferry Village for Jinli Zhen (津里鎮), Lone Hamlet for Gucunzhuang (孤村莊), Bell County for Zhongli Xian (鐘離縣), and Tiger Empress Temple for Wuhuang Si (於皇寺, which uses an old Chu Kingdom word for tiger that is spelled "wutu" in pinyin). I chose this method in hopes that the locales would be easier to remember for the reader who is unfamiliar with Chinese. In a few instances, I have also used English when the translation is straightforward: for example, Yellow River instead of Huang River (黄河), and Rooster Mountain instead of Jigong Shan (雞公山).

Chinese and English are not interchangeable languages. It is best to learn both. I have devoted much of my life to these two languages, and it has proven time well spent. As the saying goes: 熟能生巧 (practice makes perfect)!

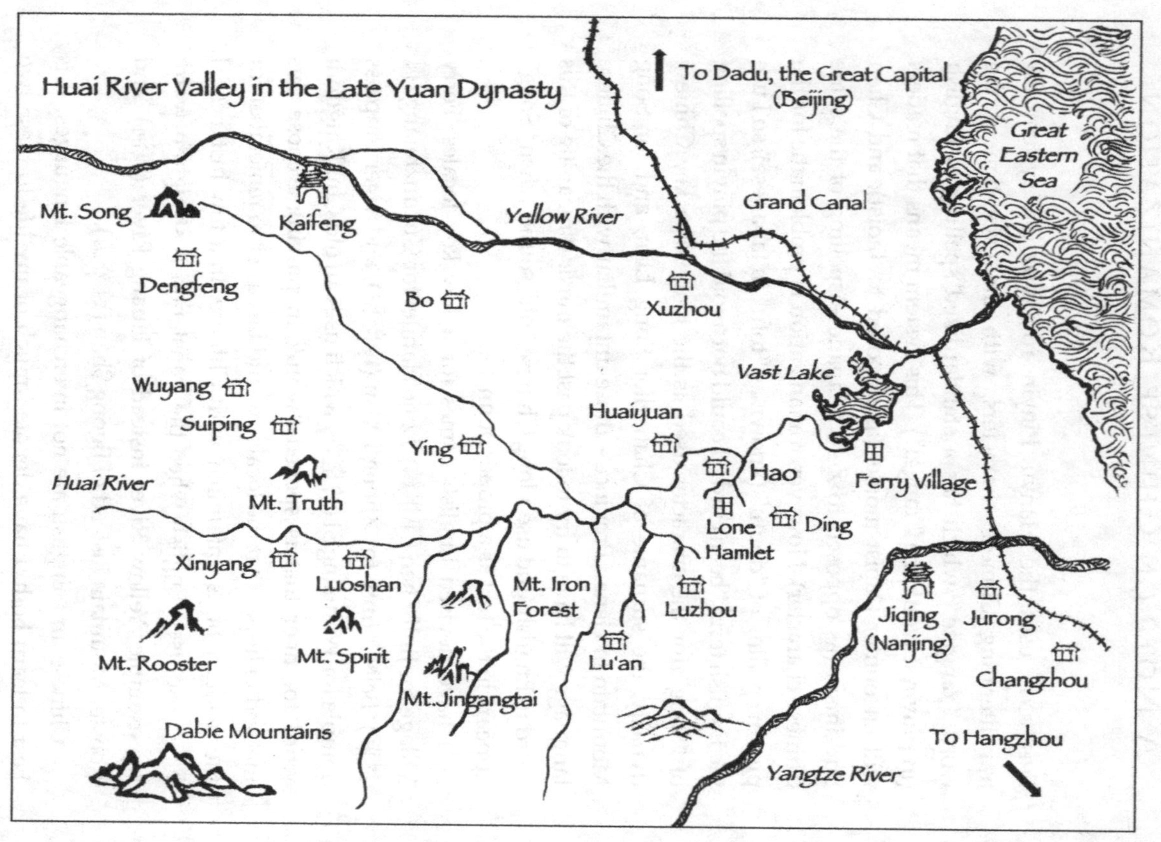

Huai River Valley in the Late Yuan Dynasty
To Dadu, the Great Capital (Beijing)
Great Eastern Sea
Mt. Song
Kaifeng
Yellow River
Grand Canal
Dengfeng
Bo
Xuzhou
Vast Lake
Wuyang
Suiping
Huaiyuan
Ying
Hao
Ferry Village
Huai River
Mt. Truth
Lone Hamlet
Ding
Xinyang
Luoshan
Mt. Iron Forest
Luzhou
Mt. Rooster
Mt. Spirit
Lu'an
Jiqing (Nanjing)
Jurong
Mt. Jingangtai
Changzhou
Dabie Mountains
To Hangzhou
Yangtze River

CONTENTS

家貧出孝子，世亂出英雄
From the poorest of families emerges the filial son;
From the worst of times emerges the hero.

—A Ming Dynasty saying

Prologue

THE IMPERIAL TOMB TABLET OF
THE GREAT MING

The year is 1375, according to the Western Calendar. The eighth year of the Ming Dynasty. The outskirts of Fengyang, a new city being built beside the Huai River in today's Anhui Province.

"When my imperial father was fifty, he moved to the east side of Bell County, where I was born," the official recited. He had been chosen for the quality of his voice, and he spoke each character clearly and beautifully, moving his eyes along the text cut into a stone tablet so large that the official had to stand on a stool to be able see the top of each line.

Everyone in the small gathering of a dozen or so officials glanced at the emperor, to see if he approved.

The emperor nodded his assent.

"Ten years later, we moved again, to the west side of Bell County."

Another nod.

The emperor knew the text perfectly well, because it was the story of his imperial life. Now he wanted to hear it recited. Seven years had passed since the founding of the Ming Dynasty, when he had assigned the writing of this narrative to a court historian.

He wanted to make sure it still sounded satisfactory. So, as part of his tour of the tomb complex where his family was buried, and which was still under construction, the emperor called for a public reading of the Imperial Tomb Tablet. Mounted on the back of a formidable stone tortoise, the tablet was placed at the center of the tomb complex, situated directly in front of the imperial grave mound and reached by a long and stately "spirit way" lined with statues of beasts, warriors and officials.

"In the Jiashen year, the Imperial Father and Mother both passed away."

After a tense silence, the emperor closed his eyes and nodded slightly.

"At that time, the family was very poor, and had no place set aside for burials..."

The emperor rose to his feet.

"Is that all it says about that terrible year?"

The reciter froze. No one dared reply.

"It should say that calamities gripped the land and my family met with disaster," the emperor exclaimed.

He stepped closer to the tablet.

The reciter jumped from his stool and moved aside. The entourage of court officials, local leaders and construction tour guides pressed in, murmuring nervously and peering up at the tablet text.

"Stand back," the emperor commanded, waving his long silk sleeve at them. "Go wait for me over there, on the other side of the bridge."

The emperor turned his back to them. He was a large, imposing man, his hair graying at the temples. He clasped his hands behind his back and stared up at the massive tablet, which was more than twice his size. Jasmine bloomed from an array of tastefully displayed ceramic pots, the scent wafting in the morning breeze. It was early spring, the start of what promised to be a lovely day.

"It was this time of year, but much hotter, when my parents and brother died," he thought, and turned to gaze at their burial place in the distance. "I remember talking about all the deaths with the court historian. A learned man. But I don't think I mentioned how hot it was that spring."

The historian had served the previous dynasty, the Mongols, the house of Khubilai Khan. When the wars ended, the historian was in a group of officials who had come to the new capital to offer their services to the new Ming Dynasty. It was pointed out that among the duties of a conquering dynasty was compiling and maintaining the previous dynasty's annals.

"He was such a respected writer," the emperor silently recalled. "I thought he would be the best person to write my story. So many officials were speaking beautiful words to me then, and so many decisions had to be made right away — everything was rushed."

The longer he reviewed the columns of words, the deeper the emperor's discontent. He paced in front of the tablet, stopping to contemplate the burial site one final time. Turning to his ministers, he made his decision.

"This tablet is to be taken down and destroyed," he declared.

The ministers all knelt and bowed their heads. The emperor ran his eyes across the tops of their elegant hats and noted the fine silk of their robes. He doubted such men as these could herd goats or sow millet. They could never imagine biting into tree bark or clay to ward off starvation.

"How could they ever understand a story like mine?" he wondered to himself. "That's why I didn't bother to speak of such matters with the court historian."

He looked down at the even finer embroidered yellow

brocade of his own robes, and he laughed. How could he ever explain to his ancestors how it had come to this?

"You may rise," he said aloud to his ministers.

He gestured for his secretary to take notes. "This tablet spends too much time on the glories, and not enough on the bitterness. This is not the fault of the author. He wrote what I asked him to write at the time of the founding, but this text will no longer suffice. Mine is not a story for a court scholar to interpret; it should come directly from the brush of a filial son. I myself will write the new text, which will be erected on this spot to instruct future generations."

Returning to the capital, the emperor cut short court sessions and canceled audiences so that he could devote precious hours to his writing. He spent as much time as he could alone in his writing chamber, thinking about his family and his youth. Sometimes he ran his fingers through his hair, reaching for the row of "incense scars" on the top of his head, the mark of an ordained Buddhist monk. This was when he reflected on all that he had learned during his years in temple sanctuaries and his wanderings with an alms bowl. However, he mostly recalled his family, his uncle and his father and their eight sons, the eight boys in the Chong generation.

"And I am the eighth and final Chong."

His story would be the words that his descendants would read forever. The revised tablet would resume its place in full view of his family graves, which meant the text would attract the wrath of his family's spirits if his description proved inadequate or boastful or disrespectful.

The emperor sighed deeply. He selected the appropriate calligraphy brush, unrolled a blank piece of paper and secured it with bronze weights. Grinding his gilded ink stick into water, he thought of his maternal grandfather, a fortune teller who knew how to write Daoist charms to ward off illness or dispel evil. Charm writing is meant to summon the gods and so is not like regular writing. It brought a smile to the emperor's face to recall how proud he had been to assist his grandfather in preparing charms, and how eagerly the recipients had reached for the finished paper squares. The emperor nodded his head, inspired by such a lucky childhood memory.

He dipped the tip of his brush into the black ink and started to write.

THE LACQUERED TALISMAN

PART ONE

FORTUNE
朱重八

如璞玉渾金，人皆欽其寶，莫知名其器

"He is like uncut jade or unrefined gold. Everyone admires his worth but no one knows the shape he will take." —Description of the sage Shen Tao in fifth-century author Liu Yiqing's *A New Account of Tales of the World*

1

MASTER CHEN FIGHTS AT YASHAN

The late 1200s, according to the Western Calendar, during the reign of Khubilai Khan. Jurong County, in modern Jiangsu Province.

THE RULING MONGOLS assigned the Zhu clan from Jurong County, south of the Yangtze River, to be a gold-panning household. This was unfortunate, because the streams trickling down Precious Mountain, upon which the Zhu family lived, offered nothing but grit and pebbles. But the fact that the gold was not there did not mean the gold quota was reduced. It meant the Zhus had to go to the market at tax collection time and trade their pitiful belongings for the requisite gold dust, to avoid penalties and punishment. Old Zhu, himself the oldest of four sons, decided to break from this impossible situation by leaving his brothers, parents, uncles, aunts, cousins and even the graves of his ancestors. He took his wife and two young sons and fled the tax collectors by heading north, crossing the Yangtze River and not stopping until he reached the Huai River. Old Zhu settled in Ferry Village, on the south bank of the Huai, where he opened a bean curd shop, arranged marriages for his boys, and lived long enough to welcome into this world all but the eighth — the last and most remarkable — of his grandsons.

Old Zhu's two sons were known as Fifty-one and Fifty-four.

They were named for the combined ages of their parents at the time of their birth, which was the local custom. Of course, the family hardly used these number names among themselves, addressing each other instead according to birth order. "Come here, second son," Old Zhu might say while beckoning to Fifty-four. "Elder brother, why must I always fetch the water?" Fifty-four might ask of Fifty-one.

After moving to Ferry Village, Old Zhu joined the circle of men who enjoyed drinking bowls of warmed wine with Master Chen, the eccentric but respected local fortune teller. These were long evenings, ending inevitably in tearful sorrow over the loss of the Middle Kingdom to the Mongol invaders — no matter that four decades had passed since the Mongols founded their Yuan Dynasty.

"My father once took me down the Grand Canal," Old Zhu reminisced one night when just he and Master Chen remained drinking in the local tavern. "We stopped at Changzhou and there, outside the city's eastern gate, we saw the towering mound that holds the bones of the women and children massacred by that butcher, General Bayan. His Mongol soldiers piled up hundreds, maybe thousands, of bodies like bricks for all to see. They eventually tossed some dirt over them, but that's no proper burial. The mound is higher than the city gates, which stand two stories high!" The two men sighed and shook their heads.

Once Master Chen established that the Zhu patriarch had the correct attitude toward the Mongols, he was amenable toward allying the Chen and Zhu houses through marriage ties. Master Chen had two daughters, but lacked sons. This was a point of merriment among the tavern drinkers, and Old Zhu was first introduced to Master Chen, as "the man with two sons for your two daughters." Master Chen's oldest was already promised to another family, but the youngest, Second Daughter, was the lustrous pearl in the palm of her father's hand, and he had not found a match worthy of her. Second Daughter had the Chen clan's square chin and prominent eyes. With her hair tied up in adorable little buns, a lucky red dot painted on her forehead, she was a delight.

The political attitudes of a potential family for his beloved youngest daughter mattered, because as a young man, Master Chen had fought on the side of the defeated Chinese armies and was in the final battle at Yashan where all was lost forever.

"Is it true that you fought at Yashan?" Old Zhu asked Master Chen on another occasion, this time as they walked home after a game of cards.

"Mmmm."

"But that battle was far, far to the south. How did you end up in such a place?"

"Because General Zhang was a man of the Huai River Valley."

Old Zhu frowned. "And so you joined his army?"

"Mmmm."

"At Yashan?"

"No, no," said Master Chen, shaking his head. "When I was a boy, everyone in my village was terrified of the Mongols. But at first, I was not sure what a Mongol was. The way my parents spoke of them, I thought they were demons. Later I realized the Mongols were the soldiers heading down to invade us from the north. Everyone told tales of what they would do to our village if they ever reached us, about how they would make pudding out of our eyeballs and sacrifice all of the village babies to their wolf gods. So when my friends and I heard that General Zhang, who was from my county, needed more soldiers to stop the invasion, we left home and headed south to join his army."

It was a warm night and the two men were in no hurry. Master Chen pointed toward the path that led to Vast Lake and Old Zhu, his hands clasped behind his back, nodded in agreement. The pair strolled side by side toward the lakeshore.

"So you wanted to join the army," Old Zhu prodded.

"Yes. But after the siege of Xiangyang, Khubilai Khan's army ignored the Huai River Valley and instead headed down the Yangtze, aiming for the prize of Hangzhou," continued Master Chen, pointing outward to illustrate the drive for the capital of the Song Dynasty. "My friends and I were new soldiers and we had joined General Zhang to fight the Mongols so we thought we were finally going to get to take our revenge on them. As you well know, when the emperor died, the Empress Dowager put the oldest of the three young princes on the throne —"

"But then she surrendered to the Mongols," objected Old Zhu.

"Yes, but she handed the two youngest princes to General Zhang and told him to flee for the South."

"And you went with him?"

"Yes, we were the army of the loyalists."

Old Zhu stopped short and gasped. "You were a true Song Dynasty loyalist," he stated, his tone reverential. "I heard someone saying that at the wine shop, but I did not realize you fought to the end." He took a step back, his eyes wide.

Master Chen stopped too, and warded off a wave of veneration with a wistful smile and a gesture that they should keep walking.

"It was not like that," he said. "I was too young then to know what it meant to be a Song loyalist. Really, I was only a few years older than those boy heirs. None of us knew what we were doing. We were all just following orders."

The pair made their way in silence until they reached the lake and stood watching the waves rock the moored fishing boats.

Old Zhu glanced at Chen, "Did you ever see them, the princes?"

"Oh, we all did. The oldest brother became sick and soon died — he was one of many who perished during those miserable months of fighting and retreating. But everyone attended the ceremony to enthrone little Prince Bing. He was only six years old when he was named emperor."

"The doomed boy," lamented Old Zhu.

"The last emperor of the Song."

The two fell silent yet again. Master Chen stared intently at the expanse of water, his eyes seeing not the little fishing boats on Vast Lake, but rather a vision of the great warships of the Song army, amassed around Yashan Island in the southern sea. "We were backed up against what seemed like the edge of the world," murmured Master Chen.

"Eh?" Old Zhu asked.

"The Mongol ships appeared one day on the horizon," Master Chen went on, lost in his memories. "By then it was a naval battle and we had all become sailors. We expected a frontal attack and a short battle and we knew that we outnumbered the Mongols. General Zhang evacuated Yashan, so everyone, even the women and children, boarded ships. We lashed our front warships together to form an impenetrable bulwark. I tied huge mats of woven bamboo to the sides of our ship."

"What was the purpose of that?" interrupted Old Zhu.

"To guard against the fire arrows of the Mongol archers," Master Chen explained. "The burning mats could be untied and dropped into the sea. Anyway, the young emperor and his top advisors were on the imperial ship, safely tucked behind our line but visible to us all as a source of inspiration. At first the Mongols did nothing. We could only wait for the order to fight, but it did not come. Then one morning we woke to a blanket of mist and rain showers, which we all knew was a dreadful portent. When a corner of fog lifted, there were shouts and drumming because some of the Mongol ships had taken advantage of the tide coming in to swing around behind us and attack."

"Where were you?"

"I was on a large vessel near the center of the front line," Master Chen answered. "I remember flaming missiles lighting the sky and masts splintering and billows of black smoke and men screaming. The Mongols did not have many ships, but they could maneuver what they had much better than we could, so it turned out to be an even fight. Toward the end, a huge smoking fireball ripped through the vessel tied to ours and set it burning, threatening our own ship, so we had to cut it loose. While I was hacking at the rigging, a lone survivor staggered out toward us, but before he could be rescued his armor burst into flames and he fell into the water below."

Master Chen stopped then and wiped his mouth slowly with the back of his hand. He sucked in his breath and pointed upward, frightening Old Zhu, who also jerked his head back to stare at the starry sky.

"Then the last archer in a cage at the top of one of our ship masts was killed and he fell to our deck." Master Chen slashed his arm down and now both men stared at the weedy sand and gravel at their feet. "My commander strode over and threw the dead sailor's bow toward us. The bow skidded and stopped at my feet. I could hear the order to replace the archer, but I couldn't believe it, even as I was reaching down to pick up the bow. I ran my eyes along the length of the exposed rope ladder leading to the mast cage. It was certain death. My commander kicked me toward the mast ladder and the other sailors all tossed me their spare arrows. My hands were shaking so hard that I could not curl my fingers around the ladder rungs." Master Chen gazed at his hands, distractedly opening and closing them.

"And then what?"

"That's when my commander pulled out his sword. He swore he'd slice me in two if I didn't move faster, but I still could hardly get my feet and hands to make their way up those swaying ropes. Then suddenly there was no sound and I felt like I was all alone and I realized I was halfway up the ladder. I couldn't understand how I could still be alive. That's when I saw the most terrible sight of all."

Master Chen gulped hard and squeezed his eyes shut, shaking his head against the memory.

Old Zhu leaned toward him. "What, what did you see?"

"The fight was almost over," Master Chen continued. "Many of the ships down the Song line were sinking or had lowered their banners in surrender. We all knew this marked the end of the Great Song Dynasty. However, the Song loyalists — the ministers and the court ladies and their children on the protected interior ships — refused to surrender, even in this final defeat. So they started climbing over the railings and jumping into the sea. The martyrs were all moving slowly and calmly, making death shouts of Song allegiance as they fell. The sight was so shocking that even the Mongol sailors stopped to watch."

"And where was the boy emperor at that point?" asked Old Zhu.

Master Chen held up his palm, indicating that his friend should be patient. "I heard General Zhang call for the warning fire to be lit, and we all knew that that was the signal to the emperor that all was lost. Martyrs kept dropping into the ocean. I continued to hang from my ladder, my back exposed, staring at the imperial ship. I could just make out the yellow-robed boy emperor, who was leading a procession to his own ship rail. The boy held out his arms so that the golden seals of his royal station could be strapped around his waist. An elderly official, who I knew must be the esteemed Counselor Lu, bowed repeatedly to the boy and then crouched down. The emperor walked behind the counselor and reached around the old man's neck, clinging to his back as the counselor stood up. All who remained alive under the Song banner dropped to their knees — except for me, because I was dangling in the mast ropes. The old man, with the emperor on his back, stepped carefully over the rail and, without a word, plunged to his death. In the silence, in the complete silence, we could not see but we all heard the splash of the two hitting the water."

Master Chen pressed his lips together and sighed deeply, his shoulders drooping, dejected. For a long, long time, the two men said nothing, tears trickling down their cheeks. Master Chen reached under the folds of his robe and pulled out a lacquered box that hung from a leather cord around his neck. He slowly rubbed his thumb along the box's carved lid, an old habit that always brought him comfort. Old Zhu did not notice. He raised his arms into the air, lifted his chin and chanted in a low clear voice the lines of a forbidden poem about the fall of the Song Dynasty:

> Bravely arriving at the southern sea,
> Men die, tangled like cords of hemp.
> The foul waves pound my heart until it is broken,
> The gales blast my hair white.

Master Chen joined in for the final lines, their combined voices ringing out over the rippling waves.

> We lost on the mountains and now we have lost at sea,
> If I have no state then I have no home.

Master Chen did not tell the last part of his story to Old Zhu or to anyone, because he knew that no one would be able to make sense of what happened next. He had made his way back down to the deck and was beckoned by a shipmate to board a lifeboat and escape the sinking warship. The emperor's ministers and courtiers were willing to be martyrs; Master Chen and his mates were not. They were Song defenders, and intended to continue the fight, but their little lifeboat lost whatever remaining favor it might have had from Heaven and was broken apart in a hail of catapulted rock. As they flailed in the water gasping and screaming, Master Chen was sure that he and the others were about to die. He closed his eyes to this earthly world of suffering and death and slipped down into the tropical waters.

Something hard brushed against one of his hands. Master Chen opened his eyes and saw a giant turtle swimming by. He reached out to caress its leathery carapace, and realized with a start that he was not struggling to breathe. He was overwhelmed with the sensation that the turtle was trying to help him. Master Chen obediently held on to the shell and glided past bodies and debris. He wondered if he was being escorted to the Pure Land, or to see the Dragon King, or maybe to serve the drowned emperor? But then he realized the turtle was taking him up to the surface.

Master Chen burst out of the water, his chest heaving and his sight blinded by the sun's rays. "There's another one!" cried an old fisherman, who reached out to Master Chen's extended arms, and pulled him safely aboard his boat.

2

A RUFFIAN WREAKS HAVOC IN THE ZHU FAMILY BEAN CURD SHOP

The third year of the Yuan Wuzong Emperor's Greatness Attained reign period (1310).
South bank of the Huai River in modern Jiangsu Province.

THE QUALITY OF the bean curd from the Zhu family shop in Ferry Village attracted faithful customers. Old Zhu had to rise long before dawn to prepare for the morning shoppers who would line up with baskets in hand, wanting a fresh brick of white tofu to take home to their kitchens.

The best seasons for making bean curd are the spring and the fall. In the cold winter months, the Zhu family had to leave their warm bedrolls in the morning darkness to scoop up ice-cold soaked beans for grinding in the stone mill. In the thick heat of the summer, they had to endure a stifling room veiled in steam and humming with the gurgle of simmering soy milk. And yet, when the weather edged back from its extremes, making bean curd was not the worst kind of work a person could find. It suited Fifty-four, the second son, a quiet, moody young man who liked to work alone. Shivering or sweating, he was content to stir his vats while his cheerful elder brother handled the counter sales.

Fifty-four knew that his parents were intent on arranging good marriages for him and his elder brother. A daughter from the Liu family was selected for Fifty-one. The Lius grew the soybeans that the Zhus needed for their shop, and it was Old Liu himself who had arranged the household registration change that had made it possible for the Zhus to rent the bean curd shop after the flight from Precious Mountain. Fifty-one's marriage produced first one grandson, and then another, to the delight of Old Zhu.

"What about your second son?" Fifty-four heard the matchmaker ask one afternoon. "The shy one? Have you saved enough yet for a second bride price?"

But Fifty-four heard nothing more for months and assumed the matchmaker had forgotten about him, until one day he heard his father arguing with her.

"We agreed to this long ago," his father said. "Just ask him."

"The youngest daughter of Chen the fortune teller?" the matchmaker asked, looking skeptical. "He has turned down every match I have brought to him."

"That's because he's been waiting for you to bring him the name of my second son," boasted Old Zhu.

Fifty-four's spoon clattered to the ground. Old Zhu turned and beamed at him.

On the day the Chen girl's bridal sedan chair arrived, announced by gongs and flutes, Daughter-in-law Liu was near the end of her third pregnancy. The wedding guests cheered this sign of fecundity, urging her two little boys to guide the veiled bride around the courtyard.

"I have had only daughters, so I expect nothing but grandsons from you!" Master Chen toasted Old Zhu.

Later, when no one was paying any attention to them, the fathers of the bride and groom had a second toast.

"It was fate that caused us both to land in Ferry Village and raise our children here," said Old Zhu. He regarded his drinking companion with the heightened affection that many cups of wine can inspire. "I have told you how I escaped from the tax collectors at Precious Mountain to start a new life here, but what about you? How did you land in this village, of all places, after the war ended?

Master Chen smiled and glanced at all the boisterous wedding guests, a joyous scene, an occasion for setting aside worries and difficulties. "I spent several months wandering back home to the Huai valley, and I learned how to write magic charms after —" But he stopped himself from saying, "after I received the gift of divination from a sea turtle," which is what he believed. Clearing his throat, Master Chen changed course, " — after spending time with some Daoist monks. And then I made my way down the Huai to this village, where I found my late wife and stayed."

Old Zhu nodded. "I am honored to have my son married to the daughter of a Song loyalist."

Master Chen waved away such sentiment. "I was just a sailor. I told you that I did not understand what it all meant back then." He poured more wine for them both. "But we will soon have another generation to regale with our old stories of the Great Song."

The two men stood and drained their cups. Old Zhu steadied himself as another guest helpfully replenished their drinks. Old Zhu laughed and shook his head at the thought of drinking more, but Master Chen grabbed his own refilled cup and lifted it as he recited a famous heroic poem:

> The great river flows east,
> its waves washing away
> all those heroes of the past.

Master Chen clapped a hand on the shoulder of Old Zhu.

The two belted out the poem together, with various others who recognized the lyrics joining in. Old Zhu glanced around for his son, but could not see Fifty-four among the wedding guests. He turned back to his old friend, now his new relative. Tears filled Old Zhu's eyes as Master Chen grandly spilled a libation onto the courtyard paving stones and launched into the poem's conclusion:

> My melancholy makes you smile
> and note my hair whitening too soon.
> This world is like a dream.
> So I pour out my single cup of wine,
> an offering to the river moon.

During the wedding feast, Fifty-four had stared at his bride's red silk gown and brocaded shoes, and his gaping wonder caused the wedding guests to guffaw. However, left alone in the bridal chamber, after the delicate, tantalizing moment of lifting the red wedding veil, Fifty-four was confronted by his new wife's face. She blinked several times, her eyes adjusting to the light.

Fifty-four knew it was his duty to lift the red veil, but he had not thought about what he would say or do next. Now here before him was his bride, expecting things from him. He knew he would disappoint her, like he disappointed his family.

"I'm sorry," he stammered, raising his arm as if to shield himself. He stumbled back onto their new quilt, hastily blew out the red wedding candles, and huddled in a corner until he fell fast asleep.

Left standing alone at the foot of the bed, the Chen girl clutched her hands at her chest.

"He thinks I am ugly," she thought to herself. "It was that

horrible veil; it rubbed my face all day and probably made my skin blotchy. And as soon as he lifted it, I squinted at the light. I look terrible when I squint."

Afraid of what would happen next, she stayed frozen until she realized from the sound of Fifty-four's breathing that her groom was asleep. Quickly she slipped out of her outer gown, yanked off her headdress and sank, defeated, into the corner of the bridal bed opposite her new husband.

When she woke the next morning, the Chen girl found that she was alone, but her wedding silks had been carefully folded and placed on a shelf. She heard a commotion outside and then suddenly what seemed like a crowd filled the tiny room, though it was only Old Zhu's wife, Daughter-in-law Liu and her two boys. The women noticed immediately that the quilt had not been pulled back.

"You did it on the quilt?" Eldest Daughter-in-law snorted.

Old Zhu's wife ran her hands over the material, looking for bloodstains. Finding none, she sighed and tossed the shivering girl a bundle.

"It's your regular clothes, that your father left for you," she said. "Hurry up, you have work to do in the shop."

For days, Fifty-four would not speak to or even look at his bride. The newlyweds could not avoid each other in the bean curd shop, and each night had to crawl under the same quilt, so they lived cramped together in a state of mutual embarrassment and fear. Old Zhu was irked, and of course he blamed his new daughter-in-law, forgetting all the warm sentiments of the wedding feast toasts. Little Chen, as she came to be known in the household, was miserable and sullen, thinking only of her desire to return to her father, who loved her.

Eldest Daughter-in-law, uncomfortably pregnant, seemed to view Little Chen as her assistant.

"Have your wife empty my chamber pot," she called out one morning to Fifty-four, who had just emerged from his bedroom and was still tying up his hair. "It is too much for me to take care of this morning."

Little Chen's discontent worsened once Eldest Daughter-in-law's baby came out, a third son, and the month-long lying-in period began. Now, not only did Little Chen have to serve the convalescing mother, whom she despised, she also had to listen to all the villagers praising Old Zhu over his Three-Sons-In-A-Row Daughter-in-Law, which was usually followed by raised eyebrows aimed her way. The situation became more than Little Chen could bear. One night, Fifty-four slipped into their bedroom as usual, head down, and almost fell over Little Chen, who was kneeling on the ground. In her lap lay her red silk wedding dress, brocaded shoes and veil.

"I have failed you as a bride and will now return to my father," Little Chen said, not daring to look up.

Fifty-four was caught by surprise. "She thinks she is a failure?" he wondered to himself. "Does this mean she wants to be my bride? Does this mean she is not repulsed by me?"

Fifty-four stared at the beautiful red material in Little Chen's lap. He reached down to run his fingers along the lustrous folds. The fabric felt as beautiful as it looked, like a peach blossom petal. For the first time since his wedding night, he spoke to his wife.

"Put it on," he whispered. He swallowed hard and then added, "The veil too."

Soon enough, a pregnancy was on the way. Alas, the baby was a girl. This was a disappointment to Old Zhu and did not impress the neighbors, who joked that it would be Fifty-four's fate to match his older brother's parade of sons with a den of daughters.

Only one member of the household took an interest in the newborn. Pushing aside the cloth over Little Chen's bedroom doorway the day after the birth, Eldest Daughter-in-law appeared at Little Chen's side with a steaming bowl of red bean porridge.

"Along with the porridge is a fresh egg that my father brought this morning with his delivery of soybeans," she said. "Don't be a picky eater like you usually are."

Eldest Daughter-in-law plunked the porridge on a side table. She leaned over Little Chen to rub a raw knuckle gently against the swaddled baby's downy cheek, murmuring, "What a pretty little pearl."

As the seasoned mother stood admiring the newborn, Little Chen held her breath, afraid to break the spell. Eldest Daughter-in-law rarely spoke to her except to ridicule mistakes or shout orders. And yet here she was offering delicacies. Maybe she is just happy that I did not have a son, Little Chen thought. The baby stirred. Eldest Daughter-in-law reached out both hands so that Little Chen had no choice but to lift the newborn into the waiting arms.

"Wah, there you are," Eldest Daughter-in-law cooed at the baby, who opened an eye, looking as wary as Little Chen. To Little Chen's surprise, Eldest Daughter-in-law's face broke into girlish smiles, and she swayed and laughed, rocking the newborn in the tiny space around the bed until she was interrupted by a customer calling from the front of the compound.

"I'm coming!" Eldest Daughter-in-law hollered back. Then she carefully returned the baby to Little Chen's lap. "You stay resting here," she insisted, tucking the blankets around the baby and mother. "And don't pay any attention to Father-in-law. What does he know? After three boys, this Zhu family could use the good influence of a girl. You know the saying: Girls are made of clear water, boys of dirty mud."

Though she did not shed her commanding tone and continued to find faults in Little Chen, especially when it came to parenting, the birth turned Eldest Daughter-in-law into an ally. Her improved disposition meant that she would not tolerate her younger brother-in-law avoiding his duties as a husband and father. She promised Little Chen that Fifty-four, who had resumed his attitude of cringing embarrassment in Little Chen's presence, would return to his proper bed as soon as the confinement month was complete. True to her word, Eldest Daughter-in-law marched up to Fifty-four the evening after the baby's thirtieth day.

"You can't keep sleeping in the courtyard," Eldest Daughter-in-law announced to Fifty-four, who was squatting on the ground, unrolling a mat. She kicked him toward his own bedroom. Not knowing what else to do, Little Chen opened the door wider to let him through. "Your daughter is getting bigger every day and yet you are still out here acting like a turtle."

The next morning, Eldest Daughter-in-law gave Little Chen a knowing nudge. "Eh?" she said, grinning. "Did you experience 'clouds and rain' last night?"

Little Chen did not return her smile. "It's not what you think," she said and turned away, her face crumpling. "I will never have another baby."

"What nonsense are you talking about?"

Little Chen pulled her down a hallway, away from the rest of the family. Brushing tears from her eyes, she took Eldest Daughter-in-law by the arm. "I need a bolt of silk."

Eldest Daughter-in-law burst out laughing. "I thought you were worried about your husband and here you are thinking about shopping."

"No, no, you don't understand," Little Chen said. She glanced away, covering her mouth with one hand.

Eldest Daughter-in-law looked exasperated and glanced around Little Chen toward the shop. "I don't have time to stand out here and blow farts with you," she said, crossing her arms.

Little Chen closed her eyes and blurted out all at once, "I need to wear a silk dress to bed."

Now she had Eldest Daughter-in-law's attention. "Is that so?"

"Yes," continued Little Chen, grimly. "I had to return my bridal silks to our mother-in-law after the baby was born and I don't know what she did with them."

"She sold them."

"But Fifty-four... nothing works with him. He is very shy, you know. And if anyone scolds him, he becomes even more withdrawn. Except that, when he sees silk... "

"Yes?"

"Everything changes."

A smile spread across Eldest Daughter-in-law's face and she leaned against the passageway, chuckling. She poked Little Chen in the ribs teasingly.

"Everything changes?"

Ignoring the taunt, Little Chen went on, "I have the loom that my father made for me." She was speaking almost to herself and beginning to pace the hallway. The loom was a wedding gift. It belonged to her mother, who died when Little Chen was just a baby, and had sat in a corner, unused for many years. But it was a favorite plaything for Little Chen. Master Chen had repaired it to working order and supplied a new bench before presenting it to his daughter. "I thought about trying to get some silk thread to weave, but Mother-in-law will notice and it will take a long time to weave enough silk to make a simple shift and that's really all I need is a simple shift—"

"So you want me to help you get a piece of silk that you can secretly turn into a seduction dress?"

"Yes," said Little Chen, nodding her head vigorously and ignoring Eldest Daughter-in-law's mirth, "and I thought you would be able to help because you are good at these kinds of things."

Eldest Daughter-in-law drew back and frowned. "What do you mean, I am good at such things?"

"At acquiring useful things. After all, you got those fresh eggs and other treats during my lying-in month."

"Oh," replied Eldest Daughter-in-law, looking mollified.

"Besides, where would I find money to buy silk?" asked Little Chen. "You know that would be impossible."

Eldest Daughter-in-law studied her thoughtfully and tilted her head. "I will see what I can do."

And that is how it came to pass that Fifty-four pulled aside the curtain over his bedroom doorway one evening to find his wife seated demurely on the center of their bed, dressed in a beautiful rose-colored silk shift. The baby slept serenely in a crib on the side table.

Fifty-four gulped and stepped back.

Little Chen did not raise her eyes or make a sound. Her long hair was undone and she had let it fall over most of her face.

"Is this some kind of trick?" Fifty-four whispered under his breath, glancing warily around the room. He was on the verge of backing out to escape whatever ridicule he assumed was in store for him, when Little Chen caught his eye and smiled. A shy, sweet smile.

"Do you like it?" she asked.

"What?"

"The dress," she replied smoothing the fabric over her knees. "I had it made for you."

Fifty-four flinched. "How could that be?"

Little Chen had the good sense not to explain her sister-in-law's role in the matter. She just shrugged. "I could tell that you like silk," she said. "Who doesn't like silk? So I managed to find some for us." Now she smiled conspiratorially at him. "It can be our secret."

Fifty-four took a hesitant step forward, and then another, reaching the bed. "It is very nice," he managed to say, as his hand slid slowly along the fabric, all the way down to the end. Little Chen leaned back and sighed as Fifty-four's hand slid beneath the shift. He enjoyed the exquisite luxury of feeling silk over his hand and flesh beneath it. His own clothes, mere homespun cotton, were thrust aside and it did not take long for the torrential rain to erupt from the billowing clouds.

Their second child was a boy. The third was a daughter. Then Eldest Daughter-in-law had her fourth son. To this, Little Chen added another son, and then another.

During the years when all these cousins were being born, emperors came and went from the Dragon Throne. The virile Yuan Dynasty expanded to its full size and then, like any phallus, began to shrink, though the decline was not at first apparent. Born and raised during the Yuan era, the Zhu sons and grandchildren did not question the Mongol right to hold the Mandate of Heaven.

Old Zhu was resigned to this situation and no longer shed tears over the loss of the Song. Instead, he took pleasure in sipping tea in his courtyard while watching his daughters-in-law rush about to keep up with their children.

"What a long addition they will make to the Zhu genealogy. The scribes will grow tired writing down all the names of my grandsons!" The old man recalled the desperate escape from Jurong, and scowled at the memory of the hulking, gold-less hill he had fled so long ago. No matter that Old Zhu could barely afford to feed and clothe his brood. What mattered was the satisfaction he would get in being able to die surrounded by his wailing offspring and then report to the ancestral spirits on how his branch of the lineage had flourished under his guidance.

"Think of how they will all gawk and stare!" he said to himself. Old Zhu took another long drag at his tea and spat out a few leaves with a loud smack.

The seven grandsons born during the years that the Zhu brothers lived together in Ferry Village were given names that reflected their place in the family, all beginning with the character "Chong," the generation marker, followed by the birth order number, to distinguish the individual boy. In this way, Little Chen and Fifty-four's first son was named Chong Four, because he followed the first three boys born to Eldest Daughter-in-law and Fifty-one. This naming method tied all the male cousins into one neat family knot. The two girls did not have names beyond "First Daughter" and "Second Daughter." Old Zhu arranged for a record of the Chong generation to be written down and sent south of the Yangtze River to the Zhu clan hall in Jurong County.

The seventh Chong, the last one born in Ferry Village, was the most colicky. He would cry and cry through the night so that all anyone wanted from Little Chen was for her to take her baby outside and away, anything to get some peace from that piercing sound.

The first night that Little Chen dared to step outside the gate of her compound, the figure lurking in the dark alley almost sent her straight back in. She did not recognize her father until he started to laugh.

"Baba!" she exclaimed with a surge of relief.

"I could hear that baby crying all the way from my neighborhood," he complained.

Stepping closer, Master Chen pulled aside the blanket to catch a better look at his new grandson, only the wet eyes discernible in the shadows. The baby stopped sobbing altogether. Master Chen nodded his approval and beckoned for his daughter to follow him. They wound through the crooked lanes and turned past a public privy to a dark footpath behind a boulder that led up a hill and onto a clearing in the woods at the village's edge. With the baby content in his mother's arms, father and daughter sat on a smooth rock and crooked their necks at the starry heavens.

"Watch over there," Master Chen instructed.

Little Chen scanned the region of the sky known as the Palace of the Blue Dragon. At first she saw nothing unexpected, though the sky was like a quilt padded thick with extra stars, puffed up by the lack of an obscuring moon. Then sparks of light appeared, streaking and darting in short bursts near the horizon, until a shower flooded sideways across the palace.

"What can it mean?" she gasped.

"Last night, the shower was even heavier and brighter," he said. "It is a sign that the people in a certain part of the realm are restless and have nowhere to go."

The shower diminished before them, but for the baby, the sky was no match for his mother's fingers, which the infant reached for and gurgled at until he blinked drowsily as the haze of sleep descended.

Reading the skies was a skill Master Chen had learned from his own father and passed down to his daughters. Little Chen's most treasured childhood memories were of sitting in her father's lap, wide awake through the dark night, watching him trace the constellations.

"Follow the handle of the Northern Dipper," he would say as she placed her little hand in his, sitting forward so she could reach his palm, and reciting along with him the old Daoist names of all the glittering stars: Heaven's Gate, Reaching North, Cinnabar Tip. He made little rhymes and stories to help her remember the mysterious appellations.

Seated on a cold rock under the fading shower of star sparks, Little Chen realized that her father had not said much about her new baby boy.

"Where was the moon lodged on the night my third son was born?" she asked. Her father pointed to the constellation Woman. "Is it favorable? For my first two sons, your readings were favorable."

Master Chen grinned. "I liked the portents for your first boy because I learned he would be one of several grandsons. And your newest proves that I was correct." He nodded his head sagaciously, looking pleased.

"But what about this boy?" Little Chen asked again.

Her father sighed and would not look at her. Then he reached down to pat the fat little exposed cheek of the sleeping infant. "As for this one, he will have a good nature and marry well," he said.

Little Chen smiled. "Why so grudging with good news?" But the smile faded as she recalled an old saying. She looked at her father and uttered it aloud. "To be born under the Woman constellation: a portent of a house soon divided."

Chong Seven grew into a chubby toddler nicknamed "Puppy" because he was always underfoot. Little Chen did not worry over his birth reading until the day the Zhu family patriarch clutched at his chest while drinking tea with old friends and fell to the ground unconscious, tea leaves spilling everywhere. He was dead within the week. The Zhus thus had no recourse at all when the henchmen of Arig, the Kipchak from the capital in charge of Magistrate Li's district, started showing an interest in the family bean curd shop, extracting higher and higher fees for the curdling jars of black salt syrup and demanding free cakes at every visit.

"Good morning, shopkeeper," began one of these visits, the tone of Arig's emissary cheerful. Two attendants filed in behind him.

"Good morning, Honorable Elder," Fifty-one carefully replied.

"And a special morning it is, don't you think?" the man continued, a malicious grin spreading across his face. Fifty-one smiled wanly and said nothing. Nearby, Fifty-four closed a lid over a jar and stood warily. The brothers awaited the inevitable extortion. The man leaned against the counter, where the abacus sat. "Don't you want to know what day this is, shopkeeper?" he asked.

Fifty-one could only raise his eyebrows, to indicate that of course he wished to know the importance of that particular day.

"Why, it's the birthday of our Lord Arig's uncle in Dadu!" exclaimed the man, glancing back at his attendants, who nodded their heads and folded their arms. "I'm sure Uncle would appreciate a special batch of your best bean curd today to express your birthday wishes for his health and prosperity."

Fifty-one looked down at the cakes on the counter, and seemed uncertain over what amount would be appropriate. As he hesitated, Fifty-four's voice cut sharply through the room.

"I can't see how a brick of bean curd will be able to fly all the way to the capital in time for birthday wishes today," Fifty-four blurted out.

A simple statement, and yet so unlike Fifty-four to utter it. Fifty-one glanced back at his younger brother with surprise, and Fifty-four himself stood gaping at his own words. A few quick syllables strung together into a cheeky retort. That was all it took to change everything.

"How dare you!" shouted the henchman. His attendants

lunged across the room, hurling trays of bean curd, containers of whey, buckets, bowls and whatever else they could get their hands on.

Little Chen and Eldest Daughter-in-law rushed their children away through a back door as the two Zhu brothers ducked and tried to shield each other. "Elder, Elder, he meant no disrespect, he was not thinking, our father recently died, please excuse us, we are still in mourning... " Fifty-one pleaded, stepping forward to trail the ruffian until he seemed satisfied with the level of destruction and called back his raging attendants. That is when the ruffian pointed at Fifty-one.

"You," he said, nodding his flaming red face, "you I will excuse, just this once, but that one," and now he flung his arm toward Fifty-four, "that one better leave before my attendants use one of your vats of boiling water to silence his impudence forever."

Then he grabbed a basket, helped himself to a pile of bean curd cakes, and led his men back out to the street.

The brothers stood facing each other in the dim, steamy light of their family shop, which was now strewn with slop. Fifty-four hunched over, his chest heaving. His elder brother reached out to put a hand on his back, but could offer no words of comfort. The two women slipped back into the room and fell to their knees to clean the floor. The children peeked in from the back doorway.

Of course, Fifty-four had to leave, and he was gone by sundown, together with his wife and children and a few meager packs of food and belongings, including Little Chen's bulky loom. They had only enough time to bow before the family altar, which now included a spirit tablet for Grandfather Zhu, and share a quick, final meal to gather strength for the journey ahead.

"It's just for a little while," the two brothers kept saying.

Only Eldest Daughter-in-law was able to speak clearly. The

children crept about warily as she sat the adults around a table to make plans. The two brothers and Little Chen drew strength from her sober logic and tried to hear her words through the churning dread that filled their ears.

"You can take the road west to my father's farm. You know where that is, don't you?" she said to Fifty-four, stretching her hands across the table to grasp his knuckles and looking deep into his fearful eyes. "Ask Father to tell you how to get to Good Mountain on the edge of the county. Father's neighbor left for there a few years back. This neighbor was a close friend of ours and he will help you."

Eldest Daughter-in-law leaned back in her seat and put her hands in her sleeves, regarding Little Chen and Fifty-four with consternation. Then she sighed and stood up.

"Little Chen, all this sniffling is no use," she finally said, prodding everyone to stand up. "Get along there. Why are you dawdling at a time like this?"

Eldest Daughter-in-law seemed so stern and impatient, but she was the one who would not stop crying in the days to come.

They all gathered in a nervous cluster, shuffling at the back door of the family compound. Fifty-four broke away, and went to his mother, who sat in her chair where she always sat in the days since her husband's death, sunken and withdrawn, her mind receding back in time.

"Mother, I have to leave you now, I am sorry," he said, kneeling at her feet.

"Aiya," the old woman sighed, lifting her chin and rousing herself. "Are you leaving Precious Mountain?"

"No, Mother, we are leaving here, Ferry Village, to seek Good Mountain."

She nodded, and patted her son's hand. "Maybe it is for the best. There is no gold here."

"Yes, mother," he answered. He rose and picked up his shoulder pole. He could not look at his brother, the one he had followed all his life, the one he could not match, the one he had failed. They all spilled into the street. It was a sad, downcast clump, with half breaking away and the other left depleted.

"Little Brother," Fifty-one called out, stepping forward to clasp Fifty-four's shoulders. "I am glad you stood up to that old bully. He deserved it." Then Fifty-one smiled. "Who would have guessed that it would be you, my quiet brother, who would refuse to let the tiger pounce on his prey? Father would be proud."

The little group bound for Good Mountain consisted of Fifty-four, Little Chen, and their three sons and second daughter. Their eldest daughter had recently been married away.

As they walked on, Little Chen waited for her father to appear. Just as she despaired that she would not be able to say goodbye to him, he emerged from some trees at a bend in the road, his conical bamboo hat casting shadows over his face so that it was hard to see his eyes. They all stopped and Fifty-four set down his pole. Master Chen placed his palm on the head of his oldest grandson, Chong Four.

"So big, my child," Master Chen said, with great tenderness. "You'll be brave, and help take good care of your mother?" Then he turned to his daughter and caressed her cheek.

"Can you go to my eldest daughter and tell her what has happened?" she asked.

Master Chen nodded and placed a piece of paper in her hands. It was a charm, a small square containing magic words.

"I will find you, wherever you end up," he promised, wiping tears from Little Chen's face. In an instant, the old man vanished back into the woods and the Zhu family resumed their journey.

They eventually stopped to rest at a wayside inn. As they were eating, the innkeeper walked by their table, returning from an errand. He was a gruff and disagreeable man, but Fifty-four struck up a conversation with both him and his brother while checking directions to Good Mountain.

"You are looking for work?" the innkeeper guessed.

"Just so," Fifty-four replied. "Unless there's anything to be had here?" His demeanor revealed his desperation.

The innkeeper's brother shook his head slowly while his eyes flickered to the table where Little Chen and her children were waiting. "No work here, no, not in times like these," he said. "But I myself have nothing but girls in my house, and a wife who is sickly. The doctor says she will have no more children."

Fifty-four did not see where this was leading. He only nodded and offered a sympathetic, "Ah." Little Chen stopped fussing with her children and turned to listen more closely to what the men were saying.

"I could use a strong boy around the house," explained the innkeeper's brother. "One like that son of yours there."

Surprised, Fifty-four followed the man's gaze to his youngest child. The seventh Chong. "But he's only five years old!" Fifty-four exclaimed.

"And yet I can see from here that he's a strong one, big for his age, a boy who could be a help around my house of girls," the man went on. Then he made a small gesture to the innkeeper, who nodded his head and left to fetch something. "I'll buy that boy from you, and when he's old enough, I'll marry him to one of my daughters. I'll give him my name and make him my heir."

Fifty-four backed away, giving slight, jerky little shakes to his head, afraid to offend the man, but wanting to escape. That is when the innkeeper returned holding copper coins. The brother kept talking at Fifty-four, his voice as mesmerizing as the money, which the innkeeper jingled tantalizingly.

"I'll buy that boy for four strings of cash," the man said.

"You'll have one less mouth to feed, and that much more money to get by with. I'll make a good home for your boy, better than you could offer him."

Fifty-four had no money to speak of. His family had just paid for Grandfather Zhu's funeral; they were all still dressed in mourning clothes. Though Fifty-one and Eldest Daughter-in-law had given their fleeing relatives all the cash they could muster, it amounted to a mere handful of coins, hardly enough to make even a clink from within the little money bag tied around Fifty-four's waist. And yet, Fifty-four, who knew no other trade beyond making bean curd, now had a wife and four children to care for. How was he to do it? And how was he to know that four strings of cash, which seemed like a lot when it jingled before his face, was a shamefully cheap offer for an indentured servant?

"Chong Seven, come here," he said.

The boy came forward, shy and frightened. Little Chen gasped and stretched out her hand but the boy was already beyond her reach.

Fifty-four saw then that his little boy had no prospects, and in a moment of bitter truth, Fifty-four looked from the child to the man before him, and recognized a better life. The man wore a well-cut gown with no patches, and had strong teeth and clean nails and good shoes. He looked well-fed, and was related to the owner of an inn.

"I am Zhu Fifty-four of Jurong, most recently of Ferry Village, and this is my youngest son," Fifty-four declared, launching the business deal. "Sir, what is your honorable name?"

The innkeeper's brother replied that his surname was Na, and that his home was down the lane. Fifty-four squatted down then to the level of his child and took the young boy's hand.

"This is a good place for you to stay, and you are a lucky boy," Fifty-four said softly. "Your mother and I need to keep going, but the Na family will take care of you here. You belong to this man now and you must do as he says. Goodbye, Chong Seven."

Little Chen stepped forward, her mouth open but no sound coming out. Fifty-four moved to her side. He restrained her with one hand, while clenching the strings of cash in the other.

"This is better," he murmured to her. "It is better for us, it is better for the boy."

"How can you say that?" she demanded.

"Look at these men," Fifty-four spoke softly into her ear. "At least we can be sure that one of us will survive."

Her eyes flickered from the large and imposing brothers to her small son. Little Chen swallowed hard and looked beseechingly into her husband's eyes. "We can come back later and buy him back," she said.

Fifty-four smiled weakly and offered a slight nod, but Little Chen could see that her husband did not think that likely.

What could she do? What could she do? She saw the innkeeper's brother pat Chong Seven's shoulder and smile reassuringly down at him. Fifty-four herded her away to gather their belongings and leave. Chong Seven smiled politely back at the man and in that instant, Little Chen realized she had lost him. He would go on to have a life without her. She lunged forward and placed the charm from her father in the hands of her littlest boy. It was all she could do.

The wandering Zhu family found Good Mountain, but there was nothing "good" about it for them. That friend of Eldest Daughter-in-law's father had moved even further west by then and once Fifty-four found him, he did not remember the Liu family with much fondness. The friend's neighbor told them of a landlord who might hire them. So Fifty-four and Little Chen continued westward, landing in a decrepit, mud-walled shack in the East Ward of Bell County, part of Hao Prefecture. Henceforth they were tenant farmers, working in the fields from sunrise to sunset. There would be no more of the camaraderie of making bean curd in a family shop, no more listening to the idle chatter of cheerful customers.

For Little Chen, the loss of her youngest child left her despairing and weary. Her second son, Chong Six, was only a year older than Chong Seven, and the two had been close playmates. At first, Chong Six had threatened to run away and find his little brother and never return, and then he turned sullen. But no one had time to worry about Chong Six. The Zhu family of shopkeepers had to become farmers, and their new landlord would expect a portion of their harvest. Meanwhile, in the midst of all this turmoil and change, Little Chen realized that she was about to have another baby. Forty years old, far from home, still grieving for her lost child, with three hungry children and a rock-strewn patch of earth to grapple with and now she was pregnant. Fifty-four refused to acknowledge her bulging stomach, and this only added to Little Chen's anxiety. At night when she could not sleep, Little Chen would place her hands on her belly and offer silent prayers to the Metal Mother. At first she prayed for the baby to disappear, to melt back into the great void it had arisen from and leave her alone. But the Metal Mother, goddess of birth and rebirth, the queen who feasts on peaches from the slopes of Mount Kunlun, would not accept this prayer. Instead, the Metal Mother filled Little Chen's dreams with visions of dragons and tigers and told her that this baby was formed in Ferry Village and would be her last link to her old home and her bridge to prosperity. By the time the birthing pains clenched at her waist, Little Chen was ready.

"Come along, daughter," Little Chen snapped at her child, who jumped up from the loom and ran to fetch the gourd of water, oil lamp, cooking pot, implements, rolled-up reed mats and wadding her mother had already set aside. Fifty-four and his two remaining sons were out in the fields hoeing the winter wheat. Little Chen walked at an urgent pace along a path through the wooded hill behind their shack. Now and then, contractions forced Little Chen to stop and grip her stomach or grab onto a tree branch for support. At last, the pair came to a clearing, where an abandoned temple stood in the twilight, or rather half-stood, on the point of collapse. Little Chen had discovered the temple one day while searching for firewood. Alongside it she had found an overgrown garden, from which she had gleaned greens and even a few apples from the tangled branches of an old pair of fruit trees. Little Chen did not mention the temple to her husband and he was too tired to ask where the food had come from. She knew she could have the baby there and even rest for a few days undiscovered, so that she could bring home a healthy infant.

Little Chen pulled aside the spider webs over the temple gate, perspiring despite the autumn chill, and stepped over the threshold. Her daughter followed close behind. The girl frantically lit their lamp with her flint and rolled out the reed mats. Soon the contractions were circling hard around Little Chen's abdomen, but still the baby relaxed in the womb, unwilling to leave it. In between the birthing pains, Little Chen tried to control her breathing by staring at the flickering flame of the lamp. Under the rotting eaves of the temple, a dove cooed several times. Then Little Chen was gripped by a different kind of pain, and cried out, "The baby is coming!"

The girl at her side trembled with fear and pressed her palms in prayer. Little Chen reached out and grabbed one of her daughter's shaking hands, squeezing hard. In one long and agonizing wringing of all Little Chen's strength, the baby came out. Little Chen fell back onto her mat, her chest heaving. The baby made no sound, but the tiny slick heels kicking at the inside of her thighs made Little Chen smile. The baby was alive.

Little Chen's daughter reached for the newborn. Cobwebs swayed in the unfamiliar dark rafters above as the girl picked up the bright red baby. "Ma, it's a boy!"

Back in Ferry Village on the night of the birth, Master Chen was chewing on a stem of grain and deep in his reverence for the skies when he was startled by a most unusual sight.

"Aiya!" the old man said, to no one but himself, and he stepped back in alarm, the stem dropping from his lips. There, in the center of the sky, a star descended. As big as a peach and glowing orange-yellow, the fireball exploded and then rumbled across the heavens to fall in the direction of Hao Prefecture.

This was a message from Heaven. But what could it mean? Master Chen pulled out a fresh piece of straw to chew on. It could be an omen of a great disturbance emerging from the vicinity of Hao, he thought. Or perhaps a sign of the birth of a great king, who will one day rise like a dragon and fly all the way to the throne. He tilted his head and wondered. "But how could a dragon rise from a place like Hao? It must be that some disturbance is coming." Then he shrugged and smiled up at the stars, content to spend another fine evening contemplating their glittering commentary on his world of red dust.

3

GRANDFATHER CHEN HANDS OUT
NEW YEAR'S GIFTS

*The second year of the Yuan Wenzong Emperor's Heavenly
Calendar reign period (1329).*
*Bell County's East Ward, near the Huai River in modern
Anhui Province.*

THE EIGHTH AND FINAL Chong had ragged breathing and was so
prone to coughs and fevers that his mother did not know if he
would survive. Fifty-four avoided the baby as a reminder of all his
recent misfortunes. Then one spring afternoon, as Fifty-four and
his sons were working in the fields, Chong Four started hollering
and running at a small group of travelers in the distance.

"What is it?" Fifty-four called out with alarm.

"Baba! It's Auntie and Uncle!" Chong Six called back over his
shoulder as he ran after his brother. Indeed, Fifty-one and his
wife and children were making their way down the road with all
their belongings in hand.

Little Chen and her daughter burst out of the house as Fifty-
four ran to embrace his elder brother and led him by the arm
to the house. "He found us! He found us!" Fifty-four shouted
over and over again to Little Chen, his voice high-pitched with
incredulous joy. Everyone tried to find room in the dusty little
yard. Nearly a dozen people crowded around the millstone, all

talking at once, spilling out from the tiny yard and trying not to trample the furrows of the vegetable plot.

"Eldest Daughter-in-law, why isn't your second son traveling with you?" asked Little Chen, looking confused.

The question was like an icy wind that whipped away all the guests' warm smiles. Auntie Liu sank onto a rickety wooden bench and closed her eyes, as if in prayer. The three sons at her side all stared at their feet. Uncle sighed and rubbed at his whiskers, which had gone completely gray. He could not avoid speaking aloud the harsh facts. Squinting at the rolling hills in the distance, hazy blue shadows against the departing sun, he answered Little Chen's question.

"Chong Two was killed by a horse that shied in a narrow lane, throwing the rider into the dust and kicking Chong Two in the head," Uncle said, speaking in a flat voice. "The rider was some important official who claimed Chong Two had caused the accident. We were forced to pay a big fine because the official hurt his shoulder and tore his robes. This happened not long after you left Ferry Village, and shortly before our esteemed mother left this world. So we also had to pay funeral costs... for two."

Fifty-four covered his face with his hands and the rest of the adults fell silent, leaving no sound but the cicadas humming from the trees.

Auntie Liu turned to look at her husband. "You haven't spoken to the end," she said.

Uncle nodded and sighed again. He had to lick his dry lips, but Little Chen did not get up to bring him hot tea. Uncle sat down on a stool and glanced sadly back at the hills.

"You remember Arig the Kipchak? His men continued their pressure on our family business, and then our customers, in our misery, started to shun us," Uncle explained. "We had to sell everything and leave. We came to find you to see if there's any chance for us here. And that's not all. Little Chen, your eldest daughter became pregnant but died giving birth last month. The baby died with her."

Little Chen nodded briskly and stood up. She did not utter a sound or look at anyone, walking quickly toward a path through the fields. Chong Four, who had been closest to his oldest sister, dropped to his knees and broke into sobs. This was when Auntie Liu noticed the absence of Chong Seven and asked why he was not in the yard.

"We sold him," Fifty-four replied. The words made him angry.

Fifty-one stared at him, open-mouthed. A movement in the basket at Auntie Liu's feet caught her eye — it was the infant waking up. Tenderly, Auntie Liu lifted the baby to her shoulder, swaying and cooing. She hugged the baby close, breathing in the fresh newborn scent. Her husband and brother-in-law regarded her in silence, lost in their own thoughts.

"You never know how much time you have with a child," Auntie Liu said, her eyes filling with tears. She held out the baby to Fifty-four.

He took the warm bundle into his arms. Auntie Liu did not realize this was the first time Fifty-four had held the child, and he knew better than to reveal his neglect to her. One of the baby's little fists had come loose from the swaddling, and when Fifty-four dipped his chin to look down at the face of his youngest son, he startled the infant, causing the tiny hand to fling wide. Fifty-four gently reached for it. The baby took hold of his father's index finger, and held on tight.

"Look at that strong grip," Auntie Liu exclaimed. When he did not respond, Auntie Liu nudged him.

"His grip is strong," he agreed, fighting back his own tears.

"Now I'd better take your second daughter and go find Little Chen," said Auntie Liu, marching off.

Fifty-four returned the baby to his basket, taking care to tuck in the blankets and resting his palm on the small exposed forehead in a brief caress. "Chong Eight," he whispered.

The Zhu brothers naturally wanted to rejoin their households, the better to hold together all the remaining boys in the Chong generation. Fifty-one and Fifty-four talked at length, and with mounting excitement, about how living as one family under one roof would honor their deceased parents, and allow them all to resume hopes for prosperity. However, the twin demons of Misfortune and Poverty got wind of these aspirations, and took offense. They promptly kicked the households apart, whispering into the ear of Fifty-four's landlord not to accept any more tenants. Uncle and Auntie learned of an even more desolate and infertile corner of the county and decided to try their luck there.

At least this time the brothers would be separated by no more than a day's walk.

"Maybe it's better to head in different directions for a little while and learn more about Bell County," Fifty-four said, consolingly, as he held his elder brother's hands in parting. Then he leaned in close and lowered his voice so that he would not be overheard by any malevolent spirits as he added, "then later we will know of the best place to open a bean curd shop and resume our family business."

"Yes, yes," agreed Uncle. "This time apart will only last for a little while longer. And we can pool our money to buy back Chong Seven."

The health of the newest Chong among the progeny of the Zhu brothers did not improve over time. During Chong Eight's second year, the "heavenly flowers" of the pox bloomed in profusion, covering his face and spreading even to the palms of his hands and the soles of his feet. Little Chen wanted to stroke the miserable child's cheek, but the angry lesions made her afraid to do anything more than dab with a soft cloth at the tears forming in the corners of her son's eyes. When his fever rose and the pitiful creature stopped nursing altogether, lying listless on his mat, Little Chen expected to lose him. She prayed to the Metal Mother, and also to the God of the Northern Dipper, who can take names off the death rolls.

And so the fever broke. The hundreds of pustules scabbed over and dropped off, and the child's body slowly returned to its normal shape. Little Chen was astonished and thankful for her son's recovery.

"It was the Metal Mother and Dipper God who saved him," she exclaimed to her husband.

"And my prayers to the Lord Buddha," added Fifty-four. "I went to the temple you know."

"You did what?"

Fifty-four smiled proudly. "I put a coin in the collection box and told Lord Buddha that if he would protect our son this once then when he's old enough, I will give him to the temple as a monk."

Little Chen frowned with displeasure. She did not mind entreating the Lord Buddha for his matchless compassion, but to promise her baby to service in a temple was quite another matter. Little Chen harbored her father's suspicion of Buddhist monks as greedy and unscrupulous.

"How could you make such a promise?" she asked, but her husband was already heading back to the fields.

Chong Eight's scabs faded and, over the course of the next few years, puckered up and retreated, but the child's face was forever dotted conspicuously with pockmarks. When Grandfather Chen first encountered the boy, during the old diviner's one and only trip to Bell County, he drew back with a look of astonishment. The boy was already almost six years old, four summers past his bout with the pox.

"What is it, father?" Little Chen asked. She stood with her hand on the shoulder of her youngest son as she presided over the meeting of grandfather and grandson.

"Nothing, nothing," Grandfather Chen replied. He took off his conical bamboo hat and leaned down to peer into the boy's face, running his finger slowly along the pattern of the pockmarks. Chong Eight froze, awed by the scrutiny. "Why," Grandfather Chen continued, "he has red marks in an unusual pattern. It brings to mind the heavenly constellations."

Little Chen frowned, but then Grandfather Chen grinned at the little boy and wagged a finger in his face. "You have the iron chin and the hawk eyes of a Chen!" he exclaimed.

The three standing there together were unmistakably related, their cheekbones sharp beneath the same piercing eyes, their chins the same kind of square, though the old man's sprouted a white beard. Only in his long, flat ears and high-bridged nose did the boy bear the mark of his father's line.

While Grandfather Chen may have been surprised by his youngest grandson's face, he delivered an even greater surprise to his daughter's family: a wife for the oldest son of the household, who was now a young man of marriageable age. The girl, who had the family name of Wang, kept her eyes down during introductions and did not speak to anyone. Grandfather Chen never explained the details of this match, but the girl later revealed that he had banished an evil spirit from her family's home. The grateful Wang family had offered their daughter as a match for one of Master Chen's grandsons. The girl proved an excellent wife. She was quiet, helpful and practical. Best of all, she and Chong Four were clearly attracted to each other.

This fourth-born among the Chong cousins was also known as "Cattail," because he was so tall and thin, and also because the number four, pronounced *si* in Chinese, is the most unlucky of numbers, having a sound close to the word for "death." Who would want a name like that? As for the middle boy in the household, Chong Six, he had the nickname "Luo-bo," which means "Radish." The nickname fit the boy's ruddy cheeks and thicker stature. Radish could be moody and withdrawn at times, but Chong Eight could always cheer him up. Now, Chong Eight was such a good name that there was no need to cover it up with a nickname of any kind since in Chinese the word "eight," or *ba*, is like the opposite of four. It has the luckiest of all the number sounds, being a close homonym for "wealth." Paired with the generation marker "Chong," which also sounds close to the word for "double," calling out this name was like saying "double the fortune." Even a simple sentence like "Chong-ba, come here," was like uttering a small blessing on the boy. To Little Chen, the name "Fortune" helped reverse the circumstances of the boy's birth, and was a small reminder of the debt she owed her lost son.

Lined up from oldest to youngest, the Chong generation of boys presented to Grandfather Chen when he arrived in Bell County were: nineteen-year-old Cattail, thirteen-year-old Radish and five-year-old Fortune. Grandfather Chen did not ask about the missing Chong Seven, but at one point he did murmur to his daughter that he had divined that Chong Seven was safe and in good health.

There was also the daughter. "My lotus flower," Little Chen had named her, "a second daughter, just like me." The lotus plant sets its roots deep in the watery pond muck, but when it blooms, the flower looms high and pure, like the radiant truth of the Buddha. It is not necessary to give daughters official generation markers, but the family called the second daughter by the nickname her mother gave her: Lotus.

When one side of the kitchen area washed away in a rainstorm, Cattail saw a way to tuck an extra private area into the Zhu cottage for himself and his new bride. He repaired the wall by adding a new alcove and strategically hanging a cloth across the entrance.

"It is the Treasured Bridal Chamber," Fortune declared when he first saw it.

Neither Radish nor Fortune cared much for Sister-in-law Wang at first. They addressed her as "Sao Sao," which means "elder brother's wife," and she ranked as yet another lord over them. When Fortune complained that Sao Sao was too bossy, Lotus smirked and poked Fortune's shoulder, saying, "Sao Sao doesn't realize yet that you're the little prince of the family."

Perhaps it was because he was the youngest. Perhaps it was because his parents had almost lost him to his sicknesses. Perhaps it was due to their sorrow over selling their third son to another family. Whatever the reason, this fourth son reigned as prince of the Zhu yard and often avoided his chores by practicing headstands and martial moves or reenacting stories with his brother Radish about their hero, the great General Yue Fei of the Song Dynasty.

"I am the young Yue Fei in the arrow contest!" Fortune announced one autumn evening, planting his feet and lifting his arms in the attitude of an archer. He was dressed in indigo homespun, a long-sleeved shirt belted over loose trousers, his head shaved except for one boyish tuft over his forehead. The mock warrior squinted into the sunset and gravely lowered his chin. But then he halted, stomping a cloth shoe in indignation. "What! That's no contest!" he shouted at the imaginary soldier in charge of the target board. "Move the target back to twice that distance, you drooling cur!"

The curse startled Grandfather Chen, who was wintering

with the Zhu family after arriving with Sao Sao. "What kind of General Yue Fei is this to be shouting insults for no reason?" he objected.

Fortune gave a brisk nod and resumed his stance. "The great general drew back the first of his eight arrows..."

"No, no," interrupted Radish. "It was nine arrows!"

"But our actor is Chong Eight, so I think it's right that he release eight arrows," suggested Cattail, who had just returned from a long day of repairing tools with his father. Cattail stretched out to rest on the ground. Shirtless despite the crisp air, he was enjoying the performance.

All this distraction made Fortune's brow furrow in irritation, which had the benefit of adding to his heroic appearance. "The great general drew back the first of his NINE arrows," he said, pulling an imaginary shaft slowly across his face until his fist was level with his ear. There was a suspenseful silence. Lotus twisted around from her work on the loom to follow the story.

"Pah!" shouted Fortune, making the sound of the arrow's release. With practiced flair, the marksman let loose a volley, his brothers chanting out the numbers. "... seven, eight, nine!"

Now Radish leaped up and presented a pretend target board to the audience. "Can you believe it? Nine arrows hit the target, but only one hole is left in the wood!"

"My heaven!" Grandfather Chen cried out in mock disbelief. "And what shall be the prize for this amazing feat?"

Cattail waved a hand to signal that he had the answer, though he was too tired to do anything more than prop himself up on an elbow. He stroked a pretend beard and affected the exaggerated speech of a grand official. "I am the magistrate here," Cattail said.

Grandfather Chen laughed. "What kind of miserable town would put such a scrawny, half-naked field hand at its helm?"

Cattail waved off this critique. "Young archer, it is my

understanding that you are not married. Would you accept a match with my only daughter?" He let go of his chin and stretched out his hand, fingertips extended, palm upward. His eyebrows arched as he awaited an answer. Even Little Chen and Sao Sao, who had been shaking their heads at all the foolishness as they rinsed chopsticks and bowls, burst out laughing.

"But he cannot make his own match!" Lotus objected.

Radish took on this task. His voice lowered into his best baritone, his chest thrust out, the youth addressed the reclining magistrate. "May I make an introduction?" Radish inquired. "I am Master Zhou from west of the mountains, and I adopted Yue Fei as my own son when his father was lost to the river floods. I have overseen his training these past years in archery and sword fighting and, honorable magistrate, I would be overjoyed to sponsor this match."

And so the scene concluded, with Fortune looking bashful and the rest of the audience calling out their wishes for long life and a happy marriage. All but Fifty-four, who watched in silence. He was resting on a stool in the corner, his hands on his knees. Marriage. Lotus was already seventeen and he needed to find a match for her. And soon enough, Radish and Fortune would want to bring home brides. Where would he find the money for all that? And what about Chong Seven? Had he been married into the Na household as promised? Fifty-four sighed and shook his head, oblivious to the merriment around him. The strings of cash that came from that terrible contract had long ago been spent. With each new growing season, Fifty-four found his debts to his landlord increasing. How long would he be able to keep a claim to this shack and these fields?

This was a period of unusually bitter winters for the Huai River Valley. Snow shrouded the fields during the coldest months, and villagers in the corner of Bell County where the Zhu family lived shivered under their padded jackets, hands in their sleeves, hungry and miserable.

"Grandfather, how can you sleep outside every night when it is so cold?" Fortune asked. He marveled at the strange warmth that the old man exuded. "Even my cough goes away when I sit outside by you. Is it magic?"

"Of course it is magic," Grandfather Chen replied. "How else do you think I made this brazier full of embers appear at my feet?"

"You didn't make the embers appear — Mother brought them out here to you. I saw her do it!"

"Is that so? Then how did I make your mother appear?"

The boy had no answer to that one.

Grandfather Chen laughed merrily and pulled Fortune close. "Look there, what is the name of that star at the top of the Big Dipper?"

The boy frowned, trying to remember. "Heaven's Roof."

"Heaven's Gate," Grandfather Chen corrected, and then continued with the same lesson he had taught long ago to Fortune's mother until the boy rolled over, fast asleep.

During the day, Grandfather Chen would not lift a finger to help with household chores, and indeed added to the workload as an extra mouth to feed. Guests frequently came by to consult with him. "I am here to see the diviner," an anxious visitor would say. Grandfather Chen could usually be found on his stool drinking black tea or carving wood. After discussing the guest's concern, Grandfather Chen would reach into his hemp-cloth satchel and draw out his charm tools.

Grandfather Chen used his gift of divination in several different ways — he could read faces and discuss astrology and feng shui — but he was best known for his charm writing. Because Fortune was still a boy, and because it was the slow winter portion of the farming year cycle, Fortune was usually allowed to spend the day with his grandfather, and this often meant experiencing the superlative wonder of watching a charm form.

"My daughter's youngest son is a lucky boy, I will have him set things up for us," Grandfather Chen announced at the end of one typical consultation session, for a woman worried about her sick father. Having sensed that he was about to be summoned, Fortune was already lurking nearby, holding his grandfather's bag. The boy eagerly placed the red cloth package on a small table and revealed writing tools and special yellow charm paper. Wordlessly and with exaggerated professionalism, Fortune placed the cake of ink on the black slate inkwell slab and took the carved cap off the bamboo writing brush. He lovingly topped a stack of small paper squares with a bronze weight, his fingers lingering over its turtle shape, oblivious to the amusement on his grandfather's face. Then the boy ran to fetch a ladle of water. He dropped just the right amount into the inkwell, so that Grandfather Chen could grind the cake across its surface and turn the water into a pool of ink. Dipping the tip of his brush delicately into the pool, Grandfather Chen prepared to write.

This was not normal calligraphy; instead, it moved like nature, with rippling waves and animal tracks and star patterns, all mixed in and around auspicious characters. Charm writing is meant to summon the gods and cannot always be deciphered like regular writing. Grandfather Chen added an unusual finishing touch to all of his paper charms. Once the ink dried, he would reach for the chop seal around his neck. The chop was a small, rectangular piece of polished dark green soapstone stored in a thumb-sized wooden box that hung from a leather necklace.

Grandfather Chen would dip the end carved with his chop in red paste and hold it over the charm paper. After a reverent pause, his onlookers breathless, he clamped the seal down, rocking it back and forth, and then lifted it away. The resulting scarlet image of his talisman balanced the magic writing. Depending on its purpose, Grandfather Chen would either fold the finished charm into a triangle and use a piece of twine to turn it into a necklace or hand it unaltered to the recipient with instructions on how to paste it up in a house or near a grave.

"Take this home and burn it over a bowl," Grandfather Chen instructed the woman. "Then mix in some water and have your father swallow the entire compound in as few bites as possible."

Fortune made a face at the thought of having to eat burned paper, but the woman reached eagerly for her charm, nodding her head in gratitude.

Within days the woman returned carrying a basket.

"My father is in better health now than he has ever been!" she exclaimed, opening the lid to drop a squawking and flustered chicken into the yard, her payment for service.

Fortune tried many times to get his grandfather to teach him more about charm writing, but Grandfather Chen always refused.

"You are not old enough and I am not wise enough," was all he would say.

But Grandfather Chen eventually relented somewhat and agreed that if he would not pass on the charm writing arts, he would at least make something special for Fortune. It would be a kind of compensation for the boy.

"Bring me some good wood," he instructed. But he rejected all the samples Fortune brought him.

"This is too old and wormy," he clucked at a hunk of pine. "Too light," he said of a willow branch. "Won't work," he said after one quick glance at a log of cypress.

Fortune had spent hours hauling in the cypress, his hungry stomach rumbling the entire way at the wasteful expense of energy. The next day, Fortune continued to ignore his hunger pangs, which were incessant in the winter, and climbed to the forest on a nearby hill, searching at length through the snow-dusted landscape for something his grandfather would accept. He stamped his feet to keep them from freezing. His breath frosted the air and his hands went numb. He could see nothing unusual and had not the slightest idea what his grandfather was seeking. Dejected, Fortune reached up to loosen a half-fallen peach tree branch, and then grabbed a walking stick poking through the underbrush for the trip back home.

"Excellent!" his grandfather exclaimed, snatching up both the branch and the stick. He seemed especially impressed with the latter. "Wah, this is from a *qingtan* tree!" he said, weighing in his palms the stick Fortune had leaned on during his walk home. The old man headed to his seat by his brazier, spending almost a full day gazing at the two pieces of wood, all the while chewing on straw and humming a song. Then he took up his carving tools, supervised knife sharpening by Fortune, and finally started to whittle. He would not let anyone see what he was making, repeatedly shooing away Fortune and Radish. He spent days on this task, but appeared to be finished when the family set off for the trip to see Uncle Fifty-one and celebrate the Lunar New Year, which marks the start of a new cycle for the farming calendar.

"Our Chong Three has produced the first member of the next Zhu generation!" Uncle shouted, unable to contain his pride, as soon as his younger brother arrived.

"Let him sleep," Little Chen protested when Auntie Liu put the baby into her arms. The two women stood with shoulders touching, gazing down at the contented little slumbering face.

The rest of the family moved past them, unloading bags and shouting greetings.

Auntie Liu glanced at her sister-in-law. "Do you still have that silk shift that you needed to get your first boy?"

A sly smile spread across Little Chen's face and her eyes twinkled at the baby, but she did not reply.

Auntie laughed and nudged her. "You do still have it," she exclaimed. "After all these years, you still need that old thing?"

"I brought it in my bag," said Little Chen. "It is in your house."

"I will need to change your room then," Auntie exclaimed. "And here I thought it would be your eldest son and his new bride who would be needing more privacy." She stepped back to regard Little Chen, folding her arms. "The merchant I bought that piece of silk from did not realize it would be used to produce four sons. Why, just think how much I would have had to pay if he'd known! He sold me four-son silk!"

And so the reunion began. At the stove, the women chopped and rolled and pounded and sliced. Their hands stayed raw and wet and their hair dusted with flour as the cooking preparations continued for days on end. They wrapped dumplings and steamed buns and pressed dough into molds and created aromas that put everyone in a mood of dizzy anticipation. In the yard, the men made fishing poles for getting at carp through the ice along the river bank. They pasted up a new picture of the red-faced Demon Queller door guardian, to protect the household from evil spirits, while Grandfather Chen prepared a special banner of magical writing for the same purpose. Radish and Fortune joined their only unmarried cousin, Chong Five, in setting off firecrackers and running along the village lanes to watch processions of singing and drumming intended to ward off evil influences.

On the eve of the Lunar New Year, that harbinger of spring,

everyone at last was able to crowd together, chopsticks in hand, and select from baked carp, dumpling soup and long noodles. The meal naturally included dishes of bean curd. There was stinky tofu and spicy tofu and even balls of caramelized sweet bean curd. Best of all was that chicken given to Grandfather Chen. Auntie and Little Chen had argued at length over how to cook this prize. They finally decided to soak it in soy sauce to enhance its flavor and then plunge it into hot oil to turn the skin golden and crispy.

At midnight, the family ritual was held. First, Uncle unrolled his father's portrait and hung it on the wall. Next he lit incense sticks and set them in front of the small wooden spirit tablets carved with the names of Old Zhu and his wife. Then Uncle made a brief family report to his parents' spirits and led the bowing to the Zhu ancestors. Each member of the family, from the oldest, Uncle Fifty-one, to the youngest, Fortune, stepped forward — except for the new baby, who was carried on his mother's hip — to take a turn at the solemn rite of kneeling three times on the dusty red cushion and bowing until the forehead touched the floor. The family was so large that the line spilled out into the yard, with Fortune the last to kneel. The moonless night was dark and still and cold. Waiting in the yard, Fortune hopped from one foot to another to keep warm, burying his chin in the scratchy straw lining of his newly-padded jacket, the recent feast churning in his belly in a most satisfactory way.

"Zhu Chong-ba," his uncle called out, his deep voice dwelling on each syllable of Fortune's name, especially the last.

The family parted so that Fortune could make his way into the hall. It was a simple peasant's hovel, made festive on this special occasion by the scroll of Old Zhu staring down from the bare wall, and the flickering light of the red candles illuminating the spirit tablets on the altar table. Faces turned toward him from every direction, so that Fortune felt as if he was entering a grand and important place. He stepped over the threshold and breathed in the thick smoke from the incense.

"The first prostration... to your Grandfather Zhu," Uncle instructed, gesturing to the pillow. Fortune dropped to his knees, setting his hands flat on the cold earthen floor. He breathed in its rich acrid odor, his dirty fingernails visible until his forehead lowered over them.

"The second prostration... to your Paternal Grandmother." Fortune jumped to his feet and stood up straight. His uncle nodded for Fortune to continue. The boy dropped back to the cushion, sneaking a glance at the unusual view of everyone's shoes as he dipped his head back down to the floor.

"The third prostration... to the Zhu clan." The family, crowded into the room, bent over the boy's small form like a stand of bamboo, all eyes following his movements. Little Chen smiled fondly at this youngest child, grateful to the ancestors for their help turning her sickly baby into a healthy boy, glad to have her own father at her side this year.

Grandfather Chen was not a member of the Zhu lineage, but as an elder he was seated in a place of honor next to Uncle. There was nothing ornate about the offerings — a chipped bowl of grain holding a few sticks of incense, some small dishes of delicacies from the feast table and the red candles were all that sat before the tablets. It was the sincerity in the eyes of the worshippers and the simplicity of the proceedings that gave them dignity. Grandfather Chen glanced with renewed respect at the portrait of the family patriarch, his old friend from Ferry Village.

As for Fortune, being the youngest member of the family made the ceremony seem all the larger and more significant. Memories of his relatives looming above him as he prayed, his uncle calling out the order of prostrations, were seared deep into

PART ONE: FORTUNE

Fortune's understanding of righteousness. Later, when he would remember the New Year's Eve rituals at Uncle's house, or think back to the years when he was surrounded by a large family and did not know about loss and grief, Fortune would feel a fondness and gratitude that came mixed with pangs of indebtedness.

The next morning, with the family rituals complete, it was time to relax, open the doors to visitors, and drink bowls of warmed wine. This was when Grandfather Chen dispensed the results of his whittling. He handed a fan of carved peach-wood slats to his own daughter, a bracelet of wooden beads etched with her namesake bloom to Lotus, and a flute to Radish.

"What's that by the side of the house?" he asked Chong Five and Cattail.

The young men dashed off to where he pointed and discovered a pair of stilts. How could Grandfather Chen have hidden away something so big? No one could say. There were even delicate wooden wine cups for Uncle and Fifty-four. Through all this Fortune's anticipation grew. What was in the bag for him? After all, the whittling started as a way to take Fortune's mind off of his desire to learn about charms. But Grandfather Chen did not seem to notice his youngest grandson. Fortune crept forward to catch his attention. Nothing. Around him everyone was distracted by all the wonderful gifts being passed out. Cattail was like a little boy himself, out in the yard trying to knock his cousin Chong Five from the stilts. Grandfather seemed immersed in teaching Radish how to put his fingers along the flute holes. Fortune sat cross-legged and forlorn, his elbows on his knees, his eyes filling with tears.

"Grandson, come over here and listen to your brother play the flute," Grandfather Chen called to him.

Fortune trudged over but would not look at his brother, his

hurt feelings hardening into a stubborn resentment.

So it was Radish who first noticed the little pouch in Grandfather Chen's hand. "Grandfather, what is that in your hand?"

Grandfather Chen looked at the pouch in surprise. "Well, I don't know," he said. "It was going to be a gift for a good boy, but there doesn't seem to be anyone like that left without a gift, does there?"

Fortune grinned. He glanced shyly up at his grandfather, who held out the pouch to him. It was a square of leather tied up into a container. Fortune dropped to the ground to untie it, his brother leaning over his shoulder. Fortune pulled loose the strings, which fell back to reveal that the inside had been painted with squares for a board game. The bag contained thirty-two small wooden disks, each engraved with a single character on one side and a picture on the other, with half of the engravings dyed black and half red.

"What is it?" asked Fortune.

"Why, child, it's a chess set," his grandfather exclaimed. "They play it in the cities. I learned it when I was a soldier because our general was fond of the game and liked to make us all play in tournaments."

Grandfather Chen spent the rest of the afternoon explaining Chinese chess to Fortune and Radish. A knot of interested onlookers changed throughout the day, according to who happened to be visiting and offering New Year's greetings. Grandfather Chen showed the boys how to set a row of five soldiers in the front rank, flanked by two cannons, the only pieces that can jump, and backed by a crowded row of chariots, horses, elephants and advisors, with a general at the back center.

"The elephants cannot cross the river," Grandfather Chen stated firmly, indicating the blank space that divided the board in half.

Fortune gravely nodded his head. It was a lot to take in.

At first, the boys played with the picture sides of the round wooden pieces facing up, but once they understood how the pieces moved, Grandfather Chen made them flip the disks over and use only the sides with the written characters. Fortune had trouble with this, since he could not distinguish the pattern of strokes that made up each word. "That's your soldier, not your advisor, you duck egg!" Radish corrected Fortune as they set up a new game. Fortune was so humiliated by his constant mistakes that he refused to play and stomped off.

Grandfather Chen gave him some time to calm down, and then walked over to the boy's side holding a pair of sticks, one of which he handed to Fortune. They squatted together over a patch of dirt, a peasant's writing tablet.

"You write the character for 'soldier' like this, starting at the top and working down, with a quick left-falling stroke and then a vertical stroke beneath it and then across and down again," said Grandfather Chen, watching his pupil's progress. "Yes! Now make the most important line, the long horizontal one, which holds the entire character in balance, and finish with two dots below. Very good!"

Soldier, cannon, horse, general. The first words that Fortune learned to write.

4

BEANS BOIL IN THE POT

*The fourth year of the Yuan Shun Emperor's Primal
Attainment reign period (1338). Bell County's East Ward.*

"MA, TELL ME the story of the 'Seven Paces Poem.'"

Intent on her weaving, Little Chen jumped at the sound of
her son's voice. She turned around to find Fortune seated on
the ground behind her. She wondered if he had seen her talking
earlier that day to a messenger. She had not thought anyone had
noticed. But why else would Fortune be sitting here wanting a
story, in the middle of the day, if he was not worried about her?

"You know the poem well enough," responded Little Chen.
"Why not recite it for me like your grandfather taught you?"

Fortune shook his head. "I want to hear the story of the
poem," he insisted.

Little Chen relented and set down her shuttle, resting her
hands in her lap before launching into the story.

"The emperor of Wei during the Three Kingdoms era was
jealous of his younger brother, the poet."

"Was the poet the youngest brother like me?"

"No doubt. And the most talented. Hoping for a chance to
find fault and perhaps even do away with the poet, the emperor
one day challenged him to compose a poem within the time
required to walk seven steps. If the emperor was pleased with

the poem, he would spare the poet's life. The poet began to walk. Let's see you do it."

Fortune jumped to his feet. He took a grand step forward and then looked over at his mother. "How many paces do you think he took before he started the poem?"

"He would have only taken a few steps to think up the words, and then he would have started saying the poem while he finished."

Fortune took a second step, and then a third. He lifted his chin and began to recite:

Beans boiling on a beanstalk fire.
Step four.
A voice cries out from within the pot:
Step five.
"We sprang from the same seed."
Step six. A triumphant smile spread as Fortune concluded with his foot outstretched for his final step:
"Why cook us with anger hot?"

Little Chen could not help laughing as Fortune landed his seventh pace.

"Tears of remorse and guilt sprang from the emperor's eyes," she continued, caught up in the tale. "He, like all in his clan, enjoyed poetry and here was his younger brother…"

"His youngest brother."

Little Chen acknowledged the correction. "And here was his youngest, smartest brother reminding him of his responsibilities. The poet obeyed the rules of poetry even as the emperor disobeyed his parents by not protecting his family. The poet was an innocent bean in the pot."

An innocent bean. Little Chen looked at Fortune, her innocent bean. The news she had received would make him sad.

"You saw me talking to the messenger earlier today?"

Fortune nodded.

"Your grandfather is not well. I have been summoned to his side."

Fortune swallowed. "Ma, is Grandfather going to die?"

"He has lived a long, long life," she answered, to herself as much as to her son.

Fortune stayed close by his mother for the rest of the day, until she sent him to collect more water for dinner. When he returned from the well, he noticed Lotus' red-rimmed eyes when she came over to help him unload the bucket from his shoulder pole.

"Is it Grandfather?" he asked. But Lotus shook her head and turned away. Fortune continued with his chores, nervously eyeing his parents as they bent their heads together, talking intently. Fortune realized that his brothers also seemed sad and subdued. And then he saw that Lotus was packing her belongings.

"Where are you going?" he asked, and the fear in his voice caused Little Chen to look up. She came to her youngest son's side and took his hand. With that, everyone drew in closer. Fifty-four pulled up a stool and sat down. Radish squatted at his feet. Sao Sao stepped over to link arms with Lotus. Cattail stopped adding kindling to the hearth and came to linger in the shadows. They all listened as Little Chen explained that she needed to return to Ferry Village to take care of her father, and that she had decided to use this time also to arrange a marriage for Lotus.

Fortune nodded and looked from his mother to Lotus.

"You will not come back?" he asked.

Lotus covered her face with her sleeve and turned away.

"Lotus is already twenty-one. There is no one here for her to marry, so your father and I want to marry her to someone from Ferry Village," Little Chen explained. "I will ask my father about this, if I can make it to him in time. He picked out an excellent bride for your oldest brother. Now it is Lotus' turn to marry. I will take her with me and find a good family for her."

"Then take me with you to take care of Grandfather and find Lotus a husband," Fortune begged, his eyes filling with tears.

His mother insisted that Fortune, who was by then ten years old, was too young and needed to remain at home.

"Radish will be our escort," she said. "Cattail needs to help his father in the fields, and besides, he has a family of his own now," she added, since Sao Sao had given birth to a boy the winter after her arrival in Bell County.

"But I need to say goodbye to Grandfather," Fortune implored, but he could see that his mother had made up her mind, though she was wiping away her own tears.

When it was time for Lotus to leave for the journey to Ferry Village, Fortune could only give his sister a piece of quartz he had found in the woods, an unusual chalky-green stone embedded with a lotus-shaped purple crystal.

Lotus smiled at the gift, holding the stone in one hand and using the other to caress her youngest brother's pockmarked face. "I remember the day you were born, little brother. Our mother squeezed my hand till I thought it would break as you appeared in this world," she said. She bit her lip and struggled to speak. "You must not cry, or I will not be able to bear this."

Lotus dropped her hand to Fortune's shoulder and looked away from his face, gazing instead at the sky. "While I am gone, you can remember me whenever you can see the Weaving Maid star. Doesn't the Weaving Maid get to cross the Celestial Silver River and meet her true love, the Herd Boy, once each year?"

"Yes," Fortune solemnly answered.

"Well, you can be the Herd Boy's little brother and come visit me, too. Think of me whenever you watch my star, and I will look for you next to the Herd Boy."

Little Chen put her arm around Lotus' shoulders and said it was time to leave. Lotus picked up her basket and said goodbye to her father. As she headed down the road, trailing Little Chen and Radish, she turned back once, to open her palm and show Fortune that she was holding tight the piece of quartz.

It took several weeks for Little Chen to arrange her father's funeral and her daughter's marriage. Exhausted, she looked forward to returning home to her husband.

"Radish, there is one more task for us, but we will take care of it as we leave Ferry Village," she said, and then refused to elaborate. Little Chen wanted to visit the inn where she had last seen her third son.

Radish's pace slowed when they neared the inn and he recognized the unchanged surroundings. "Ma, we should not pass by this place," he warned.

"Radish, I want to see him," Little Chen said. "You can wait down the road or join me." So the two sat at a table, tense and fidgeting. Soon a young man shuffled through a doorway. He was tall but thin and shabbily dressed; his shoulders slumped in the way of a broken spirit, his eyes on the ground. Little Chen could not restrain herself. She leaped up and called out, "Chong Seven!"

The young man froze and there was an awful silence. Then he shook his head. "No," he said firmly, ducking back into the room from which he had emerged.

Radish grabbed his mother's arm and dragged her away. The two did not slow down until they turned a corner in the road. Then Little Chen looked back, thinking that Chong Seven, her long-lost son, had stuck out his square chin, which was just like hers. He had a red thread around his neck and she wondered if it was wrapped around the charm she had once thrown at him.

The years after the season when Grandfather Chen died and Lotus was married away saw one bad harvest after the next. Fifty-four's debts reached a breaking point. When the crops were reaped in the tenth month of the year that Fortune passed his tenth birthday, the hulled grain poured only to the three-quarters level of the large earthenware storage jar. This was the millet needed to survive through the winter. With a heavy sense of foreboding, Fifty-four gathered his sons to help haul the fall harvest tax to the landlord's granary.

"Young Master, good afternoon," said Fifty-four to the landlord's son.

The young man replied with a scowl as he gestured with his long fingernails to step forward for a turn at the scales.

"Quickly, quickly," Fifty-four urged. The three brothers stumbled over themselves in their rush to help Fifty-four load the tax grain baskets onto the measuring stand. A clerk handled the weighing. All eyes focused on the balance arm to see if it would lift to the sufficient level. It did. The brothers smiled, but Fifty-four could sense from the tax agents that there was more to come. The landlord's son rose from his seat and strolled haughtily over to the balances. He stuck his hand into a basket, spilling grain to the floor.

"It feels too moist to me," he said. "You're just like the rest, adding water to fool us on the weight!"

Stunned by the accusation, Fifty-four decided against protesting.

The landlord's son turned to the clerk and instructed him to deduct one catty per basket from the total. Then he continued examining the baskets, setting one aside. "This one is moldy and full of thistle besides. Disregard it."

The landlord's son returned to his seat and examined his books. Fifty-four stood before him across the accounts table. Fifty-four had heard rumors that the landlord intended to give some of his fields to a recently-married son, who had been seen inspecting the area for a building project. It was only a question of which fields. The landlord's son scowled again and folded his hands. "You are already in arrears with us and while we did not expect much from you, even I am surprised at this meager result," he said, his words slow and even and false. But, really, the landlord's son had no choice — he was just following his father's instructions. "Our family does not want your services any longer. You are to vacate the land at once."

Fifty-four blinked and waited to see if that was all, but the landlord's son was ignoring him and waving forward the next group of tenants. Fifty-four backed away, making small bows and repeating his thanks for the landlord's benevolence to his family. Behind him, Fifty-four could feel the wrath of Cattail, who had sweated the most to harvest the maligned crops. Fifty-four was struck with the memory of a flaming red face shouting at him in his old family bean curd shop. He remembered the slop strewn everywhere and the overturned trays. Fifty-four thrust out his arms to keep his sons at bay, pleading with them under his breath to keep silent. Outside the building, Fifty-four drove his sons quickly away, but once all four were safely alone on the road Cattails fury burst open.

"Father, that was all lies!" Cattail shouted. "Lies! How could you let him say that?"

Fifty-four looked past his bewildered youngest son to the angry expressions on the faces of Cattail and Radish. He prickled with the thought of his own youthful defiance against corruption and inequity, which had cost him so dearly.

"Do you think protestations would have helped us?" he asked. "Did you stop even once to notice the guards in all the corners? Do you think they would have hesitated in conscripting you, at the least instigation? You are a fool!"

Fifty-four walked briskly forward. "How did I raise such ignorant boys?" he muttered to himself. He wanted them to understand, in ways that he himself had not understood at their age.

He stopped short, turning abruptly to face them.

"Don't you have any memory at all of what happened to Old Hu? He was in the same situation as us. When the debts were tabulated and the grain weighed, the Hu family came up short like we did. It may be that the landlord just wanted to get rid of Old Hu, like he wants to get rid of us so he can give our land to one of his sons. Old Hu had a bad temper and tried to argue that the measurements were wrong, so then he was ordered to pay up immediately. I was not there to witness it, but I was told that Old Hu raised his fists and pushed the scales over in his anger. And what do you think happened to Old Hu then?"

"The Hu family left suddenly," Cattail recalled, frowning.

"They did not leave, they were scattered, because Old Hu was beaten to death on the spot by all the guards and thrown out to the dogs," said Fifty-four, shaking his head at the gruesome image. He spoke his next words so softly that his sons all stepped closer to hear them. "His young daughter was taken by the landlord, to be a slave. I saw his wife holding their baby and leaving late one evening. With nothing. I'm sure she's a beggar now, if she survived at all."

Fortune reached up to take his father's hand. They continued on in silence and soon passed a neighbor, who greeted Fifty-four with a cheerful, "Have you eaten?" The standard peasant greeting. The neighbor changed his tone after taking in the disconsolate faces of the brothers and their father. Fifty-four apprised him of their unfortunate circumstances and said they would soon be leaving the village.

"Where will you go?" asked the neighbor.

"We haven't yet decided."

Back at home, Sao Sao, now the mother of two young sons, did not take the news well. She was still struggling to recover from the birth of her second child and did not want to travel. Radish remembered the last time his parents had wandered in search of a new home — the trip had cost the family a son. Fortune worried that Lotus would not know how to find them if they moved. But Little Chen immediately grasped that things could have been much worse.

"The young master did not demand full repayment of our debts?" she asked, incredulous. She agreed with her husband that the family should leave quickly before the landlord's son changed his mind.

As they packed their belongings, the neighbor who had passed Fifty-four and his sons on the road appeared at their door, holding a lantern. Fifty-four went out to talk with the man, and the two conversed at length in hushed voices. When at last he stepped back inside, Fifty-four lifted his hands in a gesture of relief. "He knows of a place we can go."

Once the Zhu family crossed Red Heart Bridge, following the directions of their former neighbor, the scenery became increasingly desolate. Their path climbed ridges and was often overgrown with weeds from lack of use. Cattail walked ahead with a reaping knife to cut through the brush, while Radish and Fortune took turns pulling a small cart loaded with their meager belongings, including Little Chen's loom, the big millet jar, and pots of pickled vegetables. Sao Sao's strength ebbed as the hours passed. She could no longer hold anything, not even her toddler's hand, and she trudged along with her head down until her body tired of the abuse and she collapsed in a faint.

Little Chen, who had Sao Sao's infant strapped to her back, kneeled carefully to the ground and was the first to see the blood trickling down her daughter-in-law's legs. Sao Sao had hemorrhaged with the birth of her second son the previous month and she was still weak despite all the herbal concoctions Little Chen had given her. The men and boys worked to clear some space and start a fire while Little Chen watched over Sao Sao and chanted prayers to the Metal Mother. Everyone but Sao Sao and her babies looked fearfully into the woods, hoping none of the wolves they had heard howling would catch the scent of blood in the air.

"It shouldn't be far now," Fifty-four kept saying as they made their way slowly forward the next day, having endured a cold and harrowing night.

Finally they reached the ferry that led to their destination — Lone Hamlet. As they waited for the ferryboat man to pole his way across the river, they took in the outline of the village that was about to become their home.

Lone Hamlet was a small village of about fifty households. It sat between two branches of the Hao River, which is a twisting tributary of the Huai. This tributary gave its name to the prefectural seat, the walled city of Hao, strategically located at the place where the Hao forks off from the Huai. Lone Hamlet was at the edge of Great Peace Ward, which was itself at the most remote corner of Bell County, one of three counties forming Hao Prefecture. Back during the fighting between the Mongols and the Song armies, the inhabitants of this area deserted it, fleeing in all directions. For several decades, the land was abandoned, until the Mongols sent down an army charged with the fearsome duty of clearing the area of tigers. Commander Yesunge, leader of this unit, became known in the region as the tiger tamer. It is said that he collected a thousand skins during his eight years there. A memorial arch for Yesunge stood in the center of the village.

Fifty-four and Little Chen knew nothing about the place beyond that a certain Squire Lin lived there. They had learned he was willing to take on more tenants.

"Old Grandpa, why is this place called 'Lone Hamlet?'" Fifty-four asked the gaunt old ferry man. He was dressed in a waterproof reed hat and cape, and poled them slowly to their destination.

"Because it's the only place where smoke has returned to the chimneys," the old man replied, his eyes fixed on the shoreline.

Fifty-four thought this over. Such a response naturally raised a few more questions.

"And what about the neighboring villages — why haven't people returned there?" he finally asked.

The old man did not seem keen on conversation. He spat into the water and answered crossly. "What a lot of farting!" he exclaimed. "Everyone else feared the tigers, of course!"

"Ah," Fifty-four replied. He did not ask any more questions, focusing his attention instead on the forest as the ferry approached the shore.

Squire Lin was the richest landlord in the village, which was dominated by the Lin family. Fifty-four's friend from the other side of Bell County had given good advice; the squire was still looking for tenants to clear land into new fields. More fields meant more money for Squire Lin. He lived in the fanciest compound in the village, with fat goldfish swimming in the pond at the center of his main courtyard and anxious servants hurrying through his rooms. Squire Lin's clerk pointed Fifty-four toward the place where he would find new living quarters. The location was across the main thoroughfare, which had been paved when the memorial arch was erected and given the grand name of Flagstone Avenue. Turning left at the village's public water well, the Zhu family headed down Mulberry Lane, which ended in its namesake grove of mulberry bushes. The squire's clerk had said they could live in the empty cottage at the end of this lane. At first, Fifty-four and Little Chen could not find any vacant structure, but Cattail poked through the underbrush and called everyone over. He pointed wordlessly to barely discernible collapsed mud walls overgrown with weeds. Their new home.

Exhausted already, Fifty-four and his three sons stood mute until Fifty-four rubbed his brow and cleared his throat.

"First, we clear a place to sleep," he said, glancing grimly at the setting sun.

The area appeared deserted; though Fifty-four was sure they were being watched from the doors of cottages in the distance. Fortune also seemed on edge. The boy jumped at the rustling of a bird in the bushes behind him, at the chirping of the crickets, at a branch that swung loose from all the commotion. Little Chen fussed over Sao Sao and then went to collect enough kindling and stones to start a fire and cook some porridge. The mood of the brothers improved when they discovered hidden treasures in the underbrush. By nightfall they had amassed the following collection: a broom, two bamboo baskets (one in good shape, and one not), a wooden hair comb, three cracked terra cotta bowls, a three-legged stool with two legs missing, and, to their delight, a hatchet in good condition.

"If you head past those three pine trees, you'll find berries that are still ripe," said an old woman who appeared the next morning. This was Old Mother Wang, a neighbor and a widow with three boys of her own. She was a small, tidy, matter-of-fact woman. In her hands was a tray of fried cakes made from taro root that made Fortune sway with desire. She passed the tray to Little Chen and also handed her a gourd full of cooking oil, a precious gift. She did not need to ask if they had eaten. Instead she asked where they were from.

"I am Zhu Fifty-four of Jurong, south of the Yangtze," said Fifty-four. "We came to this corner of Bell County from the East Ward, and before that a county in Si Prefecture."

Old Mother Wang nodded politely and warned them away from the mulberry bushes, which she said were tended jealously by a family across the lane. Then she left them to their work. Thinking first of the tigers, the family set about constructing a fence around their cleared yard. Then they repaired the mud walls and put thatch overhead, ending up with a one-room rectangular cottage. Along the back wall, facing south, Little Chen set small clay statues of the Metal Mother and Lord Buddha on the household altar, along with a charm from Grandfather Chen and a metal incense burner. At one side of the cottage interior was the cooking pit, at the other the sleeping and sitting area. Outside, extending from the wall closest to the fields was the manure shed for collecting privy waste, sweepings and ashes. With winter fast approaching, the family also began the backbreaking labor of clearing stumps and underbrush from the closest unclaimed land.

Old Mother Wang came by again one evening carrying melon seeds to crack with Little Chen. The two women sat in the lengthening shadows, spitting out shells and saying nothing. Little Chen was consumed by her fears. They did not have enough to eat and she feared foraging alone too far into the unfamiliar hills. A worry wheel turned round and round in her head, blocking out everything else. Daughter-in-law will not make it through the winter without more to eat. The baby is still nursing and cannot survive without his mother.

"You have too many mouths to feed," said Old Mother Wang, abruptly interrupting the wheel. "Your second boy, he needs a wife. What are you going to do about it?"

Little Chen grasped her father's chop seal on the leather cord around her neck. The wheel resumed again, with marriage worries added in. There is no money for a bride price, to say nothing of a matchmaker. There is no hope of ever getting a bride for Radish. Daughter-in-law will not make it through the winter...

"I will see what I can do," Old Mother Wang interrupted again, as she straightened her creaking knees and left.

Two days later she returned.

"There is a farmer across the rope bridge over the South Branch," she said, leaning against the new fence around the Zhu yard. "This farmer has no sons. He is willing to accept your second son as a 'married in' son-in-law for his daughter. And he wants to hire your youngest boy to herd his goats."

Fortune accompanied Radish the day he was sent to join the household of the farmer with no sons.

"What is a 'married in' son-in-law?" Fortune asked as they followed Old Mother Wang's instructions, heading toward the bridge over the creek that led to the Tang Family Settlement.

"It means I will join their household, and my children will take their surname," Radish stated.

"Is that bad?"

Radish shrugged. "It's not what you are supposed to do. A man is supposed to bring a wife into his family home and give his children his own family's name. That's what Cattail has done. His children will all have the Zhu name, and Sao Sao lives with us."

Fortune mulled this over as the two crossed the rope bridge single-file. He glanced at his brother's back. "Are you angry?"

Radish stopped, which made Fortune stop. He turned around to face Fortune and gripped the bridge's rope railings. "You remember about our other brother, Chong Seven?"

Fortune nodded solemnly. This brother was only mentioned rarely, and always with an expression of anguish.

"Families are supposed to buy daughters-in-law for their sons. When I was a boy, a family brought us gifts and paid money for our oldest sister and so she moved away to become their daughter-in-law. Then our mother took Lotus and found a family that wanted to pay for her. That's why Lotus didn't come back. But if a family does not have money, then instead of buying a daughter, the family has to sell their son. We had to sell Chong Seven. Now we have to sell me." Radish looked back over the bridge to the path they had just walked down. "At least I will be close to home."

"Will I get sold?"

"Who can say?"

On the shore below them, a woman washing clothes called out to ask who they were looking for. When Radish answered, the woman pointed out the correct compound for them to enter. The two brothers stood awkwardly inside the doorway. They watched the chickens peck at the earth floor, until Radish's new father-in-law strode into the room and waved at the family altar.

"Kneel!" he demanded, glaring at Radish.

Fortune shrank back into the shadows. His brother stepped forward and dropped to his knees before the Tang altar.

"You will keep your Zhu surname," instructed the father-in-law, who was known as Tang the Old Wolf, due to his ferocious, biting temper. "But your first three sons will all be Tangs."

"What about a fourth son?" Radish asked.

"Impertinence!" Radish's new father-in-law cried out. "I am not yet convinced that your seed will produce anything worthy of my clan!"

Radish glanced warily back at Fortune, which caused Tang the Old Wolf to notice the boy too.

"What are you doing here?" he shouted at Fortune. "I did not hire you to follow your useless brother around."

Fortune fled the compound before matters could get any worse, escaping through the doorway to find a boy about his own age leaning against a wall, laughing. The boy threw a switch at Fortune.

"What's this for?" Fortune asked.

"Herding goats," the boy replied. "I am Harmony. You must be the new goat herder. You've been hired because I do such a bad job."

"Are you in trouble, then?"

"Oh, no," Harmony answered. "Old Wolf thinks everyone does a bad job at everything. But things will go better with two of us running after all of the Tang clan's goats. The herd has gotten too big for one herder. Let's go."

"Aren't you a Tang?" Fortune asked. He wondered if anyone in this strange clan was actually a Tang.

"I am now," said Harmony as the two boys walked toward the goat pen. "I am Old Wolf's nephew. I live with my aunt, who is his sister."

"But where are your parents?"

"I was born in a different part of Bell County," Harmony explained. "My parents were kidnapped by bandits when I was still a baby, but they were kidnapped by mistake — the bandits were trying to raise a ransom on the wrong husband and wife. I guess the bandit chief felt sorry for me, because after he killed my parents, he put me in a shoulder-pole basket and sent one of his men to deliver me to my mother's older sister. Here. In the Tang Family Settlement. My aunt was glad to have me, because her husband had run off on her and she had no children."

"So what is your original surname?"

"No one could remember my father's surname by the time I was old enough to ask about it," said Harmony. "So now I am a Tang."

At last it came time for the first planting of grain on the land reclaimed by Fifty-four and his sons. Fifty-four brought out the seed grain that the squire had given the Zhu family as an advance on their harvest. The seed mix consisted of foxtail millet with some broomcorn millet, since the almanacs all advise, "Red broomcorn with mottled foxtail," to increase the chance of success. Once harvested, the millet would be cooked with water into porridge, steamed with malt into sweet syrup, combined with barley mash to make vinegar, ground with wheat to make dumplings, and sometimes — after a good harvest — distilled into liquor.

Since Radish now lived with the Tangs and Fortune spent every day herding goats, it was left to Fifty-four and Cattail to arrange a turn with one of the squire's oxen. They could not get an ox until a day in the cycle of ten Heavenly Stems that was taboo for planting millet, so it was not until the next day that the actual planting could begin. Cattail poured the seeds into the drill box and harnessed the plough-seeder to the ox. As the animal lumbered forward to turn the soil, the seeds were shaken to the ground through the five small "plum blossom holes."

Fifty-four watched with satisfaction the scene of his eldest son guiding the ox through the fields. Fifty-four was well suited to farming. His quiet nature, which had focused long ago on the swirling soy milk steam, now scanned the horizon and understood its earth language. While his wife could read the stars, he could read the fields. She advised him of happenings in the Gourd constellation favorable to planting, but he noticed the willows opening their leaves and the peach trees budding. These were also signs that it was time to sow the millet, as Fifty-four explained to Cattail.

In the evenings, when the goats were back in their pen, Fortune could seek out the sons of Old Mother Wang. Fortune tagged along with Second Chao, who was closest to his age, on adventures across the village. Sometimes Second Chao even took Fortune to play ball or dice games in the courtyard of Lin Ying, the grandson of a retired Yuan official and a nephew to the squire himself. Ying was admired by the other boys for his skill at keeping a shuttlecock in the air using only his feet to kick it about, but Fortune felt shy in the Lin courtyard. Lin Ying's clothes and shoes showed no signs of mending and he had servants hovering nearby.

Fortune did not feel shy around Harmony, even though Harmony was two years older, and his clan was tight-knit and aloof. Perhaps this was because Harmony himself was an orphaned outsider, and he resembled Fortune in his rebellious nature. The Tangs were the first to return to the village when peace was restored. They had learned from the Mongol soldiers to raise goats and sheep, and became known for their goat meat and wool. Harmony grew up in the Tang barns, tending horses and goats.

"I'm better with horses," Harmony claimed to Fortune.

"Then why do you have to spend most of your time herding goats?" Fortune asked.

Harmony frowned. "Old Wolf is always saying that 'boys tend goats, men tend horses,'" he said, imitating Old Wolf's gruff voice. "But eventually I won't be the youngest boy in the settlement, and then I can be promoted to groom. Your brother

Radish needs to hurry up and make some baby boys."

"I've never ridden a horse," Fortune confided.

Harmony smiled devilishly back at him. "Then you're lucky that I'm your friend."

The very next day, when Fortune arrived at the goat pen, he found Harmony waiting for him on horseback. "We can take this pony for as long as the goats graze in the meadows by Tiger Mountain," Harmony said. "You can ride behind me." He reached out a hand.

Fortune backed away shaking his head. "You know I don't know how to mount a horse. I told you I've never ridden one. And where is this one's saddle?"

Harmony jumped neatly to the ground. "I'm going to teach you to ride bareback, like a Mongol boy."

Harmony lectured his new student on horsemanship for the rest of the day, offering lessons in mounting and dismounting, along with lengthy demonstrations of his own prowess. The goats were largely ignored. Fortune slid right over the pony the first time he tried to mount it and Harmony could not stop laughing.

"Not so much force, you're not trying to hurdle him," Harmony advised as he walked around and pulled Fortune to his feet. Harmony brought Fortune back to the pony's left side and told him to try again.

"Almost, almost... pull with your right hand... wah!" Harmony called out through Fortune's second attempt, which did not use enough force and thus had the same result of Fortune landing in the dust.

Fortune stood up, breathing heavily. He wiped the dirt from his face, furrowed his brow with determination, grabbed a handful of mane, and threw his leg over the pony's back.

"You did it! You did it!" shouted Harmony, waving his arms.

But the yelling excited the pony and made it bolt forward, leaving the rider back in the dust for a third time, and scattering the goats.

The pony became the focus of Fortune and Harmony's days, and soon enough Fortune was learning to trot and gallop. This mastery of the most basic skills made Fortune all the more impressed with his friend's horsemanship. When Harmony rode the pony, the animal moved entirely at his command, and could sidle up along the goats to pack them together or dart to outmaneuver a stray.

"Hold out your switch and stand still right there," Harmony commanded one day. "I have a new trick I've learned."

Fortune dutifully held his switch at arm's length and watched Harmony ride off, turn the pony around, and gallop full speed forward. Fortune assumed Harmony was going to grab the switch from his hand, except that Harmony was not approaching close enough.

"What is he going to do?" Fortune wondered. "Is he going to cut toward me at the last minute?"

The earth shook as the pony approached at full speed. Fortune kept his arm extended until, with a wild look of glee, Harmony suddenly stretched out and down and seemed to dangle from the horse's back as he neatly plucked the switch from Fortune's hand before snapping back upright. Harmony let out a loud whoop as held the switch aloft, cantering casually away.

"How did you learn that?" Fortune asked as they picked up their belongings and prepared to head back to the Tang Settlement.

"I once saw a horse competition at a market town near here," Harmony said. "It was a long time ago, before you came to Lone Hamlet. The riders could do all kinds of tricks like that. I've been practicing ever since. I'm finally getting good at 'side-snatching,' don't you think?"

"Yes, but have you ever fallen trying that?"

"Many times. But I'm good at falling too."

"Have you broken bones?"

"Only once, and even then not too badly."

Fortune was impressed. "You are the best horse rider I have ever seen," he said. "You are the Number One Stallion under Heaven!"

"It's a good name!" Harmony declared. He leaped onto their pony and galloped off to the Tang barns.

The next morning, though, Harmony arrived at the goat pen alone.

"Where's the pony?" Fortune asked.

"We can't take him anymore," Harmony said, his tone flat.

"Why not?"

"Because Old Wolf says we can't, that's why."

Harmony turned away to unhook the pen gate. The goats, bleating and bumping against themselves, poured out of the pen and took off down the path.

Fortune frowned as he absentmindedly guided the goats along. "Did he say why?" he yelled across the jostling animals.

Harmony whipped his switch against the pen posts as he walked. "Because he thinks I ride too rough and will crush one of his precious goats," Harmony yelled back. "And because he's that way. He's mean."

5

THE HERD BOY MEETS HIS MATCH
BUT LOSES HIS MEAL

*The first year of the Yuan Shun Emperor's Correctness
Attained reign period (1341). Bell County's Lone Hamlet,
near the Huai River in modern Anhui Province.*

TOWARD THE END of Fortune's third season as a herd boy, when he
was thirteen, a drought threatened the harvest. No one wanted
to see the herd boys heading anywhere close to the crop fields,
where the millet was needed for food, the hemp for cloth and
sesame for oil. There were also a few incidents of loose goats. Old
Wolf sent Fortune and Harmony off to the hills beyond the South
Branch and told them not to return until after the new moon,
when the harvest would be in.

Little Chen did not like the idea of sending her youngest son
away for such a long time and into such wilds. She prepared
a bedroll and mat for him and packed a basket with grain,
dried food and pickles. "Watch out for tigers and be wary of
bandits," she warned. "Be careful not to offend any mountain
spirits. If you run out of food, look first for berries. They should
be plentiful in the mountains. Remember that the chive sprouts
are especially tasty at this time of year. You know what they look
like, don't you?"

Fortune nodded impatiently as his mother continued with

her instructions.

"If you can, bring some back for us when you return. Those hills are said to be full of caves, so maybe you can find some shelter, but watch out for animal dens. Keep a strong stick always handy. I've packed fish hooks and also a flint stone, see?"

"Ma, I should go."

"Use the salve wrapped in sorghum leaves if you get any cuts..."

"Ma!"

Fortune gestured for his mother to cover the basket and let him take it, promising that he would be careful. Then he broke into a run, eager to reach Harmony and set off. The two headed east to a new plank crossing of the South Branch. Once they made it to the other side, the goats could not decide which looked tastier — the fields of sorghum to their right or the marsh weeds on their left. The boys' long switches solved the dilemma. Alas for the goats, chewed crops would mean a beating for the boys and soggy marshes were too likely to swallow up stray animals. The boys rushed the herd along, keeping them in a tight formation so that they rolled forward like a wave of brown and white fur. At last, goats and boys could linger in the small glens along the base of the Three Peaks Range. The goats munched on thistle and tree shoots while the boys fished and set a trap that Harmony had brought along for squirrels and rabbits and other small creatures.

"Do you miss your parents?" Fortune asked one night as the two were stretched out around a fire, a few goats snuggled next to them, the rest of the herd nestled in clumps nearby.

"I never knew my parents, so how would I miss them?"

Fortune was on his back, staring at the stars, remembering his Grandfather Chen and wondering what his family was doing in Lone Hamlet. "I can't imagine not being raised with my parents watching over me," he said aloud without thinking, and then glanced to see if he had made his friend angry. Harmony was gazing thoughtfully into the fire and did not respond. The moon was rising in the east and almost full. Fortune pointed to the brightest star in the sky that night, high in the northwest. "See that star there," he asked. "That's my sister's star."

"What does that mean?" Harmony asked, tilting his head back to view the sky.

Fortune explained that Lotus had left home and married someone in a distant place, which left him with nothing but the Weaving Maid star overhead to remember her by. "She is my second sister. My oldest sister died when I was still a baby, and I have an older brother who was sold away right before I was born and so I never met them, but I've always known about them and wished I'd known them. I guess that must be what it is like for you and your parents."

"Yes," Harmony agreed. He watched the bright Weaving Maid outshining all but the moon. Then he leaned on his side, and looked straight at Fortune. "Do you know that I sometimes wonder if maybe my father was a Mongol? Maybe that is why I have always liked horses and can ride so well. Because it is in my blood."

"Do all Mongols ride horses?"

"They do," said Harmony, nodding his head with the confidence of youth. "And that would explain why no one can seem to remember my father's surname. Mongols don't have surnames, you know."

Fortune had also turned away from the sky, to give his full attention to what Harmony was saying.

"Sometimes I think my aunt knows much more than she will ever say about my father," Harmony continued. "I think it must have been my mother who told the bandit chief, before he killed her, to send me here, to the Tang Family Settlement, because my mother knew my aunt had married a half-Mongol and so did not hate them like so many people do."

"Your uncle is half Mongol?"

"My Uncle Buqa," said Harmony. "He is the son of one of Yesunge's lieutenants, the tiger tamers, and grew up here in Lone Hamlet. But he left long ago to join the imperial army."

"He's a Mongol soldier?"

"That what I've been told, but no one has heard from him since he left."

Fortune thought of the stories his mother and Grandfather Chen had told him of the Battle of Yashan, when the Song Dynasty was lost forever. Grandfather Chen had always spoken of the Mongols as his foes, but Fortune decided not to mention this to Harmony.

"Someday I want to learn archery," Harmony said wistfully, staring into the embers of the fire. "I'm going to run off and try to find my Uncle Buqa." He looked fiercely at Fortune. "You can't tell anyone that."

"Why would I?" Fortune replied, and then he pointed with equal fierceness back at Harmony. "But you'd better not run off any time soon or else I'll be stuck all alone with all these goats all day." They both laughed. Fortune resumed his musings on the stars. "I will never run away. I couldn't live away from my family."

The two boys were alone in a rugged, parched landscape of rocky hills and patchy forests. They spent their days lazily guiding their herd along the base of Chive Mountain, seeking out clear streams, which they could hear before they could see. They were slowly heading toward the more distant Big Sister Mountain, a place they had never explored. Whenever the goats were settled in a good spot for grazing, Harmony and Fortune whiled away their time throwing stones into the water or playing chess with Fortune's set.

"Are those our goats?" Harmony asked one morning, jumping up in alarm during the middle of a game that he was losing.

"What are you talking about?" Fortune grumbled, but then he too heard bleating in the distance. "How can they have gotten so far away?"

The boys stood still, confused, until they spotted another group of herders approaching over a rise.

"We are herders from Perpetual Harvest Ward," called out the tallest of two boys who emerged from the trees.

"Then we are your neighbors," Harmony answered, his posture wary, his grip tight on his switch. "We are from Lone Hamlet in Great Peace Ward."

"This drought has sent us all far from our mothers' kitchens," the tall boy observed, sizing up the pair from Lone Hamlet.

"Just so," replied Harmony. He and Fortune exchanged glances as the taller boy admired their herd.

The boy laughed when he saw their nervous faces. "Oh, you don't need to worry about us! We have no need of even more smelly goats to keep track of," he said, as one of his own goats bumped its nubby horns against his thigh.

A third herder appeared in the distance, driving some stragglers. He was dressed in tattered clothes, and had a round face, a dark complexion and squinting eyes. The boy was small and not much to look at, yet the trees rustled overhead with excitement at this first encounter.

"Who is that one?" asked Fortune, jutting out his chin.

The trailing boy seemed accustomed to neglect and kept his eyes trained on his feet, except for quick sideways glances to check for wandering goats.

"He is from the Xu clan like us," said the tall boy, uninterested. "We don't pay him much attention. We call him Da."

Xu Da. There would come a day when the banners of the greatest armies in the land would bear his name.

The other two herders were brothers — the taller, older one went by "Senior" and the other "Junior." Senior laughed when he learned the names of the Lone Hamlet boys. "It is good to have Fortune and Harmony on our side!" He suggested that the five join together for companionship and also for safety. "We have heard that bandits are hiding out in this area," he said.

The forested hillsides were also sheltering autumn fruits and nuts: walnuts and gingko nuts, persimmons, pomegranates and even some late plums. And there were waterfalls to splash through and rock formations to climb. The five boys, relieved from all oversight, spent their days in raucous contests of strength. They found the crumbling ramparts left by a local hero from the Song dynasty and spent days playing "General Wang fends off the Jin invaders" or "General Yue Fei brings his army to rescue General Wang at the last possible moment." The boys also conducted regular group searches for wayward goats. The Xu brothers came equipped with a slingshot. As Da watched in silence, the brothers taught Fortune and Harmony how to use it to down small birds and rodents, which they roasted at night.

One languid afternoon, tired of climbing trees and wrestling, Fortune and Senior were stretched out in a patch of shade playing chess. Da, the youngest, was sent to keep watch over all the animals, but he had edged up on the older boys, and Fortune could see that he was trying to keep track of the board game. At this point, it appeared that Fortune would win. However, when Fortune foolishly exposed his general, Da gasped, which caused Senior to notice his presence. Senior grabbed a rock and threw it at Da, yelling, "Get out of here. You're too stupid to play this game."

Da ducked with surprising agility and turned away. Fortune had noted with mounting disapproval the way the Xu brothers treated their cousin. Fortune knew little about the three, but he could gather that the brothers despised Da's more humble family background, and that Da was resigned to their attitude of superiority. Fortune had grown tired of this. He snatched up his board, which ended the game. Senior jumped to his feet. The two boys stood glaring at each other.

"What's wrong with you?" Senior shouted at Fortune.

"How can you treat your own cousin like a slave?" asked Fortune. He stomped off to find Harmony.

Da stayed rooted in place, only his eyes moving to follow Fortune's loud departure through a gap in a thicket that led to the boys' campsite. "No one has ever spoken up for me," Da thought to himself. He had been treated so badly for so long that he had learned to expect the worst from everyone but his own parents. Da's father had been tattooed on the face with the word "robber" as punishment for stealing a knife, but this had happened during a fight, and everyone knew the charge was unfair. And yet Da's cousins had used this humiliation to force Da and his parents out of the Xu compound, sending them into a miserable hovel on swampland. Da had learned from his father to maintain dignity from within, regardless of circumstances.

"Your eyes betray you," his father had warned, more than once. "Best to keep them trained on the ground when you are dealing with ignorant people. Otherwise, you will get yourself in trouble. You are still very young, and you are small for your age. Heaven knows we've had trouble enough from my bad temper."

Even though he knew better, Da could not resist shifting his glance, slowly, from the thicket that Fortune had disappeared around to the frowning Senior.

"What are you looking at?" Senior retorted, but then he abruptly turned and strode away.

This left Da standing alone in the patch of shade. His face

broke into a smile that no one witnessed.

The boys were less quarrelsome after dining on rabbits skillfully skinned and cooked by Harmony, and the Xu brothers seemed to be making an effort to speak more courteously to Da, out of respect, no doubt, for their older and stronger new friends.

They sprawled on their bedrolls that night. When the embers of the fire were almost extinguished and the goats sleeping in a pile against a smooth rock face, Fortune found that he could not sleep. He reached to adjust his mat, and realized that Da was perched wide awake next to him, lying on his stomach and elbows, with his chin cupped in his palms, as if he had been waiting to talk. Da whispered to him, "It was a mistake to expose your general in the corner of the palace."

"What?"

"In the chess game with Senior," Da continued. "If he had brought his chariot forward, your general would have been forced up, where he could have easily been pinned down by Senior's horse. This would have been a fatal trap."

Now Fortune sat up, confused. "You are right," he said slowly, "but you said you'd never played chess."

"Of course I have played," Da replied.

"None of you had even heard of the game when I first pulled out my set."

"That's right," agreed Da.

"But I know that you haven't played a game on my set," said Fortune. He looked suspicious. "Have you been stealing my set while I sleep?"

"Why would I need to?" Da scoffed. "You don't need an actual set to play once you know the rules. I play in my head." He stretched back on his bedroll and gazed up at the stars twinkling between the tree branches. "When I'm stuck alone with the goats I think about chess moves," Da explained, yawning. "Sometimes when I can't figure things out clearly, I sketch a game board in the dirt and go from there. I'm grateful to have learned the game from you. Remember what I said about letting your general out from his file in the mid-game."

The moon, visible in the morning sky before dawn the next day, was in its waning crescent phase and the boys' food stores were running low. It was time for Fortune and Harmony to return to Lone Hamlet. However, the dawn also revealed storm clouds in the distance, an angry roiling mass heading their way. Senior told them of a large cave on the slope of Big Sister Mountain. The boys agreed to move all the goats there until the storm passed; then they could part ways and set off for their home villages. Under a blackening sky, with cool storm gusts jostling the goats, the boys hurried along, intent on reaching their cave.

"What if there's a wolf waiting to eat us in the cave?" worried Junior.

"We'll send you in first to check," promised Harmony, shouting to be heard over the wind.

But the cave was empty. As soon as the boys were settled in, they realized that their stomachs were also empty. Lucky for them, the storm was the kind that vents its wrath quickly and then moves on. So, leaving Junior and Harmony with the goats, the other three headed out to hunt sparrows.

They crept stealthily through the dripping underbrush of the mountainside, glancing this way and that with hunter eyes, mistaking the sounds of dripping raindrops for birds flitting in the leaves. Then all at once, the three boys froze. The sound of men's voices cut through the air, perilously close. "Bandits!" whispered Senior. Hunched down together, the hair on their arms standing on end, the boys tried to make out what the voices were saying.

"They went down this way, I'm sure of it," said one.

"I'm so hungry for goat meat it's hard to walk straight," said the other.

Senior, in a panic, realized the men were searching for their herds. "They're headed right for the cave!" he said, too loudly.

The two men halted and turned toward the sound. The taller of the pair spotted Senior and lurched toward him. Senior stood up and tried to launch a rock from his sling, but his target was nimble and crafty. The man sprang like a cracked whip, snatching Senior's throwing wrist and twisting the boy around to grip him tightly from behind.

"Why, here's a little goat herder right where we want him," said the man, his whiskers scraping Senior's cheek.

The lanky bandit's thicker, burlier companion chuckled and swaggered up to Senior. "Where's your herd, you sniveler?" he growled.

Da, still crouching in the bushes, reached for the solid stone tucked away for safekeeping in the pouch on his belt. He wriggled it out and grabbed for the sling Senior had dropped. Rising smoothly to his feet, Da took aim and released. The stone thumped hard against the temple of the man holding Senior.

The man howled and fell hard on top of Senior. The lanky bandit looked back with surprise and grunted at the round-faced child who had scored such a resounding hit. Da offered a proud smile, but by then Fortune was on his feet and pulling Da away. The two fled, paying no heed to where they were going.

The unharmed bandit took off after them. Fortune and Da hurtled through the trees, running madly, without enough of a lead to outrace a grown man. Fortune caught sight of a rock outcropping and headed straight to it, Da on his heels. Leaping onto the rocks, the boys could sense without looking that their long-legged pursuer was bearing down on them. The rain had stopped, but the rocks were still wet and slippery. They climbed hand and foot, making their way upward. Da swung on a tree branch down into a gap. "This way!" he shouted, and Fortune followed.

They landed in a bizarre, heaven-carved maze of narrow pathways through eroded chasms that channeled in unpredictable directions, like the interior of a cave that had lost its roof. The walls of gray karst sediment had trees sprouting at intervals from crevices and glowed yellow in the sunlight that now streamed from the storm clouds. The passageways were close and deep, giving the boys a size advantage. The bandit thudded down behind them, spraying mud and grit, but Da and Fortune were already scrambling in the dirt below a boulder suspended inside a gorge. The bandit was able to squeeze through too, but only with considerable cursing. The boys had by this time moved further through the formations.

The fissures steamed gently and smelled of the recent rain shower. Fortune rocketed through them with Da at his heels. They scraped hands and knees along the rough rocks until both were bleeding and bruised. Fortune winced each time he approached a corner, expecting to crash around it into the chest of his pursuer. His fear almost came true — he checked around one opening and caught a glimpse of the bandit. Fortune stopped short, backing into Da, who grabbed Fortune's shoulder and silently pointed up at a rugged, slanting crevice. Da leaped up the rock face, climbing like a tiger until he reached a higher ledge along the hillside. He turned to haul Fortune up with him. The man below heard the gravel spilling from beneath the boys' feet. He lumbered in their direction, but made a wrong turn and had to backtrack.

Perched on their ledge, the boys crouched together well above their furious pursuer, who had not yet thought to look up. "I'll catch you both, you little stinking monkeys," he hollered, his voice ricocheting through the chasms. "I'll skin you alive along with all your goats!"

Da reached for a handful of rocks, and Fortune followed his example. The two boys were poised to throw with all their might if the bandit spotted them, and were so intent on following his progress that they were caught completely by surprise when they were grabbed from behind and pulled back into darkness.

"No sound, no sound," a voice whispered urgently in their ears. A single pair of arms gently released them. The boys spun around to face a beefy Buddhist monk. He was frantically gesturing to keep quiet and follow him. With remarkable deftness, the monk led them through the rocks and ducked into a chain of low caves that gradually became caverns. Along the walls were niches holding Buddhist statuary and burning candles. Moisture leaked from the limestone, trickling down the walls and pooling through the passages. At one point the trio had to step carefully from stone to stone to cross a rivulet. At last, the monk led them out, emerging on the other side of the mountain, in the midst of a temple complex. He escorted them into one of the halls, where a senior monk was seated cross-legged on a cushion, gesturing for them to join him in a cup of tea. The boys, their chests heaving, could only stand blinking and speechless at this unexpected turn of events.

"Welcome to Chanku Temple, my young friends," said the senior monk. "We became aware of your predicament when some of our brothers here were out on the cliffs meditating and heard a commotion. We found your companion, who has been injured, and then, it appears, Brother Pu found the two of you."

The boys had not, until that point, had a chance to think about Senior's plight, and they both opened their mouths to speak, but the older monk raised his hand for silence.

"Don't worry, we are few, but we are enough," he said.

"Interestingly, one of you managed to knock down a large bandit. If he has wounds, they will be cleaned and bandaged but we will not allow such lawless men sanctuary here. Your young companion is being carried back to our halls." The old monk lapsed into silence. He studied the boys carefully. "Children, may I ask your names?" he inquired.

"Your insignificant visitor is the youngest son of the Zhu household in Lone Hamlet," Fortune respectfully replied. "This is my friend, Xu Da, from a village in Perpetual Harvest Ward."

"I see — Young Master Zhu and his companion, Xu Da, finding a path through a world of menacing fools," mused the monk. He could not take his eyes from Fortune's angular, pockmarked face. "My son, you have a most unusual face. I wonder…"

But he was interrupted by the arrival of a messenger, who whispered into his ear.

"Ah, that is a good idea," the monk said. He glanced at the boys. "Your companion has urged us to send another brother out to protect your herd." The senior monk turned back to the messenger. "Send Brother Iron Fist," he said. The messenger bowed and departed. Turning back to his companions, the monk smiled pleasantly. "Please excuse the interruption. As Brother Pu can attest, our Brother Iron Fist has a, well, a colorful background for a monk."

"Yes, yes, it is true," Brother Pu agreed. "And he has dogs that I am sure he will take with him. Large dogs that can be even fiercer than Brother Iron Fist."

Two more monks appeared, both out of breath. They bowed at the senior monk and then consulted with Brother Pu. Fortune thought he heard the two asking about cooking meat. Brother Pu scoffed and shook his head, saying, "Well, there is nothing that can be done about that."

"Teacher," Brother Pu said to the senior monk, "our brothers can take our guests to their companion."

"Have you finished your tea, boys?"

Fortune and Da had been savoring the delicious hot drink throughout all the commotion of messages and consultations. They both jumped to their feet and thanked the senior monk, though he continued to sip his tea, and made no move to dismiss them.

"Do you know, I had a strange dream last night," the senior monk commented.

"Is that so, respected teacher?" asked Brother Pu.

"Yes. A green dragon rose from the pond as I was meditating in our pagoda. It hovered above our temple looking down at me and then floated away, toward the southeast. It was a particularly vivid dream and the dragon seemed important."

The monks stood in silence pondering this.

"Do you think the dragon referred to one of the boys who landed here in our midst today?" asked Brother Pu.

"Perhaps, but which one?" the senior monk mused. They all turned to regard Fortune and Da, who smiled brightly at the thought of being associated with such a powerful creature. Fortune pointed at Da, which made the monks laugh.

"It certainly did not refer to the injured boy," snorted Brother Pu. "He keeps asking for a dish of meat for dinner. At a Buddhist temple. Surely he knows we are all vegetarians here."

This made Fortune and Da laugh.

The senior monk threw up his hands, finished with his contemplations. "Off you go then, Merciful Buddha," he said, waving them away.

Fortune and Da found Senior on a pallet. Da's stone had enraged the injured bandit, who had hurled Senior against a tree and then staggered off, blood running from his temple. All the wadding in Senior's quilted vest had helped buffer his fall against the tree trunk, which had left him winded and bruised, but not seriously hurt. A monk was feeding him a bowl of soup.

"I want to go home," he told his companions as soon as they reached his side. They wanted some of his soup.

It is remarkable that not a single goat was lost during that month in the Three Peaks Range. When the herd was returned to the Tang Family Settlement a few days after the incident on Big Sister Mountain, Old Wolf expressed no interest in stories of bandits or temple monks. He counted his goats, nodded his head, and went back into his house.

Yesunge's memorial arch on Flagstone Avenue marked the heart of Lone Hamlet, small reticent heart though it was. On one side of the paving stones were the Lin clan hall, compounds belonging to various members of the Lin family, a distillery, and the family granary. On the other were a fish pond and several shops, including a forge and a carpentry shop and an inn with a stall that sold wine and bowls of bean curd. Fifty-four, whenever he needed to walk through the village, always slowed his pace when he came near that bean curd stall. How he longed to work again in such a shop! How he missed the sound of those gurgling vats! He would call his brother to join him and they would all be together again, as it should be. He had heard that the inn owner, an old woman, was in bad health. If the harvest turned out better in the fall, maybe he could talk to the squire about a loan and try to take over the little stall.

This was the fantasy that Fifty-four, with his deeply creased face and stooped shoulders, nursed through those years as the fields steadily wore him down. "Ai, so many rocks to move," he often muttered to himself, "such endless hoeing." And yet, after a good spring rain, when he entered his fields with a son at his side, the rows of millet green and healthy, Fifty-four sometimes gazed up at Heaven and smiled.

The fall when Fortune returned from herding goats in the Three Peaks Range was the same season when Sao Sao gave birth to another baby, a girl. She had fully recovered by then from the birth of her second son, the baby who had caused so much bleeding during the journey to Lone Hamlet. Little Chen doted on the new granddaughter, like her own father had once doted on her. Three grandchildren. The oldest clamored for stories of Great Grandfather Chen in the Battle of Yashan, and then retold them, in enhanced detail, to his father, when Cattail returned from the fields at night. Cattail was the family workhorse, his frame sinuous, his temperament withdrawn and moody like his father.

It was Fortune who most resembled Little Chen, both in looks and in spirit. The only surprise was that he had grown so tall. By his fifteenth birthday, Fortune stood a head above his mother, one of the tallest youths in the village. Hard to believe he was once a sickly baby, though he still had the pockmarks to prove it.

"Do you know you were once so feverish and gasping that I had to pray to the Lord Buddha that I'd give you to the temple if you ever recovered?" Fifty-four joked with his son one afternoon as they worked in the fields.

This was a not a story Fortune had ever heard before. He stopped his hoeing and glanced up sharply. "You promised me to a temple?" he asked. But his father looked away, not wanting to say any more.

That evening, Fortune asked his mother if the story was true.

"Your father said this to you?" she asked angrily. She had been working serenely at her loom, lost in her own thoughts, until Fortune interrupted with his question. She made a fierce stab at her piece of cloth. "Monks," she sputtered, jutting out her chin, her hand jerking back and forth over the threads. "I've never seen an honest one. If you look back after placing an offering before the Lord Buddha, you'll see the nearest monk popping it in his mouth. It's a disgrace."

"But, Ma, not all monks are like that... " Fortune protested, thinking of Brother Pu, who had saved him from bandits.

"The Lord Buddha has plenty of monks to take care of him," his mother said firmly. "He doesn't need you in his temples."

His parents did not mention the temple promise again, at least not in Fortune's hearing.

Fifty-four and Cattail eventually reclaimed so much land that they needed Fortune's help and could not spare him for herding goats. Instead of lazy days prodding a herd into meadows, Fortune spent the growing seasons toiling alongside his brother and father in the fields. When the harvest was in, and the ripe grain beaten from the stalks and tossed into the wind and stored away, Fortune resumed work for Radish's father-in-law, Old Wolf. Fortune and other young, unmarried men from the hamlet walked together behind water buffalo, driving them up to the hill pastures during the day and returning them home by evening, fattening them up so that they would have the energy to plow the fields in the spring. Fortune did not like draft animals. The goats from his herd-boy days were playful and curious, entertaining when they butted horns, affectionate when they nuzzled. The wide-horned water buffalo were tedious, lumbering creatures, with dull, passive eyes.

One afternoon near the top of Dumpling Hill, as the group of herders squatted around a small fire to keep warm, their talk turned, as it always did, to their hungry stomachs. Nearby, their cattle, which included two calves that year, grazed slowly on the sparse and rocky hillside.

"Ai," sighed one boy, the youngest among the four, "my belly growls like a wild dog at this time of the day."

Fortune hunched down, rubbing the stubble on his jutting chin, encouraging the few wisps there to curl into a manly beard. He, like the others, was dressed in a worn and faded blue quilted jacket with sleeves that extended past his wrists. It was lined with wadded fibers to guard against the cold and tied in the front over lumpy, quilted pants. His hair was long, held in a topknot by a strip of cloth.

Fortune had been brooding during the walk up the hill and had hardly spoken to the other herders. A few days earlier, Harmony had finally kept his vow to run off and join his Uncle Buqa. Harmony had heard that his uncle was at a Mongol cavalry camp stationed north of the Huai River. Fortune had watched him gallop off. "I helped him leave when I should have joined him." This is what Fortune had been repeating to himself ever since. Fortune frowned at the horizon, wondering about his adventurous friend, the Number One Stallion under Heaven. He felt restless and irritable.

"Every day, it's the same thing—noodles and cabbage, noodles and cabbage, and never enough of even that," said another young man, called Five because he was the fifth-born in his family.

Five's complaints brought a whistle from a herder who was known as Darling. "Do you know what I would like more than anything?" he asked in a low voice. Darling looked dreamy as he answered his own question, "A meaty bone in my bowl of noodles."

"He's talking about his meaty bone!" shouted one of the boys, pointing to Darling's crotch.

"I don't want to think about your meaty bone in my noodles," complained another, which caused the group to fall back laughing. Even Fortune chuckled.

Darling ignored all the comments. "Really, though, I dream sometimes of eating a thick piece of meat," he said. "I wake up salivating and cursing that the dream is over. I wonder when it will be that I'll get to eat meat again?"

"The fields could use your dream shit if it's wet and made from juicy meat," said Five. "The summer heat has dried up everything, as if there had never been any rain in the spring. My father just sold our last pig. We had nothing to feed it. My mother wanted to cook it up but my father said we'd do better selling it for more grain so that we can make it through the winter. I really wanted to eat that pig."

"We'll never get our hands on any meat," Darling said, shaking his head and tucking his hands into his sleeves for warmth.

At this, Fortune snorted and the rest all looked over to him. "What are you talking about?" he asked. "Look at where we are. Look at what we're up here doing. We're surrounded by meat! We're meat guardians! We spend our days going where the meat goes!"

The other three looked around at their cattle in surprise, having forgotten the animals could become the tasty meal Darling desired.

"But these are all draft animals," said Five. "And none are ours."

Fortune stood up, restless. He paced near the fire. In all directions, the landscape was rocky, brown and bleak. Even the cattle seemed scrawny. He mused silently on his fate. "Brave people like Harmony will leave, but I will never leave. I will stay here with my family and watch them suffer." Fortune thought of his father and Cattail, toiling in the fields every day. Lately they hardly spoke because they were so worried about the drought. Every morning they walked outside and scanned the sky for signs of rain. And every morning they were disappointed. His mother had been spending more and more time praying to the Metal Mother. "If there is no harvest this year, will Squire Lin turn us out?" he wondered.

Fortune remembered the flight from their former home, when he was ten years old and the landlord rejected their tax payment and sent them away. How many years ago was that? He counted back. "It was five years ago," he murmured to himself. "And things have not gotten better." He pinched his chin, lost in angry thoughts: "We had to give Radish to the Tangs, and he has had only one son. He has to have two more before he can give his own son his own Zhu name. Old Wolf treats Radish like a slave. It's not fair. We are always at the mercy of people like Squire Lin and Old Wolf. The same people who never have to work in the fields. They never suffer any losses. They all just make the rest of us suffer."

"What is it, Fortune?" asked one of the herders, interrupting Fortune's ruminations.

Fortune turned and looked hard at one of the calves. "What's so wrong with us eating too?" he asked, his voice low and dangerous. Fortune swallowed hard and wheeled slowly back to his companions, furrowing his brow as he turned over his words carefully. "Have we ever lost a single animal?" he asked. "How many wolves have we chased away to protect this clan herd? And what have we ever sought in return?"

None of the boys offered an answer. They all began to breathe faster, and salivate. Fortune gazed again at the complacent calf, its tail swishing. The rest of the herders stared with him, lustfully, hearts beating. All consumed with the same desire: I want to eat it.

That simple thought overwhelmed all others. For a fleeting moment, Little Chen's worried face hovered at the edge of

Fortune's consciousness, but he scowled and brushed this aside. I want to bite into meat. That was what mattered. When Fortune grabbed the axe for cutting firewood, the others jumped up and urged him on. The calf munched blithely at a tuft of grass, unaware of its impending sacrifice. The first chop fell, propelled by Fortune's anger. He breathed deeply, the pressure finally vented through action. He was no longer a helpless bystander.

"I have done it," he realized. "There is no turning back now."

In short order the calf was hacked to pieces, its haunches roasting over the campfire. The rest of the cattle stamped fearfully and formed ranks, braying at the unconscionable feast before them. This chorus only served to raise the feverish pitch of the group. Their laughter could be heard far down the hill as they gorged themselves, the meat half raw and roughly skinned, its juices smeared across their mouths.

At last, satiated, they lay back on the ground. Their greasy hands rested on their full bellies as they breathed in the beefy air. In the distance, the temple bell tolled, the sound that usually sent them on their way home.

Five sat up with a start. He swiped at his bulging eyes and rasped out, "What will happen to us?"

The youngest herder began to cry. The spell broke and fear descended on the gluttonous group. Fortune was as frightened as the rest. As the dusk deepened, he pinched again at his chin and tried to think of what to do next. At last he stopped and turned to face the others, his expression firm and grim. He told his companions to bury what remained of the calf, except for its tail, which he cut off himself and set aside. The other three worked in silence, their hands still shaking, but glad to have orders to follow. Fortune used a leaf to wipe the meat grease from his hands and face and then gestured for the three to follow him toward a pile of rocks. He surveyed the rocks at length, the calf tail in his hand. Then he selected a crevice between two boulders and jammed the tail deep into it. He turned to face his three friends.

"We'll say the calf wandered by these rocks, which tumbled down all at once and trapped him, even though we tried with all our might to rescue him," Fortune said. "I will explain this to Old Wolf, since this was all my idea."

The other boys dipped their heads in relief, mumbling that it was a good plan. It could work. They gathered their herd and headed back down the mountain in silence.

Fortune's mistake was in thinking that he could have a conversation with Old Wolf, who had no interest in hearing why his animal had not returned. His interest was only in the fact that it did not return. That left Fortune responsible for the loss, whatever the reason.

Fortune uttered a stream of explanations related to the tail in the rock crevice, but this amounted to nothing more than an irritating whine in Old Wolf's ears as he walked slowly and maliciously across his yard toward the young man who, in Old Wolf's opinion, lacked the appropriately groveling attitude of his station. Old Wolf sniffed the air, catching a whiff of charred meat. He noticed the bag around Fortune's waist and reached forward to yank it free. It fell open to expose the little wooden disks of chess pieces. Old Wolf regarded them in silence, poking at the pieces.

"You've been playing games with me," he said slowly. He turned and called forward a servant girl. "Take this mess and throw it into the fire."

Fortune watched mutely as the servant gathered up the treasured hand-carved gift from his grandfather, now worn with use. He began then to understand the scope of his transgression. If all the herders felt they could partake of the herds they guarded, then the world would be turned on end, and order would wobble in all directions like a spilled plate of boiled eggs.

Old Wolf picked up a stout wooden rod. He leveled his first blow with all his might. The beating that followed brought up all that remained of the beef meal in Fortune's stomach. The cool night breeze was punctuated by the loud blows, which knocked Fortune to the ground and scrambling to get away.

"You'll never take a herd to the hills again," Old Wolf shouted as he chased Fortune into a corner. "I should never have let the likes of you near my herd in the first place."

Fortune curled into a ball and tried to turn away from the rod until he could no longer see it. His eyes rolled into his head. His breath turned wet and foamy.

Radish, cowering behind a wall and grimacing, at long last heard the bloody rod drop to the ground and the sound of receding footsteps. He rushed to Fortune, saying "Little brother, my little brother," over and over again.

By this time it was dark out, and across the creek Little Chen was wondering why her son had not returned home. She headed down Flagstone Avenue, which was empty and eerie in the moonlight. As the rope bridge over the South Branch came into view, Little Chen saw Radish, with Fortune on his back. Radish was grimacing with the effort of placing one foot in front of the other while clenching the rope railing with one hand and balancing his brother with the other. Little Chen could only watch helplessly as Radish slowly made his way across the narrow, swaying bridge planks. She held Radish's gaze and willed him across, ignoring the black waters below.

"Good, good," she exhaled when she was finally able to reach out and pull her two sons away from the bridge to safety.

She helped Radish roll Fortune off his back. She and Radish positioned themselves on either side of Fortune, who was only semi-conscious but able to stumble along.

"Who did this?" whispered Little Chen as they turned onto their lane.

"Old Wolf."

Little Chen gasped, but she kept moving forward. Her mind reeled over what this could mean for her sons, for the family.

"What did Fortune do?"

"I think he ate a calf."

Little Chen staggered and stopped. "What?"

As Fortune moaned between them, Radish leaned forward so he could look his mother in the face. "Ma, Fortune ate one of Old Wolf's cattle. He tried to tell Old Wolf that the calf got lost but the beating made him throw up, and his vomit looked like beef."

Little Chen's free hand fluttered to her chest, as if to calm her pounding heart. "Does Old Wolf think that Fortune butchered one of his calves?"

"Old Wolf left him for dead."

Little Chen nodded and readjusted her hold on Fortune. "But he's going to survive this," she said firmly.

Together, Radish and his mother were able to drag Fortune back home. The family worked by the light of oil lamps to clean and dress gashes and probe for broken bones, which were found along Fortune's rib cage and right forearm. His face was bruised and scratched, but Little Chen was still able to lay her cool hand on her son's cheek and stroke his forehead.

"My son," she whispered to him, "my foolish boy. What were you thinking?"

6

THE RAT FLEA PICKS ITS VICTIMS

The third year of the Correctness Attained reign period (1343). Bell County's Lone Hamlet.

FORTUNE RECOVERED slowly from Old Wolf's beating, and the family decided to leave town. It was almost the New Year, so they would not be missed. Better to move Fortune away for safekeeping, if only until the spring planting. Besides, Fifty-four had not been able to join his elder brother for the previous New Year, and now he longed to see him again.

"We were hoping and hoping that you would make it this year," Auntie called out when the travelers arrived.

This festival included only four of the Chong generation. In the household of Fifty-one, Chong Two was by then long dead, and Chong Five, the only one of the generation who could be described as handsome, had died of a winter illness not long after his only child, a daughter, was born to his wife, Meadow. Meanwhile, in the household of Fifty-four, there were only Cattail and Fortune because Radish was now part of the Tang lineage, and Chong Seven had been sold away. Thus, the set of eight Chongs in the Zhu clan had by then already lost half of its pieces.

It was still an occasion worth celebrating to be able to bring so many together — it was no small matter that the four remaining

Chongs had already presented the Zhu family with seven boys, if you add Cattail's two to Chong One's firstborn and the four boys in a row that Chong Three's fertile wife had turned out. In addition, there were two girls, Meadow's daughter and Sao Sao's most recent baby. Though the times were hard, the two patriarchs, Fifty-one and Fifty-four, were able to toast each other a long life and begin the New Year with veneration of the spirit tablets. The feast was highlighted by fresh bean curd, which Fifty-one had managed to procure.

"It's a shame, isn't it, that we have to go out and buy bean curd after all those years of selling it?" Little Chen asked her sister-in-law as they strained and sliced and soaked the ingredients for spicy ginger-sesame bean curd.

"And this is such bad quality," Auntie Liu complained, pointing her cleaver at the offending cake. "We would never have sold such a dry and tasteless thing from our shop. It's a disgrace."

The journey had proved perilous for Fortune, causing the wounds along his ribcage to fester. He was placed in Meadow's tiny room, in the very bed where Chong Five had wasted away. The infection quickly sent Fortune into a delirium. He spent several days tossing and turning on Meadow's bed, his hair loose and tangled. His mother spent sleepless nights at his side and directed Meadow in how to prepare a medicinal broth that both women worked to spoon into Fortune's mouth. At last, Heaven took notice and the fever subsided. When Fortune's eyes finally blinked open and focused, Meadow burst into tears and crumpled to the ground. Little Chen had to turn away from her son to tend to the distraught girl.

"I thought it was my fault," Meadow kept repeating.

"What was your fault?"

"I thought..." but the girl's chest heaved too violently for her to get out a sentence.

"Meadow, child, what is wrong?" Little Chen asked, pulling her niece close and stroking her hair until at last the sobs subsided.

"I thought I had some sort of curse on me," Meadow explained. "My beautiful husband died suddenly, and then Fortune, as soon as he fell into my bed, grew worse... "

Little Chen firmly shook her head. "No, no, it is not like that," she said, lifting the stray wisps away from Meadow's eyes and smoothing them back into her bun. "It was the beating by a bad man that almost killed Fortune. Then it was me dragging him along a dusty road that almost killed him again, even though I knew I had to get him away. It was only when my son could rest in the safety of his uncle's home, in the safety of your room, that he finally recovered. Meadow, you did not curse him, you saved him."

Fortune remained weak and convalesced for several more days in Meadow's husband's bed. Soon enough, though, he was playing clapping games with her daughter and looking stronger. He was helped to a chair for the New Year's feast, and drank more than one toast to his own health. Uncle later claimed the sorghum liquor was what finally restored him.

One afternoon, as he watched Meadow sweeping the floor, Fortune recognized the folk tune she was humming. "How can you hum such a song?" he asked her, surprised.

She tossed her head, as if she did not care who heard. So Fortune sang the next verse out loud. The words were from a ballad by the great Tang Dynasty poet Du Fu, and it was popular in the Hao Prefecture because it referred to Bell County:

> I have a sister, a little sister
> she lives in Bell,

> Her husband, he did not survive
> fatherless their baby.
> The Huai is long, its waves high
> the flood dragon angry,
> Ten years since I have seen my sister
> this year maybe.

He finished, and gave his cousin an impudent smile.

"People will hear you singing that to me and think you are callous," Meadow scolded.

"But you are the one who started it," he reminded her. "And I miss my cousin. Chong Five was my favorite."

Meadow leaned on her broom with both hands, looking out at the courtyard, where her little girl was playing with Cattail's baby daughter. "Your aunt is convinced I will disgrace the Zhu family and marry again," Meadow said. "She talks so much about this, sometimes I want to offer myself to the next man I see, just to silence her! She is constantly watching me, and for no reason. And it doesn't matter what I do to serve this Zhu family — it's like playing a lute for a cow. My mother-in-law wouldn't notice."

Fortune nodded sympathetically. "Maybe you'll get a nice stone arch in town after you die, honoring you as a chaste widow — then what will Auntie think?" he said. "Anyway, you have it good here, compared to us in Lone Hamlet. The spirits have been cursing our fields, no matter how many offerings we make to the Earth God. We have nothing to eat anymore."

Meadow grinned mischievously. "That's not what I hear," she said.

"What?" Fortune asked, perplexed.

Meadow backed away, her smile widening as she shot back, "I hear that some of the herders in Lone Hamlet eat full beef meals!"

Fortune threw a rag at her as she skipped out the door, but

then he burst into laughter, wincing from the pain in his shaking ribs. No one else would dare speak out loud about the incident that had led to his beating. Instead it lurked in whispers and innuendo as a simmering source of consternation, evident in his elders the instant their worries over his health diminished. Fortune knew the family considered his behavior dangerous, and even unfilial, since Old Wolf now bore a grudge against the Zhu family. They wanted to crush whatever it was within him that led to such a rash act, but the shame of mentioning the butchered calf kept anyone from lecturing him. What a relief to hear Meadow make a joke of it.

While Little Chen wanted to keep away from the Old Wolf for as long as possible, Fifty-four feared they would lose their house on Mulberry Lane if it stayed vacant too long. As soon as Fortune seemed strong enough for the walk back home, Fifty-four insisted that they depart. Uncle and his household stood in a group to see off the other half of their family. It was not until Fifty-four finished his goodbyes and began to lead his wife and children away that Meadow's daughter stepped forward and tugged at Fortune's sleeve.

"What is it, little cousin?" he crouched down to her eye level though his ribcage was still tender and ached at the movement. The rest of the family also stopped to see what the child wanted. She was only three or four years old, but she was a bright little girl, and had already memorized many children's poems and rhymes. In a sweet singsong voice, she recited the one known as "Bidding Elder Brother Goodbye."

> We part on the road, mist rising in the air,
> Around the pavilion, leaves are now rare.
> I sigh — oh, how we differ from the wild geese,
> When they set off to travel, no one is left behind.

The family murmured in surprise. "Such a fitting poem." "What sorrow that our family cannot always fly together." "So clever."

Fortune held the girl's hand. "Goodbye, little one," he said, his voice barely louder than a whisper. Fortune glanced up at Meadow, whose somber face reflected his own melancholy. Then he stood and turned to leave. Auntie took Fortune by the arm, walking along for a bit with him. The shrunken old woman hanging onto the tall young man trailed the rest of Fifty-four's family, moving slowly and reluctantly down the road toward Lone Hamlet.

"Do you know that when your parents first had to move away and leave us, long ago back in Ferry Village, why, I did not think they would last long," Auntie Liu said.

Fortune glanced at her in surprise. Neither she nor his parents had ever talked about their feelings on this matter.

"Yes, yes, it's true," Auntie kept on. "But you see how they have prevailed, enduring so much hardship. They had to give away your third brother and then they lost your first sister to the childbirth sickness. Terrible, terrible. But look how we have all kept together, working so hard to keep the Zhu clan vital." She stopped and faced Fortune, reaching up to pat his cheek. Her thinning gray hair was neatly pinned back from her lined face. "Now we are trusting you, our unpolished jade, with our family's fate," she said. Smiling fondly, Auntie sent him on his way.

When the road curved, Fortune turned for a last look back. His aunt and uncle and cousins were still standing in the road, watching. Fortune's heartbeat quickened with a surge of affection. He raised his hands in a farewell salute.

The sun was already too hot over the fields of Bell County when it came time for the first spring planting. Farmers were apprehensive as they took in their meager, withering winter wheat to clear the fields for the next crop. Not a drop of rain. To sow the millet in the cracked furrows was like scattering seeds onto a tortoise shell. The hot sun in a cloudless sky glazed the fields, producing the worst drought anyone could remember. Farmers drenched in sweat looked to the horizon for a hint of a rain cloud, but saw only the worst kind of shadow — the kind that turns into a black humming horde of hungry locusts. With drought comes famine. With famine comes disease.

As spring progressed toward summer that year in Lone Hamlet, the villagers stripped the bark from trees and scrounged desperately for roots. They dug "Goddess of Mercy Powder," a kind of white clay that rips through the intestines. But even as they starved, a worse calamity loomed, the specter of a deadly new disease heading their way. In Lone Hamlet, the first warnings were vague. A plague had entered the city walls of Hao. No, the plague had not been seen south of the Huai River. Yes, it was south of the Huai, but not yet east of the city of Kaifeng, which was still a good distance away.

"It doesn't matter where the plague is," Fifty-four grumbled. "What matters is that we are going to lose all of our crops to this drought. The plague demons will starve like the rest of us if they dare come to Lone Hamlet."

Then one day, a man fleeing the walled city of Hao came across the ferry in search of a relative who, as it turned out, was no longer in the village. This starving refugee appeared at the well on Flagstone Avenue, sitting listless in a patch of hot shade, answering questions in a dull monotone. Fortune was there with Little Chen, helping guard her fair share of water. Mother and son stood in the blistering heat and listened to the crowd questioning the weary man.

"Has the drought hit the fields closer to the Huai?"

"No place I've seen is free from this drought," said the

traveler. He ran his tongue over his dry lips and looked up at the one who had asked the question. "Could you bring me another ladle of water?"

"How are the grain supplies inside the city walls at Hao?"

"There is no grain to be found in the city," the man responded. "That is why I left. The magistrate distributed the relief grain during last season's drought. The rest went into the storage jars of the wealthy households, or sits rotting under guard. Everyone who can is leaving the city in search of food."

"And what about the plague, has it hit Perpetual Harvest Ward?"

The man had just passed through there, and said the plague had not descended on that ward yet. Fortune thought of the herd boy Xu Da and their adventure in the Chanku Temple caves, and he felt relieved.

"Is the plague in Good Mountain?" asked Little Chen. No, the man did not think the plague had headed that way. Little Chen sighed, grateful that Chong Seven — and also Lotus, who lived even further in that direction — might be safe from at least one menace.

But then someone asked after the fate of Vast Virtue Ward, where Fifty-one farmed with his two sons, the place where the reunited Zhu family had passed the New Year only a few months ago.

The refugee glanced up in fear, his eyes bulging from his emaciated face. "Stay away from that ward," he gasped. "The plague is like a blood-sucking insect feasting on the villagers there."

Little Chen and Fortune backed away in shock, as did others who had relatives in Vast Virtue Ward. How could this be? The two ran home and called Fifty-four and Cattail from the fields.

When Fifty-four heard the news he covered his face with his

hands. The image of his cheerful, hardworking, honest older brother's face welled up before him. Fifty-four's eyes brimmed over with tears and he kneeled keening to the ground. Sao Sao's children cried at the sight of their grandfather suffering so.

"Baba," Cattail said, leaning down at his father's side. "We don't know that the plague demons have taken Uncle's family. This is only the gossip of one foolish traveler. Come now, have a seat."

Sao Sao turned to fetch her father-in-law some water, but then she caught sight of her oldest child, Precious, a boy already nine years old. He was holding a rat by the tail. "Precious," she scolded him. "Throw the rat away."

The boy smiled sweetly at her and swung the rat, not wanting to let it go, but not wanting to disobey his mother either. Cattail walked over to his son and took the rat, which appeared half dead. Cattail licked his heat-chapped lips, and held up the weakly protesting animal to show the others. "This one's not as skinny as the rest," he said. "Why let it go while we starve?"

Sao Sao gazed at the rat and felt hungry. But Little Chen was struck with foreboding. She grabbed a broom, crying, "Drop it! Drop it!" Startled, Cattail flung the rat down and Little Chen swept it away with all the force she could muster, chasing after it until it was well clear of the yard and scurrying toward the mulberry patch. The rest of the family stood soberly watching Little Chen's back as she in turn gazed out at the rodent. The little creature fell over on its side, its paws raking the air until it righted itself, lurching jerkily out of sight.

Sao Sao cleared her throat. "Old Mother Wang told me she saw two rats cough up blood and die in the lane the other day," she said. "It's strange. It can't be a good omen. Best to stay away from rats."

The next morning, Fifty-four noticed the rat lying stiff in

the dirt not far from where Little Chen had swept it away. He squatted down to examine it, his stomach churning, but when he flicked the corpse over and brushed away the fleas, he could see that the animal was too diseased to eat.

The plague entered Lone Hamlet through the Tang Family Settlement, and not one of the five households there was spared. Harmony's aunt and Tang the Old Wolf both died. One day a boy appeared at the Zhu fence with news of Radish's fate. Little Chen called for him to enter but he refused.

"Your second son wants you to know that he and his wife and their baby are free from the pestilence and are nursing the few who remain in the Tang Family Settlement," the boy said. "He dares not come to tell you himself for fear of bringing sickness on his beloved family. He called this to me from across the rope bridge. He threw this steamed bun to me as payment, but said the Earth God would know if I ate it before delivering his message." Then the boy turned and ran off, biting hard into the stale crust of the bun.

Little Chen clasped her hands to her chest in relief and whirled around to tell Sao Sao, who was inside the cottage. Bursting with the good news — fear for Radish had been tormenting her — Little Chen rushed to Sao Sao's side and started to pour out the message from the boy at the fence. But then she realized Sao Sao was not listening. Instead she was leaning over her son, Precious.

"Daughter-in-law, what is it?"

Sao Sao, her hands shaking, glanced up at Little Chen and offered her a weak smile. "Oh, it's nothing," Sao Sao said. "He doesn't have a fever. I'm sure he doesn't have a fever."

But the boy's skin was burning hot and he was limp in his mother's arms. Little Chen reached into her tunic and pulled out her father's chop seal talisman, gripping it tightly in her hands as she prayed for the Metal Mother to evict this evil. Then she caught sight of Sao Sao's two other children, the baby girl barely old enough to sit upright. Little Chen scooped them both into her arms, and ran out of the yard and down the lane, not stopping until she was inside Old Mother Wang's cottage. She set the children at the woman's feet and then kneeled before her.

"Everyone knows that your house has a special kind of good luck to it," Little Chen said. "Take these grandchildren of mine for a while, until it's safe for them again."

Little Chen rushed away before the astonished woman could say another word, the frightened left-behind children crying at the sight of their grandmother's retreating back.

Sao Sao was suffering helplessly through Precious' first convulsions. As the day wore on, she and her mother-in-law used damp cloths to try to cool his little body. Sao Sao's dread welled and subsided in waves within her. She grew desperate to have her husband back from the fields. However, when he finally walked in that evening, Cattail had his father's arm around his neck and was half-hauling a feverish Fifty-Four into the yard. Sao Sao looked into Cattail's face and saw there a reflection of her own horror.

"No!" Little Chen cried out as she ran to her husband.

But Sao Sao did not notice her father-in-law.

"Precious."

She uttered that one word. In Chinese, the boy's name was pronounced "Bao-er." It is a full, round, healthy sound. When it rang in Cattail's ears that bleak evening, all the fulfillment and pride that "Bao-er" had brought to Cattail ever since the word had been assigned to his son, all that happy feeling fell away. Cattail dropped to the ground and crawled on his knees to his son's sickbed. He pronounced the beautiful name over and over as he reached for his son's burning hot hand. Lifting it made the boy cry out in pain, because at his armpit the buboes that are the unmistakable mark of the plague had already begun to turn black.

Fortune was not in the village when the plague descended on his family. His mother had sent him with a basket and a trowel up into the hills and told him not to return until he had gathered some roots to relieve everyone's hunger. He walked through the cool shade of the mountainside trees with his neighbor, the second son of Old Mother Wang, who was skilled at foraging. Other villagers were bent on the same task, but the two young men ran ahead up a steep hillside along Cloud Mother Mountain. There they found mushrooms and leeks and a few other edibles. Second Chao captured a cricket in his hands and dared his friend to eat it. Fortune popped the struggling insect in his mouth and crunched cheerfully.

"You eat that like you've done it before," said Second Chao, laughing.

Fortune grimaced at the aftertaste. "I think once was enough."

In all, it was a pleasant, carefree day.

When the evening bell tolled the two young men headed back to the ferry. Recognizing Fortune, the ferryman drew back in fright and told the pair to stand at the far side of his boat.

"What's this all about?" Second Chao asked. The ferryman would not speak, but poled through the water with all his might.

Second Chao glanced at Fortune and shrugged. "Crazy old man," he said. The two laughed together. A fish splashed nearby. On the village bank, a kingfisher was perched in a dead tree at water's edge, its blue-green feathers reflecting clearly in the rippling waves.

The peaceful vista of Lone Hamlet before them, the two friends moved forward to disembark. Baskets in hand, they stepped to the shore. The ferryman shrank away again as they passed. This was the last moment of unsuspecting contentment for Fortune. This was when the ferryman released the nine dagger words that changed everything:

"Run home, son. The plague has struck your house."

When Little Chen saw her youngest son enter the doorway, she uttered a cry of relief that he had not come staggering in like his father. The two embraced. Little Chen allowed herself to hang on the shoulders of her healthy, strong son and weep into his chest. She allowed herself this moment of weakness, releasing some of the terror gripping her heart. Then she opened her eyes and turned back, still shuddering from her tears, to nurse her stricken husband and grandson.

The plague turned from Precious and Fifty-four to claim a third Zhu victim. But while the first two fell into a pitiful, moaning state of unconsciousness, Cattail was struck with a violent delirium. He kept rushing out into the yard, gasping for air and screaming gibberish warnings. Fortune chased after him again and again, calming him with ladles of water and dragging him back into the cottage.

Little Chen stayed at her husband's side, feeling his pulse and murmuring prayers. Sao Sao held Precious in her arms rocking and singing to him.

On his last night, Fifty-four's eyelids flickered briefly and then opened. He turned toward the candlelight. Little Chen sat up and nudged Fortune, who was sleeping at her feet. The two leaned over Fifty-four, smiling down at him.

"Baba," Fortune said, "we are here with you."

Fifty-four's vision cleared and he reached for Fortune, making a sound like a cough, or perhaps a sigh.

"Stay with us," Fortune begged him, grabbing onto his

outreached hand, but Little Chen knew better.

"Rest now, husband," she said, placing her palm gently over her son's. "You can rest now."

Fifty-four died on the same day as his grandson — the child took a last sweet breath at dawn; Fifty-four's rasping ended at dusk. Cattail's agonies continued for another three days and then abruptly ceased. The women washed the bodies and arranged them side by side, three generations of Zhu males.

"Wait," said Little Chen when Sao Sao picked up the coarse shroud cloth.

As Sao Sao stood expectantly with the cloth in her hands, Little Chen went to the corner of the room that contained her bedding and pulled out a small bundle of rose-colored silk. Kneeling down beside the bodies, Little Chen gently placed the bundle into her husband's hands, taking a few moments to arrange the material to her satisfaction. Her own hand lingered over her husband's cool fingers and she kept it there, unwilling to let go, gazing wistfully at her husband, tears dripping onto his sleeves.

Behind her, Sao Sao worriedly gestured to Fortune to intervene. He stepped forward and put his arm around his mother's shoulders. Little Chen let him help her to her feet. She turned away as Sao Sao spread the cloth cover.

Only a small piece of sackcloth remained. Little Chen ripped it into two strips, tying one to her forehead and handing the other to Sao Sao. The white marks of mourning. White, the pallid color that is left when you drain out the vivid red, the color of life.

The fields, baking in the heat, had been surrendered to the locusts. The millet crop was a complete loss. Little Chen boiled one of their last handfuls of grain together with some bark chips and leaves and one of the mushrooms Fortune had dug with Second Chao. She stared down at this pathetic meal and tried to focus on it. She struggled to see anything through her thoughts and memories of the family members she had just lost. They were all she wanted to think about, and she kept whispering her grandson's name aloud and calling out feebly for Cattail and her husband, unable to accept that they were gone and would not be eating this food she had just prepared. "The dead are dead," she said to herself, speaking firmly. "I need to think about those who are still living." Little Chen forced herself to pack up her loom, the wedding gift made by her father's own hands, and told Fortune to carry it for her down Flagstone Avenue. They sold it to the squire's clerk in exchange for seeds of the fifty-day variety of millet, used in times of severe drought.

Little Chen placed the seeds in Fortune's hands. "The rains will come soon enough," she said.

Little Chen also consulted the ancestral spirits. Kneeling before the family altar, the corpses at her left, she sought guidance. She stared, blinking now and then, breathing in and out in short puffs. Though she tried, she could not fill her lungs or sink into slow, meditative breathing. Her chest remained tight, her lips clenched, as she trained her eyes on the figurine of the Metal Mother, her patron goddess. "Queen Mother of the West," she prayed, using the goddess's more formal name, "You preside over life and death, disease and healing, and you determine the life span of all beings. We beg you to let us survive as a family." After some time elapsed, Little Chen stood up. She walked out of the yard and down the lane and over the rope bridge toward the Tang Family Settlement. She returned holding onto Radish's arm. His wife trailed closely behind with their baby boy tied to her back. The three adults halted briefly before the village shrine to the Earth God.

"I am bringing my second son home," Little Chen told the clay image inside the waist-high shrine near the well and memorial arch on Flagstone Avenue. "Because of unforeseen calamities we can no longer allow him to continue as a Tang. He and his son are now responsible for carrying on the Zhu line."

Behind his mother's kneeling form, Radish looked in surprise at his wife. Then the two hurriedly bowed to the image. They followed Little Chen down Mulberry Lane and into the Zhu yard. There, they joined the ritual wailing for the dead.

Back in the Tang Family Settlement, among all the five households, only an old man and his daughter-in-law remained. The rest had either died or fled. The old man, a brother of Old Wolf, sent his daughter-in-law back to her parents. He wandered out into the Tang graveyard, picked the spot among the burial mounds with the best feng shui, lay down, and died.

At first, it seemed that Little Chen had succeeded in grabbing her eldest remaining son back into the Zhu lineage and flouting the elaborate rules of heredity. Old Wolf had died thinking he had set a healthy grandson in place to carry on the sacred duties of ritual worship before the Tang ancestral tablets. His last order had been to lock up his daughter and grandson. No one was to enter their room until the plague had passed, to keep the child safe. Radish had broken through the lock while his father-in-law's corpse was still cooling.

Little Chen took this baby, her blood grandson promised to the Tangs, even though the Zhus still had intact lines of heredity through Fortune and through Sao Sao's surviving son. Little Chen recognized that calamity presented an opening, a brief chance at circumventing the iron laws that favored wealthier men like Old Wolf. The voice inside her head cried out, "There are no Tangs remaining to point out that our marriage contract promises three sons to Old Wolf." She wanted to snatch up for her family all the lines of continuity available. You could never have too many.

PART ONE: FORTUNE

Even though Little Chen knew she had fooled the world of mortals, she realized there were other forces to consider. That is why she had promptly informed the Earth God of her intentions. She had hoped he would understand her situation. Still, in her heart she expected retribution. She was not surprised when she felt the fevers and chills come on shortly after retrieving Radish.

She was able to disguise her symptoms for an entire day. This gave her time to accept her fate. But as she was suffering on her sleeping mat at the dawn of a second feverish morning, she worried that she would soon slip into the plague delirium. She needed to hurry and say her goodbyes. Little Chen sat up and looked over at the peacefully sleeping form of her youngest child, thinking "he is already a man." She gazed into his pockmarked, unusual face, and through the dizziness and nausea, she reminded herself of her blessing in having been allowed to keep him at her side for so long.

Fortune opened his eyes and saw the wet streaks down her face, her tears the first thing illuminated by the weak light of daybreak. "Ma," he whispered.

She took his hand and he jerked upright, fully awakened by the chill of fear he felt at the unnatural warmth and clamminess of her skin. "I have the plague," she stated softly, her voice gentle and peaceful. "There's no use in making a fuss."

They sat holding hands for some time, the dawn stars succumbing to the light flooding gently into the yard. They were sleeping outside, across the doorframe to guard the entrance to their cottage from evil spirits. Inside, Radish, now the eldest son, slept closest to the corpses. Sao Sao was next door with her two remaining children, under the care of Old Mother Wang.

"I won't have time to make any more funeral arrangements. You'll have to find a place to bury us. Maybe you can ask the landlord..."

"Ma," Fortune said again.

"Don't be afraid," she said. "Do you know that once, when you were still an infant, you slipped out of my hands when I was giving you a bath? Yes, I dropped you — it was terrible. But you grabbed hold of me with your juicy little baby hands, gripping my fingers so tight, dangling in the air. I couldn't believe it! I grabbed your slippery body back up into my arms."

Little Chen folded those same arms now, rocking gently and remembering, a weak smile on her starving, sick face. She clung to the memory of holding her small baby tight to her chest, their hearts beating together, so forcefully alive. "I knew then that you had within you a special kind of will to survive," she continued. "Many times after that I've seen signs that you are different. My father knew it too, but he refused to share his thoughts about you. Still, I could tell that you surprised him, almost frightened him. He promised me once that your future held marvelous things in it." Little Chen reached over to take her son's face in her hands. She smiled again. "You have the iron chin and the hawk eyes of a true Chen," she whispered, repeating the line her own father had said upon first seeing this last son of hers.

Her tears were finished, but now Fortune began to cry. His lips trembled and his vision swam.

Little Chen caressed his shoulder, thinking it was a pity, such a pity, to have to leave him in the midst of all these other deaths. She reached around her neck and took off the leather thong holding its talisman. "This was not much help to me, but I think that's because it was never intended for me — my father's talisman was meant for you," she said, placing the necklace over her son's head. She held up the chop box in her palm, studying it fondly. Then she looked firmly into Fortune's eyes. "My son, you will survive this terrible plague. You have a special fate and you will find out what that is soon enough. You are stronger than all the rest of us. I am trusting you to take care of our family." She leaned against his shoulder and said no more.

Fortune helped her gently back onto her sleeping mat. He rose to get Sao Sao and begin the ordeal of nursing his dying mother.

And then there were four bodies under the coarse cloth.

Sao Sao was consumed with fear for her two surviving, starving children. Fear for their fate came running at her with clubs raised in both hands before grief could make much headway. She headed to the Zhu family altar and prostrated repeatedly, wailing with abandon. In this way, she bid her dead husband and son goodbye. Sao Sao strapped her daughter to her back and took her son by the hand. Before stepping over the threshold, she paused and looked back over her shoulder at Fortune and Radish, who had been mutely observing her preparations.

"I am going back to my parents in Ferry Village," she explained.

"Sao Sao, where should we bury the family?" Fortune called after her.

But she had nothing to offer. "It's no use," she said. Then Sao Sao was gone.

Fortune looked to the ones who remained: his brother Radish, Sister-in-law Tang, and their baby boy, known ironically as Plenty. Fortune could see that Radish's spirit was ebbing, leaving behind a listless shell. Sister-in-law Tang was tireless in her search for food and miraculously found scraps to share with Radish and Fortune and produced milk for her baby. But Sister-in-law Tang was a silent and passive woman. She watched her husband succumbing to his despair, but could offer no suggestions.

Fortune had no one left to guide him. He needed to find a resting place for the four bodies moldering in the cottage. "Ma, what should I do?" Fortune decided to take Radish to the compound of Squire Lin.

Before the main gate, he whispered into his brother's ear. "You are the elder, you are the one who should present our circumstances to the squire," Fortune said, willing Radish to summon back his vigor. "You must do this." Fortune placed a hand on Radish's shoulder and tried again. "Elder brother, think of our parents and our eldest brother. They are waiting. They need our help now."

Radish sighed heavily at these words and lifted his eyes, meeting Fortune's.

The squire was seated behind a mahogany desk in his Hall for Receiving Guests. He faced the entrance in the position of authority. Before him was a beautiful set of writing brushes resting on a blue porcelain stand near rolls of documents. A delicate cup of tea steamed at his elbow beside a plate of sesame cakes. Along one wall was a carved display table holding a blooming gardenia in a vase, its ivory petals emitting a pleasing fragrance. The squire did not invite the two members of the Zhu family to sit down. He regretted having allowed them to enter his hall at all. He knew that in such times they could only be asking for charity. Worse, they could be contagious.

"What is it?" he grimly inquired.

Radish swallowed and licked his lips. He opened his mouth and took a long breath.

"Well?"

Fortune leaned closer to his brother and gently nudged his arm. Radish swayed and looked as if he might faint. Fortune had no choice but to begin himself. He cleared his throat. "Honorable Squire Lin, we are all that remains of a large family devoted to working your fields," he said, turning to Radish, who nodded that he was ready.

"And so," Radish took over, "we would like to know when

you would recommend that we set a date for burying our parents?"

The squire sat back in his chair, surprised and somewhat gratified by the request. He mused and reached for an almanac, turning the pages and muttering to himself as he weighed the options. He looked up, his finger resting on a line of text. "Days for burial remaining in the fourth month include the 25th and the 29th," he said. "You must avoid burial on the 26th at all costs as that would be exceedingly unlucky. The days in the fifth month look more auspicious, but I assume you do not have time to spare."

The two before him nodded and bowed their thanks. They backed toward the door a few steps and hesitated. Fortune nudged Radish, urging him to get to the main purpose of their visit before it was too late.

"Squire Lin," Radish mumbled, "we have one more request. We wish to know if you have a spare corner of land ... " Radish's voice broke and he could not go on.

Fortune finished the sentence. "... where we could set our parents to eternal rest?"

The brothers did not dare look up.

A long, uncomfortable silence followed. The squire's chair scratched along the slate floor as he stood up. "Come with me," he demanded.

The squire marched angrily out of the room. The two young men rushed after him, crossing the courtyard to a storage area in a corner. The squire wrenched open the door and gestured inside to a long dark object against a wall.

"Look there," he told them. "What is that?"

Radish and Fortune leaned cautiously into the room and peered through the dusty shadows at the place the squire had indicated. They saw a coffin. An empty coffin resting on its side, handsomely carved with flared edges at each end.

"Squire, it's a coffin," Fortune answered carefully.

"That is correct," said the squire. He stepped back and lifted his chin, his hands clasped behind his back, his long silk robe stately. "That is entirely correct. It's a coffin. It's made of solid cedar, the best wood for coffins, brought here from the South more than five years ago. And what do you think of that?"

Radish looked at Fortune with dull eyes and was not sure what to say next.

"Ah," Fortune stammered. "It's wise, squire."

"Very wise," the squire nodded his head vigorously. "Very wise indeed! You are right!"

Now the squire raised one of his hands, the silk sleeve falling back in folds. He jabbed a finger in the air to emphasize Fortune's rightness. The squire began to pace as he launched into a lecture.

"You can see how I have made plans and preparations. Knowing that I will proceed to my next life, as we all must, I have thought ahead. And if I already have in my possession such an excellent coffin for my burial, you can imagine the thought that has gone into the place for my interment."

For a fleeting, incredible instant, Fortune dared to hope that the squire was going to offer to help them. Maybe he wanted to sell them this coffin? But that was impossible. Indeed, it was unthinkable, as the squire made clear.

"Now we have the example of your family," said the squire, his tone changing from long-winded arrogance to dry contempt. He stopped pacing and faced the two young men. "Your father clearly made no preparations whatsoever for his passing. And you have failed in your filial duty to serve your parents, having no notion of what to do with their bodies. It is a disgrace to see such vulgar ignorance. Why, you are not even dressed in mourning. You are no better than dogs running loose in the alley.

I do not allow animals in my house. Get out at once! Get out!"

The two retreated from the courtyard as fast as they could. Back in the street they could finally raise their humiliated heads and squint into the harsh sunlight. They exhaled, gasping for air as if they had just emerged from a pool of water. Fortune was seething. He took one look at his stunned brother and broke into a run, propelled forward by his own anger. He ran past the memorial arch and the Earth God shrine, startling two women at the well. He turned onto his lane, brushing past a neighbor, who shook a fist and shouted for him to slow down. Fortune kept running until he burst into the yard of his cottage, out of breath, but still enraged. Grabbing a stool, Fortune hurled it into the fence, shouting curses. He grabbed the fence too, though when he did so, he leaned forward and in this way he caught sight of Radish turning into the lane. Fortune loved this downcast brother, his last remaining elder. Radish's grief was more than Fortune could bear. A single glance at Radish had set Fortune running; now the same sight was all it took to arrest his fury. Fortune dropped his hands to his sides. He walked back down the lane toward Radish, weeping.

"What will we do now?" Fortune cried out in a high-pitched, anguished voice. "What will we do?"

Fortune took his brother's arm and the two trudged inside the cottage. Sister-in-law Tang brought them cups of hot water. Fortune was not able to stop crying. His tears spilled out in bursts. He kept wiping at his nose and cheeks, but could still taste his tears and snivel every time he licked his lips. Radish picked up a cup and slowly drank from it, his expression wooden. The shadows lengthened across the room and still the two sat there, the one keening, the other vacant.

Sister-in-law Tang reappeared at their side. "Little brother," she said, tapping Fortune's knee. "There's someone here to see you."

Fortune stepped out to the yard and saw a messenger from the family of Lin Ji. This Lin Ji was the father of Ying, whom Fortune had met through Second Chao and had sometimes played with as a boy. The messenger told Fortune that Lin Ji had a matter to discuss with the Zhu family. The two brothers were to come at once to see him. They had no choice but to follow the messenger back across Flagstone Avenue and through the gate to Lin Ji's compound. The two were ushered into yet another gentry hall, the second in a single day. Again, the two peasants from the fields faced the long gown of a gentleman. Neither brother dared lift his eyes higher than the pattern in the silk that decorated the wearer's chest. Again the pair stood in straw sandals and tattered trousers breathing in the aroma of tea leaves and ink. This time, however, the gentleman behind the table rose slightly and gestured for the messenger to bring his guests cups of tea and a plate of melon seeds, treats neither Radish nor Fortune had been able to savor since the New Year festival. Ying was seated near his father, dressed like a young man now in a long robe and a scholar's cap.

Lin Ji expressed his sorrow at the deaths in the Zhu family. Then he explained his purpose in summoning Fortune.

"It has come to my attention that you are looking for a place to set your deceased family members at rest."

Lin Ji had too much dignity to reveal what had led to this conversation, which was the news from his son that the arrogant squire was bragging about his coffin again, this time doing so at the expense of a poor family in mourning. The squire was Lin Ji's younger brother. In such a small village, the commotion of the summoning, the shouting, and the furious flight of Fortune through the streets was being commented on and exaggerated well before matters could get properly concluded. Ying had told his father that Fortune was a childhood friend. He had asked his father what could be done? This had shamed Lin Ji into action.

"I have a piece of land you can use for this purpose," Lin Ji said, at which point both Fortune and Radish fell to their knees, choking on their tea to express their thanks.

Forgetting himself, Fortune looked straight at Lin Ji and blurted out, "Respected sir, why would you do such a thing for us?"

Radish cringed, but Lin Ji waved the young men up from their knees and answered carefully.

"Do you know the expression, 'crossing the river in the same boat'?" he asked, with his words directed at his son as much as at his two guests. "It refers to a time long ago when the kingdoms of Wu and Yue were bitter enemies. One day two families, one from Wu and the other from Yue, ended up having to sail down a wide river in the same boat. Neither group would have anything to do with the other, biding their time until they could go their separate ways. Well, suddenly the winds changed and the skies darkened and they all found themselves in great danger. It turns out that these unlikely companions made it through the storm safely only because the one side started to bale water while the other helped with the sails. What would have happened if they had done nothing out of contempt or spite? They would have all drowned! What if we here in Lone Hamlet turn from the duty of burying our dead? We would all suffer the wrath of the offended spirits! You and I may not be from the same family, but why should we not work together to save our village from this pestilence?"

Fortune listened closely and nodded his head.

"Besides," Lin Ji continued, "it gives my family merit before the Lord Buddha to be able to offer some of our land to comfort the dead. You grant us merit in allowing us to grant you this favor."

He could have added, but did not, that this good karma might also help cancel out the disgraceful behavior of his brother, Squire Lin.

Sister-in-law Tang helped Radish and Fortune wrap the four bodies in their sleeping mats. Cattail was wrapped together with his son, leaving three bundles. Little Chen had woven extra reed mats for this purpose, which Sister-in-law had finished. Little Chen had also directed her living sons to build a bier from planks, with carrying poles at each end like a stretcher. Now the brothers stacked and tethered the bodies to the bier, which they carefully set onto a cart.

"You need to offer a sacrifice at the household altar," Sister-in-law reminded the brothers. Only a single bundle of incense remained, so Radish pulled out just one stick, which he lit and set in the burner. Fortune placed a precious pinch of grain into an offering bowl. The three took turns at prostrations.

"You need to walk three times around the bier to show that we cannot bear to part with the dead," Sister-in-law said, her voice barely above a whisper.

She took her husband's hand and the pair circled the bier, with Radish closest to the bodies. Fortune followed behind. They all wailed in the manner of mourners.

This done, Fortune and Radish stood waiting for further instructions from Sister-in-law. She had a worried frown on her plain, wide face as she intently examined the two young men. She did not want to make any mistakes.

"Undo your hair," she said.

The brothers reached up to untie the cloth covers over their top knots. They shook out long black locks that had never been cut. Sister-in-law looked around the yard and went to grab some hemp rope and a knife. She cut off a length for each of them to tie around their foreheads.

"I remember doing this for funerals," Sister-in-law said. "I don't remember the reason." She bit her lip. "I think we have done everything."

Radish and Fortune hauled the cart; Sister-in-law, holding her son in her arms, made up the rear. Not a grand procession. They made their way past the village fishpond and through the dusty fields where soybeans would have been flourishing if not for the drought. Locusts crunched underfoot and circled overhead. Sister-in-law angrily swatted the insects from her baby. They came to the burying place, a small, rocky rise covered with poplar trees and pine near the South Branch of the Hao River. The brothers, drenched in sweat, struggled to wheel through the brush. They untied the stretcher from the cart.

"Can you lift it, Elder Brother?" Fortune asked.

To drop the stretcher would be a terrible thing. Radish nodded.

The air was hot and exceedingly humid, causing the bundles to reek. The two brothers heaved the stretcher up an incline to the place they had previously selected, a slight depression near a stand of pine midway up the hill. Sister-in-law handed Fortune the spade. They all paused, looking down in sorrow at the uncoffined reed bundles before them. The baby, Plenty, was sound asleep, his sweaty cheek resting on his mother's shoulder. Intent on their duties, the young farmers forgot about the sky. A bank of dark clouds billowed unnoticed above them, rushing into the void left by months of empty blue. Whipped into frenzy, wrathful at the inattentive gathering on the hillock below, the clouds burst open and unleashed a deluge.

Rain! At last! After so many months of drought. It was the kind of pelting downpour that blots out all else, forcing Fortune to drop his spade and run for shelter beneath a nearby tree. Radish grabbed his wife's hand and did the same. Thunder crashed overhead and the baby screamed in terror, though the sound was muffled by the torrents and rumblings. The clouds released sheets of water, but the parched ground proved incapable of receiving it. Rocks and mud tumbled down the hillside. Saplings sagged over. Fortune pressed against a boulder, his eyes shut tight.

Then it was over, the ground steaming. Everyone stood up and looked for the hollow, the place chosen for a grave. Gone! The spade had washed down the hill, but the reed bundles on the stretcher were buried beneath a thick layer of sediment and an overturned tree trunk. The three mourners gaped in disbelief. Sister-in-law began to weep, shaking her head and complaining in a screechy, choking voice that this was not a proper burial.

"The bodies are all jumbled who knows where, when they should have been set carefully one next to the other, heads to the north, feet to the south," she shouted, gesturing wildly. "This family is cursed with bad luck at every turn."

She became increasingly agitated. She bounced and bounced the whimpering baby on her hip. Radish backed away from his wife and said nothing.

Fortune cleared his throat. "Heaven has chosen the manner for burying our parents," he stated. "So be it."

The tone in Fortune's voice made Sister-in-law catch her breath and stop ranting. They picked out rocks to set around the place where they thought the bodies were buried. With the grave marked, they returned home.

7

OLD MOTHER WANG OFFERS GOOD ADVICE

Summer of Correctness Attained, fourth year (1344). Bell County's Lone Hamlet.

AT FIRST THE midsummer deluge that buried the Zhu dead was welcomed, as holding the promise of drought relief. However, when the rain clouds lowered and refused to leave, coughing up a continuous stream of heavenly discharge, the dikes to the north along the Yellow River burst. Seventeen walled cities flooded. The hordes of refugees soon sprouted bandits like mold.

The Huai River also rose with the rainstorms, but the dikes around the City of Hao were not breached. The flood dragon, who is fickle, flicked his tail away from the Huai tributaries. Instead, he sent the ravenous torrents of the Yellow River northward, to eat out an entirely new bed in the rush to the sea. And what did that mean for the Huai farmers? In a matter of months an entire region that had soaked its roots in the drool of the Yellow River was left gagging on dust with no relief in sight. The farmers had gone from drought to flooding to worse drought and could not recall such bitterness — this was unprecedented suffering. Even farther to the north, the emperor in his palace wrung his hands and asked his ministers what he should do. His chancellor resigned. Everyone else in the court averted their eyes, knowing this series of disasters could only be a portent of heavenly disfavor.

Radish was gone. Unable to withstand the forces of starvation, disease and loss, Radish's despair had turned into an unquenchable restlessness. His mind wound back in time, lingering over the flight from Ferry Village, when Chong Seven was sold for four strings of cash. Radish watched the rainstorms from inside the cottage, mumbling nervously over his memories.

When the showers finally stopped, Fortune rushed outside with the seed grain his mother had traded her loom to obtain. But while Fortune threw himself into the planting, Radish slipped into a deeper haze.

His wife brought their son to his side, hoping to rouse Radish. Fortune came home in the dark exhausted, but still found the energy to fill his brother's ears with the promise of a quick harvest of ripe grain. None of this seemed to matter to Radish anymore. His listlessness was pricked only by the desire to escape. He became convinced that he and his wife and baby should not stay in Lone Hamlet. One afternoon, speaking to himself in phrases that Fortune struggled to decipher, he began to pack a bundle.

"We have to leave," he said, his eyes flickering but refusing to meet Fortune's gaze.

"Where?" asked Fortune. "Where will you go?"

Sister-in-law Tang appeared in the doorway, her son on her hip. "We can seek out my mother in the county to the west of here," she said, "maybe she's still alive. Maybe things are better there."

Fortune looked at her in surprise.

"Yes, that's a good idea, that's where we will go, that's a chance for us," Radish muttered.

They all stood up. Sister-in-law took a shoulder pole with a basket at each end. In one went the bundle Radish had packed, in the other went the baby. And they left, just like that.

Fortune ran out after them and caught Radish by the shoulders. "Don't go, brother!" he pleaded.

Radish blinked and stepped back. Fortune briefly recognized the brother he had grown up with, the one he loved. Radish reached out and ran his fingers across Fortune's cheek, smiling.

"Do you remember when that old savage beat you in his yard that night?" he asked.

Fortune nodded. Sister-in-law and her baby stood waiting.

"I thought you were dead," Radish said. "I rolled you onto your back, blood everywhere. Do you know what you sang as I dragged you out of Old Wolf's yard?" Radish laughed and started to hum the opening lines to General Yue Fei's famous song, "The River Runs Red."

The two brothers sang the opening line together:

In wrath, my hair bristles till it pushes up my helmet...

Suddenly Radish's voice broke and he crumpled to the ground, weeping. He wrapped his arms around his gaunt ribs and heaved out bitter sobs.

"I can't save you, I can't save you," he said over and over again in a rasping voice, glancing up at Fortune and trying to see him through his tears. "There is nothing I can do. There is not enough food for even one person, and we are four."

Fortune stumbled back, reeling from his older brother's agony. He opened his mouth, but no words came out. He breathed in, trying to regain his voice and stay on his feet.

"Don't go, brother," was all he could offer, his voice no more than a croaking whisper, his tears disappearing into the dust.

Then Radish changed once again into the flickering-eyed

madman. "I have to go, I have to go," he muttered, staggering to his feet. He grabbed one of Fortune's shoulders and tapped frantically on the other. "You stay here. It's safer for you to stay here. Maybe mother's seed corn will sprout and there will be enough for you to eat. You have to stay and take care of the spirits. You have to stay behind, little brother. It's too dangerous out on the road."

Fortune wiped away his tears and tried to reassure Radish, nodding his head and saying that he need not worry.

Radish kept muttering. "I'll find some food for us," he said. "My wife will find us food. We'll come back with it. Maybe I'll even find our lost brother."

"What?" Fortune asked, trying to keep up with Radish's racing mind.

"Chong Seven! Don't you remember your own brother? We used to call him Puppy."

Fortune kept nodding in agreement. In truth, Fortune was terrified by this manic version of his brother and did not know what to do to soothe him. A part of him just wanted this Radish to go away.

"Yes, we'll come back," Radish continued. "We will hire monks then, and hold a proper funeral for our parents. You stay here." He shuffled off and did not look back.

Fortune stood in the middle of the lane, rooted to the ground, his mouth gaping open. When he could no longer make out the figures of his last remaining relatives, he turned back to the Zhu family cottage. This was the same mud-walled home rebuilt only six years earlier to shelter a husband and wife, their three grown sons, their first daughter-in-law, and their two grandsons — all dead or gone now. All but one.

Fortune was utterly alone. The cottage that had always seemed crowded was now so empty that glancing around it made Fortune's hands tremble. He breathed hard, and this made a loud sound in the still room. His throat was dry and he gulped, and this made a loud sound too.

He pulled his mat out into the yard and rested on his back, wrapped in quilts that still held the scent of his dead and departed relatives. He stared sleepless at the sky. The sun lowered and the moon rose and still Fortune did not move or close his eyes. Stars made their way across the sky. He picked out Weaving Maid, his sister's star, high and bright in the northwest.

"Perhaps Lotus is safe; perhaps I will see her again," he thought to himself, fervently wishing this could be true. "But what about Second Brother? How long will he last as a wanderer with no place to go?"

As dawn approached, Fortune observed the Triple Terraces constellation, which glittered weakly that night. This was his Grandfather Chen's asterism, the one the old diviner had worshiped. It consisted of three stars in a line, close to the Northern Dipper. The Triple Terraces is associated with the Perfected Warrior, the Black Tortoise who rules the North.

"Grandfather Chen considered the Perfected Warrior to be a special guardian of all the Daoists."

Thinking of his grandfather made Fortune sit up and reach for the charm-making talisman hanging around his neck. He had not yet bothered to examine it. Now, in the soft morning light, he studied the small box. Carved out of peach wood, it had been lacquered red and had a hole drilled into the top, through which the leather thong was threaded. The box was the length of a finger. The top was grooved underneath so that it could slide off to reveal two compartments inside: one was a long rectangle containing the chop; the other consisted of a small square, half filled with oily-red stamping paste.

Fortune glanced inside and was pleased to find his

grandfather's green soapstone chop as he remembered it. This made him smile. Now Fortune slid the cover back in place and puzzled over its design. Carved into the lacquer on the front of the box was a curious image, a square toad-like creature with a single eye and a watery body. What could it mean? He sighed and rose to his feet. It was a new day. He headed into the fields and wandered aimlessly. As he walked along, he counted the days since his father had died and was relieved that he was still well within the seven-times-seven days it takes for a soul to be assigned a new path in the cycle of rebirth. Offerings and special prayers during these important days can help the spirit of the deceased get a good assignment from King Yama, the ruler of the underworld. Fortune hurried along to his parents' grave to bow and pray that the souls of the dead would be released from all suffering.

Radish's parting words troubled Fortune. His brother had said he would seek to hold a proper funeral when he returned.

"How would we do that?" Fortune wondered. "And what should I do now to help Mother and Father and Elder Brother and Precious?"

He thought of the rituals on the Lunar New Year at Uncle's house, performed with such ease and dignity. In contrast, he knew that nothing had been dignified about the mudslide burial of the plague victims.

"We didn't know what we were doing and everything went wrong," he fretted.

Fortune's deepest fear was that his parents and brother and nephew would become Hungry Ghosts. These are the tormented wretches who wander the realm with unquenchable thirst, unable to swallow anything because their necks have narrowed into needles. Fortune's father had said Hungry Ghosts are the souls of the dead who received an improper burial or who have been neglected. Fortune worried that both conditions could apply to his dead — and he had so many souls to take care of all at once. He could not undo the funeral. Now he feared that if he made a mistake in the mourning rituals he further increased the risk of turning one of his beloved family members into a wretched ghost or even a vengeful demon.

Fortune shuddered at these terrifying thoughts. He sank down on a boulder near his parents' grave. Everyone has left me. This single thought reverberated relentlessly inside his head. He stood up to escape it, pacing in circles, his pain and helplessness coiling together. The talisman around his neck swung against his shoulder. He grabbed it and wrenched it over his head.

"You did not protect my mother," he shouted at the little box in his palm. "You have not protected my family."

Then he threw the necklace into the forest as far as he could hurl it. There, it was done.

Fortune remained staring after his lost talisman until he was startled by a voice at his back.

"The trees can take a great deal of abuse, it is true," said the voice.

Fortune turned and saw Old Mother Wang standing at a short distance, her youngest son at her side. They were searching for berries, baskets over their elbows.

"Your stomach is another matter," Old Mother Wang continued. "Lucky for you, I have found some ripe hackberries and the taro roots in my garden are fat now. Come home with me, my poor child, and I'll make you something to eat."

Fortune followed her meekly to her cottage.

Old Mother Wang's husband and daughter had drowned in an accident several years before the Zhu family moved to Lone Hamlet. She had three sons, the oldest apprenticed to the blacksmith on Flagstone Avenue. Her younger two, including

Fortune's friend Second Chao, lived at home with her. Old Mother Wang stuffed Fortune with fried taro root cakes, and even pulled out a gourd of fermented sorghum beer. She sat with Fortune, drinking and humming old songs.

"Stay here with us now, child," she said. "You can't live alone in that empty cottage."

And so he did. For the next few weeks, Fortune and Second Chao worked together in the fields. The village had emptied out by this time, with only a few chimneys still sending up cooking smoke in the evenings. Such an unprecedented sight — a vacant expanse where there should have been oxen dragging ploughs, farmers calling to each other as they worked their hoes along the furrows, children scampering underfoot. Instead there were just Fortune and his friend. The special millet that Fortune had planted after the rains ended turned golden, ready to be harvested.

"It has been fifty days, as my mother said," Fortune exclaimed to Second Chao.

Tending the fields required all of Fortune's energy and attention. However, in the evenings when the work was over and Fortune could rest in Old Mother Wang's cottage, his worries would swarm like gnats.

"Old Mother," Fortune hesitantly began one evening.

"Yes, my child?" she responded.

"Old Mother, I wonder," Fortune stammered. "Could it be that my parents committed terrible sins in their past lives? Is that why the Zhu family is suffering this fate?"

"Who can say?" Mother Wang replied without looking up from the cloth she was mending as Fortune finished his dinner. "But Heaven did not single out your family for punishment."

Now she set down her needle and focused on Fortune.

"Why, there are those in the village who are worse off than

you — look at the Tang clan with all its many sons and daughters. Gone!" she said, her gestures made all the more dramatic by their companion shadows in the lamplight. "And they were not the only ones wiped out completely. Your mother, she was one to watch the stars. She knew that sometimes we are all swept up in the great forces. Sometimes the punishments that rain down from Heaven are not meant for us at all. Oh, no! Sometimes our suffering is a message from Heaven to the Emperor, the Son of Heaven, and it is just our miserable fate to be part of it."

"So it can be like that," Fortune wondered, hoping.

Old Mother Wang stood up then. "Are you full?" she asked solicitously.

Fortune clutched at his belly in great satisfaction. The face of his host wrinkled in a smile of delight.

As the summer turned into fall, Old Mother Wang realized that Fortune's circumstances would soon need to be clarified. In this, she was thinking of the squire and his accountants. She addressed the matter one morning, sitting forward on her stool, looking intently at Fortune.

"Child," she said. "Tell Mother Wang, are you planning to keep farming your father's fields alone?"

Fortune said nothing.

"Have you spoken to the squire? His clerk will come asking for the tax soon, you know."

Fortune gritted his teeth. He had no intention of ever returning to the squire's house.

"Then have you thought of a relative in another village who could take you in?"

Fortune pinched his chin. He had nothing to say. After the warning of the first refugee at the village well, others had confirmed that the plague demons had claimed Uncle and his family. As for his sister Lotus, Fortune knew only that she was married to a fisherman named Li. Fortune had never been to Ferry Village and knew of no way to find her.

"Ai," Old Mother Wang grimaced. "You're a stubborn one, like your mother. It's time to remember your father's wishes. I heard that he promised you to a temple. Let's talk about that."

Fortune shook his head adamantly. "My mother did not like the Buddhist monks," he said. "She would not let me speak of becoming a monk."

"Do you know what your mother hated?" Old Mother Wang asked, reaching over to jab Fortune's thigh for emphasis. "Your mother hated the thought of her favorite son starving. That's what she hated." Now she leaned back and folded her arms, nodding her head in agreement with herself. "Yes, yes, your future is with the temple," she said.

Fortune frowned and left for the threshing grounds. As he and Second Chao threshed and winnowed the millet, Fortune had no time to ponder the Buddhists, but as he walked home he mulled over Old Mother Wang's words.

"Second Chao, do you think monks know how to make spirit tablets?" he asked his friend as they trudged along a footpath.

"How should I know something like that?" Second Chao answered absently. "We have no spirit tablets. You know how it is, though — the Daoists search for the elixir of immortality, and the Buddhists chant for those who died without it. The temple monks are the ones who do the ceremonies for the dead, I've seen that myself. So they must know how to go about setting up spirit tablets."

As Fortune sat with his neighbors that night slurping lustily at millet gruel, he took up his questions again. "So, Buddhist monks learn the chants for the dead?" he asked.

"What?" asked Old Mother Wang. "Why, yes, they do. This is

true. That's who you call for the services. And that's who takes your money when the chanting's done!" She chuckled to herself as she took away the chopsticks for rinsing.

That evening, Fortune walked alone along Mulberry Lane to his old cottage and sat down at the center of the empty interior. He eventually drifted off into a fitful sleep. This is when his Grandfather Chen first came to him in a dream. The old man stood before him, dressed in his conical bamboo hat and homespun gown. He glared down at Fortune. "Where is the chess set that I made for you with my own hands?"

Fortune rose to his knees and explained how Tang the Old Wolf had destroyed the chess set. He begged his grandfather's forgiveness.

"Bah," the old man waved his hand in a dismissive gesture. "It doesn't matter. Didn't you learn anything from your friend, Xu Da? Didn't he teach you how to play without a set?"

Fortune nodded, hoping desperately that his grandfather would not ask about the chop talisman he had foolishly, foolishly thrown into the hillside.

"Do you have any questions for me?" Grandfather Chen asked.

"Where is mother?" he quietly asked, his brow creased with despair. But he needed to know. He lifted his eyes to meet his grandfather's. "The family. Did King Yama assign them to one of the heavens or one of the hells?"

Grandfather Chen's stern expression softened and he gazed away into the distance. He seemed troubled. "It's not yet resolved," was all he would offer.

Fortune woke in the pitch dark of a moonless night. He returned to Old Mother Wang's house with the contents of his family altar packed into a cloth. He set this down on the table, where Old Mother Wang had a candle burning. She sat up in her bed and rubbed her eyes, waiting to hear what Fortune had to say.

"Can you help me join the temple?" he asked.

"Mm," Old Mother Wang answered simply, nodding her head.

After that, and for the first time since the plague deaths began, Fortune slept soundly.

Old Mother Wang selected an auspicious day for entry into a temple. On the chosen day, she handed Fortune a basket containing a bowl of offering grain, a jar of sorghum beer and two red candles. Old Mother Wang instructed Fortune in how to approach the temple abbot. Then she called over Second Chao and told him to escort Fortune to the temple gates.

"Child, do not look so forlorn, you are choosing the right path," she said to Fortune, her voice strong and reassuring. "Your father made a vow to the Lord Buddha and you are fulfilling it. The Buddha's boundless compassion will now be yours. They say the monks never run out of food. They say their cheeks glow from all the fine meals."

Fortune thanked her and turned to leave with Second Chao. Old Mother Wang called her youngest son over, the same one who had been in the field with her the day she had come upon Fortune shouting in the woods. The boy smiled mischievously and held something behind his back as he sidled up to Fortune. He pulled out his hand and opened his grimy fist. The chop box talisman, still hanging from its leather thong.

"This is yours, Uncle," the boy said.

The joy spread across Fortune's pockmarked face. He dropped to his knees and let the boy place the necklace over his head.

Old Mother Wang smiled. "It's a good omen," she said. "Off with you both, then!"

She held Fortune's arm as she walked him out of her house

and then she stood smiling and waving as Fortune and Second Chao departed. When the pair were well beyond earshot, her smile faded. Sadly, she shook her head and uttered aloud the famous verse by the banished emperor of a conquered dynasty:

> How much can the burden of sorrow on one man be?
> As much as the river water in spring flowing to the
> sea.

PART TWO

VESSEL
朱盛

蒼蒼竹林寺
杳杳鐘聲晚
荷笠帶夕陽
青山獨歸遠

Green, green, the bamboo forest temple,
Distant, distant, the sound of the evening bell.
His lotus hat carries the sunset,
As he retreats alone into the darkening mountain.

—"On Parting with the Buddhist Master Lingche," by
the eighth-century poet Liu Zhangqing

8

THE NOVICE SHAVES HIS HEAD AND LEARNS HIS NEW NAME

Autumn of Correctness Attained, fourth year (1344). Tiger Empress Temple, on a hillside above Lone Hamlet.

FORTUNE AND SECOND Chao walked respectfully past the gate guardian statues. They headed into the weedy courtyard before the Hall of the Heavenly Kings, where a lone attendant lay snoring on a bench. Proceeding around the image of the fat Laughing Buddha, the two visitors stepped over the high threshold leading into the heart of the temple — the courtyard of the Great Hall. There, they could hear the monks in session, their sonorous chanting punctuated by the rap of a wooden mallet and the chimes of bells. Billows of incense wafted out of the open doors. A monk rushed by. When Second Chao called after him, the monk halted, looking impatient.

"Well?" he asked.

Second Chao cleared his throat and blurted out, "I have brought you this new monk for your temple."

The monk eyed Fortune, unimpressed. He shook his head and waved his hands in disapproval. "This will not do," the monk said. "We are in the middle of a ceremony. There is no time to help you today."

Second Chao may have been nervous about helping Fortune

join a temple, but he was not ready to accept defeat. So he nodded and let the monk go on his way. "Keep your distance from that useless fart," Second Chao advised Fortune. "Let's find a different monk."

Fortune nodded numbly, but he was not listening. He was fighting the desire to flee. Fumbling for the newly-reclaimed talisman around his neck, Fortune could think only of his mother's hostility toward Buddhist monks. He squeezed the talisman with his right hand and reached for Second Chao's arm with his left, holding desperately to both. Fortune felt overwhelmed by reluctance and foreboding, to the point that his feet dragged.

It was all he could do not to speak aloud his thoughts: "I want to go back to our fields. I want to go back now. I don't care if it causes me trouble. This unfriendly place does not hold my destiny."

A senior monk dressed in flowing robes emerged from the same side door that had swallowed up the "useless fart." This temple elder held a string of prayer beads, absently running his fingers along the grooved wood. He was a stout fellow with a firm mouth and heavy-lidded but observant eyes. Known by the religious name of Balance, he continued to whirl his beads through one palm, but lifted the other to welcome the visitors, striding toward them.

Second Chao bowed and raised his clasped hands in respectful greeting. Fortune tucked his talisman back under his jacket. He felt sure that the monks would disapprove of something his grandfather had carved — or worse, try to confiscate it.

"Esteemed Elder, my family would like the honor of presenting this young believer for service to Tiger Empress Temple," Second Chao announced, launching into the speech he had rehearsed the night before with Old Mother Wang, but forgotten until encountering the senior monk.

Balance pursed his lips. "Who is to be the sponsor?"

"My family, the Chao family of Mulberry Lane in Lone Hamlet," Second Chao replied, lifting his basket and pulling off the cloth cover. "We have brought along this worthless offering for the temple altar."

Balance ran his eyes along the broad shoulders and homespun clothing of the proposed monk. Turning slowly from Fortune's captivating face to the offering of candles, grain, and oil, Balance smiled and reached for the basket.

"The Goddess of Mercy has marked her feast day by sending us a novice," he commented.

Having accepted the requisite offering, Balance nodded a curt dismissal of the sponsor.

Fortune did not want to let go of Second Chao's arm, but he had no choice. Second Chao was only escorting Fortune to the temple, and now that task was finished. It was time for Second Chao to return home to Old Mother Wang.

"Goodbye my friend," Second Chao murmured. "It will be alright."

How Fortune wished he had a mother waiting for him back in the village. But he did not. And so he could do nothing but stand mutely as Second Chao retraced his steps and exited the courtyard, disappearing into the known world, the place outside the temple gates. Fortune, on the other hand, was sent deeper into the temple, and soon found himself alone in a spare, low-ceilinged room with a sleeping platform along one side. He held in his arms the wad of bedding straw and the reed mat handed to him by the clerk in charge of guests. The clerk had forgotten to provide a candle, so now Fortune sat warily in the gloomy twilight with his arms full and his stomach growling.

The clerk had told Fortune that the session in the Great Hall was a special service for the Goddess of Mercy, ordered and paid for by Squire Lin. The religious services would conclude with a vegetarian feast, which was about to start. "You can follow me to the dining hall and take your meal there," the clerk had said, grudgingly.

Fortune was startled by the mention of the squire's name. Surely the squire will recognize me and remember my harvest debts? He declined the offer of a seat at the feast, much to the incredulity of the guest clerk, who left shaking his head.

Fortune could hear the happy gathering in the dining hall nearby. Ladles clanged against cauldrons as the food was dished into bowls. Monks called out to each other. Fortune heard a man, probably the squire, making what sounded like a speech. Friendless and forgotten in the guest chamber, Fortune shook his head to rouse himself from his stupor. He stood up. Finally noticing the bedding straw in his arms, he felt his way in the darkness, working to spread it in one corner of the platform. A ray of light pierced the tattered paper window pane at the other end of the narrow room — perhaps a torch had just been lit? Fortune walked toward the light, wanting a glimpse of his new surroundings. The window faced out, giving a view of the hillside woods. The light came not from a torch but from the rising harvest moon. Its pure brilliance was perfectly centered within the window sashes, a crisp contrast to the frayed remains of the pane.

"Oh!" Fortune exclaimed, bathed in the companionable glow.

In his solitary reverie, Fortune wondered if his brother Radish or his sister Lotus were still alive, watching this same moon. Old Mother Wang, at least, would be thinking of him on this first evening in the temple. The words of a famous moon poem came to mind. Fortune whispered them, though the sound of his raspy voice made him feel even lonelier:

PART TWO: VESSEL

The autumn dew has just turned white,
The moon is the same one shining on my old home.
I have brothers but they are all scattered,
No place remains for me to ask after their fate.

The window being small, the moon soon rose above its frame. The room plunged back into darkness.

At dawn, Fortune emerged from his quarters, suffering the discomfort of the unfamiliar on top of a churning stomach. He was in a side corridor which ran parallel to the temple's main public axis. This corridor gave access to the temple's private areas: the monks' quarters, the dining hall, the bookkeeping office and a reception room. Hearing movement in the reception room, Fortune looked in that direction. A monk emerged from a doorway. Fortune recognized him as the guest clerk.

"Aiya," the clerk said. "You are already up. I'll go and see what's to be done." The monk started to walk away, but then realized Fortune was still lingering in the hallway. "Go on, back to your room," the monk waved him off.

Fortune was not in an obedient mood. He decided against returning to the gloomy guest quarters for another interminable wait. Instead, he walked up the sloping corridor and peered through an archway, gazing at the carved eaves and carmine red walls of the Great Hall. Morning sunshine illuminated the massive bronze incense burner at the entrance. Turning back into his corridor again, Fortune discovered stairs leading down to a low opening in the exterior wall. A chance to relieve his bladder! He ducked out into the forest.

Returning, Fortune found a young monk staring down at him. This monk was about Fortune's age though much smaller in stature. "We have a toilet area, you know," the monk informed him. "You don't have to piss on the trees."

Fortune shrugged. "It won't hurt them."

The young monk grinned and led Fortune back to the reception room. "I am Emptiness," he said. "The Abbot sent me to arrange for the shaving and to give you this."

Emptiness set down the tray he had been carrying and uncovered a bowl of noodle soup and a cup of tea. Fortune devoured the humble meal at once, and Emptiness ran off laughing to fetch some oiled sesame cakes to further stem the new guest's hunger. Fortune was still enjoying the cakes with Emptiness when the head monk, Balance, swept into the room, the guest clerk close behind.

Calling for Emptiness to clear away the food tray and set out writing utensils, the clerk fussed about. Balance waited at the room's center, observing everyone from under his heavy-lidded eyes, his prayer beads clicking between his fingers.

"We shall begin," he finally announced in a deep, gravelly voice with the accent of the southern provinces.

The clerk took a seat and lifted a writing brush. His hand poised over a registry book, he looked up at Balance. "Will there be any lay family or sponsors for the candidate?" he asked.

Balance raised his thick eyebrows.

"Esteemed Elder, my parents are dead," Fortune replied. "I lost my family to the plague demons. My sponsor is the Chao family of Lone Hamlet."

The clerk clucked in disdain, as if to say, "Have we stooped to accepting ragged orphans who have to run and find a neighbor to sponsor them?"

But Balance tapped a finger on the registry book, encouraging the clerk to concentrate on writing out Fortune's name and the date of his arrival at the temple.

Balance picked up a bundle of incense which Emptiness rushed to light. Once the flame was extinguished, the room filled with the scent of sandalwood. Dividing the bundle in two, Balance handed half to Fortune and, with a stately grace, stepped to the north wall of the room, where a low altar held a statue of the Maitreya Buddha, the Buddha of the Future, also known as the Laughing Buddha, part of the pantheon of Enlightened Ones. Maitreya was the same fat and jolly fellow with a seat in the temple's Hall of the Heavenly Kings, to greet visitors. On this smaller room's altar, he served in a more sanctified capacity — the welcoming of a novice to a religious life.

Balance kneeled on a cushion, bowed deeply, and placed his incense sticks in the metal censer before the deity. The pungent smoke drifted upward, a tangible request for communion with the gods. Balance rose and, beckoning for Fortune to kneel in his place, he launched into a sermon.

"There was once a young prince born under auspicious signs who possessed the stern dignity of a tiger and the virtuous wisdom of a sage. This prince sought to cultivate his mind. One night he stole away from his father's palace, riding out on a white horse. He left his family, shaved his head, and achieved Nirvana under a Bodhi tree. He became the greatest of the Enlightened Ones, the Shakyamuni Buddha."

Balance paused to gaze down at Fortune.

"If you renounce lay life," Balance intoned to the upturned face of the young man before him, "you too will be severing your family ties and leaving behind all attachments."

Fortune had not expected this. He knew that a monk lived in a temple, not with his parents, but he had not considered the implications of such a fate. Did not Fortune enter the temple to learn funeral rituals, so that he could better care for the spirits of his parents? Now, in this first ceremony, he was being asked to do the opposite. Fortune frowned.

Balance spoke again. "If you wish, you can bow one final time to your parents."

Fortune's expression hardened. A final bow — would it not be better to starve to death? And yet, refusing to survive would also be unfilial. Where did he have to go besides this temple? That was the other, more practical, reason he had resolved to become a monk. With his thoughts in this kind of turmoil, Fortune reached for the talisman around his neck.

"What's that?" cried the clerk, pointing accusingly. "Candidates enter the temple with no possessions!"

Startled, Fortune flicked his eyes to the clerk. "It is only my grandfather's chop seal," Fortune answered in a tight voice.

The clerk rose from his desk to get a better look at the little lacquered box, and then his face flushed. "It's a pollution!" he shouted. The clerk pointed at it, outraged. "It has marks on it, like the Daoist charlatans make!" he said to Balance. "And it is hanging on a cord of animal skin! We are vegetarians here! We can't allow this!"

Fortune sucked in his breath. He clenched his fists. "The conceited cockroach," he thought to himself. "Is this how monks behave? Was my mother right about them after all?"

"Brother," Balance said gently to the clerk, "I will deal with this. Please take Emptiness to the supply area to oversee the selection of the monk robe. I will finish here."

The guest clerk clucked his tongue once again, but stood up to leave with Emptiness. Balance waited until the pair was gone. Then he turned back to the candidate still kneeling on the altar cushion.

"We ask you to enter our community willingly, with the understanding that you are entering a new life and breaking with your past." Balance added carefully, "But this does not mean you must forget your parents or their sacrifices. It means that you are changing households. We will become your new family and this temple will be your new home. You will be secluded here in our halls, living the simple life of a monk."

"Can I still tend my parents' graves?"

"That is permitted," Balance said. "Living here as a monk you can accumulate merit on your parents' behalf. And here you will find the Great Compassion of the Lord Buddha and the Goddess of Mercy. Here we understand that life is suffering. Here we can help you find an inner peace."

Balance's words were firm and solemn. The monks at Tiger Empress had been summoned to perform many funeral services in Lone Hamlet during that season of drought and disease. Balance had been confronted before with the kind of misery and grief that the young man kneeling before him had endured. Balance raised his palm above Fortune's head and recited the Three Jewels, which are the three sacred faith vows of Buddhism.

"Take refuge in the Buddha, take refuge in the teaching, take refuge in the disciples."

He reached for the razor that Emptiness had left for them and held it up before Fortune.

"A monk becomes his own lamp and looks inward to conquer cravings. His mind is like a clear mirror which he strives to keep polished. Are you ready to shave your hair as an outward mark to the world of your commitment? Are you ready to abandon all attachments and become my dependent and disciple?"

Fortune nodded.

"Can you follow the first Five Precepts? This means you cannot take life, nor can you steal, commit sexual immorality, speak untruths, or drink wine. Can you follow these rules, as all monks must?"

Again Fortune nodded.

"We do not offer ordination at such a small temple. We can only shave heads and set you on the monk's path," Balance explained. "You may choose to take the rest of the ordination vows later at a monastery."

He instructed Fortune to untie the blue strip of cloth that held his topknot in place.

Fortune's hair had rarely been trimmed and hung well past his shoulders. Did not Confucius say that our hair, like our skin, is a gift from our parents and should not be damaged? Every morning of every day, Fortune, like all the men in his family, pulled his hair to the crown of his head and wrapped it tight inside a cloth tie. The only exception to this was the time after the death of his parents, when Fortune and Radish had let their hair hang loose and uncombed as a sign of mourning. To shave his head — was this not unfilial?

Balance stooped over to place a basin at Fortune's knees.

Fortune felt the top of his head being pressed down, down until he was blinking at his own reflection in the porcelain glaze. It was time to shave off the long locks. They dropped softly into the basin, tuft by tuft, blocking Fortune's reflection and sprinkling a downy coating on his knees. Fortune stared at the severed pile of his own hair and was surprised at how much his head had produced.

With one handful in the center still remaining, Balance paused and resumed the liturgy.

"One tuft remains," he said. "It is not too late to be released from this path. Do you consent to having it clipped?"

The last of Fortune's black hair draped over his eyes. He stared at it, thinking, "there is no release from this path for me. I can walk down this path or starve to death and join my parents' corpses."

Fortune cleared his throat and raised his almost-bald head to look at Balance.

"I consent," he promised.

PART TWO: VESSEL

"Without reservations?"

"No reservations."

"One last time I ask you: do you consent?"

"I consent," said Fortune, his voice strengthening with each promise. "And I will never regret."

With one final flick of the razor, Fortune became a monk.

In the hallway came the sound of the guest clerk returning, the sign of the end to all solemnity. Balance leaned down to his new tonsure disciple and whispered, "Keep the seal of your grandfather, my son, but keep it out of sight."

The constraint of a tunic against his thighs and the bizarre sensation of air passing over his bald scalp made Fortune feel ridiculous as he trailed a fellow monk up a steep temple passageway. Fortune had never dressed in anything but trousers and a short jacket tied by a cord, with padding added in the winter and taken away in the summer — the clothes of the poor farmer who toiled in the field. The robe, on the other hand, was the mark of a man who was not a laborer. Not that Fortune's new robe was in any way striking or finely cut. In fact, it was shabby and patched and too small for Fortune's large frame so that the seam came tight under his armpits and the hem stopped at his knees. At least the long sleeves ended past his fingertips, as was proper, but they lacked the wide flare of the Azure Ocean robe worn by monks at wealthier monasteries. The cloth had been dyed a weak gray color. It smelled dusty and felt bulky. Fortune was shuffling along, trying not to rub his shaved head, when the monk he had been following turned into the dining hall.

"Stand there," the monk said, gesturing inside the doorway.

The rest of the monks were seated around two sets of wooden tables, with benches on only one side so that the sets faced inward to a center aisle. At one end of this aisle was the high abbot's chair. It faced the doorway, where Fortune now stood alone, the object of every other monk's interested gaze. Fortune recognized Emptiness and the guest clerk among the twenty-some faces of his new brothers. The old abbot entered followed by Balance.

The abbot was a small thin man, with the religious name of Prayerful Virtue. He was absent-minded, and his eyesight weak, so he did not notice Fortune until Balance coughed politely and stood before the abbot's seat.

"Venerable Master," Balance addressed him, "the Feast of the Enlightenment of the Goddess of Mercy brought us a novice. This morning I shaved his head and presided over his taking the Five Precepts."

"Eh?" Abbot Virtue responded, peering out until his eyes rested on Fortune. "Ah. Yes, yes, so I see. Blessings of Buddha. Blessings, blessings."

The abbot raised his chopsticks and plucked up a mouthful of pickled plum, in a hurry to begin eating, since the monks would not start their meal before him. "Come closer, young novice," the abbot called out, gesturing with his chopsticks. "Let me get a look at you."

Abbot Virtue studied Fortune while chewing at his pickles. Then he turned to Balance. "What do you make of such a long face and such a heavy brow?"

Balance pursed his lips, as he tended to do when thinking something over. He gestured at a monk seated on the western side of the room, the side for the higher ranks. "Our Great Hall attendant can speak better to this," Balance said. "Tell us, brother, what do you make of the novice's strange face?"

The Great Hall attendant put down his chopsticks and stood up to better scrutinize the visage in question. Fortune obligingly looked back, blinking his hawk eyes and lifting his iron chin. He had never received a detailed analysis of his features.

PART TWO: VESSEL

"Well, I'm no expert, but I would call this a 'wood' face," said the Great Hall attendant, referring to the element — as distinct from fire, earth, metal or water — that is linked to such matters as the tiger, the color green, the number eight, the planet Jupiter, the season of spring and the direction of east.

A monk entered the hall from the kitchen, lugging a bucket of steaming noodles. This monk, who was the grain steward, set down his bucket near Fortune and turned to join the speculation over the novice's physiognomy.

"It's a wood face all right," the grain steward agreed. "But see how it's unbalanced. Look here at the chin, it's sticking out too far. This can only mean turbulent changes after middle age."

"Just so," said the abbot, nodding. He drummed the fingers of his left hand on his table, but was careful to keep the chopsticks in his right hand poised over his dishes of noodles and vegetables, so the others could continue eating. "But what about his brow? It's quite pronounced."

"It's in the sector of the face that governs youth and this monk is past his youth, so what does it matter?" said the grain steward, who was a matter-of-fact fellow.

"How can that be?" asked the striker of the drum, who sat on the east side of the room among the lower ranks. "I thought a high forehead signaled a long life."

This was too much for the rule-oriented guest clerk, who waved his chopsticks in consternation. "See here, this is all nonsense," he complained. "It is all superstition."

Well acquainted with the guest clerk's views, the abbot paid him no attention. Instead, he looked down at the novice, taking in more than his face this time. "Young novice, why aren't you eating?" he asked. "Have you already eaten?"

Fortune stammered. It would not be polite to suggest he was salivating with hunger, weak at the knees, longing for his own bowl of noodles. "Venerable Master, it doesn't matter."

The rest of the monks knew better. The grain steward ladled out two bowls, one of noodles and one of pickled cabbage, and the guest clerk pointed Fortune to his new seat in a back row. It was the place for the brother with the lowest rank of all.

When the meal was over Fortune noticed two young women, neither with the shaved heads of nuns, enter from the kitchen to clear away the dishes. He wondered at the presence of these women among the monks. But Balance beckoned to him and so Fortune left, his questions forgotten.

The pair, now linked as tonsure master and disciple, passed from the long side corridor to a courtyard in the main public axis of the temple. Walking behind the Great Hall and around a pavilion holding the bronze statue of a tiger, they climbed the steps to the abbot's quarters at the rear of the temple complex. Here, after a short wait, they were joined by Abbot Virtue, who took a seat in his reception room with Emptiness, the abbot's acolyte, who poured everyone a cup of tea.

"Venerable Master," Balance began. "We need a religious name for our novice."

It was the tradition at Tiger Empress Temple for the abbot to select the religious name for every novice, no matter who his tonsure master might be. Abbot Virtue asked Fortune some questions about his family and why he wanted to be a monk.

"My father told me that, when I was a baby, I had a bad case of the 'heavenly flowers' disease," Fortune said. "My father thought I was going to die, so he asked Lord Buddha to spare me, saying that if I survived he would give me to a temple when I grew up."

"You have the marks to remind you of this promise," the abbot noted. "Perhaps they will begin to fade now that you have fulfilled your father's vow."

He turned to Balance, who held the rank of rector, the second in command and the supervisor of all the monks in their daily affairs.

"What will the novice's duties be?" the abbot asked.

"This strong young man will be a great benefit to our temple," Balance replied. "He will be our new verger. He will be the one who keeps the incense smoking and the candles lit and the oil burning. This will be his primary duty to the Lord Buddha and to our Tiger Empress Temple. He will sleep in the dormitory next to the bunk of our head verger and he will report at daybreak to the tea steward to assist with the boiling of water and the preparation of the offering to the Hungry Ghosts. After the morning meal, this novice will report to the Great Hall attendant for instructions on upkeep of our halls. In the afternoons, before the dinner hour, this novice will report to the firewood attendant and keep our stoves supplied with kindling."

Balance told all this to Abbot Virtue, but the speech was really for the benefit of Fortune, who knew nothing of what it meant to be a verger or to work in a temple.

Emptiness, standing beside the abbot, seemed confused. "But who is our head verger?" Emptiness asked.

"Piety was our verger. Now he is our head verger," Balance stated.

The instructions over, it was time for the naming.

"When you meet a monk, you ask him, 'What's your upper and lower?' because monk names have two parts to them," Abbot Virtue explained to Fortune. "Our Balance is actually 'Exalted Balance' when we introduce him to monks who are not from our temple. In the same way, my acolyte, 'Emptiness,' is really 'Bright Emptiness,' and I am 'Prayerful Virtue.'"

The abbot closed his eyes and breathed slowly in and out, in and out, his hands settled loosely in his lap. The others watched in silence. Fortune observed with interest this display of the meditation practice for which the Chan sect is famous. He admired the peaceful feeling in the room, though his own eyes flicked from the abbot's hands to his face, to the faces of Balance and Piety, to the steam rising from the teapot. After several minutes, Abbot Virtue serenely opened his eyes, and waited for them to refocus on Fortune's face.

"When I clear away all extraneous thoughts, what remains in my mind's eye are the novice's arresting features," he explained. "My son, your face speaks of great vicissitudes, though I cannot say if they will bring you calamities or blessings. We shall encourage the blessings. I will give you the name 'Vessel,' because you will be the container for our high expectations."

"Cheng," Balance repeated, nodding his head. "It is a good name. This will be his 'lower,' the name we will call him by. But what of his 'upper'?"

Abbot Virtue considered the red spots dotting Fortune's cheeks. "Vermillion," he said at last, reaching over and patting Fortune's knee, "to remind you of the promise your father once made and which you, in filial love, are now fulfilling."

"Ah!" cried Balance, slapping his own knee in surprise. This word "vermillion" was the exact meaning of Fortune's surname "Zhu," but the abbot had not asked for the clan name and did not know it. Balance was amazed, but decided against telling this to Abbot Virtue. Instead, he softly repeated the name. "Zhu Cheng."

"Vermillion Vessel," Fortune echoed.

Ah, but no longer Fortune. Chong-ba, the Eighth Chong, that name of good fortune, is Vessel. He is now a novice.

9

TENDING THE HUNGRY GHOSTS
AND SPIRIT TABLETS

"WHO IS THE Tiger Empress?" Vessel asked on the day after receiving his new monk name. He was still adjusting to having a new name, and so names were on his mind.

"Our temple was named for an empress who was raised by tigers," said Piety, who was in the midst of showing Vessel where he should sweep each morning. "That is why we have a tiger pavilion."

Vessel frowned. "Why didn't her parents raise her?"

"It is said that her parents left the baby in a Goddess of Mercy grotto when they were fleeing the border wars between the Song and the northern invaders," Piety answered. "The Goddess must have summoned the tiger family to take care of the baby. Some say the tigers were actually immortals. The baby grew up to be a beautiful lady and so she was sent to court to be a consort. Before she died, she gave her best jewels to a monk at court and told him to use them to build a temple in honor of her tiger protectors near the place where she was raised." Piety paused. "You know about the gilded monk, right?"

Vessel smiled. "Oh yes, it's famous in Lone Hamlet. I even

came here and saw it once during a temple fair. That was the only time I ever visited this place until the day before yesterday."

"The 'meat body' is right over there," said Piety, pointing to a pedestal at the far side of the Hall of the Temple Guardian. The two walked over and stood before it, gazing up at the gilded death grimace of the monk, who was seated in the lotus position — feet crossed, soles upward, hands loose in lap.

"He is our temple founder," said Piety reverentially.

"You mean the one entrusted with the empress's jewels?"

Piety nodded.

Vessel smirked. "I guess he'd need to be saintly to be given a job like that."

Piety looked askance at Vessel and lit a stick of incense, which he set on the monk's altar.

"How did he end up like this?" Vessel asked.

"Abbot Virtue told me that the monk asked to be placed in a ceramic container when he was about to die, seated just like that. Then after he died, his disciples pickled him in salt and sealed up the jar. When Commander Yesunge, the tiger tamer, came through here, his men found the sealed jar. They broke it open and saw that the body had been perfectly preserved. So the monks took up a collection to have the body gilded and displayed on its own altar."

"And who are the women in the kitchen?"

"They are the wife and daughter of the Abbot," Piety replied in a low voice. "You must address the wife as 'Master Mother' and the daughter as 'Elder Sister.'"

"But how are there women in a temple of monks?" Vessel pressed. "Isn't that forbidden?"

Piety glanced cautiously around as he led Vessel out to the main courtyard. The area was deserted. He turned back to Vessel.

"Abbot Virtue started out as a young monk at a monastery to

the south of here, in the district where the Bell Bandit rebelled," Piety explained. "The imperial troops swept in and destroyed our abbot's home temple. He was forced out of the fold and returned to lay life, but he continued to honor his vows and he remained a vegetarian. Then he married and had two sons and a daughter, but his life was bitter and both his second son and his daughter's betrothed died young. It is said that bodhisattvas began to visit our abbot in his dreams and they pleaded with him to return to the temple life where he belonged. When this temple was restored by the tiger tamers, monks were called back and some of them knew Prayerful Virtue and invited him to become our abbot. He accepted the invitation, but refused to abandon his family. The women in the kitchen are his wife and his daughter. They have taken the Five Precepts of the laity. Abbot Virtue's son could not bear the cruelty of the outside world, so he shaved his head and became a monk too. He is our tea steward."

"Ah, the tea steward," Vessel remarked, nodding his head. He had met the tea steward that morning, having been instructed to head at daybreak from his dorm to the kitchen, where he was expected to fetch water for the cauldrons. Vessel had not slept well and rose before dawn from his bunk on the sleeping platform. Making his way down a still-dark passage to the kitchen entrance, the magpies just beginning to rustle in the trees, he had found a middle-aged monk seated in deep meditation on a low stone pillar. Vessel had waited awkwardly to be noticed. When this did not happen, Vessel became anxious and finally interrupted him.

"Elder brother, can you tell me where is the tea steward?" Vessel had asked.

That made the meditating monk's eyelids pop open. He had paused to refocus his vision and then swiveled his gaze across the courtyard until noticing Vessel. The monk finally spoke in a tranquil voice: "I am the tea steward."

Piety broke into Vessel's recollections to add, "I have heard that the tea steward held his baby brother in his arms and watched him die of starvation and the fevers." He shook his head sadly and sighed.

Resuming his instruction, Piety stepped over the threshold of the Great Shrine Hall.

"You will need to light the candles and start the incense every morning before the worshipers arrive," he said, lifting the cover off a burning oil lamp inside the entrance.

Piety lit two incense sticks in the lamp flame and handed one to Vessel. The pair walked slowly to the main altar and then crossed to the side ones. At each image, Piety stopped to kindle a new stick of incense and place it in a bronze burner. Vessel copied him, listening solemnly as Piety chanted over and over again, "May all beings in the three evil paths of existence who suffer the eight kinds of disasters be released from afflictions."

Tiger Empress monks ate regular meals, like Old Mother Wang had promised, but their grain came from the nearby fields, which were once again cursed by drought. Balance increased the number of fast days, but still the grain supply dwindled. The monks ate twice each day: a breakfast of millet gruel and steamed buns; a dinner of noodles and pickled vegetables. But to Vessel, who had not long ago dined on boiled tree bark and white clay, the temple meals were generous.

While the meals may have satisfied his stomach, nothing could stanch Vessel's deep chasm of sorrow and loneliness. Under his monk's robe, Grandfather Chen's talisman drummed on Vessel's chest, a constant reminder of his duty to serve the dead. The solitary drudgery of stoking fires and hauling in buckets of water and sweeping halls offered no escape from the festering worries in Vessel's head. Is Radish still alive? Did he find Sister-in-law Tang's mother? What about the souls of my parents and Cattail and Precious — are they at peace? In the midst of chopping wood for the temple kitchen, his muscles warmed by the exertion, his breath exhaling in white frosty puffs into the crisp fall air, Vessel would become locked in a kind of stupor, gazing into the distance, unable to recognize his temple surroundings, his axe poised over his shoulder, lost in a haze of sorrow.

"Eh, young novice, what's the matter with you?" the firewood attendant would call out, jerking Vessel out of his torpor.

It turned out that this firewood attendant was none other than the monk Second Chao had labeled as a useless fart. Second Chao was right. When Vessel reported to the firewood attendant in accordance with Balance's instructions, this monk in charge of keeping the kitchen supplied with kindling took one look at Vessel's wide shoulders and tossed aside his own axe. The useless fart took to bringing along a small stool during trips to collect firewood, the better to rest in comfort as he watched Vessel toil.

So it was not when working alone but rather in the warm dining hall, the monks conversing jovially around him, that the thorns of grief stopped scratching across Vessel's chest.

"You have finished eating, novice?" Abbot Virtue would ask at the end of each morning meal.

"Yes, Venerable Father," Vessel always replied.

Then Abbot Virtue would hand him a flat wooden board and send him to make an offering to the Hungry Ghosts. Vessel would bow to the abbot and collect a pinch of millet grain from the dining hall Buddha's altar. "Don't spill any," Balance urged the first few times, but Vessel was unfailingly careful as he placed the offering on the wooden board and carried it to the low pillar outside in the courtyard, opposite the pillar the tea steward used for meditation. Vessel had to clear away any fallen leaves before he could tip the board to spill the offering onto the pillar. Then he would snap his fingers to let the Hungry Ghosts know they were not forgotten, and recite this verse:

> Hear now, o spirit world,
> This grain is meant for you.
> May it be enough.
> May it be enough.
> And may all who need it find it.

Vessel always stood in silence after finishing this prayer. He would close his eyes and fervently pray that some of the offering be transferred to the souls of his parents and brother and nephew. Then he would open his eyes and smile, glad to be a monk.

One morning not long after his arrival at the temple, just when he was beginning to feel familiar with his routine, Vessel nearly collided with the guest clerk at the entrance to the Great Hall.

"You careless dog's leg!" the guest clerk shouted.

"Watch out yourself, you bald ass," Vessel retorted, though he should have known better.

The enraged guest clerk stepped back and pointed imperiously to the gate through which Vessel had come. "To the rector with you," the clerk hissed.

Having no choice, Vessel pivoted and marched off toward the bookkeeping office, the guest clerk at his heels. The fuming pair burst into the room where Balance was immersed in documents. Glancing up at the testy old monk and the willful novice, both red-faced with anger, Balance reached for his prayer beads.

"Yes, brothers?" he asked, his tone weary.

"Rector," the clerk began, "the Great Hall attendant mentioned to me at breakfast that rodents had eaten away the altar candles, which as you know are quite expensive. I went at once to check and saw with my own eyes that this is true. Nibbled down to nubs, they are, and yet when our novice here recently came to me to get more candles I reminded him to keep watch for this very problem." The guest clerk paused to turn and glare at Vessel, who was baffled by this unexpected complaint. "He eats up our grain as fast as the bowls can be set before him, just like a rat, and yet this novice is too lazy to shoo away mice!"

The guest clerk had worked himself into a fine state and would have continued but Balance raised a palm to cut him off. Nonetheless, the guest clerk leaned with both hands on Balance's table and dropped his voice, finishing off by saying, "What's more, just now this novice dared to insult me. He called me, he called me ... a bald ass."

Balance gave a slight dip of his chin, as if to acknowledge the seriousness of the charge, and then took a deep breath before addressing Vessel.

"The temple is no place for such vulgar talk," Balance sternly instructed. "You must learn to control your temper. You can meditate on that on your bed bunk while the rest of us take the evening meal."

The guest clerk vigorously nodded his head in support of the punishment. Balance pursed his lips and glanced vaguely at the room's altar.

"We must watch our supplies more closely," he worried. "It seems we are always having to buy more candles, more oil, more paper, more incense. What's to be done about it?" With that he waved his hands to dismiss the pair and turned back to his documents.

Stung, Vessel strode blindly through the corridors, heading in the opposite direction of the guest clerk. Outside the Hall of the Temple Guardian, Vessel snatched a broom left propped up near the entrance and stomped into the dim interior. Sweeping with reckless gusto, he sent great clouds of dust over the meat body and other statues until the motes made him cough and blink in irritation. Vessel threw the broom to the ground. The feeling that he had been treated unfairly churned within him, causing his hands to tighten into fists. His anger thrummed in his ears, turning them red.

Outside in the courtyard, an old granny making her way through the halls and altars thumped her cane over the Temple Guardian threshold. Vessel spun in her direction. He threw up his hands and shouted at her, "Can't you see that I am trying to clean this hall right now?" Startled, the old woman shrank back. Then she peered into the shadowy hall and drew her bottom lip over her two remaining teeth as she glanced from Vessel's angry face to the broom on the ground. She used both hands to rap her cane hard on the floor as a rebuke of the young monk's rude behavior.

Vessel watched her slow retreat, his nostrils flaring and his chest heaving. The old granny reminded him of his Auntie Liu. He was struck by a vivid memory of how Auntie Liu and his entire family had been angry at him for getting caught eating one of Old Wolf's calves.

"They'd all been angry with me, even though Old Wolf had nearly beaten me to death. No one had been angry with Old Wolf."

Vessel's mind spun back even further to the landlord's granary in the village where he was born, back to the time when the landlord's son had rejected the Zhu family's basket of millet, calling it moldy. Vessel remembered his elder brother's anger and how his own father had called Cattail a fool.

PART TWO: VESSEL

"Why didn't father listen to Cattail, and let Cattail complain to the landlord's son?" he wondered. "After all, the millet had not been moldy. Why was it always so important to keep quiet and stay out of trouble?"

And now Cattail and his father and all the rest were dead from the plague. What good did staying out of trouble do for any of them? No good at all! It led to Squire Liu calling the Zhu family a disgrace for not having a burial plot. That is all the good it brought. It led to Vessel left alone in a temple, accused of being lazy and greedy and vulgar.

He said the words aloud: "It's wrong; it's wrong and unjust and unfair."

Vessel covered his ears with his hands and squeezed shut his eyes. He turned in furious blind circles around the hall interior until he knocked against a pedestal, which caused him to lose his balance and slip to the ground.

"You evil demon!" he cursed the pedestal, jumping to his feet and kicking at the unmoving carved stone.

He grabbed his discarded broom and used the handle to beat at the place where he had tripped, leaving splintered gashes in the wood. Throwing the broom down for a second time, Vessel whirled around to face the room's main altar, which held an image of the red-faced Lord Guan Yu, the god of war and righteousness, the temple guardian himself. The young monk in his straw shoes and plain gray robe stood with his fists out; the majestic god dressed in elegant armor held aloft his famed crescent-moon blade known as the Green Dragon. The god leered. Vessel's breath curled out through the chilly air like horns, like an angry dragon. Vessel had not dared to defend himself to his tonsure master, but he would not be silent before the gods. He shouted at Lord Guan Yu, "You are the temple guardian. It is your responsibility to watch over us. How could you let mice eat the candles at my expense?"

The god did not answer, but a sudden gust of wind whipped through the hall and doused one of the altar candles. Vessel stared at the trail of smoke that rose from where the flame had been, wondering what it could mean. He heard the sound of monk shoes slapping on the pavement and turned to see Piety rushing up.

"Who were you yelling at?" Piety asked, out of breath.

His anger spent, Vessel stood limp, his hands dropped at his sides. He could not think of how to reply. Piety came inside and pulled at Vessel's sleeve.

"It doesn't matter," Piety said. "I'll walk with you to the dormitory."

Piety knew Vessel had been banished from the evening meal. Before leaving Vessel alone at his bunk, Piety reached into his robe and dropped two steamed buns onto Vessel's lap.

"Don't tell," Piety whispered, grinning.

Tiger Empress was not a large temple and it was understaffed. Vessel could not avoid the guest clerk or the useless fart, his two least-favorite brothers. However, Vessel found most of the other members of his new community to be congenial. Abbot Virtue's wife liked to pat him on the arm and call him her dear son, and she usually had a snack waiting for him when he returned to the kitchen from chopping wood or fetching water. The head verger Piety was always looking out for him. The grain steward was a hilarious storyteller and entertained everyone at night with tales from his days of wandering with a begging bowl. Among all the brothers, though, Vessel's favorite was the librarian.

This monk, who had the religious name of Jewel, was a serious, introspective fellow, several years Vessel's senior. He had solemn, expressive eyes and a fleeting smile. When the monks relaxed and joked at meals or in their sleeping quarters, the librarian rarely spoke, but during the morning prayers and the various temple ceremonies, his deep voice rang clear, easy for Vessel to pick out and follow. Jewel spent most of his time in the back section of the temple complex, furthest up the hill, working alone in the Patriarch's Hall, surrounded by the dusty shelves of sutras.

Vessel did not encounter Jewel during his first few weeks at the temple. Then one blustery fall day Vessel carried a heavy load of fresh-cut jujube wood to the lazy firewood attendant, who no longer bothered to accompany Vessel out into the woods. The firewood attendant picked up a piece and admired it.

"This you should take to the librarian," he said.

Vessel nodded and continued on with his load, balanced in two bundles tied to each end of a shoulder pole. He passed into the leaf-strewn courtyard of the Great Hall, went around the tiger statue pavilion, stepped over the threshold to the next courtyard, and climbed the stone steps to the Patriarch's Hall.

"Eh, it is our new verger," Jewel announced, hurrying politely over to escort him in. "The novice with the necklace!"

Vessel kept his grandfather's talisman hidden beneath his robes, but the leather thong was visible around his neck.

"Elder brother," said Vessel, "the firewood attendant asked me to bring you this load of jujube wood."

Jewel bent down to examine the wood. He selected a wide piece and weighed it in his hand. "This is excellent," he noted approvingly. "And we were almost out."

As Jewel picked through the pile, Vessel glanced over the monk's bent form and noticed the work table at the center of the room. There, on a space littered with carving tools and wood chips, was a half-finished spirit tablet. Next to it, an older, weathered tablet with gilded lettering stood mounted on a small lotus-shaped pedestal.

Jewel sat back on his heels when he noticed Vessel's interest. "Do you know something about wood carving?" he asked in a hopeful tone.

Vessel shook his head. "I...," he stammered, "I did not know you carved the spirit tablets here."

"Where else?" Jewel asked with a shrug. "So many funerals these days, it's hard to keep up."

All the plague deaths meant more work for the monks. Any family that could come up with the money hired monks to hold a service for the souls of the dead. A basic funeral service required at least five monks, but a wealthy family might ask for more. Everyone also wanted spirit tablets carved, so they could properly house the souls of their ancestors. Vessel's Uncle Fifty-one had kept the Zhu family spirit tablets on an altar along the main wall of his house in Vast Virtue Ward. They were small, plain rectangles of pine board carved at the center with the names of Vessel's grandparents, Old Zhu and his wife.

Vessel wondered where those tablets had ended up. Even more, he wished he could get tablets made for his own parents. Vessel stepped across the dim chamber to the table and looked down at Jewel's work. He wanted to trace the beautiful characters with his finger, but was afraid to touch the tablet.

Jewel set aside the jujube. "It is for an old widow in the Lin clan," Jewel explained. "I am trying to copy the style of her husband's tablet, which I did not carve. The family let me bring the match back here so that I could copy the technique. I think they wanted the spirit of Old Benefactor Lin to keep watch over my progress." Jewel chewed his lower lip as he regarded the workmanship of the husband's tablet. "Look at all this intricacy," he said, pointing to the "mystic knot" design around the facing. "It's really taking me a long time. Widow Lin died last month and the Abbot is ready to hold the ceremony for transferring her spirit to the tablet. I need to finish it."

"You carve all of the spirit tablets," Vessel said, more to himself than to Jewel.

Vessel blinked several times and pinched his chin as he admired the pair of tablets. Then he glanced around the room and noticed another, larger carving project in the far corner of the hall. "And are those more tablets?"

Jewel took the novice's arm. "No, no, this is not a spirit tablet," he said, escorting Vessel across the room. "See for yourself."

Vessel leaned over the workbench to peer more closely at the woodblock carving, which depicted the Goddess of Mercy seated on a billowing cloud. She was shaking a willow branch, the little finger on her right hand raised high, spreading a long stream of sweet dew over the bottom of the page, which was still blank. The image was chiseled in startling detail, the eyelids of the goddess lowered yet revealing a sliver of contemplative iris, the hair swept in elaborate coils over long earlobes.

"I'm working on the text, which will call on the Bodhisattva's saving power," Jewel said. "The text will go here, in the lower section, inside the sweet dew. When I have finished with the carving work, I will ink up the blocks and print many copies to distribute to those who are suffering in this drought."

"Elder brother, this will be of great merit," Vessel said in a respectful voice.

Jewel shrugged. "Our treasurer wants to sell the copies, which was not my intent, but I'm told the temple needs the money," he said, frowning. Then he shrugged again. "We've run out of paper, though, and I don't think we will be able to buy more any time soon. At least not in the quantities I want."

From that day on, Vessel spent as much time as he could with the librarian, working to saw and plane the jujube wood into a neat pile of trimmed boards ready to be carved into spirit tablets. Vessel ran errands for the librarian, brought him tea, and even discussed funeral procedures with him.

One day when Vessel had a question about a particular aspect of the funeral ceremony, Jewel went to his book shelves and started to pull out sutras and commentaries he thought Vessel should study. The pile grew, yet Jewel showed no sign of being finished. He appeared to have forgotten about the novice, flipping through the pages of the string-bound volumes, stopping here and there in apparent interest at various passages.

Vessel finally broke into Jewel's musings. "Brother," he exclaimed. "It doesn't matter. I cannot read them."

Jewel looked up in surprise, his mouth open, arrested by this idea that the bright young monk before him was still illiterate.

"Ah," Jewel said.

10

MONKS TAKE LEAVE OF THEIR TEMPLE

It is now late autumn of Correctness Attained, fourth year (1344), at Tiger Empress Temple.

WEEKS PASSED AND the number of worshipers in the temple halls dwindled as the weather turned cold and the daylight shortened. Vessel had to spend more and more of his time alone on the hillsides behind the temple, gathering firewood. One evening, burdened with a heavy load on his back, Vessel rushed as fast as he could toward a shortcut to the cooking hall, thinking the dinner bell would be sounding at any minute. He burst into the kitchen only to find it deserted. Confused, he unloaded his firewood and walked into the dining hall. Tension gripped the room. The monks appeared to be fearfully awaiting the Abbot Virtue and Balance. Vessel slipped into his seat, next to Piety.

"What is it?" he asked.

Piety turned to him with a grave face. "The guest clerk is gone," he said. "The treasurer left the keys with him yesterday, as is always done when the treasurer has to go into town overnight to arrange for supplies and such. The other brothers say this time the guest clerk used the keys to rob us and now he has disappeared."

"How can this be?" Vessel asked, but he fell silent at the

arrival of the abbot.

Looking exhausted and leaning heavily on his staff, Abbot Virtue did not climb into his seat as usual. Instead, he announced that everyone should take their bowls of noodles and bring them to the grain storage room. A line of monks chanting, "Homage to the Amitabha Buddha," snaked out of the dining hall, down the slanting corridor, past the kitchen, and into the granary. This was a small room fitted with shelves, designed for holding baskets of millet, not a crowd of monks. However, the grain was almost gone — all that remained was a single, opened container of millet, three-quarters full. Several of the brothers wept at the sight.

"Emptiness, light the incense," the abbot instructed his acolyte.

Emptiness went to the altar table and lit a handful of incense sticks. These he set in the burner before a small image of Skanda, the mighty protector of the law who oversees temple affairs. Skanda was dressed in armor, with one hand on his hip and the other grasping the fat club for punishing transgressors.

"Raise your bowls before Skanda," Abbot Virtue commanded. The assembly faced the image and held high their bowls of noodles, which steamed in the wintry air of the unheated room. The abbot slowly intoned an invocation:

> Give praise to the Three Jewels!
> Give praise to the Buddha and the bodhisattvas!
> Give praise to the Lord Skanda!

"Homage!" the gathering responded to each summoning call.

Abbot Virtue turned away from Skanda and gestured for the monks facing him to sit down on the dirt floor. He insisted that they eat their noodles even though he himself did not have a bowl. The monks pulled chopsticks from their belts and hurriedly slurped down dinner.

"Disciples, my cherished ones," the abbot began in a gloomy voice, "I am ashamed. As the master said, 'I may know people, I may know faces, but I do not know hearts.'"

He ran his eyes along the twisted wood of his staff, which was topped by a metal finial holding two sets of three rings. It was a cherished gift, presented to him when he left lay life for a second time to lead Tiger Empress. Gripping the smooth, worn wood with both hands, he shook the staff until the rings jingled. Then he tapped it on the ground and looked straight into the faces of his monks.

"What you have heard is true. Our guest clerk used the keys that had been left with him to open our treasury and clear it of all our coins and notes and our precious items. He used a cart to drag away the grain baskets. We think a relative was waiting for him with a packhorse at the side door. The guest clerk has fled and he is gone. We must make do with what we still have."

Mouths gaped as the monks turned to look at one another, twisting this way and that, but no one could think of what to say. Balance stood grimly near the door, observing. He was the one who first pieced together what had happened.

"How could I have left him alone in the document storage room?" Balance muttered, still berating himself for letting the guest clerk become so familiar with the contents of the cabinets in the place where the coin donations and other valuable were kept.

Vessel did not look at the others. He was reliving his encounters with the guest clerk, and silently naming each sin. "That stickler for the smallest of rules, that trumpeter of errors by others... " The guest clerk reminded Vessel of Squire Lin, the haughty landlord. Vessel remembered the last time he had seen the squire — he had been standing in his storeroom with his fancy coffin, shouting at the Zhu brothers for not having made arrangements for their parents' graves. Vessel could imagine the squire buying the stolen grain from the guest clerk.

"And then he would hoard it all for his own family," he stewed, his face flushing with anger at the thought. "And no doubt he would still curse the starving beggars at his gate."

From the muttering at Vessel's side came the sound of a monk rising to his feet. Everyone turned to look at him, a stoic elder known as Old Hawk who was spending the winter at the temple. He was one of the pilgrims, the ones who travel with no destination and are known as the wandering monks.

"Headmaster," Old Hawk said, addressing Abbot Virtue, "The wandering brothers have enjoyed enough of your hospitality. We will leave at once."

The five other pilgrims rooming at the temple also stood and bowed.

The abbot sighed. "It is just as well," he said. "We have nothing left to feed you with."

At this the temple's treasury officer collapsed into a heap, uttering loud, groaning sobs. He crawled to the abbot's feet and knocked his head on the ground several times, weeping and wailing. At long last, the pitiful monk blurted out, "It is my fault!" His voice was broken and barely coherent.

"Brothers, it is I who left the keys with the guest clerk, it is I who am to be blamed," he sobbed.

Most of the other monks looked away in embarrassment. Abbot Virtue nodded patiently as the treasurer continued to apologize.

"I will be the first to leave ... and I will wander ... I will beg for forgiveness and seek out hardship until ... "

The abbot raised his palm to silence the treasurer. "You

may leave to wander in penance, but only until you sense Lord Buddha's compassionate desire for your return to the fold," he ruled.

The treasurer mutely nodded his head. Rubbing at his swollen eyes and wiping his nose, he crawled back to resume his place among the other monks.

Vessel did not look away or feel uncomfortable at the outburst of remorse. Instead his anger rose as he dwelled on the injustice that had been done to his temple. Vessel's eyes were trained on the treasurer, but what he saw was his brother Radish with Squire Lin. The look of shock and guilt on the treasurer's face reminded Vessel of the way Radish had looked back at the squire when they were being berated for not having coffins ready for their parents. This, in turn, reminded Vessel of the way he had felt, back when he was a herd boy, when Old Wolf ripped away his chess set and threw it into the fire, and then almost beat him to death.

"My brother is the one who carried me away from Old Wolf and brought me home to my mother," he thought to himself. "No one ever treated my brother with kindness even though my brother never harmed anyone. Why is it that people like Old Wolf and Squire Lin and now the guest clerk can do whatever evil they want and no one ever does anything about it?"

Vessel's rage returned, that same surge of emotion that had enveloped him in the Hall of the Temple Guardian, when he had faced off with the red-faced Lord Guan Yu over rats eating the candles. Vessel jumped to his feet. Everyone turned to him in surprise, as he was still, in their view, a mere novice, not expected to speak.

Vessel raised high his left fist and slapped his right hand over it in a salute to Abbot Virtue. The muscles of the young monk, who had just passed his sixteenth birthday, flexed beneath his robe and his iron chin jutted out. The monks around him were confused by this militant demeanor.

"Venerable Father," Vessel said in the deep voice of a young man passing out of adolescence, "I will also leave this temple. I will not let the guest clerk destroy Tiger Empress. I will seek him out…"

Balance raised his palms in objection. "Vessel, you will not seek him out," he stated, slowly and clearly.

Abbot Virtue agreed. "The rector is right, we will not seek vengeance. That is not our way. We will report the theft to the magistrate; we have already reported it before Lord Skanda. Beyond that we will do no more."

Vessel remained on his feet and did not drop his salute.

"I will leave this temple," he said again. He had let go of his memories, but still burned with anger, though his voice sounded calm and firm. "I will not be a burden."

The other monks around him, floundering and panicky, seized on this determination like cranes snatching up fish. Eyes brightened with the sense that this was the correct path. One by one, the rest of the monks rose, saluted the abbot, and repeated the phrase, "I will not be a burden."

Abbot Virtue and Balance were astonished and looked at each other in confusion. The treasurer, unable to ignore the ledgers even in the grips of guilt, wiped away his tears and cautioned everyone against acting rashly.

"Brothers, wandering for a brief time, why, it might not be a bad idea to relieve the temple burden, but you cannot all go at once," he said, wringing his hands in consternation. "We need a core of monks here to tend to the temple." He put a finger to his nose in concentration, and listed the people who should not depart. "We have to keep at least five here or we will not be able to offer funeral rites — the abbot, the rector, the acolyte, the tea steward, and the striker of the drum. The gatekeeper should stay too. The women can continue to cook the meals. We need to keep the librarian for carving the spirit tablets." He mulled over the matter for a few seconds more. "I guess the rest could try wandering, though not for too long, or the burden of running the temple will be too much for the ones left behind," he concluded.

"So be it," said Vessel. He bowed to Abbot Virtue and then to Balance, picked up his empty bowl and strode out of the room.

The rest of the monks filed behind him, leaving only the two temple elders.

The abbot turned to Balance. "Tell me again — where did this novice come from?" he asked.

Back in the sleeping quarters, the monks busied themselves with preparing for departure at sunrise. They grew cheerful at the impending change and joked about where they would head first with their alms bowls. The preparations went on well into the night. No one could sleep, even though they needed the rest. In the face of such camaraderie, Vessel's rage eased enough for him to turn his attention to mending clothing and assembling travel packs. In the midst of this, the librarian pulled Vessel aside. "Come with me."

Vessel followed Jewel in the darkness through a snow-dusted courtyard that opened onto the Patriarch's Hall. The two monks pulled open the heavy wooden doors and stepped into an even blacker darkness. As Jewel kneeled to light the small brazier, Vessel stamped his feet and breathed on his fingers to keep his sluggish blood circulating in the cold air. Jewel lit the lamp at his work bench, reached for a piece of prepared jujube wood, placed it before him and turned to Vessel.

"I will make you a spirit tablet for your deceased parents," he said.

Ever since the time of the successive plague deaths, Vessel had been tormented by the thought of the improper mudslide burial he oversaw for his parents and elder brother and nephew. This could mean — indeed, it seemed likely — that their souls were unable to rest peacefully. Vessel worried incessantly that they suffered under the Yellow Springs, the home of the dead. To make matters worse, he did not know if any other member of his Zhu clan remained alive. If he was the sole survivor, then he would be the only one left who could offer sacrifices. A spirit tablet would restore order to the Zhu family and preserve the bond between the living and the dead.

"But I leave in the morning," Vessel exclaimed.

"I will have it done by then," Jewel replied.

"But how did you know?"

Jewel snorted. "We all knew when you arrived that your parents were killed by the plague. Plagues, droughts, that's how most novices have landed at our gates these past few years."

He reached for a stick of pine soot and ground it back and forth in water to create ink of the proper consistency. The brazier coals and the desk lamp and the body heat from the two monks hunched over the workbench warmed the small chamber.

"What poor family cut down by the plague has time for death rites?" Jewel continued. "I knew that was why you were so curious about the funeral services. I just hadn't had time yet to take care of this matter."

Jewel pulled a small brush from a ceramic holder, dipped it lightly in the ink and held it poised over the upper right-hand corner of the blank tablet. His calligraphy flowed down in a vertical line.

"What does it say?" Vessel whispered.

"It says that I am the one writing this tablet, in this the fourth year of the imperial reign period titled 'Correctness Attained.'"

PART TWO: VESSEL

Now Jewel reached for a thicker brush, and turned to look at Vessel. "I need to write their names," Jewel said.

Vessel nodded. "Zhu Fifty-four, that is my father," he said. "Chen Second Daughter, that is my mother."

Jewel estimated the spacing in the center of the tablet. He used the dry brush to practice the inscription, narrating it for Vessel: "Spirit tablet for the Buddha-blessed Zhu Fifty-four and the Buddha-blessed Chen Second Daughter."

The names would be placed side by side, down the center of the tablet. Jewel wet the tip of the thick brush and tested the ink until he was satisfied. He wrote the first half of the inscription with the confident, relaxed hand of a practiced calligrapher. His *heng* strokes were bold, his *shu* strokes balanced.

Vessel watched, mesmerized. He saw, in place of the fluid line of black calligraphy, his Grandfather Chen's charm writing. He saw his mother's back bowed in prayer before the family altar. He heard her murmured words mingling with the curling incense plume. But she did not pray to the Buddha.

"Mother prayed to her goddess," he thought to himself.

As Jewel lifted his brush and positioned it at the start of the place where he would begin the line for Chen Second Daughter, Vessel felt a pang of alarm. He cleared his throat.

"Elder brother, perhaps for my mother it should say 'Metal Mother-blessed Chen Second Daughter.'"

"Eh?" Jewel sat up in his chair.

"The Queen Mother of the West." Vessel used the more widely known name of the revered Daoist immortal. "Could you invoke her for my mother instead of Lord Buddha?"

"Oh, yes, yes," Jewel said, practicing the revised text a few times in the air before re-inking his brush and finishing the inscription. Then he switched back to the thin brush, writing one final line down the left side of the tablet, which he narrated,

"Respectfully prepared by their pious son, Zhu..."

"Chong-ba," Vessel whispered. "The 'chong' that means 'double.' The 'ba' that means 'eight.'"

"... Zhu Chong-ba."

Jewel rinsed out his brushes and said they needed to wait for the ink to dry before he could carve the characters into the wood. He went to heat some water over the brazier to make a pot of tea. Outside the hall, in the cold predawn hours, an owl hooted. Vessel could not take his eyes from the spirit tablet. The tidy characters seemed so different from his Grandfather Chen's charm writing. Vessel pulled out the talisman around his neck and turned it toward the flickering workbench light, studying the strange carving on the chop holder's face and comparing it to the spirit tablet calligraphy.

"Ah, the novice's necklace," Jewel said softly, holding two bowls of fragrant tea in his hands. He handed one to Vessel and reached for the talisman to study it.

"It was carved by my grandfather, to hold his chop," Vessel explained, sliding off the cover to real the contents of the oval box. "He was a diviner — everyone came to him for help. He used this chop to finish his paper charms. My mother, his youngest daughter, received the necklace after he died and she gave it to me right before she died. I never asked what the carving on the box cover is all about. It looks like the magic writing he used to do on the charms."

Jewel nodded. "It is well carved," he said as he handed the box to Vessel, who slipped it back under his robes. "I think the ink is dry enough," Jewel said, returning to his seat. "There is a bedroll in the corner. You should rest while I work on this."

As Jewel carved, the sun rose, the temple bell sounded, the monks gathered for a final meal together, and then all but a remnant walked out the main gate, begging bowls in hand.

PART TWO: VESSEL

Vessel slept through all of this, awakening only when Balance shook his shoulder to rouse him.

Vessel sprang to his feet, alarmed at having slept until full daylight. "Master, have the others left already?"

"Yes, my son," Balance replied. "We decided to let you rest. Look, your spirit tablet is complete."

Vessel's head was still groggy and his back damp from deep slumber when he turned toward the workbench and first saw the carved tablet for his parents. It was mounted on a small stand and bathed in the red-tinged light of a morning sunbeam streaming through the window lattice. The characters stood out clearly, though Vessel could not read them. That did not matter, because he knew by heart what the words said. Vessel dropped to his knees and stretched a hand toward the tablet.

"For so long I have wanted this," he said in a voice that broke into sobs.

Jewel, who had stepped out to run an errand for Balance, opened the door onto the scene of the novice weeping.

"Aiya, aiya, what's this?" he exclaimed. "Your parents finally get their tablet, only to find you sniveling in front of them, your eyes still crusty from sleep?"

But Jewel was smiling. Jewel had fetched a small percussion instrument and a hand chime. With these, the three monks assembled around the workbench and chanted prayers and sutras for another hour, helping Vessel call his parents to their tablet. Then it was time to go.

Vessel carefully wrapped the tablet in a cloth together with a packet of incense. He went to the vacated monks' quarters to gather his satchel. In the kitchen, the abbot's wife served him boiled vegetables in millet gruel along with noodles and steamed buns. As she packed some provisions, Emptiness appeared, holding a prized gift of felt boots, which Vessel gratefully pulled on. The remaining monks gathered to escort the novice out the front gate.

"When you return, I will teach you how to copy out the sutras," Jewel promised, his voice hopeful and encouraging.

Abbot Virtue gripped his staff and looked up into the face of the tall young man.

"There is no parting and there is no meeting," he said. "There is no need to rejoice or to grieve. There is only the truth of the Buddha's compassion."

Balance took Vessel's arm and escorted him down the path, offering his own blessing as they walked. "You leave with your willful nature intact, despite my efforts. Do not let your anger and emotions consume you, Vessel," Balance advised. "Instead, seek to harness that spirit as you would seek to tame a strong young colt into a trustworthy mount. I wish you perseverance and the ability to see the pure white lotus that rises above the muck."

Vessel smiled. "Master, I would rather have a real horse to harness than try to imagine one." He grinned, and remembered a story from his childhood. "As soon as the sage monk Zhou Dong found the young general Yue Fei a white horse, the old monk died. So, Master, I don't want a horse from you, imaginary or not, because I wish you a long life!"

Balance stopped short, turning to face Vessel. "Do you see yourself as a young general, then?" he asked.

Vessel shook his head. "I was raised on the tales of Yue Fei, that's all," he said. "But it is true that you have been like a wise Master Zhou to me."

Balance reached out with both hands to grasp his tonsure disciple's shoulders, feeling reassured at the young man's strength. The pair regarded each other in fond silence for a moment before Balance let go with a heavy sigh and Vessel turned to the others, clasped his hands one last time in farewell and set off.

The remaining monks filed back into the temple. All but Balance, who could not pull his eyes from the retreating form of his disciple. Balance reached into his sleeves and clicked his prayer beads through his fingers. He thought of the years Master Zhou was said to have spent cultivating the talents of the young Yue Fei, who went on to defend China from the northern invaders. Balance sighed aloud over the training he had not been able to provide to Vessel, a young man with startling potential. Balance stood alone in the cold, a wool cap on his bald head, his beads clicking under the folds of his gray robe, issuing silent prayers until long after his disciple had disappeared into the forest.

11

VESSEL LOSES HIS WAY ON THE ROAD TO DING

Winter of Correctness Attained, fourth year (1344). Anfeng Circuit in modern Anhui Province.

VESSEL LEFT HIS home temple and headed south, aiming for Ding County, and from there to the walled city of Luzhou. This was the route mapped out by his temple brothers the night before. They had heard that the regions to the south and west had not suffered such an extreme drought. In his bag, Vessel carried the following: the new spirit tablet and incense, a clay begging bowl, a letter of introduction from his tonsure master, a pair of straw sandals, some packages of dry food, chopsticks, flint for lighting a fire, and a small hand drum with a mallet. The drum was carved in the shape of a fish as a reminder to stay alert because fish never sleep. Fish swim fearless and free as they roam through the water. Rolled up and tied to Vessel's back were a reed mat and a blanket. Vessel hoped he might catch up with some of his brothers. He walked at a quick pace at first, enjoying the late morning sunshine, Emptiness's warm felt boots on his feet. Too proud to beg in his own village, he skirted the main lane after crossing the rope bridge. But he did stop to see Old Mother Wang. She set him down at her table to warm his hands and eat some melon seeds as she rummaged through her storage area. She emerged with an old padded vest, covered with patches but topped by a high wool collar.

"The winter solstice is approaching," she said, insisting that Vessel put the vest on over his robe.

Old Mother Wang leaned on Vessel's arm and walked with him to his parents' burial site, where she bade him goodbye.

The ferryman recognized Vessel. "Ah, so it's true you've shaved your head," he said, his glance skeptical. But this was not a ferryman who liked to talk. He poled across the West Branch, which had started to ice over at the edges.

"Your temple brothers are far ahead of you," the old man remarked as they reached the shore.

Vessel took a shortcut through the Three Peaks that he thought would set him on the path for the Golden Dipper River, where he would find his brothers at the Chan temple of the same name. By late afternoon he had reached the far side of Cloud Mother Mountain and no longer recognized his surroundings. The winter sun was setting and his felt boots had rubbed blisters into both ankles. His forehead and ears ached from the cold. He sank his chin deep into the woolly collar of his new vest. Now Vessel anxiously scanned the forest for signs of a side path that might lead to a hermit dwelling or an abandoned shrine where he could safely spend the night. He heard a rustle in the distance and whipped around in time to see the orange and black coat of a tiger streak through the tree line. This was followed by the scream of a rabbit. Terrified, his heart racing and his blisters forgotten, Vessel fumbled with stiff fingers to pull out his fish drum and rap loudly on it, hoping to frighten the forest beasts from his path. He continued in this way until he spied a large, stout stick. He tucked the drum away and was reaching for the stick when he noticed an old man standing silent in the gloom, watching him. The man had one good eye and only a few teeth. He said nothing, but he did not seem threatening.

"Greetings, I am a monk from Tiger Empress Temple who seeks lodging for the night," Vessel began, but the old man immediately turned into the forest, gesturing for Vessel to follow. Caught between a tiger's hunting ground and a mute hermit, Vessel chose the latter. He gripped his stick and followed the old man into the fast encroaching darkness.

Vessel did not sleep well. In retrospect, the old man treated him like an honored guest, ladling a bowl of wild herb soup from his hearth and letting Vessel spread his mat close to the fire. But Vessel was too wary to appreciate any of this. The hermit rose shortly before daybreak to light his hearth fire. Vessel was relieved to have the night finished, but found that sitting up made his head ache and brought on a coughing fit. His mother's stories of malevolent fox spirits ran through his head. Was the hermit a fox spirit? Had he been cursed with an illness? Vessel folded his mat and prepared to leave. His satchel and bedroll assembled, Vessel edged anxiously toward the door. Then the hermit turned to Vessel. He held out a steaming bowl of a tea-like brew.

The dawn light filtered into the room from a small papered window pane, the hearth fire adding a warm glow. Vessel swept his eyes across the interior and realized he was in some kind of a medicinal lodge. The rafters were hung with dried animal parts and plant fibers, and one of the walls was covered with shelves of pungent preserved items. Next to the fire was a large mortar and stacks of baskets containing insect shells and fungi. In the dim morning light, with finches chirping outside, the hermit did not seem so ominous. Vessel looked through the steam rising from the bowl into the old man's eyes and reached out to accept the tea with both hands, grateful. Vessel decided the man was not a fox spirit.

"Elder Master, could you tell me what path I should take to reach the Golden Dipper River?" Vessel asked.

The old man did not reply. In fact, he did not seem able to hear. He regarded Vessel closely with his one clear eye and suddenly reached out and took hold of Vessel's wrist. Vessel gasped, but realized the hermit was feeling for his pulse. They stood in silence, Vessel tense and breathing hard, the hermit concentrating on the fluctuations in the throbbing vein, until he turned to his shelves and poured out piles of herbs onto a table. The hermit opened a jar of salve and squatted, gesturing for Vessel to sit down and take off his boots. Vessel grimaced as he complied, unwrapping his leggings to expose raw blisters on each ankle. The old man gently dabbed black paste onto the blisters and bandaged them. Then he stood and prepared a thick pouch of medicine, which he handed to Vessel, pointing for him to put the pouch into his bag. The hermit led Vessel by the elbow out of the hut and through the woods to a barely discernible footpath. The old man poked Vessel in the chest and then jabbed his finger in the direction of the path, nodding his head and grunting.

"Elder Master, I understand," Vessel said. He clasped his hands and bowed his head in gratitude and, not knowing what else to do, took the path as directed.

The tea proved strangely invigorating. Vessel walked through the wilderness. Heading southwest, he expected he would soon reach Golden Dipper River. Perhaps he would be in luck and find that his brothers had decided to stay another night at the temple there. If not, the resident monks would know where they had gone. But Vessel was nowhere near the river. He was instead approaching the desolate foothills of Mount Floating Raft. The bright morning sunshine faded into a bleak wintry haze. The air was wet and when the wind gusted, snowflakes whipped against

Vessel's cheeks and coated the grass. The birds stopped singing to huddle for warmth in the pines. Vessel did not like to be alone. He trudged along staring at the frozen ground, his toes numb, his nose running, his thoughts turning from fears over survival to a general sense of failure. He had felt helpless ever since the death of his father seven unfathomable months ago. He had not been able to prevent any of the deaths or losses that followed.

"I have lost my brother Radish," he thought to himself. "I could not protect my temple from being robbed. I could not stay at my temple. Now I will not survive the night."

Vessel wandered on. He began to feel uncomfortably warm even with toes so cold they were difficult to walk on. He pulled his monk's cap from his head and wiped the sweat from his forehead. He was seized by coughing fits. The footpath he had been following disappeared. Ah, but now he recognized the hillside.

"This is the glade where I cut wood for the fire attendant. If I head up the slope, I will no doubt find that lazy fart," Vessel chuckled.

He climbed over bushes and hoisted himself up the steep incline, shaking snow off his robes. He needed to hurry, or he would be late for dinner. He saw a small house in the distance and laughed again.

"It's the strange hermit's lodge. I've walked in a circle."

Vessel reached into his bag and took out the medicine pouch. He saw the old hermit running toward him.

"I didn't know you could run so fast!" he called out. He waved the pouch in his hand. "Here's the medicine. I forgot to ask you what it was!"

Then Vessel collapsed, his fever taking over. The boy who had been running toward him called over his shoulders for the others to help.

PART TWO: VESSEL

"There's a monk here," the boy yelled. "There's something wrong with him."

Vessel had fainted at the mountain refuge of Old Mu. Down in the county seat of Ding — which Vessel had been seeking — Old Mu had been a reasonably successful carpenter. Old Mu had also been a married man with a daughter almost ready to marry out and a son at his side learning his trade. Then the plague struck. Like a delicate rice shoot swept away in floodwaters, Old Mu's happiness was swiftly uprooted. The plague claimed his wife and his son, but before it could take his daughter too, Old Mu gathered her up and fled for the hills, where he knew of an old abandoned cottage they could use. Among the refugees on the road the Mu pair had encountered a starving boy of seven — a lost servant abandoned by his wealthy household during their flight from the pestilence.

"They said I have the sickness, but I do not," the weeping boy had exclaimed, indignant.

Old Mu's daughter, Cinnabar, had taken the boy's hand. He'd stopped crying then and looked hopefully into Cinnabar's face. She told the poor child that he could join her family. Old Mu had sighed and adjusted his shoulder pole but did not argue with his daughter. So the boy, who went by the name of Cricket, joined the Mu father and daughter. He had been with them for almost six months now. It was Cricket who spotted the delirious Vessel crashing through the underbrush.

Old Mu came running out of the cottage to help Cricket, but when he saw a man collapsed in fever, Old Mu recoiled. He reached out one arm to pull Cricket away and yelled over his shoulder for his daughter to stay back too.

"First, I will check to see what this sickness is," he said sternly.

Old Mu stepped forward and used his foot to ease Vessel onto his back. Crouching over the prostrate monk, Old Mu used a stick to poke into Vessel's mouth to see if his tongue was black. Then Old Mu loosened Vessel's vest and robe to get at his neck and armpits. Old Mu even pulled open the belt holding up Vessel's padded trousers and studied his groin, looking for the telltale dark swelling of the glands. Vessel raised his head and coughed, but did not resist the inspection.

"No sign of the plague," Old Mu declared, looking deeply relieved. He sat back on his haunches and noticed the pouch of medicine on the ground. Picking it up, he sniffed at the contents. "It's some kind of oyster shell compound," he decided.

"This monk has some other illness," Cinnabar said. "Let's take him inside."

She and her father each took one of Vessel's arms and dragged him into their cottage, while Cricket gathered up the monk's medicine and bag. Cricket unfolded Vessel's own mat and set it close to the fire. Old Mu lowered Vessel onto this pallet and Cinnabar covered him in a warm quilt. There, for the next two days, Vessel lay coughing and sleeping.

His fever broke the third night. The next morning he woke peacefully to the sight of Cinnabar approaching him with a bowl of herb soup.

"Meadow!" he cried out, thinking he was back in his uncle's compound with the widowed wife of Chong Five.

Cinnabar stopped short and almost spilled her soup.

But she was too young to be Meadow. He remembered the other reason the girl could not be his elder cousin's wife. His mother had said Meadow and all of Uncle's family died in the plague. Vessel looked away, not wanting this girl he did not know to see tears in his eyes.

"What is your name, monk?" Cinnabar asked, kneeling down to set the soup next to Vessel's pallet.

Dizzy from the days of feverish sleep and still under the

spell of the vivid memory of Meadow, Vessel could not answer. He stammered and tried to remember his departure from the monastery. Why had he left? His head would not clear.

Cinnabar smiled and stood up. "It doesn't matter," she said. "Rest some more and then you can tell us."

Vessel spent the next hours dozing, remembering and wondering. He recalled the plight of the temple, the monks' departure, and the spirit tablet that Jewel had carved for him with such diligence. Then Vessel noticed his bag and reached inside where he felt the reassuring weight of the wrapped tablet. He resolved to offer prayers and incense to his parents' tablet every morning from that day forward for the full three-year mourning period required for parents.

Vessel studied the inside of the cottage he had landed in. The simple surroundings reminded him of his former family home in Lone Hamlet. Strings of peppers and onions dangled from the roof beams, over a wooden table with stools and a small family altar. Low cots were stacked against the wall. He watched Cinnabar come and go, busy with tasks. When the winter sun was at its peak, Vessel heard a man in the distance call out to Cinnabar and the girl answer by addressing the unseen man as "father." At this, Vessel sat up and prepared to meet his host.

Old Mu was a thin, wiry man with creased eyes and graying temples. His topknot was held in place by a dark blue cloth. He wore a padded jacket of the same color over faded cotton trousers and leggings. His hands tucked into his sleeves, he appeared at the cottage entrance to check on his monk guest, with Cricket peeking from behind and Cinnabar pulling up a stool for her father.

"Eh, monk, my daughter said that you have revived," Old Mu said in a low, pleasant voice. "It was useful to arrive with your own medicine in hand."

Old Mu described how Vessel had clambered up the slope to the cottage and then thrashed for days in a fever. Vessel could remember nothing after leaving the strange hermit. Vessel told his hosts his religious name and temple affiliation. He explained that his parents and elder brother and nephew had all been lost to the plague.

"Heaven's wrath has torn at us all," Old Mu consoled him.

"Father, we can eat now," Cinnabar said, setting bowls on the table and wiping her wet hands on her skirt. "Monk, can you join us?"

They dined on stewed rabbit seasoned with wild garlic and leeks. Vessel could not resist the broth, though he did abstain from the meat. When the meal was finished, Cricket pulled out a flute and played mountain songs. Old Mu brought out a gourd of liquor, which he insisted was not wine, but rather a medicinal brew. In truth it was fermented sorghum and Vessel was soon bellowing lyrics along with his new dear friend Old Mu, their conversation increasingly unintelligible until the young musician dozed off and the men sprawled on their blankets, snoring deeply.

Cinnabar was an obedient girl. She had wide, plump cheeks and thick brows, her skin creamy and unblemished, her lips often slightly parted in a gentle, melting way. She kept her hair pinned back in two low buns, but wisps escaped at her temples over the course of a day and would not stay behind her ears. Her smile made her cheeks bunch up and almost crowd out her eyes. The sorrow of losing her mother and elder brother marked Cinnabar with a mature compassion unusual in a girl of fifteen.

Having first envisioned her as his dear cousin Meadow, Vessel was favorably inclined to Cinnabar from the beginning. He had ended his convalescence by letting his eyes idly track her movements while his mind dwelled on his past. He was not actually paying attention to Cinnabar at that point, but then their eyes met. Vessel looked away, but not before realizing that he had made the girl blush.

After the night of singing with Old Mu, Vessel woke up feeling much stronger. He rose with everyone else and slipped outside.

"The privy is over there," Old Mu said.

Vessel nodded politely, but the privy was not yet his destination. He found a low rock at the edge of the cottage clearing and set his parents' soul tablet there. Vessel lit a stick of incense and kneeled on the cold ground in prayer. Only when he finished did Vessel realize that Old Mu had been observing in reverent silence.

Vessel wanted to repay his host with service before leaving to continue his wandering. He wrapped up his spirit tablet and asked Old Mu if he could fetch some water or gather timber for the fire.

"If you are up to it, why not come hunt with Cricket and me," Old Mu suggested.

But Vessel bowed his head and looked embarrassed, saying, "I cannot take life."

Old Mu nodded his head, once again looking reverent. Then he pressed Vessel to stay for at least another night, to fully regain his strength. "My daughter will tell you what needs to be done here," Old Mu said. He picked up his hunting bow and headed into the forest, Cricket scampering along at his side, leaving Vessel and Cinnabar alone in the cottage.

Vessel kept his eyes on the ground, his embarrassment escalating. "I will fetch the water," he stated.

"Thank you," Cinnabar replied, wringing her hands nervously and also looking down.

"And, where is the bucket?"

"Oh, it is over there."

Now Vessel had to look up, to see where Cinnabar was pointing. He shuffled in the correct direction. "And where do you fetch the water?" he asked.

Cinnabar covered her mouth and laughed. "Around to the right from the door is the path. You will find a stream below the stand of pines, and there's a stick there to break away the ice if you need to."

"All right," Vessel nodded and was off.

Naturally he filled the bucket to the brim to show off his strength. Carrying it back up the hillside strained his still-sensitive lungs, making him wheeze and cough. The water splashed and sloshed until it reached the level he should have filled it to in the first place. When he caught sight of the cottage again, Vessel eased the bucket down to catch his breath. He could glimpse Cinnabar sweeping the little yard, swaying with the broom and humming a pretty tune. His eyes widened and his heart raced. He wiped at his forehead, wondering if his fever was returning.

Cinnabar ran to help the monk as soon as she caught sight of him. It would have been rude to ignore him.

"Every morning at the temple I carried in much more than this little bit," he boasted, shooing her away.

Vessel looked Cinnabar full in the eye, his timidity dissipating in his eagerness to be useful. "What can I do now?" he asked.

Cinnabar glanced around, considering. She sent him to gather lumber from the woodpile. She had him pull down a branch that had been threatening to fall near the doorway, and then she asked him to chop the branch up. She insisted that he sit and rest and drink some tea. They had a fine morning together.

As Vessel was busy sharpening Cinnabar's chopping knife, Old Mu and Cricket came rushing up to the cottage in great excitement. Cricket held by the feet a fox with a thick, beautiful pelt, caught in a trap set by Old Mu. What is more, Old Mu had shot a roebuck with a full set of antlers. "Monk, you have brought us good luck," Old Mu exclaimed. In their previous hunting forays he and Cricket had not managed to catch anything but a scrawny rabbit or two.

Old Mu asked Vessel to come with him at once to retrieve the buck. The monk hurried off behind the two hunters, vultures beginning to circle overhead. Dragging the animal up to the cottage and butchering both it and the fox took up the rest of the afternoon.

"Monk, you can be a great help to me," Old Mu told Vessel that evening. "I can take this fox pelt and the antlers and buckskin to Ding to sell at the market," Old Mu said. "I will be able to trade this for more grain and other supplies. I have been worried about our provisions since I think spring will come late this year. With you here to protect my daughter and Cricket, I can go to Ding with no fears. Could you stay, then, for a few days more? Just until I return?"

How could Vessel say no?

It was the first night after Old Mu's departure. Vessel and Cricket had spent the day merrily playing shuttlecock with an old rag and holding stick-throwing contests, occasionally stopping to help Cinnabar with cooking, drying and storing the new supply of venison. Now Cricket was fast asleep, his sweet boy's face lit by the hearth fire.

Cinnabar and Vessel sat together. The wind outside shook the bare tree branches, but inside the cottage was warm. The dancing firelight glowed in the cheeks of the two earnest youths. As the evening wore on, their conversation turned to the sorrow of their mutual losses and also to memories of their former lives before the plague demons struck. They were surprised at the similarity of their plague stories and several times one would interrupt the other to say, "It was the same for me. Just the same." They shed tears for each other over the deaths of their mothers. The two reveled in the chance to reminisce about their families. Vessel even pulled out his talisman and showed it to Cinnabar, telling her the story of Grandfather Chen in the Battle of Yashan. Cinnabar pointed to the altar table.

"That is my mother's Goddess of Mercy statue," she said proudly. "It has been passed down in our family for generations." Cinnabar sighed and leaned back on her cot, locking her arms around her knees in a wistful manner. "I cannot talk to my father about my mother. Her death caused him too much sorrow, and yet with you it makes me happy to be able to remember her again."

She asked him about life in the temple. He described his monk brothers — the old abbot and the lazy firewood attendant and the talented librarian. Vessel told a long story about the annoying guest clerk that left Cinnabar laughing aloud into both hands. Vessel tugged at her sleeve, telling her to keep quiet so as not to awaken Cricket.

"Here, sit closer to me," Cinnabar said, patting the space next to her on her cot.

Vessel did as Cinnabar requested, moving up to the cot from his seat on his bedroll. He took care to leave a wide space between them. Cinnabar blushed and sat up straight, but Vessel put her at ease, telling her more humorous stories he had learned from the monks.

Soon it was Vessel's turn to let out a pensive sigh. "That old guest clerk, how I hate him," Vessel said bitterly. "He was always so strict about the rules, and then he turned out to be the one who broke them all. It was terrible to see Abbot Virtue so saddened and upset over what the guest clerk had done." Vessel pressed his lips together and furrowed his brow.

"Is it hard to be a monk?" Cinnabar asked in a soft voice.

Vessel raised his eyes to meet hers, which reflected the burning embers in the hearth.

"Do you know, my mother never wanted me to enter the temple," he said solemnly. "There are nights when I cannot sleep because I am worried that I have angered her and the other ancestors. She was not fond of the Buddhists, even though my father thought Lord Buddha saved me from the Heavenly Flowers. My mother told me once that it was not my fate to become a monk, and yet I have disobeyed her."

"But you had no other choice," Cinnabar cried out, leaning closer toward him.

Vessel's eyes watered and his bottom lip quivered. Cinnabar slid closer and reached to brush a tear from his cheek. Vessel took that comforting hand into his own. He felt it in his palm, so small and lovely. Vessel caressed the beautiful hand and then lifted it to his mouth. He closed his eyes and breathed in the scent of Cinnabar's skin. Vessel heard Cinnabar catch her breath, but she did not withdraw her arm. Vessel opened his eyes just enough to peek along her sleeve to the curve of her neck. He studied the way her hair was gathered into tidy matching buns, catching a glimpse of her lips, parted in that irresistible manner he had already learned to appreciate. He leaned toward them, reaching, embracing.

It is true that Cinnabar at first resisted Vessel's ardor, but not for long. In fact, if the child next to them had awakened, little Cricket would have been entirely surprised at the excitement taking place in the firelight on the cot at his side.

Monks are trained to rid themselves of desire and are required to live a celibate life. Vessel pushed such thoughts away. He woke up the next morning in a delirious state of joy. He felt no pangs of sinful guilt, only a yearning to spend every moment at Cinnabar's side. He did not even take time to tend to his parents' soul tablet. And if Cinnabar felt confused or worried about what her father might think of her behavior, she was soon enveloped in the rapture of the attentive Vessel. His euphoria was infectious.

Cricket happily accommodated the joyful, playful state of his two older friends. He led them down to the stream and did not notice when Vessel caught Cinnabar's hand and kept hold of it. Cinnabar called out:

"The river is too deep to wade!"

Cricket sang out with Vessel the song's flirtatious response:

"Where it is deep, you'll find stepping stones,
Where it is shallow, you can raise your robes!"

The boy thought nothing of it. Nor did he notice when he was urged to go to sleep rather earlier than usual that night.

This second night alone together, the two young lovers spent far less time talking. Their occasional whispered conversations did not dwell on past sorrows. Entwined on that one narrow, low cot, they reveled in each other and were quite unable to sleep.

The next day, Old Mu returned.

He was a kind man, but not a foolish one. His cheerful greeting dissolved into a stony silence with one glance from his daughter's embarrassed flush to Vessel's smitten grin. He stepped into the cottage to set his pack of food supplies on the table with a thud and then he stalked back out the door, heading for the woods.

Cinnabar dissolved into tears. When Vessel knelt beside her and she was able to catch her breath, she stared up at him and asked, again and again, "What are we going to do?"

Cricket tugged at his sleeve. "What happened?" he asked. "Why is Grandpa so angry at us? Where did he go? Why did he leave after just getting back?"

But Vessel could only frown and pinch at his chin. The euphoria and desire that had consumed him over the past two days evaporated, leaving only a dull pang in his stomach. He reached out a hand to caress Cinnabar's shoulder, though she would no longer look at him.

"I will speak with your father," Vessel promised.

Old Mu was gone for a long time, but when he returned he seemed composed and determined. He called to Vessel and asked, in a grim voice, if the monk would accompany him on a walk to an old tree that had fallen and could be cut into firewood. Vessel took the axe down from the wall and followed.

Old Mu took turns with Vessel at chopping the tree trunk into logs. Finally, with two neat stacks of wood bundled and ready to load onto each other's backs for the walk back home, Old Mu pulled out a flask of water and waved at Vessel to sit next to him and rest. Their chests heaved from the exertion. Their breath created little swirling puffs of whiteness in the cold air. The evening sun slanted through the trees and felt hot on their faces.

"I don't know much about temple life, but I know you have broken some of your vows," Old Mu said, looking out at the forest as he addressed Vessel. "You do not seem like much of a monk to me."

Vessel flinched, but he wisely kept his composure and did not interrupt.

Old Mu wiped his nose and spat on the ground. "I have been thinking about this situation," he continued. "I have been thinking about my own family and my plans for my daughter."

Now Old Mu turned his head, pressed his palms on his thighs and leaned into them, the better to study Vessel. "You have no family left to make arrangements for you. I have lost my son. My daughter appears to favor you."

Old Mu paused after this series of statements, to let his words sink in.

"You are a strong, hardworking young man with no prospects and no talent as a monk. Why not marry into my family, become my son-in-law and take the Mu name as your own?" Old Mu spoke in a slow, careful voice. "We work well together — just look at this woodpile, gathered in these two piles so quickly. I can teach you my trade of carpentry. We can move back into my home in Ding and create a good life together. You can help me keep my daughter at my side. I can offer you a family to replace your lost one."

Old Mu stood and heaved his bundle onto his back.

"Think this over carefully, young man," he said, hunching his shoulders against the weight of the wood.

He turned and headed back up the hillside to the cottage.

Vessel remained frozen in his seat. He tucked his hands into his sleeves and rocked back and forth, to keep warm and to think. What a new twist this was! He pulled off his cap and rubbed the lengthening stubble on top of his head, thinking "I need to shave soon." His hand stopped, poised mid-rub. But, then again, did he? Only monks need to keep their heads shaved. A married son-in-law wears his hair long, tied up in a topknot. As it should be.

Vessel jumped to his feet. He felt excited. His chest warmed to the thought of taking Cinnabar as his wife.

"Such a sweet, gentle, well-mannered girl — could there be a better match in this vast land?"

He thought of her welcoming eyes and this made him grab the lumber left for him and toss it onto his back. He laughed aloud and would have thrown back his head, but this was not possible while shouldering such a heavy pile of wood.

"It's a good plan!" he announced to the surrounding trees. "And I'm a bad monk!"

PART TWO: VESSEL

He marched off to join his new family.

What a happy evening this unlikely group shared in their snug little cottage. Everyone seemed content. Cricket pulled out his flute, and the three others sang along to his tunes, sharing stories and jokes until exhaustion overcame them all. Cinnabar smiled demurely at her betrothed as she pulled her blanket over her shoulders. Old Mu placed his hand on Vessel's arm and said he would take them all back to Ding soon to draw up a marriage contract.

Vessel, back to his bedroll on the ground, felt elated. He had found a family. He would learn a new trade from Old Mu. He would be an elder brother to Cricket. He would soon be married to a perfect wife. He had found a place where he belonged. Wrapped in the warmth of these comforting thoughts, his hand gripping the talisman around his neck, Vessel drifted off to sleep.

The first image that came to him in his dreams was that of his Auntie Liu patting his cheek on the road outside her house. "Now we are trusting you, our unpolished jade, with our clan fate," she was saying. Then she faded away.

Next his mother appeared. Her arms were crossed and she looked displeased. "So," she said, "you have found a new family."

Vessel was kneeling at his mother's feet. He felt confused, but so happy to see her again.

"Ma!"

"What is your new name then?" she asked. "You are going to be a Mu now?"

"No," Vessel said, shaking his head, aghast at the thought. "No. I am a Zhu."

"I forfeited my life for the Zhu clan," his mother went on, not hearing him. "I pulled your brother out of the Tang clan, don't you remember? All that sacrifice and now you are ready to cast your Zhu family aside."

Vessel was shaking his head. No, no, no. His mother began to fade away.

"Ma!" Vessel cried out again, not wanting her to go. "But I thought you did not want me to be a monk! And Old Mu is right — I'm not meant to be a monk. I cannot keep the vows."

Now his father appeared in his mother's place. "Fortune, the Lord Buddha knows the monk vows are a sacrifice," his father was saying. "You have only just begun your time in monk's robes. You need patience. You have not tried hard enough."

"So you want me to stay in monk robes?" Vessel asked.

He could see his mother again, but faintly.

"My son," she said, her eyes pleading with him.

Both of his parents were on a boat, and it was floating away from him. Vessel ran along the shoreline, but he could not keep up. His parents sat solemnly in the boat, watching him, and he knew that if he lost sight of them, he would lose them forever, but he could not keep up.

Vessel awoke. He jumped into a crouch on his mat and gulped, his heart pounding. The others around him were fast asleep — Old Mu exhausted from his trip to Ding and the ordeal he had encountered upon his return; Cinnabar exhausted from the previous sleepless nights in Vessel's arms; Cricket sleeping deeply as usual.

Vessel remained in the grip of his dream. His head was cleared of all lovesickness. The vision of his dream-parents floating away seemed more real than the snoring Mu family around him.

One thought stood out, "I am all that remains of my Zhu family."

He felt the gaze of his parents, waiting to see what he would do next, waiting to see if he could keep up with them. Vessel snatched his blanket and rolled it into a neat bundle with his mat. He pulled on his felt boots and his monk cap. Vessel quietly crept out of the little cottage and into the night. In the cold air of the silent yard he stood and gathered his thoughts.

"I understand," he whispered, speaking to his parents. "I cannot change my name to Mu."

He thought back to the day long ago when he had followed Radish to the home of Tang the Old Wolf and learned what it meant to become a 'married in' son-in-law. He remembered Radish kneeling in the dirt and promising that his sons would be Tangs.

Vessel stood for a long while looking hard at the door to the snug cottage. He thought of the beautiful girl inside and of how he longed for her. But his mother's words burned. He could not take the path Old Mu had planned for him.

"I am all that remains of my Zhu family," he said again, speaking aloud this time, to the trees and the clouds and the wind. "And my parents do not want me to stay here."

Vessel turned away from the cottage. He set off into the night, walking down the hillside and away to the west, toward other places and another fate. The fate reserved for him.

12

MASTER PENG'S DISCIPLE FINDS SUPPORT IN WHITE PINE

Still winter of Correctness Attained, fourth year (1344).
Outskirts of the city of Luzhou, known today as Hefei, the
capital of Anhui Province.

VESSEL MARCHED steadily away from Mount Floating Raft. By daybreak, his path crossed the circuit road leading to the regional hub of Luzhou to the south. Vessel hesitated, looking in the direction of the walled city. He lacked the courage to take the circuit road. Even though he had lived his entire life within a day's walk of Hao and had passed more than once within sight of its walls, Vessel had never entered it. He knew nothing of city life. After a long night of dreams and escapes he did not have the stamina to approach an imposing city gate. Clutching at his grandfather's talisman, trying not to think about Cinnabar, he hurried across the deserted circuit road. He did not stray from his inconspicuous footpath through the forest.

He rested briefly in a clearing, dutifully pulling out his parents' soul tablet and offering prayers. Resuming his journey, his feet felt heavy, and each step became a reminder of the growing distance between him and the Mu family.

"Why couldn't I stay with them?"

He sped up his pace to chase away such thoughts. His

stomach growled and his face felt raw and chapped.

"I am always having to leave," he thought, "and now I don't even know where I am going."

With a sense of relief, Vessel noticed the upturned eaves of a temple in the distance. This was Spring Comfort, a small temple of the Tiantai sect located on a hillside overlooking the east channel of the Wa River. Smoke curled promisingly from its chimneys. Vessel headed to the gate and presented his letter of introduction from Balance.

"I am the novice Vermillion Vessel of Tiger Empress Temple in the Prefecture of Hao," Vessel proclaimed. The words felt like a reassurance that he was indeed a member of the Buddhist fold. The monks at the gate smiled back at him as if it made perfect sense for him to appear before them. "My tonsure master is known as Exalted Balance and he has sent me to be a wandering monk. I humbly request permission to lodge here."

Vessel passed the Lunar New Year at Spring Comfort Temple. He worked diligently to assist the handful of resident monks, who were happy to take in a wandering brother. Vessel did not reveal much about his own background, but the abbot may have guessed at Vessel's inner turmoil.

"Perhaps I can add another mantra for you," the abbot said at the end of one recitation session.

Vessel, seated in the lotus position on a prayer mat, opened his eyes and looked expectant.

The abbot rang his hand chime and intoned, "O Compassionate One! It is rare that we can be rid of doubts. It is often that we make mistakes. Desire manifests itself and cuts us off from the Dharma. O guardian of the unfortunate! Furnish us with the armor of restraint and the understanding that all things are transient."

Vessel's pressed his eyes shut and fervently joined the abbot in the response: "He guards us! The Diamond Thunderbolt of Heaven remembers us!"

As Old Mu had predicted, spring came late that year. When the forsythia at last bloomed and the grass turned green, the abbot felt confident that Vessel had reached a state of composure sufficient to allow him to continue as a wandering monk. The abbot wished the novice well and sent him on his way.

Vessel spent the next several weeks passing through the regions of Anfeng and Runing. On the advice of the Spring Comfort monks, he went south until he reached the road to Lu'an, and then he turned west. Vessel found the courage to enter Lu'an, which was not big enough to be a walled city. He marveled at the variety of goods displayed and was scandalized by the cost of everything. He turned a corner and found himself walking through a lane of high walls and lavishly decorated gates — the compounds of the wealthy. A servant staffing one of the gates watched him pass by and appeared startled.

"Monk, why aren't you rapping on your fish drum?"

Vessel nodded, embarrassed, remembering that his monk brothers had told him to seek alms when he walked through neighborhoods or markets. He fumbled in his bag for his drum and mallet and was soon tapping out an uncertain beat.

"Louder!" yelled the servant, who had stepped into the lane to observe the monk's progress.

Vessel nodded again and straightened his posture, rapping resolutely at his drum. He glanced over his shoulder and saw that the servant was satisfied and had returned to his post. Vessel strode along the quiet, tree-lined boulevard. No one seemed to be paying him any attention. He relaxed and tilted back his head, chanting to his own beat,

"Homage to the Amitabha Buddha."

All at once, two doors flew open and servants came running

toward him. Vessel jumped back in alarm, thinking he was about to be seized for some kind of violation. But the servants thrust strings of coins at him, loudly proclaiming the names of their masters. They stood back and watched Vessel tuck the coins into his satchel. They seemed to be waiting for something. Finally one of the servants frowned with impatience.

"Well, are you going to shout a prayer for my master or not?" he asked.

So Vessel complied. He shouted out a prayer of blessing, turning in a slow circle so that he could be heard in all directions, inserting the names of the masters as many times as he could.

It was a good thing Vessel had encountered that first gate servant, because when he finally found a temple for lodging, he was required to make an "alms collection donation."

Vessel spent a few nights in Lu'an before crossing the Pi River and continuing west. He took the triple-arched bridge over the White Dew River, skirted Iron Forest Mountain and climbed Mount Jingangtai, from which he could view its famous Leopard Rock. He rode the ferry across History River, using alms donations to cover his fees and meals. He learned to decipher the guttural dialect of the region and became accustomed to rice instead of noodles in the dining halls. He pushed aside thoughts of Cinnabar and instead chanted aloud the names of his family whenever he felt lonely, summoning a favorite memory to accompany each name. His mother at her loom, his father on planting days, his grandfather making a charm...

Vessel was heading ever deeper into China's interior, enjoying the warmth of spring. When he turned his head to look over his right shoulder, he was gazing north in the direction of the Huai River. Over his left shoulder, to the south, were the Dabie Mountains. He felt invigorated by roaming without a destination.

After months and months of sorrow and losses, after never knowing what to do next, after all the uncertainties and worries and disappointments, Vessel welcomed this unexpected chance to move untethered through the landscape. No one was waiting for him to arrive anywhere. No one knew where he was. As the days passed, Vessel learned how to pace himself. A discouraging day was usually the result of bad weather or a path that became a dead-end or misjudging the difficulty of the terrain. But under blue skies and pleasant walking conditions, more often than not, he encountered unexpected wonders and colorful characters — sometimes both at the same time.

"Do you see that?"

"What?" Vessel squinted, unsure if he was looking in the right place.

"That bend in the river where there is a boulder shaped like a fox sitting on its haunches?"

Vessel shaded his eyes to better see the place his companion, an elderly lacquer craftsman, was indicating. "Yes! Yes!"

"That is the place where General Sun Wu ordered his army to disembark for an avenging attack on the State of Chu," the craftsman explained. He was referring to the general known as Master Sun, author of *The Art of War*. "That was the campaign that taught Sun Wu the principle, 'Speed is everything in the conduct of war.'"

Vessel had encountered the craftsman chopping wood alone off the forest path. The scene was such a vivid reminder of Vessel's last day with Cinnabar and her father that he came to a halt, gazing wistfully at the toiling man. The craftsman had turned and called out a greeting, pausing from his work to offer Vessel a drink of water. Vessel repaid the kindness by taking a turn at the craftsman's pile of lumber. Now the two were resting at a nearby hillside pagoda, enjoying the excellent view over one of the many tributaries of the Huai.

"Sun Wu came through here in ancient times," said the craftsman. He rose to his feet. "But do you know that during the Song, another great general came through this region?"

"Yue Fei?" Vessel guessed.

"Just so," the craftsman nodded, happy at Vessel's correct answer. "General Yue made three expeditions to the north to fight the Jin barbarians. It was on his third and last campaign that he marched up from Hanyang, dividing his force into two armies for the crossing of the Dabie Range. One of the divisions came through this very place on the way to reclaim the Song capital from the northern invaders."

Vessel spat on the ground.

The craftsman stepped back in surprise. "What was that for?" he asked.

"Because you are about to say that the treacherous minister Qin Gui forced Yue Fei to halt, and convinced the emperor to withdraw General Yue from the field," replied Vessel.

"Ai," the craftsman sighed, "and then Qin Gui had him put to death."

Vessel spat again.

"My grandfather taught me to always spit at the sound of Qin Gui's evil name."

The craftsman laughed, but then he threw back his head and added an impressive arc of his own saliva.

Vessel guessed that the craftsman was an experienced storyteller. "Tell me what you know of Yue Fei's martyrdom."

The craftsman smiled. He had worked for many years as a carver in a large lacquerware shop in the valley until being appointed caretaker of a guild storehouse, a collection of buildings used by the workers who tapped juice from the lacquer trees in the surrounding forest. It was a job with few duties that came with a comfortable cottage, leaving plenty of time for the craftsman to devote to his favorite hobby, reading local histories. He was famous for his collection of gazetteers.

"Thank you, young monk," he said to Vessel, before taking a deep breath and launching into his lecture. "In the ninth year of the Song Dynasty Emperor Gaozong's 'Prosperity Continues' reign period, Yue Fei's armies pushed the Jin invaders north, clearing them out of the region below the Yellow River to the point that the captive capital city of Kaifeng came tantalizingly within reach."

"Where is Kaifeng from here?" Vessel asked.

"It is directly to the north," said the craftsman, pointing straight ahead. "It would have changed everything if Yue Fei's army could have reclaimed Kaifeng for the Song. He and his lieutenants made plans to take back the capital and march north to destroy the Jin menace once and for all." The craftsman sighed and shook his head. "Alas, alas. To the Song court, which was jealous of military power, having the upper hand on the battlefield meant an opportunity to sue for peace. The emperor agreed to a disgraceful treaty on humiliating terms. Some say the Jin negotiators demanded Yue Fei's head in exchange for accepting this Huai River before us as the new border between the Jin and the Song."

The two contemplated the river in the distance, glinting peacefully in the sunlight, giving no hint of its role in past war negotiations.

"The emperor sent word to Yue Fei's camp to stop all military action," the craftsman continued. "Kaifeng was lost forever to the Song. Yue Fei was said to have cried out, 'Ten years of merit wiped out in a single morning!' The emperor summoned Yue Fei south to court, but his soldiers begged him not to leave the front, and the people poured in from the countryside to kneel at the gate to the general's camp and block his departure. They all wept and implored Yue Fei to ignore the imperial orders. But couriers kept arriving from the emperor. In the end what could the general do but obey? As he approached the capital, with only a small escort of personal guards, Yue Fei was arrested on the ridiculous charge of fomenting revolt. Prime Minister Qin Gui…" the craftsman politely nodded at the ritual spit by Vessel, "had the general tortured but could not extract a confession. So the prime minister had Yue Fei and his son Yue Yun put to death."

"How were they killed?"

"They were hanged on Fengbo Pavilion on the night before the Lunar New Year's Eve. It is said that when the jailer came to take them to the pavilion, Yue Fei told his son, 'Men of substance should face death unflinchingly.' Then he wrote out his famous last words…"

"Heaven will prove my innocence," the two said in unison.

Vessel and the old craftsman contemplated this shameful story as they looked toward the Huai River, which Vessel had never crossed.

"At least I have never had to set foot on territory taken by the northern invaders," Vessel said, referring to the Jin. He sounded proud of himself.

The craftsman burst out laughing. He looked out at the river and back at Vessel. "My new monk friend, I think you've forgotten something."

"What?" Vessel asked crossly.

"Are there any other northern invaders who come to mind?" the craftsman wondered mischievously. "More recent invaders? Who, I might add, also came through this very region, brushing the Song out of their way as easily as you turn over your hand?"

Vessel thrust his hands deep into his sleeves, refusing to acknowledge the truth in the craftsman's words: that the

Mongols were invaders from the north before they claimed the Mandate of Heaven.

"Then this is an inauspicious land and there's nothing good to say about it," Vessel snapped. He did not like to be wrong.

"Oh, you are still young," the craftsman exclaimed. "There's no need to dismiss this place. Have you not heard the expression: 'It's easier to shake a mountain than rattle the Yue army'? The story of the martyr Yue Fei is a story of righteousness! And you cannot discount that this region is part of the last frontier that the great men crossed to defend. First the Jin and later the Mongols, and who knows who will come next? You don't fight over something that doesn't matter."

Vessel kept hold of his elbows and stared obstinately into the distance.

The craftsman sighed. "I brought you here to enjoy the view, to repay you for all your help this morning," he reminded Vessel. "I won't let you stay in a bad temper. Come back to my rooms and I will make you dinner."

Vessel's stomach prodded him to relent from his dark mood. He looked over at the craftsman and grinned.

"Grandpa, I can barely stand because my back is so sore from all the wood I chopped to earn this view," he said. "I expect a grand meal out of you!"

By late spring, Vessel's wandering had brought him to the suburbs of a river town known as Luoshan. He resolved to enter the city and reached the main gate before dusk, but the guards refused to let him in.

"You are too late, we are closing the gates now," one guard stated, as his companion waved through a merchant wheeling in a cart loaded with goods.

"But why are you letting him through the gates?" Vessel

exclaimed with impatience.

"That merchant?" asked the guard, looking lazily over his shoulder at the man hastily receding into the city lanes.

"Who else?"

"Well, he contributes regularly to our gate repair fund." The guard raised his eyebrows invitingly to Vessel. "What do you think, monk? I doubt you need all the alms you have collected today."

Vessel turned away in disgust. He headed back toward a sign for a hillside refuge he had noticed earlier. Climbing the narrow path in the deepening shadows, he slipped and fell into a creek, so that he was soaking wet when he arrived at what turned out to be a Goddess of Mercy hall. The stingy custodian would only allow him to sleep on the hard ground in the cramped courtyard. Vessel departed as quickly as possible in the morning, but not before squeezing a full meal out of the custodian.

Eager to get away from Luoshan, Vessel walked at a good clip for much of the day, encountering few distractions. In the afternoon, he stopped to eat at a small wayside inn that offered unexpectedly tasty fare. Now the light was once again fading and he needed to find yet another place to spend the night. Fireflies glowed and cicadas droned. He thought he could make out Rooster Mountain in the distance, its peak lit by the setting sun, but he was startled from his musings by two middle-aged farmers, a husband and wife, who waved him over.

"This way, Master, over here," they called out, beckoning insistently.

Puzzled, Vessel turned down the path leading to their village.

"You are early, Master!" the husband remarked.

Before Vessel could respond, the couple ushered him along a lane, taking no apparent notice of Vessel's confusion. They turned a corner and entered the courtyard before a clan hall, where a number of people were waiting. Everyone turned expectantly to greet Vessel. An older man, who had the bearing of a leader, stepped forward ceremoniously.

"Welcome, Honorable Master Peng!" the man said, raising his clasped hands in a salute. "I am the village head…"

With everyone's full attention, Vessel was at last able to resolve the confusion. "No, no," he said, shaking his head and stepping back. "I am not Master Peng. As only a mere wandering monk, I cannot be the one you are seeking."

The crowd muttered in consternation and the dismay showed clearly on the faces of Vessel's two escorts. The village head blinked in surprise, but remained unflustered. He nodded a polite acknowledgement to Vessel and sent the escorts back to their station, telling the crowd the wait would not be much longer.

"Monk, you are welcome to join us," the village head said to Vessel. "Any moment now a Maitreya master will be arriving to offer us a lecture. I think you have heard of the great Master Peng?"

Vessel uttered a noncommittal "Eh," and moved to the edges of the excited crowd, where he was ignored. It did not take long for the escorts to reappear from around the corner with a new monk in tow. This one was at least a decade older than Vessel and looked suitably prepared for a reception. He smiled regally and raised his voice to explain, "People of White Pine Village, my revered teacher, the Honorable Master Peng, could not join you tonight. Instead, he sends his regards and has given me, his humble disciple, full instructions as to his message for you."

The gathering appeared to accept this explanation, and the village head conducted official greetings and introductions. At one point, the disciple shifted his eyes questioningly to Vessel, who stepped discretely forward and explained in a low voice that he was a wandering monk from Hao traveling through the district and honored to be able to join this gathering. The disciple smiled again.

The village head led the disciple into the clan hall, and the rest filed in behind. Several villagers insisted that Vessel take a place up front, since he was a monk and moreover a guest.

The disciple took his seat on cushions, facing the spectators from a platform, which was illuminated by torches along the walls. He called for incense to be burned before all the spirit tablets in the hall and several men jumped up to take care of this task. Then the disciple closed his eyes and began to chant, repeating the same two phrases: "Homage to the Amitabha Buddha! Homage to the Venerable Maitreya!" Everyone else in the hall joined in, including Vessel, who was accustomed to this kind of group chanting.

"Na-mo A-mi-to-fo. Na-mo Mi-le-zun-fo."

Over and over again, the two sets of six Chinese syllables rang out in the same low tone, mesmerizing, unifying, intoxicating.

After chanting the mystical phrases 108 times, or one full pass through the prayer beads, the disciple rapped on a gong to bring the exercise to a close. Everyone opened their eyes and focused on the full lips of the speaker, who had a pointy bald head and a bouncy throat knot.

"Brothers and sisters, I could see all the fresh grave mounds as I walked into your village," the disciple began, in a voice that was rich and appealing, in contrast to his angular visage. "You have suffered. Everyone suffers. Think about it — the people in Pei and Feng drowned when the dikes burst. The people in Bo and Su are starving. To the north and the east there are earthquakes. To the south and the west is the plague. Where is there not suffering?"

He looked around as if seeking to find a place of sanctuary.

Then he bowed his head for a moment of sorrowful reflection. The listeners' upturned faces reflected his melancholy, Vessel's among them.

All at once, the disciple snapped his face back up, his eyes ablaze now, his skin shiny in the torchlight, the incense clouding behind him. Some of the audience members drew back with alarm at the sharp change. The disciple lowered his voice.

"And yet, the sutras say that it is exactly in the darkest of times that the Buddha light is able to shine at its brightest and most radiant. It will shine in the form of the Venerable Maitreya, the Buddha of the Future, who the sutras say will descend on his white lotus and bring us peace and prosperity. Why, the Maitreya Buddha is waiting right now up in the Tushita Heaven for the moment when he can come down among us and be reborn."

The audience became excited and Vessel noticed people sighing with hope and even crying as the disciple reviewed the many glorious transformations that would be brought about by the Maitreya. Flowers would bloom everywhere and the ground would be dusted with gold. Everyone would live harmoniously and have loving hearts; no one would suffer from afflictions like the plague.

"You will be able to plant one seed of millet and seven crops will result, one after another, with no need for tilling or hoeing," the disciple exclaimed, raising his thumb and forefinger, squeezed together as if holding the one tiny seed that could result in such bounty.

Vessel listened closely to this wondrous tale, thinking, "if only my father could have lived to farm in such an easy world!" Vessel was as familiar as the next person with the Maitreya, and knew of this Buddha's cheerful, compassionate nature and his lofty place within the pantheon. Yet, the disciple was presenting a mighty Maitreya to the White Pine villagers. This did not resemble the Maitreya that Vessel knew from Tiger Empress or the temples he had wandered through. Trying to make sense of the disciple's message, Vessel pinched at his chin, his brow furrowed with concentration. He was used to monks whose focus was on keeping the temple running and of temple leaders preaching the hard work of self-cultivation and the need to rid one's mind of desires. In contrast, here was a message that filled the listeners with covetous longing and a desire for revenge. Vessel looked around again at the faces visible in the dim light. They were glowing red from the torch flames and their glances contained a strange expression, one that seemed to say, "The Maitreya's paradise will be all for me." Vessel began to feel uncomfortable.

Now the disciple launched into a new topic. He spoke of how the local magistrates did not want to see the Maitreya Buddha descend because that would mean they would no longer be in power. The disciple spoke of how the arrival of the Venerated One might require that people like the villagers in White Pine take certain risks. And he added that the Blessed Arrival would be heralded by a sage who would prepare the way. A sage like the Honorable Master Peng.

"My revered master, who comes from the Compassionate Salvation Monastery, is a healer with amazing powers. I have seen him with my own eyes sprinkle holy water on the sick and make them instantly well again," the disciple exclaimed. Then he leaned his elbows on his knees and his voice took on a conspiratorial tone. "I will tell you the real reason he could not come here tonight to speak to you in person."

Now the hall fell silent. The spectators drank in the disciple's words as if they were a ladle of water on a hot day.

"He is in hiding," the disciple said, his voice barely above a whisper but his chin high and his eyes defiant. "It's been almost seven years now since my master called on the people of

Yuanzhou, south of the Yangtze River, to rise up and push away the evil officials who were trying to prevent the dawn of a new order. My master wrote the character for 'Buddha' and wore it on his chest so that no arrows or spears could touch him. He and many, many others fought bitterly against the imperial troops, but my master was able to escape with his followers and he has been hiding in the homes of his believers ever since."

"Oh, we are talking about Peng, the Jiangxi rebel leader," Vessel realized.

He was a mere boy of ten when Master Peng led his five thousand followers into rebellion. Most were slaughtered, with the cavalrymen's spears neatly slicing through the vests inscribed with the sacred Buddha word. This occurred far to the south of the Yangtze, but ever since, Vessel and his family had heard vague rumors of violence and disturbances in the surrounding regions. The disciple's story was not new, but it did mark the first time Vessel had heard from an actual participant in rebellion. Why, it was as if this monk favored rebellion. Vessel's sense of alarm deepened. He realized that everyone else seemed enthralled by the change in tone. The hall was crowded and hot. The scent of the incense mingled with the smell of bodies pressed together. Vessel swallowed and wished he had not taken a seat in the front.

"You all may know of Ugly Zhao and Buddha Guo, who were put to death for telling the people to prepare for the Maitreya's descent," the disciple continued, his voice rising. "Twelve years later, Hu the Cudgel raised banners emblazoned with the Maitreya name and rebelled in this very prefecture!"

A man jumped to his feet and shouted out, "Hu took his cudgel straight to Chenzhou and burned that city to the ground!"

Another cried out, "Old Hu chopped the penis off our former magistrate and fed it to the pigs!"

The audience became boisterous, but the disciple raised his voice above them. "Do you know that Hu the Cudgel was preparing a new calendar?" he asked, and this startling fact brought the focus back to him.

The disciple nodded his head many times, his bald pate perspiring and his throat knot working feverishly as he glanced back and forth across the hall.

"Yes, that's right. Before the imperial troops caught up with him here, Hu the Cudgel was about to found a new dynastic era and proclaim his first reign title for the House of Hu!"

The hall grew uncomfortably quiet at these dangerous words. Vessel could hardly breathe.

"In the end, it turned out that Hu the Cudgel was not the one destined for the Dragon Throne. And yet, is it not clear that the throne awaits a true ruler? My brothers and sisters of White Pine, have we not seen more than enough signs that the Mandate from Heaven has been revoked from the Yuan Dynasty?" the disciple asked.

Vessel heard a few of the nearby listeners gasp, but no one interrupted.

"How many more floods? How many more plague demons must we endure? We have suffered enough under the Mongol rulers in Dadu!"

He reminded the gathering of the evil Chancellor Bayan, who hated the Chinese. The disciple said Bayan had called for the massacre of the five most common Chinese surnames — Zhang, Wang, Liu, Li and Zhao — as a way to improve the ratio of Chinese to Mongols. This was a well-known tale. The disciple passed along the latest rumor that the reigning emperor, Toghon Temur, was the son of a Turkish mother, not a Mongol at all, and so not regarded as legitimate even by his own court.

"Wait for the sign," the disciple told the audience. "Wait for the sign that the Maitreya Buddha has descended to launch a new era. The sign could come any day now. The Honorable Master Peng will let you know."

The disciple concluded by asking for contributions to support the work of Master Peng and his followers. The village head stood up, gesturing for the presentation of a tray of coins that had already been collected.

His work finished, the disciple led the gathering in a recitation of the Lotus Sutra and then everyone filed back out into the night, talking excitedly among themselves as they dispersed. Vessel tried to slip away, but the disciple suddenly appeared at his side.

"Brother, I would welcome your thoughts and comments," he said to Vessel.

"Ah," Vessel mumbled uncertainly, nodding his head a few times, "it was all very interesting... "

"You said your home temple is in Hao Prefecture?"

Vessel was surprised that the disciple remembered. "Yes. Tiger Empress." As soon as he said the name of his temple, Vessel wished he had stayed silent. He did not think his abbot would condone Master Peng or his disciples, nor would he allow his monks to go around stirring up trouble like this one was doing.

"Tiger Empress," the disciple repeated, seeming to think this over. "A Chan temple south of the city of Hao. I have not been to it."

"It is just a small hereditary temple."

"Who is the abbot?"

Vessel did not want to answer. He looked away, trying to think of how to avoid a reply without being rude. Luckily, the village head was striding their way, waving at the disciple to try to get his attention.

"Our host is coming," Vessel said, smiling and pointing, but to Vessel's dismay, this did not prove a distraction. More and more villagers were gathering around, pressing in, wanting to be near the disciple, who seemed interested only in Vessel.

"In these uncertain times, why would a strong young wandering monk like you return to such an unimportant temple as Tiger Empress?" the disciple asked pointedly. Around him, the villagers nodded approvingly, eager to agree with the disciple. "I will recommend you to Master Peng. You could become a leader among his soldiers."

"But I am not a soldier," said Vessel, his voice sounding nervous and foolish in his ears, especially in comparison to the confident baritone of the disciple.

"We are all soldiers for the Maitreya Army," the disciple sternly advised. "We need to be in the right place when the Venerable One descends. What place could be better for a monk than at the side of Master Peng?"

The crowd parted for the village head, who bustled forward to announce sleeping arrangements for his important guest. The disciple suggested that Vessel room together with him, but Vessel managed to be assigned instead to the home of another, less important family. This arrangement met with the approval of the village head and the matter was settled, with plans to gather again in the morning for tea and a sending-off breakfast.

"We can talk more in the morning," the disciple told Vessel before heading off with the village head.

Vessel's assigned host escorted him to his sleeping quarters, brought him a bowl of stew, and showed him where to unroll his sleeping mat.

"I will take you to the sending-off breakfast, and it's a good thing, because you will surely be seated close to the disciple and I will be seated next to you," the villager happily prattled on as Vessel unpacked his bedroll. The host reached for Vessel's emptied bowl. "Remember me when you join with Master Peng."

Vessel drew back. "Why do you think I am joining Master Peng?"

"Didn't you hear the disciple say he would recommend you?"

"And you think that means I am joining him?"

"Who would not join Master Peng?" replied the villager, looking incredulous. "You'd better do as that one commands. I hear Master Peng has the tongues sliced from the mouths of dissenters and fear-mongers. He mounts the tongues on a Buddha wall and has his monks pray before it."

"What would you pray about at a wall like that?" Vessel wondered aloud.

"For their continued silence, I suppose!" The villager blew out the oil lamp and headed for his own bed.

Vessel could not sleep. He lay listening to the sounds in the lane outside, trying to remember the way back to the main road, trying not to think about the disciple or his lecture. When his host's snoring became unbearably loud, Vessel rose, gathered his belongings, and crept out into the dark village lanes, which were thankfully empty. Vessel felt the same sensation as when he had stood outside Old Mu's winter cabin a season ago — an overwhelming desire to get away. This time, however, he left with no regrets.

Vessel headed westward, following footpaths and watching the sky as the red-tinged Fire Star set before him. The constellations faded peacefully into the dawn light, serenaded by roosters. The sun rose behind Vessel to reveal fields of bright green winter wheat in all directions. Farmers appeared, crowding the paths, nodding friendly greetings to Vessel as they hurried along. Vessel breathed in the fresh scent of the dewy fields as he watched the farmers with interest and remembered his own days of helping his father and brothers bring in the winter wheat and clear the fields for the millet crop. Assessing the first spring crop, which appeared meager, distracted his mind from his fears that if he stopped and looked back over his shoulder, he would see the disciple of Master Peng running to catch up with him.

Vessel switched to a broader road to keep out of the way of the farmers. He continued at a quick pace. The sun rose higher and beat down relentlessly on the anxious and under-slept monk. The heat was unseasonably cloying. Vessel pulled out a rag to wipe the sweat from his face and pushed his robe off his arms and shoulders, walking bare-chested. His dusty sandals bit into his feet. Before the strange night in White Pine, Vessel had slept on the hard ground of a Goddess of Mercy courtyard, so he had not had a good rest for two nights. He was exhausted and hungry and had been walking too fast for too long. He could see no one on the road in either direction. Vessel stepped over the ditch to rest under an oak tree. He wiped his face again as he leaned against the tree trunk and considered the mountain looming before him. He longed to reach its shady forests, but did not know if he had the stamina for a steep climb. He sank down to rest, his vision swimming.

The road remained empty, with no sound beyond the buzzing of insects and the light breeze rustling the leaves in the trees. And then the buzzing turned into a cheerful whistling. Vessel blinked and tried to focus and realized the whistling came from a monk. "No, no," Vessel shrank away as the monk stopped whistling and rushed toward him. Vessel rose to his knees, and tried to stand, swaying and dizzy as the monk kept coming for him. Vessel had no place to hide and could not flee. He could see now that the approaching monk was not the disciple from White Pine.

"Master Peng?" Vessel cried out, fearing the worst. He shrank back. "I will not go with you!"

But this monk was not trying to grab him. "Water, you need to drink my water, my friend," the monk was saying, as he fumbled to pull the stopper from his gourd bottle.

Vessel took a deep drink. He wiped his mouth and felt his mind clearing.

"Are you with Master Peng?" Vessel asked warily.

The monk recoiled. "I am not!"

Vessel glanced anxiously down the road. "I think one of Master Peng's disciples is chasing me."

The monk frowned and encouraged Vessel to take another drink. He was about the same age as Vessel, though he was a full head shorter. "Don't worry about that lot," he said. "I am called Diligence and I am a monk at Spirit Mountain Temple, which is near here. I was heading to the market, but my shopping can wait. Let me help you back to my temple."

Vessel spent the next few days at Spirit Mountain, whose monks had in common an intense suspicion of the followers of Monk Peng.

"I know all about Monk Peng and his band of incense burners," growled one jowly monk as he and Vessel swept a courtyard. "I've seen him with my own eyes, down in the village markets. He always pulls out his so-called magic healing water, sprinkling it on the villagers and promising them all kinds of nonsense. What a fox he is. He speaks in a language that bewitches the villagers. I have seen men leave their fields and family duties to run off and join him. It's a great folly."

"Farmers deserting their own fields?" Vessel asked, sounding skeptical. He thought of his own family, and what a disaster it would have been if his father had suddenly run off and joined a Maitreya preacher. But his father would never have committed such a rash act.

"Oh yes," the jowly monk answered. He paused from his sweeping, leaning thoughtfully on his broom. "You know, young brother, Master Peng's disciple won't like it that you managed to slip from his clutches. They're a secretive, suspicious bunch. They'll think you plan to report them to the magistrate."

Vessel stopped sweeping then, too, and frowned.

The monk swiped his hand across the air. "Oh, now, forget about it," he told Vessel. "You're safe with us."

The monk was right to be concerned. The very next morning Diligence rushed into the wandering monks' hall looking for Vessel, who was busy sewing a patch into one of the sleeves of his robe.

"Vessel," Diligence whispered in an urgent tone. "It seems that your White Pine village disciple is looking for you after all. He's just down the hall with the guest clerk, asking questions. Stay here. No, no, that won't do. Come with me."

Vessel dropped his needle and pulled his robe back on, slipping out a side door behind Diligence. The two rushed around a corner, passing other brothers, who stopped their work to join in hiding Vessel.

The guest clerk could be heard speaking in a loud voice to warn the others in his path. "We have no guests in our wandering monks' hall at the moment, I'm afraid," he was saying.

Diligence had stopped to listen, but once he heard the emphasis on "wandering monks' hall," he gestured frantically at a nearby brother. "He's headed for the dorm. Quick, Dumpling, run and clear out Vessel's belongings."

Brother Dumpling ducked through a doorway. Seconds later, Vessel's satchel and also his bedding came flying out into the hallway. Diligence and the others caught the items in the air and tossed them to Vessel. Brother Dumpling slid the door shut, staying back to greet the disciple.

"Welcome, guest!" he shouted in what must have seemed a strangely loud voice.

Vessel and Diligence did not wait to hear more. They dashed further down the hallway, their robes flapping.

"Get down behind the well," said Diligence. "That old demon has no business coming this way. I'll go help clear him away."

Vessel crouched low and did not dare glance over the top of the well. He could hear nothing over his own labored breathing and was left to his own thoughts. Wiping sweat from his temples, Vessel settled into a more comfortable position and reflected on how the disciple had agitated the crowd at White Pine. He wanted them to rise up against their magistrate. What fools! Would they leave their crops in the field for a man like Monk Peng? The disciple had gone on and on about how much easier it would be to farm once the Maitreya descends. "Even I started to think of how wonderful that would be. But it was all lies. It was just a way to get the villagers to fight for Monk Peng." Vessel shook his head. "That's no way to start an army," he whispered to his sandals.

The frantic escape through temple passageways brought back another, older memory. This time Vessel smiled, remembering the beefy monk who had grabbed him and his fellow goat herder, Xu Da, whisking them away from bandits. "That was so long ago," Vessel whispered to himself. He wished he could tell Da about Monk Peng's disciple. Da was a smart one, he would have seen right away that the disciple was no better than the bandits at Chanku Temple. Vessel absently traced a chess board in the dusty ground, thinking of the clever skills of his old friend, who learned to play chess without needing to pick up any actual chess pieces. This naturally led to the image of Old Wolf destroying his treasured chess set. So many trying to cause such havoc everywhere. He wondered wistfully if he would ever see Da again. Da or Harmony, the Number One Stallion under Heaven. "What would Harmony say about Cinnabar? Would he escort me back to the Mu family and tell me to ignore my dreams?"

As he was lost in this reverie, the brothers returned, chuckling and elbowing each other.

"Shhhh," said Diligence to the rest of the group. "Keep your voices down. We don't want him to hear us — he's only just left."

Vessel rose from his hiding place. The brothers smiled back at him from across the well.

"He found me with your sewing kit!" Dumpling said, bursting into laughter. "I had the needle right in my hand as he walked through the door. Looked very proper. Good thing my robes are in such bad shape!"

Diligence smiled broadly. "What an interrogator that one is," he exclaimed. "I decided to tell him that you had been through our halls, but that you'd left the day before for Rooster Mountain and had never once made mention of Master Peng. I even showed him your name in the registry and our guest clerk was kind enough to have marked you as having already left!" Diligence turned to ask the guest clerk how he had managed to accomplish such a clever feat.

"It must have been a mistake," the guest clerk said, looking embarrassed. "I must have made a mark in the wrong place when I filled in the registry for our guest's arrival. But I would have noticed this when our guest actually left. I would have corrected it at once ... "

"Well, it was a fine mistake to have made," Diligence said happily.

Although the monks all assured Vessel that he would see no more of Master Peng's disciples, Vessel decided to leave. He felt that he was causing too much trouble for this jovial group of brothers. He enjoyed one last meal with them and then set off the next morning. Diligence escorted him far past the outer temple gate, an expression of his high regard for his new friend. As they parted, Diligence presented Vessel with the gift of a folding fan.

"So that you won't be so likely to faint on the road again," he joked.

Vessel turned north to head in the opposite direction from Rooster Mountain and at last crossed the Huai. As he stepped down from the bridge near the city of Xinyang and his feet touched the northern bank of the river, Vessel thought of the lacquer craftsman who had teased him for forgetting about the Mongol invasion. Vessel dipped his head in acknowledgement of the craftsman's superior knowledge of history and maps.

For the next few weeks, Vessel spread his sleeping mat under the stars. He burned incense to his parents' spirit tablet every morning and contemplated the constellations every evening. He climbed Truth Mountain and rested under Longevity Temple's pair of ancient gingko trees. He picked juicy peaches near Suiping and roasted chestnuts with a wild-haired hermit outside of Wuyang.

The more Vessel mulled over his night in White Pine and the words of the monks at Spirit Mountain, the more revulsion he felt for the disciple of Master Peng. That misguided monk was no better than a bandit. He frowned at this thought. Vessel had heard the voices of the men exiting the clan hall in White Pine, and they had been talking not of self-cultivation or the Three Jewels but of their complaints against local government leaders. Vessel cursed his own behavior that night, feeling he had simpered like the rest when the disciple had asked for his opinion.

"People are weak and easily misguided," Vessel exclaimed to the hermit with the chestnuts in Wuyang.

"Ai," the hermit agreed, taking a long swig of water from a jug and then splashing a handful onto his face. "And it's hot."

PART TWO: VESSEL

Indeed, though spring had arrived late, the weather had progressed quickly to summerlike heat. The two were fanning themselves in a patch of shade as they ate. Vessel admired his new folding fan and then lazily continued to ponder the lecture at White Pine as he crunched his way through a handful of the delicious nuts. Several of the disciple's claims had been puzzling, and even frightening.

"Old hermit, could it be that the emperor is not considered legitimate by his own court?"

The hermit scratched his head and looked bored. "Who is the emperor these days?"

Vessel burst out laughing. "It doesn't matter!"

"Ai," the hermit said again nodding his head complacently. Then he pointed a bony finger at Vessel. "Young monk, you have a lot of questions," he said. Then he heaved a deep sigh and mumbled distractedly, curling a tangled lock of loose hair in a finger. "If you are trying to understand that which cannot be known then you should first seek the center of things."

Vessel considered this opaque statement and frowned. "Do you mean I should go to Dadu, the capital?"

"Where is that?" the hermit asked, looking genuinely confused.

"Who is asking more questions, then?" Vessel retorted, grinning.

The hermit swatted at Vessel with the edges of his own fan, which he had crafted himself from bamboo fronds.

"You are an impudent fellow!" the hermit growled. "I mean that you should go to the Central Peak. It is to the north of here. That is all I will say. It's too hot for all this chatter."

Vessel took leave of the old hermit the next day and wandered on, with no particular destination in mind. However, as he weighed the hermit's suggestion, he decided it made sense after all to seek out the Central Peak, one of the five sacred Daoist mountains. He took out his grandfather's talisman and studied the strange markings on the wooden box cover. He ran his fingers along the deep red grooves. Grandfather Chen had loved the mountain wilds.

> Who can vault over worldly entanglements,
> and join me in the white clouds?

It was a well-known question posed by the Cold Mountain Master, a poet recluse of the Tang Dynasty. Vessel wiped the sweat from his forehead. How he wished he was on a cold mountain peak. He headed north.

13

SILVER CRANE SEES TO THE UPKEEP OF THE STARRY REGISTER

Early summer of Correctness Attained, fifth year (1345).
Near the town of Dengfeng, in modern Henan Province.

VESSEL ESTIMATED that he was about a half-day's walk from his destination of Central Peak. However, it was evening, and storm clouds were churning in the distance. Vessel quickened his pace, hoping to find a safe place to take shelter. Reaching an intersection with a smaller trail, Vessel glanced down it and saw an elderly monk hailing him.

"See here, you aren't from my temple!" the monk called out abruptly. He walked with a hitch to his gait, his progress aided by the use of a cypress cane.

Vessel waited for the monk to catch up so they could exchange greetings.

"Come along, then, novice," the monk said after hearing Vessel's introduction. "You won't make it to Central Peak tonight. And if you don't hurry, you won't make my monastery before this storm is upon us."

The two hustled single file along the narrow path. After they crossed the bridge over Babbling Stones Creek, the monk led Vessel through an unguarded side entrance to a large and imposing monastery. The skies had turned black. A rush of cool air swirled as the first drops fell.

"This way," the monk shouted to be heard over the storm.

He pointed Vessel along the edge of a small courtyard garden. As the rain pelted the ground, the monk pulled Vessel into a tiny cottage in the far corner. Safely inside, the two grinned at each other, exhilarated at having beaten the heart of the storm. Vessel set down his bag and shook the drops from his robe as the elder monk fussed around the room to heat a pot of tea.

"Don't bother," Vessel urged politely, but his host ignored him and soon the two were seated comfortably with their hands wrapped around fragrant cups. Vessel learned that the monk's formal name was Silver Crane, perhaps due to his silky white whiskers. He served as some sort of record keeper for Tripitaka Monastery, where Vessel was now a guest.

As Vessel described his wandering time for the past few months, Crane latched onto Vessel's casual mention of the wanderer's freedom to watch the stars.

"You like to watch the stars, eh?" the old monk asked, leaning forward and peering intently into Vessel's eyes.

When Vessel nodded and added that he had learned from his mother and maternal grandfather to study the heavens, the old monk leapt up with surprising vigor, snatched his cane, and threw open his door.

"Look, the storm has spent its fury," he announced. "Let's go."

Vessel had no choice but to hurry out the door behind Crane, who was marching in his unsteady gait past the garden outside his cottage. When Vessel ducked through the low archway of an interior monastery wall, he pulled up sharply. Bathed in the moonlight was a brick tower unlike anything Vessel had ever encountered. It rose above the trees, a flat-topped pyramid looming directly before him.

"What is it?" he gasped.

"Eh?" Crane glanced over a shoulder at Vessel. "Oh, yes, it's marvelous. Come on then."

But Vessel was transfixed. Crane finally turned back again and, looking impatient, explained.

"It is a special tower, commissioned by the Dynastic Ancestor," he said, using Khubilai Khan's formal title. "There's a terrace at the top. I want to take you up to it so we can see the stars better."

Through the dusky post-rain steam, the face of the tower appeared to be cleaved in half, with a long waist-high wall extending out along the ground from its center.

"What is the long wall for?" Vessel asked.

Crane looked in the direction Vessel pointed. "Oh, that," he said. "It is a dial for measuring the shadow of the sun."

Crane gestured with his cane toward a wide, exposed stairway that Vessel realized led to the summit. They began to climb. Vessel placed his feet carefully on the wet stairs, which were difficult to see in the lengthening shadows. However, once they reached the platform at the top, Vessel was impressed with the view, both of the monastery complex below, dotted here and there with lamplight, and of the starry canopy above, from which the storm clouds were quickly retreating.

"The clouds are shielding the Herd Boy and the Weaving Maid in the region of the Black Tortoise, but we will see them meet next month on the bridge across the Silver River," Crane explained. Vessel looked wistfully at his sister Lotus's star high to the south. "Now, young novice, can you see the Great Horn of the Blue Dragon?"

Vessel tilted his head as far back as he could to look straight up at the center of the sky, where the brightest star of the evening presided. He nodded.

"Would you say that it is twinkling and shaking or does it

seem calm? My eyesight is so weak now that I cannot trust it for the record keeping."

Crane shuffled over to a desk in a small, covered alcove at one side of the platform. He opened a string-bound record book, lit a thin candle and picked up a writing brush. Vessel did not pay attention to these preparations, concentrating instead on the Great Horn, eventually judging it more disturbed than calm. Crane noted the observation, his eyes shining in the tiny candle flame.

"Very good, very good," he said. "The Great Horn will not remain still. That could mean a disturbance for the emperor." Crane pointed next to the northwest horizon. "I am most interested in the Five Barons. They have almost set in the Vermillion Bird region of the sky. I need you to consider all five. Novice, which seems the brightest?"

"Master Crane, the second one is bright and clear and outshines the others tonight."

The old monk nodded slightly. "And which has the least luster?"

"The fifth baron."

Crane sighed dejectedly and shook his head as he dipped his brush in ink to record this finding.

"It is as I suspected." he muttered. "Indeed, just as I suspected."

Once he finished making notations, Crane pulled out a fresh piece of paper and moved his brush boldly down it. Vessel found the old monk eccentric but companionable. Studying his features in the soft red glow of the desk candle, Vessel saw that Crane had a broad, square face and a precisely chiseled mouth. His eyebrows were as silky white as his drooping mustache and beard. Vessel thought his host seemed sagely, which led Vessel to conclude that Crane was an important leader of the monastery.

PART TWO: VESSEL

Finishing his writing, Crane blew on the ink to dry it and then handed the paper to Vessel.

"It is late, so I do not want you to disturb the guest clerk," he said in a stern voice. "It so happens that I am a senior monk here, so this paper will get you a bunk at the end of the closest dorm." He took Vessel to the opposite balcony and tried to point out the path to the dorm in the shadowy maze below.

The pair climbed back down the observatory steps. At the bottom, Vessel thanked the old monk for the night's viewing.

"You have a keen ability to observe the skies," observed Crane, his eyelids lowering thoughtfully as he leaned on his cane. "I myself learned to interpret the skies from a great master, some say the greatest astronomer of all. He is the one who built this tower."

Vessel raised his brows at this. What a remarkable place he had stumbled upon.

Crane seemed to be weighing something in his mind. He studied Vessel and then vigorously nodded his head. "Yes, yes, I am right in this," he agreed with himself. "I will accept you as a student. You can report to me tomorrow after the first meal but before the sun is overhead. I will explain the shadow measurer then. You will also assist me in the nighttime record keeping."

Vessel drew back in surprise and could only blurt out, "Master Crane, I was planning to head next to the Central Peak..."

"Bah," the old monk brushed this idea away. "Summer is not the time to visit that mountain. You can visit it in the fall. You'll have plenty of time then." He turned on his cane to walk back to his quarters, adding over his shoulder, "I have written in your note that you will begin the ordination training, which starts tomorrow morning. Your timing is excellent."

Vessel opened his mouth to protest, but Crane had already stepped through the gate that led away to his courtyard room.

Vessel looked down at the piece of paper in his hands. He realized his bag remained in Crane's room. Should he run after him and ask for it? Vessel felt this would be rude. He decided he could retrieve it the next day.

The dorm attendant was clearly confused by the note from Master Crane that Vessel presented the next morning, when he surprised everyone by his presence. The attendant read the note through several times and looked hard at the signature.

"I need your letter of introduction from your tonsure master," the attendant said. Vessel sheepishly explained that his bag was not yet available to him. The attendant nodded and waved him on, telling him to follow the rest of the novices heading to the training rooms, where he could present his note again. The attendant wanted someone else to make a decision on the matter.

The ordination officer took Vessel's letter without looking at it, filing it away in a stack of papers where he would not be able to find it again. The ordination master assumed that Vessel had been properly checked in with the guest clerk. And there were so many new novices taking their seats, who had time to bother with so much paperwork? He was also distracted by other concerns — the monastery's elderly abbot had recently died and the senior monks had begun to consider the question of a successor.

Tripitaka was a large and strict monastery of the Chan sect, and a famed ordination center. The small temples, like Tiger Empress in Hao, were where monks entered the fold, took the initial vows and had their heads shaved. To become ordained, a monk needed to enter an ordination center like Tripitaka. At such a place, novices could spend a semester of preparation, and seek to be among the group selected for the annual ordination ceremony. Novices preparing for ordination were trained in every aspect of proper behavior, from how to remove and arrange each sandal when taking a seat in the meditation hall to how to recite all the important sutras. Even in the dining hall discipline was maintained. At Vessel's first meal in Tripitaka Monastery he was rapped on the head by the patrolling monk for slurping his bowl of noodles.

As the sun approached its zenith, Vessel made his way to the rear of the monastery complex, gaping once again at the brick observatory which lurked with its back to the monastery halls, facing out onto the plain. In the glare of the midday sun, Vessel was able to appreciate the tower's brick pattern and design features. But not for long. Crane was waiting for him, looking impatient and holding Vessel's satchel in one hand.

"Let's get ready," Crane said, tossing him his bag and hurrying off to the front of the tower.

Crane directed Vessel to stand alongside the waist-high wall dial, which he referred to as the Sky Measuring Scale. It extended out at least forty paces from the front of the tower.

"The shadow will not be long today because we are approaching the summer solstice," Crane stated.

He pulled from his robe a thin strip of copper with a pinhole in its center. He carefully fitted the metal strip into a small folding stand which he had already placed lovingly on top of the low wall.

"This is the Shadow Definer," Crane explained, pointing to the copper strip. "We have to wait for the sun to rise above the tower and cast its shadow along this wall."

Now Crane turned to point up at the viewing platform where Vessel had studied the Great Horn and the Five Barons the night before.

"When you align the pinhole in the metal strip with that rod up there across the top of the tower, it will make a glorious and completely clear reflection on the Sky Measuring Scale. This will give you the exact measurement of the shadow length for this day."

Crane said no more, staring straight ahead into the trees, his hands folded over the top of his cane and his face calm as he waited for the sun to rise higher in the sky.

"Master, should I seek a measure yet?" Vessel asked, as the shadow of the tower crept along the Sky Measuring Scale.

"Not yet," the old monk answered.

The birds lazily chirped back and forth from the pines and the insects whined through the heat of the day. The two monks stood in silence for several more minutes. The hot sun beat down on Vessel's shaved head. He shifted on his feet and wiped away the sweat running down his nose.

"Master, I think the sun is at its highest point."

"I think that it is not."

But after such serene contemplation, Crane suddenly became agitated, waving a hand in the air. "Seek the measure!" he cried out as his cane clattered to the ground. "Do you see the image of the bar through the pinhole?"

"Master, I cannot see it," Vessel responded, anxiously peering through the copper strip.

"Look again, quickly!" the old monk yelled, flapping his sleeves. "It is no bigger than a rice grain! Move the Definer back and forth! Back and forth!"

With such excitement at his back, Vessel perspired even more as he nervously sought to make the reading. However, when he finally discerned the dim shadow of the metal rod through the center of the tiny disk created by the pinhole, he hollered. "I see it! I see it!"

"Fine work, novice," Crane said, slapping Vessel on his sweaty back. "Now hold your finger to mark the spot and I will note it down. Crane leaned over and peered closely at the place Vessel indicated. He limped over to his writing brush and busied himself with his charts.

"Very good," Crane said. "That is all for today."

He picked up his cane, put away his instruments, and headed back to his quarters. Vessel remained smiling happily at the Sky Measuring Scale wall until Crane turned back to shoo him off.

"Novice, this is no time for foolishness. You are late for your afternoon session with the ordination officer!"

So began a period of constant rushing for Vessel. He ran from ordination training to sky measurements, morning and night, except for those times when cloud cover or dust storms prevented sky readings. Crane wanted Vessel to go to sleep with the other monks for a short rest but then rise — without disturbing anyone — when the temple bell sounded the Second Night Watch. This allowed enough time at the observatory platform for midnight star work. Vessel became adept at slipping out of his dorm in the darkness and padding around the corner to the hallway that led to the tower.

No matter the lack of sleep, as soon as he stepped over the threshold at the observatory courtyard gate, Vessel felt alert and eager to begin his work. This area seemed even more sacred to him than the temple halls. The regal bulk of the tower with its grandiose stairs and its ingenious secrets for capturing time made Vessel's pulse quicken as soon as he caught sight of it, day or night. All of the difficulties of memorizing sutras and remembering monk rules, all of his guilt over leaving Cinnabar, all of his worries over the fate of Radish and Sister-in-law Tang and the souls of his parents and Cattail — all could be set aside in these sessions with Crane and the cosmos. During the brief noontime shadow measurements, Vessel lingered over the instruments, entranced by their beauty and power in the same way he had once admired the charm writing tools of his Grandfather Chen. At night, Vessel never tired of listening to Crane tell stories about the stars. Vessel memorized the characters for star names and also the way to write — in crude, childlike calligraphy — simple descriptions of his observations: "The moon wanes. The Year Star nears the Great White Star." When he was with the other monks, he struggled over sutras, but Vessel never needed to be shown a character twice when it came to astronomical nomenclature. In his dorm at night when he should have been trying to sleep, he liked to review in his mind what he had learned from Master Crane. Studying the skies was a family tradition, a skill that had been passed from Grandfather Chen to Little Chen to Vessel. Now, working with Crane, Vessel was able to develop this skill, and his attentiveness was due in no small part to his desire to please his ancestors.

"I remember when I was a young monk, perhaps a few years older than you are now, and I was first presented to Master Guo," Crane recalled one night as they leaned against the platform wall at the top of the tower. "He asked me to name the seven stars of the Dipper and the twenty-eight lunar mansions and when I could do these things, he seemed satisfied. From then on, I was always at his side when he was visiting."

"What was he like?"

"He was a tall man, with a long nose and tiger eyes," Crane said, smiling at the recollection. "His appearance was handsome and dignified. He was often frowning, I think because he was calculating figures and making plans in his head — our slow-moving minds in this muddled world were no match for such a one as that. My Master Guo had the ear of the Dynastic Ancestor himself."

"Why did he build an observatory here?"

"Because long, long ago, the Duke of Zhou investigated and determined that this is the exact place where the shadow of the sun was shortest at the Summer Solstice and longest at the Winter

Solstice. And it is near to the ancient capital city of Luoyang, and so was convenient to the Duke. That is why Dengfeng is known as 'the heart of heaven and the guts of the Earth.'"

This answer did not satisfy Vessel. "But I still don't understand why Master Guo would think to build such a massive tower here."

Crane nodded and continued. "When the Dynastic Ancestor ascended the throne to rule the Middle Kingdom, he was not so much interested in finding the center of the Earth as in establishing a more accurate calendar," Crane explained, choosing his words carefully. "As it is said in the histories, 'The one who can give the people a calendar is the one who can rule them.' A newly unified empire needed a new calendar. My master was known as a great mathematician, so he was summoned to the capital to demonstrate how the calendar of the Song Dynasty had become dislodged from the correct measurements. Master Guo was then commissioned to establish a new calendar."

Crane paused and looked expectantly at Vessel.

"And a new calendar requires an observatory?" Vessel asked.

"A new calendar requires measurements, and these measurements needed to be taken not just in the capital, but also in other places. So Master Guo naturally thought of Dengfeng, because of its long tradition of being the best place to make celestial measurements. He decided to build a tower here five times bigger than the standard stone pillars that have always been used for shadow readings. This would make his measurements five times more accurate," said Crane, waving his hands triumphantly at the resulting observatory platform. "And so, after collecting measurements here and in the capital and elsewhere, he was able to present the Great Khan with the Time Service Calendar."

Thinking of the Mongol khans reminded Vessel of Monk

Peng's disciple lecturing in White Pine village. Vessel opened his mouth, but found that he did not yet have the courage to voice his concerns about matters raised during that lecture. So he closed his mouth and waited.

Then one night, after the record keeping was finished and Crane was ready to head back down the tower stairs, Vessel took a deep breath and released his question: "Master, I have heard it said that the disasters ravaging the countryside — floods, drought, sickness — why, they are a sign of the withdrawal of Heaven's approval of Yuan rule."

Crane turned to face Vessel, his expression grave. "Yes, I am aware of this," he said softly.

"Some even say that the Maitreya Buddha will soon descend to launch a new era."

"It is often charlatans who say that to stir up trouble."

"Master, what do the stars say?"

"Long before my time, in the first year of the Harmony Attained reign period of the Song Emperor Renzong, the records show that one morning a strange star appeared at dawn in the eastern sky," he began, gazing out toward the horizon. "This star was said to have been as bright as a full moon and visible even during the day for a month, dazzling all the court astronomers. They argued over whether this 'guest star' was a portent of good or evil."

"Which was it?" Vessel interrupted.

"Well, not long after the star finally faded away, Emperor Renzong became ill and then he died — and since he had no sons, a crisis ensued. More than a century later, after the Song Dynasty ended, historians noticed that the fading of the guest star corresponded to the point when the Song's ruling House of Zhao moved from waxing to waning. Heaven marked the exact moment when the decline began, and the event was recorded by court astronomers, but it took many years before the sign was understood and correctly interpreted."

Crane fell silent, musing as he stroked his beard. Then he turned to Vessel and jabbed his forefinger to punctuate each phrase as he said to the young monk, "The stars do not shout out quick answers to simple-minded questions. They give a gradual and cumulative perspective to those who are patient and seek confirmation."

After a pause, Crane turned reflective once more and went on with his lecture.

"This is why astronomers must work so diligently. I say this to you, and yet I must also respond that, for the past few years, all across the starry sky there have been signs, once again, of Heaven's disfavor."

The old monk looked up into the night, raising his sleeve and drawing his outstretched fingers in an arc above his head.

"The Longevity Star, which accords with virtue, was not visible for a single day last winter and was but a faint and pale yellow the winter before that. Worse still, during the fourth and fifth months of the spring before this one a candle-flame star with a white tail as long as my finger swept across the Black Tortoise, a ruinous portent. Even the Great White One has begun to take on a fiery hue which can mean insurrection is imminent."

"Master, how can order be restored?"

At that Crane grunted and turned to Vessel with a sly smile. "Novice, that depends on a number of calculations which have yet to be determined," he said, chuckling. "At least, that is how my Master Guo taught me to reply to such a tricky question."

The pair made their way down the tower steps. In the darkness beyond the high temple walls, the frogs croaked noisily in the fields while the crickets chirped from their perches. Overhead, the stars, the message bearers, blinked and glided in agitated silence, mute faces clamoring for attention.

Vessel thought it odd that so few monks ever appeared in the observatory courtyard. The area was usually deserted, and the courtyard seemed to be used mostly for storage. Weeds sprouted from the paving stones. Vessel supposed that the area was kept apart because it was so important. The other ordination students did not seem to have any idea what the tower was used for. More than once Vessel had to explain to curious novices pointing at the flat-topped pyramid behind the monastery that it was a place for measuring the sun shadow and studying the stars. Although he reveled in his work with Crane, Vessel did not talk to others about his special duties, sensing that Crane preferred discretion. Vessel felt reluctant to say why he always needed to hurry off after the late morning meal, when the rest of the novices enjoyed a brief rest period.

Crane, for his part, seemed mostly irritated by the presence of anyone else near the observatory. If a monk entered the courtyard — to retrieve a large basket or haul in an extra bench for storage — Crane would turn away and stop talking. It was as if he wanted to disappear.

"Novice, what are you doing here?" a monk called out to Vessel on one such occasion.

Vessel felt embarrassed that the monk had not addressed Crane. As he waited, unsure of how to respond, Crane leaned close and hissed, "Tell him you were sent, as punishment, to memorize one of the stele inscriptions here."

Vessel repeated this strange statement, which made the monk laugh and head back through the courtyard gate.

Crane shook his head. "What we do here is not the concern of dimwit monks like that," he said, hurrying Vessel around to the front of the tower for their shadow measuring duties. "What we do is for one person only!"

PART TWO: VESSEL

"The abbot?"

This made Crane spin around and jab his finger at Vessel. "What do you mean, the abbot?" he spat out. "Our work here is correlated with the work at the observatory in the capital and prepared for the Son of Heaven himself! No one else can be given access to such vital information! This is why astronomers should not mix with the common people. This is why you need to turn your back to others when you are working on your measurements and sky readings. Besides, the abbot is dead."

Vessel countered that anyone could look into the heavens and see what was happening there.

"Yes, that may be true," Crane agreed. "But a farmer gazes into the sky on an unusually dark night and mumbles to himself on the phase of a new moon. A court astronomer, armed with charts and records, sees an orb on the point in its path which the astronomer knows will soon cause it to invade and cloak the sun. The farmer is dazzled by a shower of falling stars, but the court astronomer consulting his cyclical records has already prepared the emperor for this phenomenon. That, my young novice, is the difference between an idle stargazer and an imperial astronomer."

For the rest of the monks at Tripitaka Monastery, the most important place on the temple grounds was not the strange tower overlooking the plains, but the grand platform near the Great Hall. This was the ordination stage, glazed in beautiful greens and golds. It was one of the largest in the land and drew hundreds of novices from temples in the surrounding hills and valleys. Most came to Tripitaka for the sole purpose of attending the monastery's prestigious summer ordination training, which culminated in a sacred ceremony on the famed stage.

Vessel, like the other novices, spent hours working on his meditation skills, a crucial aspect of the ordination training, especially at a temple for the Chan sect, whose very name means "meditation." In the early afternoon of every day, the novices filed into the meditation classroom. They sat cross-legged at their assigned places on the floor, holding a piece of bamboo to keep their palms cool.

On the first day of training, the ordination officer had picked up a bundle of ten incense sticks, laid them side by side on a board and cut them in half along a diagonal. Picking up one of the two shortest sticks, the officer set it burning and placed it in a bronze censer. Turning to his row of students, the officer explained that they would watch the stick turn to ash until it was gone.

"Concentrate on the glowing end to cleanse your mind of all impurities and distractions," the officer instructed, glancing across the room to be sure everyone was paying close attention. "We will start today with this shortest stick. But over the course of the next few days, we will meditate through ever longer sticks of incense. You will soon find that you can lose yourself in an entire stick."

Ah, but Vessel could not do it. And practice did not help. If it was not the cramp in his leg, then it was the mosquito buzzing in his ear. As his fellow novices seemed to maintain perfect composure, Vessel fought an interior war with his body, which raged to move, to scratch, to flinch. His eyes would not stay trained on the incense. His mind would not stop wandering. The ever-longer sticks did not deliver endurance, but merely increased his agony. The ordination officer sighed and shook his head at all the squirming. It was expected that some of the novices would not be able to complete the training. And yet, Vessel stubbornly endured each session. He had to stay at the monastery that housed Silver Crane.

His relief would come when the officer rapped a wooden

board to signal the start of a serpentine chanting session. At last, the novices could unfold their knees. They lined up in a pattern that had taken several days to get right, and then marched around the central Buddha altar and looped out into the courtyard, weaving back and forth, all the while chanting the Buddha's name and following the pace set by the officer with his fish drum and mallet. The pace went faster and faster until the novices were trotting, and it was hard to suppress gleeful smiles as they bobbed among each other. Then with two raps on the board and one on the bell, everyone came to a halt. They all reassembled in formation in the courtyard and began the ritual martial exercises for which the Central Peak region of the Song Mountain Range is famous. While Tripitaka was known locally for its ordination platform, Song Mountain was heralded throughout the Middle Kingdom for the fighting monks of Shaolin Temple. No matter which particular temple they called home, all the monks on Song Mountain practice the shadow boxing routines designed at Shaolin as a way for monks of the Chan sect to stretch their cramped legs and limber up.

With the ordination ceremony only a few days away, the monk elders expected perfection in all the Chan attributes.

"Show us that you are prepared for the next step," they admonished again and again. "We will soon decide who among you will be permitted to step onto the altar and take the final vows of an ordained monk."

This warning was ringing in Vessel's ears as he came running, late again, to the final meditation practice session. Out of breath and overheated, Vessel fell at the feet of the ordination officer and bowed his forehead all the way to the ground.

"Officer, it could not be helped," he said.

"And why is that?" the officer asked dryly.

Vessel looked up but remained on his knees. The explanation came tumbling out. "Officer, it is because I am required to make the shadow measurements with Master Crane when the sun reaches its zenith. I cannot leave before this is done, and yet the afternoon meditation sessions now start too early. I cannot make it back in time and Master Crane will not allow me an exemption, not even for the final ordination preparations. I wonder, Officer, if you could speak to him about this?"

The officer gulped. He shook his head several times and gazed down at the novice before him.

"Master Crane?" he asked.

Vessel nodded briskly.

"Silver Crane?"

Vessel nodded again.

"You have been meeting him every day?"

Vessel sat back on his haunches. "Officer, I have been working with him for the entire summer — since the night I first arrived at Tripitaka, when he brought me safely out of the rain and into his room beside the observatory tower."

"But this is not possible."

Vessel did not know what to say.

"Get up, get up," the officer urged, reaching down to pull the novice to his feet. "We must inform the others at once."

The pair headed off. Inside the classroom the students remained in their places, hands folded in their laps. At the sound of the receding steps one or two leaned forward to peer out the door. "What do we do now?" one of them finally asked.

Meanwhile, Vessel mutely followed the officer back to a garden veranda inside the abbot's quarters, where he was told to wait. Vessel was left alone to admire the huge red hibiscus blooms and listen to the songbirds twittering in their delicate cages under the eaves. He ignored these pleasures, his ears straining instead to hear the senior monks, who were in a heated discussion in the next room. After some time, they filed out — the rector, the steward, the instructor, the bursar, and finally the ordination officer. They formed a dignified quintet in flowing robes and took seats facing the novice.

"Young novice — tell us again your name," said the rector, who had a long mustache and wore a lotus hat.

"Senior Master, this insignificant novice is Vermillion Vessel, of Tiger Empress Temple in Hao," Vessel answered.

"And what time would you normally meet with, well, our former Master Crane?"

Vessel stared back at the rector. "The former Master Crane?"

The ordination officer leaned forward and cleared his throat. "Silver Crane was one of our ordination officers, the same position I hold now, but he left years ago and we were told that he had died. It appears that you have been working for a ghost."

The rector ignored Vessel's look of shock and pressed on with his questions. "What time do you normally meet him?"

"During the day, as the sun approaches its zenith over the tower," Vessel murmured. "During the night, after the second bell of the night watch sounds."

The five glanced at each other and conferred briefly. Vessel continued to sit stiffly on his stool. "It doesn't make any sense," he thought to himself. "Is Master Crane some kind of immortal?" Vessel was uncomfortable in this interrogation setting and was beginning to feel it had been a mistake to reveal his work at the observatory.

The instructor, who had a fresh complexion and was the youngest of the monastery leaders, regarded Vessel with a solemn gaze. He explained, in a kind but careful tone, "Novice, we need to understand why Silver Crane has felt the need to return to our monastery as a ghost."

The others nodded their heads. The rector pointed his finger at Vessel. "Above all," he said, "we need you to ask Crane a most important question." The rector paused, and now all five of the monks looked intently at Vessel, drilling into him with their eyes the critical nature of their request. "We need for you to ask Crane who among us should take hold of the abbot staff at Tripitaka? We need the guidance of Silver Crane."

Hours later, when Vessel stepped out of his dorm into the moonless night, he found the five senior monks holding oil lamps and assembled in silence, waiting for him.

"Oh," Vessel blurted out, not having realized that he was going to have an escort.

They shushed him and then urged him forward. Vessel nodded obediently and set off. He stopped when he reached the observatory courtyard gate.

"Will you be going in with me?" he asked.

The monks shook their heads. The one wearing the lotus cap whispered that they would await his return.

So Vessel left them there, lit his candle, and entered the courtyard. He could dimly make out the form of Crane, standing with his cane as usual in the shadows at the back of the tower.

"Crane is not a ghost," Vessel whispered to himself.

But his chest welled with sorrow, because he knew the five senior monks at his back irrevocably changed everything. Vessel felt sure that the many nights he and the old astronomer had spent in leisurely study of the heavens had just been snatched up into a memory, a thing of the past.

Crane's mouth set in a grim line when the flickering candle came close enough to reveal Vessel's forlorn, and slightly apprehensive, expression. "The temple officers have finally realized what we've been doing back here?"

Vessel nodded.

The old monk looked back at the courtyard gate. "Do they think I can't see them peeking?"

Vessel grinned. Crane gestured for the two to walk around to the front of the tower, where they could not be watched from the gate. They climbed the wide observatory stairs, as if it were any other night. At the top Vessel blew out his candle and the pair leaned companionably against the back wall of the platform, gazing up as always at the heavens. The night was peaceful and still, ruffled by an occasional breeze of refreshingly cool night air.

"Master, they want to know why you are here."

Crane frowned. He turned his face eastward, looking back over the monastery grounds at the horizon.

"Since the first night we spent up here, I have paid close attention to the Five Barons," he said.

Vessel nodded.

"In all that time, you have noted how the fifth baron has remained the dim star of the constellation. Well, the reason I have been so interested in this is because that baron correlates with the emperor's Bureau of Astronomy. When that star is dim it means the work of the imperial astronomers is being neglected."

Vessel turned around so that he could get a better look at the barons. In the early evening of his first night with Crane, he had watched the barons set to the northwest. Now, in the middle of the night almost two months later, he could see them rising from the northeast.

"Then, it is not simply that the fifth baron is a dim star?" Vessel asked.

"No!" Crane replied with vehemence, using both hands to rap his cane on the floor of the platform. "When I worked here with Master Guo, the fifth baron flamed bright white! In those times, when we would finish our work, Master Guo would sometimes take out his flute and dedicate songs to that star. When I look at it now, I can still hear his melodies ringing in my ear. But tonight the baron is dull and almost indiscernible, as he has been for some time. His health reflects the state of record-keeping here and at the court in the capital. It grieves me to have to endure the baron's reproach night after night." The Crane reached for Vessel's shoulder, grasping it urgently, his eyes wide and imploring as he faced his young student. "How can the emperor rule if he does not maintain his calendar? How can the records be referred to if they are filled with blanks and lapses? That is not how sky watching is done."

Vessel nodded, reciting softly the line he had learned from Master Crane himself, "The heavens give a gradual and cumulative perspective to those who are patient and seek confirmation."

"Exactly!" Crane smiled broadly, releasing his hold on the novice's robe. "I left here in anger years ago because the record-keeping was sorely neglected under the most recent abbot — a man of no intellect who could not connect the stars with the work of a Buddhist monastery. It's as if he could only appreciate a thing if it had the phrase "Oh venerable Buddha" written across it. Why, the monks these days treat this area as if it were a storage shed!" Pushing such vexing images away with the flick of his hand, the old monk stroked his beard and added, "But then recently I heard that the old abbot had died. Contrary to what you were told, I myself was still quite alive when I learned of that."

Vessel burst out laughing. "But the ordination officer said he had heard that you were dead."

Crane raised an eyebrow. "It may be that I allowed such a rumor to be spread. I left Tripitaka and found a hermitage where I could meditate in peace. I tried to forget about the work that I had done here, but when I heard about the old abbot, I decided to return. Then I encountered you on the road back and knew it must be fate that brought us together. I resolved to study the sky with you and wait for the right moment to approach the temple leaders.

"Then shall we go back to them now?"

Crane slowly shook his head. He studied Vessel thoughtfully, drumming his fingers on the top of his cane. "I think that I shall remain a ghost."

Vessel frowned and cocked his head, waiting to see what this could mean.

"Yes, yes, I can be more effective as an immortal," Crane continued. "Novice, you have showed me how best to claim the attention of those who lead Tripitaka. They will pay far more heed to a ghost than an old monk."

This brought to mind another matter. Vessel felt inside his robe and pulled out his grandfather's talisman. "Well, then, ghost master, do you know enough to tell me what my grandfather carved on this chop holder? He used it to complete his charms, and it was passed from him to my mother to me. But I don't know what the pattern means. I did not think to ask my grandfather about it when I was a boy."

Crane took the lacquered box in his hand and studied its strange square markings. "Novice, you and I are Buddhist monks," he said. "This is some sort of Daoist magic writing. It means nothing to me."

He handed the box back to Vessel, but then slapped his palm on the platform railing at a sudden recollection. "You were headed to the Central Peak when we first met," he said. "That's a sacred Daoist mountain. Take your talisman to the Daoists at the Central Peak Temple. It's just down the road. They will know what to make of it."

"Ah," Vessel said. "And I remember now that you told me autumn is the best time to visit the Central Peak."

"Did I say such a thing?" Crane looked surprised. "I think I may have made that up. However, it is probably true. But never mind all that. Novice, I do not want you to leave this temple until you have completed two tasks. First, you must ensure that the temple will agree to keep the astronomical records."

Vessel dipped his head in assent.

"And second, you will complete the ordination."

Vessel took a step back, dismayed. "Master, I only went through the training so that I could spend time with you on the tower," Vessel said. "The ordination officer has not been satisfied with my progress."

But Crane was adamant. "Let me tell you something about ordinations at Tripitaka Monastery!" he began.

Vessel smiled to himself as the old monk set aside his cane and assumed his lecture posture of one hand folded behind his back and the other stroking his silky whiskers.

"Besides my own Master Guo, there is another astronomer who is also associated with this temple. Has the ordination officer bothered to tell you novices about the great Yi Xing?"

"You have mentioned Yi Xing, Master, but the ordination officer has not," Vessel replied.

Crane uttered a low curse under his breath which Vessel could not catch. "Yi Xing was from Nanle County to the northeast of here. He was a man of the Tang Dynasty, famed for his learning from the time he was young, but he chose to shave his head and he was ordained at this very monastery, a detail I withheld because I thought you should hear it first from your ordination officer. Well, the emperor learned of Yi Xing's great talents and invited him to court to translate Buddhist sutras into Chinese and also to adjust the calendar. Yi Xing died while he was still a young man and before his calendar work was finished, but he is forever memorialized here by the structure he built for this monastery. And do you know what that structure is?"

Vessel did not know.

"Why, it is the ordination platform!" Crane laughed in delight at the surprised look that crossed Vessel's face. "That's right! The old abbot of Tripitaka had no use for astronomy, as if it had no connection to the Three Jewels of the Buddha. As if Tripitaka's own famous ordination platform was not lovingly designed by an astronomer monk — the best kind of monk for big projects that require accuracy and measurement! That was the platform where I bowed down to take the bhiksu vows, and that is where I want you to bow down as well. The senior monks need to remember that opening one's spirit eye to the perfection of Nirvana does not require closing one's human eyes or turning away from cosmic calibrations."

Tears were still drying on his cheeks when Vessel reemerged through the courtyard gate. Hours had passed and dawn was approaching. Only one of the five escorts remained. It was the young instructor, who was seated with his back leaning into a corner, his legs sprawled out in front of him, sound asleep. Vessel stood looking down at the monk in the dim light, not sure if he should rouse him, but then the instructor shook himself awake and stood up, rubbing his face. This instructor had handsome features and a penetrating glance. Vessel thought he had the kind of fierce look that Master Guo was said to have. The instructor leaned back, regarding Vessel and taking in the significance of his red-rimmed eyes.

"You have had to say goodbye to your Master Crane?" he asked gently.

Vessel nodded and looked down. "I will miss him."

"To establish such a bond with a venerable ghost is no small thing," the instructor remarked. Then he yawned and stretched. "We should go."

When Vessel was confronted once again with the row of seated senior monks he remembered with chagrin that he had forgotten to ask Crane the question they all wanted answered. What a long night.

The rector, in his lotus hat, cleared his throat and got to the point.

"Well, young novice, who did Master Crane recommend as our abbot?" he asked.

Vessel stalled. "Honorable masters," he began. "Master Crane's concern is with the neglect of the astronomical records."

Vessel explained the work he had done for Crane and the reasons the old astronomer had given for keeping the records maintained. Vessel spoke slowly, watching the reactions of the monks facing him. He noticed that the rector started to frown as soon as the observatory records were mentioned, while the bursar seemed bored and the ordination officer looked skeptical. The aged steward appeared to be nodding off to sleep. Only the young instructor seemed to be listening closely. He leaned forward with his hands on his knees and his back straight.

"Yes, yes, that is all very interesting," the rector interrupted. "But I wonder about Master Crane's thoughts on the succession?"

The steward's eyes popped back open and there was a tense silence.

Vessel made his decision.

"Master Crane recommended the instructor," he said.

The instructor flashed a look of shock but quickly regained his composure. The other four turned to the chosen one and offered congratulations.

Vessel stood to leave, but realized he had better inform the monks of Crane's desire to have him ordained. The ordination officer snorted, but the instructor stood and placed both hands on Vessel's shoulders.

"To help the last disciple of Master Crane, himself the disciple of Master Guo, take vows at the altar built by Yi Xing — this will be a great honor for our monastery," he said. "We will assign you to the first group in the ceremony and I myself will oversee the preparation of your ordination certificate. And when the ceremony is finished, I will establish an officer in charge of maintaining the observatory records and submit his name to the court and assign to him a full roster of assistant monks. Tripitaka Monastery will never again let the astronomical records lapse."

14

DAOIST MONKS POKE FUN ON CENTRAL PEAK

Late summer of Correctness Attained, fifth year (1345).
Near Dengfeng, in modern Henan Province.

VESSEL HAD not felt so self-conscious since his first day in monk robes, back at Tiger Empress Temple. But that first shabby gown was nothing compared to the beautifully stitched and fitted full-length robe that the new Tripitaka Monastery abbot had presented earlier that morning, as a special gift, when Vessel had set off on his next journey. What is more, Vessel's head was lumpy from the incense scars branded into his scalp.

The ordination ceremony for Vessel's class was a solemn morning rite. The ordination officer nodded with satisfaction at Vessel, who recited the correct texts and maintained a straight line. When Vessel kneeled before the ordination altar and prepared to ascend it for the vows, he turned his attention from the sonorous chanting to the details of the altar itself. He took a moment to appreciate the beautiful gold and green hues of the glaze and the elaborate carving of the balustrades. He murmured a silent prayer of thanks to Yi Xing and Master Crane. Then Vessel rose and climbed the stairs, among the three in the lead group, to take his vows under the eyes of seven witnesses, including the new abbot.

PART TWO: VESSEL

Next came the branding ritual. This was done to banish distracting thoughts and also to show the willingness of the newly ordained to suffer pain for the sake of the Buddha and the faith. Vessel grimaced when the burning black cones of mugwort were crushed into his head. He had received the regular amount — three rows of three — and by the time the last mark was burned in, he felt dizzy. The branding occurred early in the day, immediately following the ordination ceremony, because it can result in a dangerous desire to sleep that must be walked off. Vessel and the others in his group were herded about the monastery in a long, merry walk, with older monks offering jokes and congratulations until at last everyone returned to the dining hall for a vegetarian feast.

That was three days ago, and the incense scars were still puffy and sore — it would be several weeks before they would fade into the silvery-white moon disks that mark the shaved heads of Buddhists monks. Vessel had resumed his wandering life and was on his way to Central Peak at last.

It took a half-day walk to reach Central Peak Temple, which sat at the base of the highest of the Seven Peaks of the Song Mountain Range. No attendant was at the main gate the afternoon Vessel arrived. So he passed unnoticed under the archway and through the huge wooden doors, which had been thrown open. He found himself in a grove of gnarled cypress trees. The gray bark swirled in fantastical patterns, this one looking like a dragon head, that one like a strutting peacock. Vessel ran his hands over the ridges in the knot of one particularly grand specimen. Its bark was smooth and dry. He wondered how old such a tree could be. Did this wise old one witness the rise and fall of the Song? Could it tell stories from the Tang Dynasty? Vessel sat to rest in the tree's wide swath of shade and idly watched a pair of red-billed magpies flick their long blue tails as they strutted about the ground. He pulled out the talisman from under his stiff new robe, examining anew the strange engraving on the cover. He slid it open to check on the red seal paste and chop inside. "Well," he said aloud, "I came here to find out what my grandfather made."

Wandering deeper into the temple, Vessel found a pair of Daoists playing cards inside a pavilion. As he approached, they leaned back from their game and turned their attention on him.

"A lumpy-headed Buddhist, with pockmarks to match," observed one.

"Monk, you are confused, your incense scars are too fresh. You are in the wrong kind of temple," said the other. He wagged his top knot at Vessel. "See, we keep our hair."

Vessel held up his palms in submission. "Brothers, I wonder if you could tell me if you know what is carved onto my necklace?" He took off his talisman and held it out.

Clearly intrigued, a monk with long black sideburns took the lacquered box in his hands and studied it. He nodded his head and chuckled, handing it to his opponent in the card game, a monk with a full tuft of hair growing out of the mole in his right cheek. This one laughed too, and soon the pair was howling. Finally the one with the sideburns wiped away tears and addressed Vessel.

"Tell me something," he said. "What's that thing in the middle of your face?"

Vessel reached to touch his nose, confused. He did not answer.

"Yes, that," Sideburns said. "I'm wondering what you would call it?"

"Do you mean my nose?"

Now the pair fell back from their card game, unable to restrain their mirth. "Yes, yes, that's it!" Sideburns yelled out, holding onto his belly. "It's your nose! He does know that much!"

Vessel felt a rising sense of irritation. He had no idea what was so funny about his nose. "See here," he said. "I have wondered for a long time about this talisman, which my grandfather carved. I have been told to come to this temple to find out about it. I have traveled far to reach Central Peak. Please tell me what you know."

The monk with the tufted mole took pity on Vessel. Still shaking from laughter, he struggled to regain his voice. He pointed over his shoulder. "Go to the next gate and look for the stone tablet standing to your right," he said, dabbing away his tears. "See what you can see."

Armed with this cryptic advice, Vessel left the monks to their cards. In the distance, he saw another gate and headed in that direction. He could see mounted stone steles on both sides of the archway. Approaching, Vessel veered to the right, where the first and largest one was covered in a lengthy inscription. He stood close to it, narrowing his eyes to scrutinize all the carved characters. Vessel could only recognize one here and another there. As a whole, the text meant nothing to him. He tightened his mouth in frustration.

The other tablet was smaller and decrepit, lurching at an angle and weathered. No matter. As soon as Vessel saw it, the rest of the temple fell away. He sucked in his breath and reached out his hand to touch the carved image. This stele also had characters that Vessel could not read, but the stone slab was dominated by five patterns. The center one was exactly the image that was carved onto his talisman.

Vessel covered his face with his hands and rocked on his feet, too overwhelmed to even look at the stele. Then he pulled his hands away and took the talisman off of his neck, the better to compare the rough carving in the lacquer box lid with the pattern in the middle of the mounted tablet before him.

A wizened old Daoist with sparse yellowed teeth and white

hair teetered over the gate threshold, approaching from the opposite direction.

"Grandfather, please, please tell me what these patterns are for," Vessel cried out, running over to the monk and pointing at the stele.

The old man grinned and nodded helpfully, taking Vessel's arm and following him. "Eh, young Buddhist, why so excited?" He squinted at the place where Vessel was frantically gesticulating. "Wah, it is the tablet that shows the patterns for the five sacred mountains."

"Each of these patterns represents a mountain?" Vessel asked. The old Daoist nodded.

"And what about the one in the middle, this square one here with the swirls inside that look like eyes?" Vessel asked, reaching out to touch the pattern in the center at the heart of the stele inscription.

But the old man pointed first to the top left pattern and moved his hand in a circle, naming the ring of outer mountains: Mount Heng, the black tortoise of the north; Mount Tai, the green dragon of the east; Blessed Fire Peak, the vermillion bird of the south; and Mount Hua, the white tiger of the west.

Vessel could barely speak. "And the pattern in the center?"

"That is this mountain, the Central Peak of the Song Mountain Range," the old man replied.

Vessel exhaled. "The nose in the center of my face," he said softly.

"What's that?" the old Daoist asked.

"It doesn't matter," Vessel said. He handed the old man his talisman. "Is this a carving of the Central Peak? It was made by my grandfather."

The old monk took the box in his age-spotted hands and brought it to his face, peering closely at the design. He turned the box this way and that, catching the light and laughing softly to himself. "I have seen this once before," he muttered in a low tone, speaking more to himself than to Vessel. "Yes, yes, I remember this." The old monk looked up at Vessel and studied his face. "But you do not look familiar at all."

Vessel gaped, his heart thudding in his chest. After all this time and all these questions asked of so many different kinds of people, he had landed on a person who not only recognized the carving, but remembered the carver. Vessel dropped to his knees.

"Honored master, you cannot know how long I have been wanting to know about this talisman, which was made by my mother's father..." he began, but the old monk looked irritated and would not let Vessel remain on his knees. Vessel stood up. "My maternal grandfather said that I have the features of his clan."

"Your mother's father, you say." The old monk looked unconvinced, putting a finger to the side of his chin and regarding Vessel again. "I remember young Chen, though it was long, long ago that he visited us here and carved this chop box. I do not think you resemble him at all. You are not good looking. It must be the influence of your paternal line."

Vessel was too pleased with the sudden turn of events to take offense, especially since the old monk spoke matter-of-factly, with no malice.

"Come back to my room," the old monk said. "I will pour us some tea."

The two spent the afternoon and evening together, eating, drinking and reminiscing. The old Daoist, known as Weng, told Vessel everything he could remember about Grandfather Chen and the temple in the time of his visit.

"How did my grandfather end up here?" Vessel asked.

"After the Battle of Yashan, your grandfather was a lost soul.

He was far from home and devastated by the defeat at sea. He told us that he could not accept in his heart that the Song had fallen. He spent a long time wandering the countryside, like you have been doing. But he was not a monk, so he drank many bowls of wine. Eventually he found this place and we let him stay with us."

Monk Weng paused to take a drink of tea.

"We treated him badly. We told him he had only come to Song Mountain's Central Peak because he couldn't read and thought the 'Song' character for our mountain name was the same as the one used for the dynasty. And we teased him for being a Loyalist too. We reminded him that long before the Song lost everything to the Mongols, they lost half their kingdom to the Jin! Why, I brought your grandfather to the exact place where General Yue Fei had once kneeled, weeping."

"My grandfather talked to you about Yue Fei?" Vessel asked.

"Everyone here talks about Yue Fei all the time," the old monk said. "It is said that the great general visited the temple during his final campaign against the Jin invaders from the north."

Vessel thought of the lacquer carver's story about how Yue Fei was summoned back to the capital from that campaign, and executed.

"It's only been two hundred years since Yue Fei died," the old monk continued. "We are all still trying to understand what his life meant to us, because he was a great hero. I told your grandfather, as I tell everyone, that Yue Fei looked at the pair of fierce guardian statues on either side of the Martial Gate by the Great Shrine Hall and cried out that the temple generals were made of wood and mud, and yet were more successful than he would ever be at banishing evildoers. Yue Fei was martyred in the autumn of the next year."

"But wouldn't such a story have made my grandfather

angry?" Vessel protested.

"Your grandfather fought the Mongols just like Yue Fei fought the Jin, so your grandfather could not see the Northern tribes as anything but invaders and enemies. We monks wanted him to realize the Mandate of Heaven had been transferred to a new ruling house and there was nothing any of us could do to change that. The Jin never amounted to much, in my opinion, but the Mongols, why, they became the legitimate rulers of China. Your grandfather could continue to cherish the Song ideals of loyalty and bravery. But the Song era ended and will not return."

The old monk's brow furrowed and he nodded his head slowly, lost in his memories.

"These conversations with your grandfather — now that we speak of them again, I remember them so vividly. He and I spent a great many hours talking about all this, and I realize now that it helped us both understand what had been happening around us. Sometimes it takes time to make sense of big changes."

Monk Weng turned his gaze to Vessel.

"Maybe I do see your grandfather's face in yours," he mused. "Tell me again what became of him after he left here. And how it is that you arrived in this exact same place."

"Grandfather did not mention this temple to me," Vessel noted. "He told us many stories of his battles, especially the Battle of Yashan, but he did not talk about what followed or how he returned to the Huai River Valley."

"This does not surprise me," said Monk Weng. "He kept his inner struggles to himself."

Vessel laughed and slapped his thigh, "Now that I think of it, he would always say 'I learned it from the Daoists in the mountains' when people asked him about his charm writing. He meant the Daoists here!"

The old monk frowned. "But we do not write charms here,"

he objected. "Your grandfather must have learned that in the villages or from some hermit he encountered on his way home."

Finally Monk Weng yawned and said he was too old to talk so much and would have to revive himself with sleep. His room was tiny, but there was enough space for Vessel to unfold his sleeping mat. It was not long before the two fell asleep.

That night, Vessel dreamed that he was wandering outside the Daoist's chamber. He came upon Grandfather Chen sitting alone on the steps to the Martial Gate, where Vessel had found the Five Mountain True Patterns stele.

"Grandfather," Vessel whispered.

The old man's affectionate smile caused his hawk eyes to crease. "Grandson, you have scars on your head," he said, jutting out his iron chin.

Vessel held up the talisman. "Why did you carve your chop box with the image of this mountain?"

His grandfather would not answer. He started to fade away.

"Why?" Vessel shouted.

Suddenly Grandfather Chen was looming over Vessel, as bright and distinct as if they were standing in the daylight. His grandfather was reaching for the talisman around Vessel's neck, smiling. "There it is! My reminder of my lofty ideals and my unavoidable truths."

Vessel awoke. He sat up and pulled out his talisman, discernible in the dawn light. Glancing around the room, Vessel realized Monk Weng was gone.

"Monk Weng!" he called out urgently.

"I'm coming, I'm coming," the monk replied from the courtyard.

Vessel was relieved to see him shuffle back into the room.

"I dreamed of my grandfather," Vessel exclaimed, relating all that he could remember, and holding out the talisman.

PART TWO: VESSEL

The old man peered down at it. "I must say, it has held up well. Your grandfather worked hard on setting all those coats of lacquer, you know. It took a long time."

Vessel tucked the box safely back under his robes. "So what does it mean?"

Monk Weng frowned. "Tell me again what your grandfather said."

"He reached for the talisman and said, 'My reminder of my lofty ideals and my unavoidable truths."

Monk Weng nodded thoughtfully. "Then it is just as your grandfather told you. The talisman has lasted much longer than anyone expected, and I can see that it has been a great comfort for you, but you should not regard it as sacred or holy, because this piece of wood will not protect you from harm. All it can do is remind you of your grandfather and his struggle to understand his purpose. It is the same struggle that we all go through."

Monk Weng pursed his lips and nodded his head, thinking about the dream.

"I think your grandfather is trying to tell you that in these difficult times, when the landscape seems to be shifting and re-forming, and when great changes seem imminent, your role is to discern righteousness and follow it. That's what he means by his lofty ideals, the best aspects he saw in the Song Dynasty era."

"And his unavoidable truths?"

"Yes, what should we make of that?" Monk Wong pondered. "For him, this meant the unavoidable truth of the Song fall and the rise of the Mongols. But you will have your own obstacles to face, your own truths which cannot be avoided." The old Daoist sat back and shrewdly eyed his guest. "Perhaps one of these truths is that you are your grandfather's grandson."

Vessel did not know what to make of such a statement and could only nod his head, bewildered.

"What I mean to say is, maybe you have a martial fate."

Vessel waved his hands to dismiss such a thought. "My grandfather was not martial. He was the local diviner."

"When I knew him, your grandfather was a soldier who had lost his army. Maybe you will find it."

"I will not join the imperial army," Vessel exclaimed.

"I did not say that you would. The imperial army is now the Mongols. The very army your grandfather fought."

"Then what army would I possibly join?"

Monk Weng shrugged. "That will be your unavoidable truth, my young Buddhist."

15

TOSSING SHELLS ON CHIVE MOUNTAIN

Mid autumn of Correctness Attained, fifth year (1345). On Song Mountain in modern Henan Province.

HAVING REACHED the Central Peak, Vessel had no further destination in mind, so he stayed with the Daoists. But as the days slipped by, he felt a growing restlessness. He worried that his home temple might fall under the influence of the likes of Monk Peng. Vessel also wanted to visit his parents' grave and report to them all he had learned about Grandfather Chen. As the maple leaves started to redden, and after passing his seventeenth birthday, Vessel decided it was time to head back to Tiger Empress Temple.

"Your grandfather enjoyed using my divination shells when he was a visitor here," Monk Weng said as he accompanied Vessel out the main gate. "You ask a lot of questions, so I carved a pair for you to take."

Monk Weng pressed into Vessel's palm two pieces of wood, shaped like clam shells with the insides painted red. Delighted, Vessel immediately squatted on the dirt path to give them a try. Shaking the wooden shells, he asked Heaven, "Will I return to this place?"

Vessel released the shells. Monk Weng leaned on Vessel's

shoulder and squinted down at the heavenly response. "They have both landed face down," he declared. "You cannot see the red insides. It is a yin response. Unfavorable. Verify it with another shake."

Once more the shells scattered on the path and said no.

"It appears you will not return," Monk Weng said. "Very well. Toss them again, and this time I will ask the question."

Vessel shook the shells in his hands while the old monk directed his voice toward Heaven.

"From now on, will this foolish Buddhist be able to find the nose at the center of his face?"

Vessel laughed and released the cups, which landed on their curved backs, red insides facing up. Monk Weng looked them over and gave a sagacious nod.

"It is as I suspected," he said. "A yang response."

"A yang response is not a yes?"

"It is not! It means Heaven is mocking the question and will not reply. To receive a yes requires one side up and one side down. Yin-yang. A completion."

Monk Weng straightened his back and reached out to pat Vessel's arm.

"My young friend, don't forget about your nose. As you continue your travels, remember that you have been to the center. Sometimes the Ten Thousand Things are not as complicated as they may seem."

And so they parted.

Heading east from the Central Peak, Vessel traveled through the Yellow River Valley, skirting the city of Kaifeng. He spent the winter at a temple near Bo, where he visited the grave of a great general of the Three Kingdoms era. Turning south, he crossed back over the Huai River at Huaiyuan. It was not until shortly after his nineteenth birthday that he returned at last to his home temple in Hao Prefecture. He had wandered for almost three years.

At Tiger Empress, Vessel found the temple relatively unchanged. He did not miss the guest clerk, whose treachery had forced out so many of the monks, most of whom never returned. To Vessel's sorrow, his tonsure master, Balance, was also gone. Balance had taken leave of his temple duties to tend to his dying mother and handle her funeral and mourning arrangements, which could last for years. Abbot Virtue and his acolyte, Emptiness, remained at the temple, as did the librarian.

Jewel worked patiently to help Vessel copy sutras and gain from them a rudimentary skill with a writing brush. Months and seasons turned into two more years at the temple. Vessel, now a young man in his early twenties, copied out long sections from the Lotus Sutra and its commentaries. The Maitreya Buddha appears in the sutra's first chapter, wondering aloud at the powerful miracles made possible through meditation. Every time Vessel read this passage, it brought to mind his night in White Pine Village and the memory of how the Maitreya could be wielded to such alarming effect. Vessel wondered if, after all this time, the villagers were still waiting for the sign.

Again and again Vessel asked himself: "Do I have a martial fate? That would mean I would have to leave the temple." He had no intention of becoming a rabble-rousing monk like Master Peng and his disciples. He would leave the fold rather than corrupt it. "But I have no desire to leave this place."

This was the thought that most vexed him. Indeed, the same young man who had arrived so unwillingly at the Great Shrine Hall, the one who had wanted to flee back to Old Mother Wang and the familiarity of the farm fields rather than have his head shaved, now dreaded the thought of departure from his temple sanctuary. He knew that a martial fate would send him far from

Lone Hamlet.

"Soldiers do not stay in one place," he fretted. "When Grandfather Chen was a soldier, he ended up at the ends of the earth for the Battle of Yashan! But if I leave Lone Hamlet, I will not be able to tend my parents' graves."

Twice each year — at the spring Grave Sweeping Festival and at the fall Goddess of Mercy holiday — Vessel headed down from the temple to visit his family's gravesite. This was when he cleared away brush from the burial marker and made sacrifices of grain and fruit.

"I've gone with you to tend your parents' graves. I can do it by myself if you run off and leave us all," said Jewel one evening as they sat together in the Tiger Pavilion courtyard, trying to hear each other over the droning roar of the cicadas.

Jewel was the only person at the temple who Vessel trusted with his worries. Vessel gazed out at the late summer sky and noticed the first stars of the evening appearing on the horizon, which reminded him of his time at Tripitaka.

"I only had that one season with Master Crane. Six summers have passed since then, and yet I can remember my conversations with him so vividly."

"That's because he left you like the Yellow Crane," Jewel declared.

Vessel looked puzzled. "My master was called the Silver Crane."

"No, no, that's not what I meant," said Jewel, shaking his head. "I meant like in the poem — the crane that rode away with a Daoist immortal on its back, leaving everyone to wish for its impossible return. 'The yellow crane, once gone, will not return, while white clouds throughout the years float in the void.' You cherished your time with your master and so your memories of him remain vivid."

"Ah, yes," said Vessel, repeating to himself the line: 'The yellow crane, once gone, will not return.' His gaze returned to the evening sky. "I remember asking whether order could be restored in a time of bad omens. Master Crane replied with the evasion that he had learned from his own master, 'That depends on a number of calculations that have yet to be determined.' I learned that 'the heavens give a gradual and cumulative perspective to those who are patient and seek confirmation.' I learned that the stars have signaled Heavenly disfavor with the ruling house. But what use is it for me to know these things?"

"It will take time to understand," Jewel counseled.

"But it has already been six years and I still don't understand."

"But you have learned much here at the temple these past six years," Jewel insisted. "And the more you learn, the more you understand what you need to learn next."

"Do you think the Mongol era will end soon?" Vessel asked.

Jewel shrugged. "In the Grand Scribe's Records, it is said that 'When the moon reaches fullness, it begins to wane.' Maybe the Mongol era is waning. How are we to know such a thing?"

Vessel nodded, but he continued to dwell on his worries. "It may be that Lord Buddha is displeased with me."

"Vessel, you must focus on the Buddha's compassion..."

"Yes, yes, but there is a matter I have not told you about: I was supposed to ask Master Crane to select the new abbot for Tripitaka, and yet I forgot to raise this matter during our last conversation," Vessel frowned as Jewel waited patiently to hear the rest. "Then when all the senior monks were gathered around me, asking me this important question about the succession, I could see they needed an answer. And it seemed so obvious that the instructor was the only worthy candidate." Vessel paused and looked wide-eyed at his friend. "So I said Master Crane picked the instructor. And the instructor became the abbot."

Jewel gaped slightly. "You picked the abbot for Tripitaka Monastery?"

Vessel nodded again.

Jewel folded his arms. "The Five Precepts command us to abstain from speaking untruths," he said. "You should not have said that Master Crane told you something he did not tell you. It is better to say nothing than to say an untruth."

"But I felt confident that I knew the correct answer."

"Vessel, you are not like any monk I have ever met."

"I suppose I should have stayed silent, but I also know that I picked the correct abbot for Tripitaka," Vessel reasoned. "I had spent enough time with Master Crane by that point to know his wishes. And I believe that Lord Buddha guided me to cross paths with Master Crane." Vessel leaned forward to add more wood to the small brazier at their feet. "Master Crane taught me to think differently about things. I am lucky to have had two wise old men as my teachers."

"I am not a wise old man."

Vessel looked up with surprise. "I did not say you were."

Jewel threw his hands in the air. "But you just said you've had two wise old men help you think things through."

"I meant Master Crane and Monk Weng, the old Daoist at Central Peak."

"And what about me?"

Vessel laughed and gestured happily at his old friend. "Yes, you are right. I have had two wise old men and one young librarian," he said, holding out first two and then three of his fingers.

"One wise young librarian," Jewel noted, with an emphasis on the second word.

"Maybe so, but you are as fussy as an old man."

It was not long afterwards that Jewel was invited to join a

Goddess of Mercy printing project at a prestigious monastery to the east. The morning of his departure, Jewel again advised patience.

"Take refuge in the Heart Sutra, which drives away evil thoughts, and also in the Diamond Sutra and its lessons on living without attachment," he said, placing a hand on Vessel's shoulder for emphasis. "Continue to copy the characters. Putting ink to paper brings its own kind of clarity. You will find the answers you need soon enough."

While Jewel was gone, Vessel vowed to set aside time each evening to empty his mind into calligraphy. For a few weeks he succeeded, picking a single character or phrase to focus on at each session, copying over and over until his concerns and worries faded into the weight and balance of each stroke. The black ink was unforgiving against white paper. It did not tolerate the wandering mind. By the end of a good session, Vessel could sit back and admire characters that were balanced and confident.

And yet, the Buddhist sutras could not calm the restive stirrings around Tiger Empress.

"If Monk Weng guessed right that I have a martial fate," Vessel wondered, "how will I recognize when it is time to become a soldier?"

Not wanting to know the answer, Vessel clung all the more fervently to the routines of monastic life and to perfecting his calligraphy. He sought to shut out signs of disorder, but the news of turmoil and disruption trickled steadily into the temple.

"The court wants to tame the Yellow River by digging a new channel, but they want to do it by conscripting all the men in the Huai valley!" visitors to the temple exclaimed.

"Take my son to be a novice," mothers begged, pushing forward young men who had reached conscription age.

"The channel diggers have risen up at Huangling and killed

their Mongol overseers!"

"The villages in Xiangyang and Nankang are burning!"

"The rebels have taken control of Yexian!"

Then one afternoon, Vessel heard an unusual tune being whistled in a temple courtyard. He followed the sound, which led him to a young man hauling in a delivery of supplies from Hao. Vessel asked about the melody. The young man broke into song:

> The imposing Great Yuan
>> held such beguiling power.
> They sought a canal but abused the men
>> and dug the chaos in.
> The laws they are too harsh,
>> the punishments extreme.
> When all are devoured and the wealth is gone,
>> who in the end will win?
> Bandits become officials,
>> the virtuous mix in with the fools.
> Now is the time for the Maitreya to come,
>> the time for the red turban.

The young man finished and stood with his hands on his hips, looking triumphantly back at Vessel.

"What do you mean by 'red turban'?" Vessel asked.

"Wah, you monks don't know anything," the young man scoffed. "When the channel diggers rebelled, it is said that they all tied red turbans around their heads."

"But why red?"

"It is also said that among the Five Elements, the rebels worship fire," the young man replied. Then he picked up his shoulder pole and left, still humming the tune.

At about that same time, the monks noticed that visitors to

Tiger Empress were ignoring the Great Shrine Hall, focusing their prayers and donations instead on the Maitreya image near the front gate. A strange monk appeared from the town of Ying, to the west, and registered with the guest clerk. This new wanderer showed no inclination for prayers or temple work and Vessel assumed he would soon be on his way. Instead, Vessel found him lecturing from the steps of the tiger statue pavilion. Vessel looked at the intent audience of young monks and felt his heart race with alarm. This was not right. This was a strange place for a lecture. The speaker had his back to Vessel, but his voice was loud enough that Vessel could hear him clearly.

"The Maitreya will soon descend, that is what the channel diggers along the Yellow River learned! They saw with their own eyes the fiery King of Light, the one who heralds the Maitreya descent!"

As soon as he heard the word "Maitreya" Vessel stormed up to the pavilion.

"You there!" he called out aggressively, "were you a conscript at the Yellow River?"

"Monks are not conscripted," the wanderer haughtily retorted.

"Then how is it that you know about the channel diggers and what they saw?"

The wandering monk gave Vessel an icy stare.

"Come with me," Vessel demanded.

Vessel was no longer a lowly verger who could be ignored. The wanderer from Ying had no choice but to follow him to the abbot's quarters. A long discussion followed, with Vessel asking pointed questions designed to reveal the visitor's true intentions to Abbot Virtue.

After the next meal, the abbot, his acolyte and Vessel escorted the guest from Ying to the temple gates.

"We love the Maitreya and pray for his descent," Abbot Virtue explained in a kind and patient voice. "But we know the Future Buddha has nothing but compassion for our suffering. There is no room for revenge in his belly, only laughter at that which is laughable. That is why he is also known as the Laughing Buddha."

"I came here to offer a righteous Maitreya service, as I have done in temples across this prefecture," the guest complained. "You are fools to turn me down."

Vessel opened his mouth to retort, but was silenced by sharp glance from the abbot.

"We are too humble a temple and would not dare host such a grand service," the abbot demurred. "You are too kind to make such an offer."

The guest snorted with contempt. He turned his back to Tiger Empress Temple and left without another word.

Abbot Virtue shook his staff, clinking its metal rings to chase away bad karma. He reached for Vessel's sleeve. "Go and lock the doors to our Maitreya Hall," he urged.

Two days later, the temple secretary summoned Vessel to the abbot's chambers.

"Tell Vessel what you just told me," Abbot Virtue instructed the secretary.

"Venerable Master, while I was leaving town to run errands in the village, a young man rode up to me on horseback and asked if I was from Tiger Empress," the secretary said, holding up a sealed envelope. "Then he gave me this letter. It was on a deserted part of the road. I don't think he wanted anyone to see us talking. He asked if I knew a large, pockmarked monk with a name I did not recognize. But I think he meant our brother Vessel."

The abbot nodded. "He wanted to give this letter to 'the pockmarked monk'?"

"Yes, and he is waiting for a reply. He says that for our own protection he dares not be seen going to and from the temple, but he will wait in the village until sunset. He told me where to send the reply."

The secretary handed the letter to Vessel, bowed to the abbot, and left.

Abbot Virtue poured tea for himself and Vessel. He blew on his cup to cool the steaming brew as he watched Vessel open the letter.

"It is from an old friend of mine from Lone Hamlet," Vessel exclaimed. His expression grew grim as he read through to the end. "Master, the rebellion has come to Hao," he said quietly. He set the letter down. "Rebels from Ding have taken over the walled city and one of their leaders is surnamed Guo. My old friend from the village has joined this leader and thinks I should join him, too."

The abbot frowned. "Your friend knows you are a monk, but he thinks you should join a rebellion?"

Vessel shrugged, not knowing how to explain that Harmony Tang likely found it hard to believe Vessel was a serious monk. "We herded goats together as boys and he taught me how to ride a horse. I did not think back then that I would become a monk."

"Is he trying to lure you into trouble?"

"Oh no, not this friend," Vessel assured his abbot. "We played at war as boys and now he wants me to come join him for the real fight. He says his commander would welcome me."

The abbot leaned forward and spoke urgently. "My son, you must be careful in how you reply to a letter like this."

Vessel stood up. "I will go to the village and talk this over with my friend..."

But Abbot Virtue adamantly shook his head. "We were given instructions on how to reply and your friend seems to think it dangerous for you to be seen down in Lone Hamlet talking with him. The secretary will take your reply."

Vessel sat back down. He murmured, more to himself, "I have been expecting some kind of sign. But this, this is not it." He wished fervently that he could discuss the letter with Jewel, but Jewel had not yet returned from his printing project.

"I will write a quick reply."

"You only need to acknowledge that you received his letter."

"Yes, that is what I will do. I will thank him and tell him I received his letter and nothing more."

The abbot sighed with relief as he gestured for Vessel to take a seat at his writing desk.

Days passed and rumors flew up from the village about the rebellion in Hao. Units of the imperial army had begun to assemble on the north bank of the Huai. The rebels had closed all the Hao gates and were said to be preparing for a long siege.

Consumed with worries about the dwindling food supply at the temple, Vessel forgot about the letter from Harmony until he was startled one evening by a young monk, who was calling and waving at him from the end of a hallway.

"Elder brother, come quickly!"

"What now?" Vessel murmured to himself, irritated at the young monk's display of urgency. But as the monk drew near, Vessel could see fear in his eyes.

"Elder brother, there is a man on horseback at the gate calling for you, using your former name."

"My former name?"

"Were you not once called Fortune Zhu?"

Vessel nodded as he turned to stride in the direction of the front gate, the young monk scurrying along at his side.

"Elder brother, there is something else…"

Vessel looked over but did not slow his pace.

"Elder brother, this man," the young monk stammered.

"What is it?"

"Elder brother, this man is dressed like a soldier and he has a red turban tied around his head."

Vessel broke into a run.

He found Harmony holding the reins for his large black mount and standing next to the well in the front courtyard, where a group of monks was rushing to draw a bucket of water. More and more brothers were spilling into the courtyard.

"Harmony!" Vessel called out.

His old friend looked up. The Number One Stallion under Heaven flashed a smile of recognition, a handsome boyish grin that Vessel knew so well and that carried memories of childhood adventures.

Then Harmony's expression turned serious. "Tiger Empress Temple is the target of a raiding party," he announced. "The men are already on their way and could arrive at any moment." Harmony gestured at the assembling brothers. "You all need to leave at once."

Harmony set the water bucket in front of his horse and adjusted his saddle before turning to face Vessel.

"Fortune, my friend, it is good to see you but we are in trouble," he said, lowering his voice. "It is complicated back in Hao. The Red Turbans are fighting with each other, and your reply to my letter was stolen from my barracks. I should have burned it, but I did not. Now the enemies of my commander have your name and the name of your temple. They consider you to be my recruit and they suspect your temple is now allied with my commander."

"But I did not say that I was going to join you," Vessel whispered back, indignant. "I merely thanked you for the invitation."

"That was enough. My commander's enemies already knew this temple closed its Maitreya Hall. Your letter offered them an excuse to send out a raiding party. They intend to destroy Tiger Empress so that my commander will no longer be able to attract recruits."

Vessel pinched his chin. "What should I do?"

"You cannot stay here," Harmony replied, "and if you leave and are caught wandering alone outside these temple walls, the imperial troops will assume you are going to join the rebellion. When I learned you were at Tiger Empress I wrote to invite you to join me, but now my invitation has put you in danger. I did not mean for this to happen."

Harmony jumped up into his saddle. He pulled a red cloth from his pack and threw it down. "Tie this like mine and jump on my horse. I will take you to Commander Guo. My leader will be your protector."

Vessel caught the cloth in his palms, staring down at it.

"Fortune, I am a Red Turban now, and so are the men headed this way, but they are a rival band," Harmony continued. "My leader is not like the other Red Turbans. He is the only one who seeks righteous change."

Vessel flinched. Could this be the sign?

"Come with me now, Fortune," Harmony urged. He extended his hand.

Vessel instinctively reached up to grasp it. As one hand locked its grip, the other, the one holding the red turban, stretched toward the saddle. His thigh muscles flexed for the jump that would send him up and into the seat behind Harmony. With one easy motion, he could leave the temple and gallop away.

PART TWO: VESSEL

"Vessel!"

A voice called behind him. As he turned back, summoned by his religious name, his glance took in the flurry of activity spurred by Harmony's warning. Emptiness was calling to him, needing help with some task. Vessel exhaled and smiled at the monk he had known since the first day he entered the temple. Vessel's leg muscles slackened. He released his grip.

"Harmony, I will keep hold of this red turban, but I cannot abandon my brothers or my abbot to raiders."

Harmony's horse tossed its head. "Then get your brothers away from here and come find me as soon as you can. Once they are settled, if you can make it to the city gates, I can bring you to my commander," said Harmony, his expression grave. "Fortune, pray for guidance over your fate and I will pray that I will soon be greeting you in Hao."

Then Harmony clicked his tongue and rode away.

Vessel hurried back through the dim passages to gather his satchel. He returned to the main courtyard at the same time that Abbot Virtue appeared. All the frantic chatter stopped as the monks turned expectantly to see what Vessel would do. He slung his satchel over one shoulder, bowed before the abbot and said, "Master, I can lead the way if you are ready."

Abbot Virtue gazed slowly across the courtyard. He pressed his palms together and raised them to his forehead, offering a silent reminder of the boundless protection of the Buddha. Then he nodded to Vessel, acknowledging his assent to flight.

Vessel took the abbot's arm and together they walked out of the temple refuge. The others scrambled behind, clutching handfuls of belongings as they stepped over the main gate's high threshold. The last two closed and barred the massive wooden leaves of the main gate before slipping out a hidden side-door and running to catch up.

As the monks crossed the long clearing in front of the exterior gate, they heard the shouts from below of the approaching Red Turbans making their way up the hillside. Vessel motioned for his brothers to hide behind a dense stand of fir trees. They crouched down in their gray and tea-brown robes, peering through the deepening shadows at the path to their temple.

The rebels stormed by on horseback, most with ragged red sashes tied across their foreheads. Several carried torches, and one pair drove an ominously empty wagon. The stragglers lurched drunkenly in their saddles.

Reining to a halt at the gate, the band's leader shouted, "Tiger Empress Temple, open your doors! We have come to bring you Enlightenment!"

When nothing happened, the leader ordered his men to scale the walls and open the gate from the inside.

"Head for the granary and supply rooms and set your torches to anything we can't carry out."

It was not long before the burning wood and thatch brightened the sky overhead. Vessel crawled forward to get a better look at the temple walls. "They are burning the dormitory," he whispered. He and the others stayed in the underbrush transfixed, frozen witnesses of ruin, as the wind gusted in their direction, raining down ashes. Some of the monks wept softly; Abbot Virtue ran his fingers over prayer beads, murmuring sutras.

"We need to go," Vessel finally urged, blinking smoke from his eyes and gagging on the thick, acrid fumes. "It will take them time to load up their wagon."

The monks moved as quickly as they could down the hillside, Emptiness and another monk gripping the abbot's elbows. They passed through the Tang Family Settlement, which had already been torched. Covering their faces with their sleeves, they stumbled through the smoldering ruin. The abbot continued to chant sutras. Some of the brothers chanted with him as the frantic procession swayed and groped along the rope bridge, the same bridge that Vessel had once been carried across on his brother's back after being beaten nearly to death by Old Wolf. The line of monks skirted Lone Hamlet, and soon turned onto a smaller and safer footpath. At last their pace slowed to a steady walk. The waning moon rose before them, offering its light as the frogs croaked and the metal rings on the top of the abbot's staff jingled. The monks shuffled past fields and marshes, heading southeast toward the Three Peaks range.

Leading the procession during the flight from the Red Turbans, with Abbot Virtue directly behind him, Vessel had glanced whenever possible at the starry heavens, mulling over his conversation with Harmony. As he scanned the Black Tortoise region of the sky, he saw an unusually bright gliding star enter the same constellation that governed the region of Hao.

"It is a summons! The stars are calling on me to stop."

In the moonlight, he realized that the hillside in the distance — at the point in the horizon where the star had fallen — was Chive Mountain, the place that he had first visited with Harmony as a goat herder. They had escaped bandits there once before, with help from the monks at Chanku Temple.

After stepping gingerly on rotting planks over a brook and proceeding for some time without rest, Vessel stopped the procession at a fork in the road and turned around.

"Everyone wait here," he instructed. "We are near a back entrance to the temple at the foot of Big Sister Mountain. I will run ahead and make sure all is safe there."

Vessel sprinted alone along the forest path and concentrated on his task. It was not long before he had roused the sleeping gate guard and returned with him to his brothers waiting nervously at the forked road.

Taking a deep breath, Vessel dropped to his knees and bowed three times at Abbot Virtue's feet.

"Venerable Master," he said, trying not to let his voice break, "the gate guards will take you to their temple, where you will be well cared for. This temple is much smaller than ours, and it is hidden in the caves so it is hard to find, but I know some of the monks there and I trust them. The gate attendant has assured me that no Red Turbans have disturbed the peace of their halls."

The abbot waited briefly. "But, my son, you speak as if you will not be joining us down this path. How can that be?"

Still kneeling, Vessel could not speak. He slowly shook his head, his upturned face lit by the moon. He took a deep breath. "I will take the other path," he said in a voice that was hardly louder than a whisper.

"My son, I will not leave you here alone in the dark."

"But, Master, I cannot continue with you," Vessel said, his voice gaining strength from his own resolve. "And I know this place. It is the area of the cave grottoes. I want to go on alone to contemplate my fate."

The other brothers anxiously crowded forward. Abbot Virtue remained still for some time, leaning on his staff. Finally he spoke.

"You feel certain?" he asked. "You feel called to do this?"

Vessel nodded. "I am certain."

Abbot Virtue placed a palm on Vessel's shaved head and intoned: "Take refuge in the Buddha, take refuge in the teaching, take refuge in the disciples."

Then the abbot reached for Vessel's arm and drew him to his feet. For the second time that evening, Vessel found himself taking the hand of someone he trusted, someone who wanted to guide him away from danger. And yet, the gliding star could not be ignored. Vessel said farewell over and over again as his brothers, some weeping, filed past. As the monk robes brushed by and hands reached out to touch him one last time, Vessel could hear the voice of his mother reciting a poem:

> Cut, it doesn't break,
> Straightened, it still tangles,
> This sorrow of separation,
> It is no ordinary flavor in the heart.

Exhausted, smelling of soot, uncertain of his future, his mind dwelling on Harmony's advice, Vessel turned away alone and slipped into a damp mountain cave. Unrolling his mat, he fell into a deep sleep.

After a few hours, Vessel emerged from the cave to follow a footpath through narrow limestone passageways that opened onto a secluded pavilion overlook. Though the wooden railings had benches built into them, Vessel did not use them, sitting instead on the stone floor, his back to the entrance, gazing out through the latticework at the predawn sky. Vessel watched the Triple Terraces constellation, the asterism his Grandfather Chen had worshiped, set to the west. The stars faded into the morning sunlight. Uncrossing his legs and reaching into a pocket of his robes, he pulled out his wooden divination shells from Monk Weng.

Vessel kneeled on the pavilion's hard paving stones and held the shells in his hands, clasped tight against his chest. He closed his eyes to the beautiful morning. This was a perilous moment and Vessel could risk no errors. He decided to address his divination questions to Lord Guan Yu, the red-faced god of war and righteousness, who served as the guardian deity for Tiger Empress.

"I am afraid," he began. "In this, the twelfth year of the 'Correctness Attained' reign period, disorder is everywhere. As you know, Lord Guan Yu, the Red Turban rebels have killed the magistrate and chased away the officials so that now they control the Hao city walls and gates. The imperial army has arrived to take Hao Prefecture back from the Red Turbans."

Vessel paused and adjusted his knees.

"To go out on the roads is to risk being seized by greedy men, who will tie a red cloth around my head, declare me a rebel, and hand me over to the imperial army for a reward," he continued. "If not that, I fear capture by one of the worst of the bands of rebels. How am I to tell the righteous ones from the mere bandits? Now, my Lord knows that I have already lost my parents and most of my family to famine and plague. I am an orphan who became a monk, and now the rebels have burned down our temple. Lord Guan Yu, I have no place to go."

Vessel cleared his throat and focused on the image of Lord Guan Yu, dressed in armor and holding aloft his crescent-moon blade, the Green Dragon. He formed his first set of questions.

"Lord Guan Yu, perhaps I could take up the begging bowl again and wander? Or should I stay put? If you think I might stay in this place and watch over my abbot and what is left of our temple, I ask that you reply to my toss of the divining shells with one yin and one yang. If, on the other hand, escape from this region of turmoil is the right path, then reply with a yang-yang answer."

Vessel shook the shells. He released them on the paving stones. The little carved wooden cups landed red side down without even a clatter. A yin-yin reply. Inauspicious.

Vessel sat back on his heels and pondered how to frame his second throw. "Lord Guan Yu, you have dismissed both of my suggestions. I will try again, hoping this time for an answer."

PART TWO: VESSEL

He gathered the shells back up in his hands, shook them, touched his clasped hands to his forehead in supplication, and released his second throw. Again, both cups clamped face down to the pavilion floor, like magnets to iron. A clear yin-yin. His third, the last allowed for this question set. Another yin-yin.

Vessel stood up. He backed away from the toss. Reaching into his bag, he took out some sticks of incense, which he lit and wedged into cracks in the railing. Vessel breathed in the fragrant smoke, a soothing aroma, which curled upward and wafted away with the breeze. He resumed his kneeling position and gathered the divining shells once again. He tried a different question.

"Lord Guan Yu, do you desire that I embark on something new? Have you seen that the net-ropes of this dynasty's rule have come untied, leaving confusion and disorder throughout the land? If it is time for me to join the rebels who seek to clear away the Mongols, I ask that you reply with a yin-yang."

He dropped the shells. One fell flat, the same as the other tosses, with the red side down. The other landed on its back, red side up. Yin-yang. Favorable.

Now Vessel dropped his face in his hands. The bold appearance of the expected answer tore away his composure. Vessel groped for the divining shells and prepared for a second throw.

He trembled as he pleaded, "Lord Guan Yu, what you ask of me is certain to bring me even more suffering and misfortune. I know nothing of warfare. Surely rebellion is not the path meant for me? Make my decision for me, I beg you. Reply with a yin-yin answer, and so tell your servant that rebellion is not favored by Heaven. Let me stay a simple monk."

Holding the shells in his right hand, he reached with his left for the leather thong around his neck, pulling the red lacquered talisman out from under his robe and grasping it tightly. Then he released the shells. One skittered along the stones and bounced clear out of the pavilion to the underbrush beyond the railing.

"Returning to the earth. Yin."

The other spun wildly and refused to land, finally coming to rest in a most peculiar vertical position that was neither yin or yang, something Vessel had never seen before. He dropped on all fours to peer at this bizarre sight, unable to comprehend how the shell could be so balanced. It stood upright, as if held in place by the invisible fingers of Lord Guan Yu himself. Vessel reached out to touch the red interior, but just as his index finger neared it, the shell tipped gently back in a yang reply.

"Lord Guan Yu has given me a miracle to assure my comprehension," Vessel whispered, overwhelmed. "You want me to join the rebellion." He crouched in silence, gazing at the shell. "I will proceed. I will present myself at the Hao city gates. If there truly is a righteous leader among the Red Turbans, I will find him. If there is not, I will form a band myself to seek righteous change. Lord Guan Yu, my time in monk robes has come to an end."

16

THE MONK RAISES A RED TURBAN

Spring of Correctness Attained, twelfth year (1352). Outskirts of the walled city of Hao in modern Anhui Province.

VESSEL SPENT THE next few nights on Chive Mountain, observing the skies. He divined that the first day of the intercalary month would be the best day to set off for Hao. That morning he thanked the old hermit who cared for the mountain caverns and departed.

Near the bottom of the mountain, Vessel reached a crossroads, and recognized it as the place where he had turned away from Abbot Virtue and his monk brothers during the long night of their flight from the burning temple. Vessel stopped to rest.

"Surely they made it safely to the temple I sent them to on Big Sister Mountain?" His thoughts turned to his wise young friend, the librarian. "Jewel does not know our temple has been destroyed. Neither does my tonsure master."

Balance remained far to the south at his ancestral home. He had not returned to Tiger Empress, but he had answered the first letter from Vessel's own hand, the culmination of several calligraphy lessons with Jewel. Vessel reached into his satchel and pulled out a scroll of calligraphy, which he untied. It contained a copy of the Heart Sutra, written by Jewel and inscribed to Vessel.

Seated under a sprawling shade tree, Vessel read the sutra aloud in honor of the monk who had so patiently taught him to read and write the past few years.

"… Go, go, go beyond, go thoroughly beyond, and establish yourself in enlightenment…"

Vessel returned the scroll to his bag and stood up. He looked east down the road toward the place where he hoped his abbot was safe with the other refugee monks. "Further to the east is Jewel," he thought to himself. "Behind me, to the south, is my tonsure master. To the west is Tripitaka Monastery, whose new abbot sent me off with a blessing, and Monk Weng, my grandfather's friend. Close by at my center are the graves of my parents and brother."

"I am not alone," Vessel said aloud, and turned north toward Hao.

His confidence left him when the city walls came in sight and Vessel realized that the countryside was completely empty, the huge metal-studded gate doors shut tight in broad daylight. It was unnatural and could only mean that the imperial army was somewhere nearby. There would soon be a battle over control of Hao. Vessel's throat went dry and he reached into his robe for his grandfather's talisman, squeezing it tight. At least the arched bridge over the moat had not been raised. When Vessel reached the top of the arch, he heard a strange sound. He glanced up and realized it was the sound of arrows being fitted into bows by archers along the top of the wall.

Vessel tucked the talisman away and cleared his throat. He raised his red turban above his head.

"I am Vermillion Vessel, a monk from Tiger Empress. I've come to offer my allegiance to the leaders of the Red Turbans," he yelled out.

No response. The bows stayed taut. Vessel kept his feet

planted on the bridge and tried again.

"Tiger Empress Temple sits above my home village, Lone Hamlet. Perhaps some of you are from this village, perhaps you know Harmony Tang of Lone Hamlet, an old friend from my youth. He invited me to come here and serve his master, Commander Guo."

Nothing happened at first, but when Vessel refused to move, a voice finally called out from behind the gate.

"We burned down Tiger Empress. That was several days ago. You are a spy."

Vessel stayed put, wondering if the gate guards were Harmony's friends or enemies. However, he had drawn a retort where he had expected no response at all, and feared an arrow.

After a few minutes, a small side door tucked into a leaf of the mighty gate creaked open and two large guards, armed with clubs, rushed at him. They grabbed Vessel and dragged him back through the side door. Inside the dark gateway interior, in a passageway leading through the packed-earth city walls, Vessel could not make out anything more than shapes of men. At the end of the passage, he could see daylight streaming in through the final archway. The entrance to Hao.

Vessel's arms were wrenched behind his back and tied with a thick rope, which was looped around his neck. He was pushed into a cell and the door was locked, but not before he heard one of the men shout out an order.

"Send a messenger to the Commander to see what's to be done with this one."

Vessel stood waiting in the dark, but nothing happened. He shuffled around the room until he hit a wall and leaned against it. Still nothing happened. Vessel sank to the dank ground and eventually dozed. He awoke at the sound of the drums in the city drum tower beating out the night watch times. Later, Vessel strained to decipher the muffled sounds of the guards' voices and guessed that a day had passed. He had spent many hours seated in meditation, his hands tied behind his back. He shrugged his shoulders to make his talisman tap against his chest until he felt satisfied that it had not been damaged by the rough treatment of the guards.

Memories of his lost family members drifted through his mind. His mother at her loom, his smiling sister Lotus, childhood games with Radish — these were a comfort, but other thoughts, especially of the plague deaths, gathered force with the surrounding gloom. Tears ran down his cheeks, but he could not wipe at them. He wondered about Cinnabar and her father and Cricket. The troubling memories entwined with the thought of his temple in ruins and his monk brothers scattered.

"I am seeking to join the very rebels who burned down my temple," he said aloud to himself, several times, incredulous.

He sifted through images from the escape that had ended in the Chive Mountain caves. He remembered kneeling at his abbot's feet on a moonlit path, and seeing his abbot's frown of confusion over why they were parting. He remembered the gliding star, the summons from Heaven to make a decision. Above all, he remembered the divination shell standing miraculously upright in an unmistakable instruction to set aside his monk robes and join a martial cause. Everything has been leading to this.

Vessel was startled from his reverie by the sound of a key turning in a lock. The cell door creaked open and a form appeared. An arm raked the air until it struck Vessel and could pull him out.

"What am I to do with this ugly monk?" yelled the guard.

"One of Commander Guo's men is asking for him," came the shouted instruction from a soldier Vessel could not see.

The guard pushed Vessel along the streets, drawing curious

glances and unfriendly taunts. They had not gone far when Vessel heard his childhood name.

"Fortune!"

"Eh?" the guard stopped as Harmony came rushing toward them.

"Why have you tied him up?" Harmony shouted. "Why did it take so long to report this monk's arrival? Cut these ropes!"

The guard spat near Harmony's feet.

"Who are you to boss me around?" he asked, giving Vessel a shove that forced him to stumble.

Harmony moved menacingly toward the guard, but decided it would not be wise to start a fight. Instead he threw a handful of copper coins at the guard.

"Get out of here," he growled as soon as the guard finished removing the ropes from Vessel.

The guard snickered and sauntered off, but not before leaning down to pick up the coins and store them away in his belt. Harmony took Vessel's sleeve and hustled his friend away, ushering him into his own room.

"Wait here," he said after setting out a stool and insisting that Vessel take a seat.

Left alone in the small room, Vessel breathed deeply, relieved to have survived entry into Hao. Harmony had rushed off to a nearby canteen. He soon returned, like a good host, with a jug of wine in one hand and, in the other, a heaping bowl of noodle soup, two meat-filled buns balanced on top. He handed the bowl to his guest.

Vessel set the buns aside and hungrily gulped down the noodles. Then he sniffed at the meat-buns and turned one in his fingers, considering his monk vows even as his saliva filled his mouth and his stomach churned. His time as a monk had come to an end. And now he was confronted by a meat bun, a small, doughy emblem of the secular life. Vessel pondered it, but not for long. He opened his mouth and bit deep into the steamed bread, relishing the spicy forbidden flavor of the pork filling. He closed his eyes and hummed with pleasure, causing Harmony to burst out laughing.

"Was it some of Commander Guo's men who burned down my temple?" Vessel finally asked.

"It was not," Harmony replied. He folded his arms and offered no further information.

"And so," Vessel pointed his chopsticks at Harmony. "Are you going to let me know who King Yama will be sending to the deepest hell?"

Harmony raised his eyebrows. "Learned monk, who seems not really a monk, what punishment would the king of the underworld order for burning down a temple?"

"Being forced to herd fiery hell-goats for Old Wolf!" Vessel answered.

This made Harmony laugh all the more. "I have not thought of Old Wolf in years," he said. "What a mean son-of-a-whore he was. But forget about him. Let me tell you what I know. Commander Guo captured Hao only about a month ago. The magistrate had not bothered to set up any defense and the city was taken as easily as you turn over your hand. There's an imperial unit that's said to be preparing a siege, but so far they have made no move other than to pay anyone who turns in so-called 'Red Turbans.'"

"The countryside was deserted when I walked to Hao."

"Hah! You're lucky no one grabbed you and tried to sell you to the Mongols," Harmony said. "Well, my commander captured Hao together with his brother-in-law and with another man, Commander Sun, who we do not trust. This Commander Sun talks to any who would listen about the Maitreya coming. Have you heard of this too?"

Vessel nodded. "During the fall and winter, villagers started to come to Tiger Empress and talk of rebellions," he said. "Then an outsider who we'd never heard of came to the temple. He sounded like others I'd come across in my travels..." Vessel broke off, remembering the villagers at White Pine, eager to hear more about how to rebel. "I told the abbot that such monks were dangerous and would bring the wrath of the authorities on us. Our abbot sent the monk away and had our Maitreya altar closed off to the public."

Harmony nodded slowly. He looked at his feet and sighed.

"Ah, Fortune," his voice was soft. "That outsider ran straight to Hao and found this same Commander Sun who I've been telling you about. They are both from Ying."

"My abbot was worried about what that monk would do next," mused Fortune. "I should have been more concerned."

"Yes," said Harmony. He glanced at the door to make sure nobody was eavesdropping before continuing. "Then, at about the same time, one of Commander Sun's men broke into my room to try to steal my arrows, though I caught him, the dog's leg, and broke all of his fingers."

Harmony sneered and shook his head, still angry at the thief.

"Somehow he snatched your reply to my letter, without my noticing until it was too late. He took it straight to the monk and Commander Sun. The monk convinced Commander Sun to attack your temple and make an example of your abbot and raid your storage hall, because we are always low on rations. That's what I rode out to warn you about the night your temple burned. It's a good thing you all left right away."

"But how did you learn of it beforehand?"

"One of Commander Sun's men came to the stable while I was there," Harmony replied. "He demanded a horse. Commander

Guo was gone somewhere that evening with one of his sons, but his brother-in-law gave permission, not realizing what the horse was going to be used for. When I asked the man how far the horse would need to ride, he said far enough to raid a temple in Lone Hamlet. Well, there is only one temple in Lone Hamlet! I did not wait for Commander Guo to return, I saddled my horse and rode to Tiger Empress. I saw the raiding party on my way back, though they did not see me. It was Sun's men who were guarding the gate when you showed up here."

Vessel studied his old friend. Harmony was dressed like a cavalry soldier, with a short jacket that had tight sleeves and was tied by a wide sash. His trousers were tucked at his knees into his leggings. He did not carry a sword, but two bows hung from hooks on one wall, above a Mongol-style quiver of arrows. A red-tasseled cloth cap held his topknot in place. Harmony was like a warhorse, strong and impatient. Now his eyes narrowed as he described the reaction of the imperial army to the sudden sprouting of Red Turban rebellions.

"It is said that in Xuzhou, the canal city that feeds the capital, a group of men disguised themselves as river channel diggers and captured the city in a single evening!"

Harmony launched into a ditty:

> The Grand Canal has been cut in two
> No more grain for fat officials in Dadu.

Vessel set down his chopsticks, thinking of the Mongol cavalry soldier his old friend had once revered.

"And what of your Uncle Buqa?" he asked.

Harmony stopped singing and grimaced. He dropped his hands into his lap and studied them with a sober expression.

"I went to the Mongol camp, but my uncle would not

acknowledge me," Harmony said in a flat voice. "So I stole his best yearling and rode off with it. That was already a long time ago."

Harmony shook his head and then his devilish grin reappeared. He glanced sideways at Vessel. "Do you know people think I am a Mongol? It's because I ride like one."

"That is because you are the Number One Stallion under Heaven!"

Harmony's grin broke into laughter. "I always liked that title!"

He gazed at the ceiling, lost in his thoughts.

"Remember when Old Wolf sent us off to Chive Mountain and we met up with those herders from Perpetual Harvest Ward? What was the name of the youngest boy?"

"Xu Da," Vessel said, without hesitating. "I've often wondered what became of him."

"Did we give him a nickname?"

"No, but he was clever, too clever for his cousins. He could play chess without a chess set," Vessel recalled, shaking his head, still incredulous. "Maybe he has become the Number One Chess Player under Heaven. We should try to find him again."

"We will," said Harmony.

Vessel swallowed the last meat bun and then wagged a finger at Harmony, "But you haven't finished your own story."

Harmony nodded. "Well, I found another cavalry unit and joined it. I looked for a chance to meet up with my uncle and challenge him, but then I lost interest in all that. Eventually, I brought my horse — the same one I stole from my uncle — to Ding, where I presented it to Commander Guo, though at the time he was just a wealthy lord known for his stable. He took me in and has treated me well. So now I am his groom."

"So you went from an imperial army cavalry unit to a Red Turban band of heroes?"

Harmony pursed his lips. "Not everyone here is a hero," he noted. "And it didn't happen like that. Commander Guo did not want to be a rebel at first. He started out wanting to restore order when things got so out of hand. It was only later that he and the others raised the banner for restoring the Song…"

"What do you mean, restoring the Song?" Vessel interrupted.

"That's what the banners all say. Didn't you see them on the city walls? We are the flying dragons who will bring back the Great Song Dynasty."

"I did not have time to read the banners with all those arrows pointing down at me."

Vessel pressed his hand against his talisman, so that he could feel it against his chest, but decided not to reveal it yet.

"Do you know that when my grandfather was about our age, he fought for the Song?"

Harmony smiled. "I only remember that you admired General Yue Fei. And now we can both fight together in his name."

"I wonder what my grandfather would make of raising Song banners after all this time?" Vessel wondered aloud, shaking his head.

Harmony took two bowls from his cupboard and set them on his table, hoisting the jug of wine from the canteen. He filled the two bowls and presented the first one to Vessel. Then Harmony took his own bowl in both hands and stood up.

"Let us drink to the end of your days as a monk!"

Vessel smiled, but it was a sad, weak kind of smile. Almost eight years had passed since that desperate day in Lone Hamlet when Second Chao walked him to Tiger Empress Temple. Eight years! The monks had been like brothers and fathers to Vessel. He thought of Jewel carving spirit tablets and teaching him how to read and write. He thought of the monks at Spirit Mountain shielding him from the zealous disciple of Monk Peng, and all the many lessons learned at Tripitaka and at Central Peak. The monks had fed Vessel — when there was food — and sheltered him during his journeys. They had protected him from harm and forgiven his transgressions. As a member of their fold, he had gained insight into Heaven's intentions.

Vessel slowly rose to his feet and took his bowl of wine in both hands, just like Harmony.

Vessel thought of his Grandfather Chen fighting at Yashan, and the divining shell standing on its end. "Maybe you have a martial fate," Monk Weng had said. His unavoidable truth.

Vessel closed his eyes and murmured a silent prayer to the Buddha, thanking all the monks who had shown him kindness: "My hair may grow out, but at its roots will always be the incense scars reminding me of my days as a monk. Three rows of three — to remind me of the Three Jewels. Take refuge in the Buddha, take refuge in the teaching, take refuge in the disciples."

Then Vessel opened his eyes.

But he can no longer be addressed as Vessel. He is no longer a monk. He is Fortune once again.

Fortune lifted his bowl and looked toward Heaven.

"To righteousness!" he declared.

Both he and Harmony drained their bowls.

EPILOGUE

THE CHANCELLOR OFFERS HIS EDITS

Yingtian, capital of the Ming Dynasty, known today as the city of Nanjing.
The tenth year of Hongwu (1377).

THE EMPEROR ushered in Song Lian, chancellor of the Hanlin Academy, and wasted no time on formalities. Gesturing at the document in Song Lian's hands, the emperor asked for comments.

"As you can see, I have written most of it. What do you think?" the emperor asked.

Song Lian unrolled the scroll onto the emperor's writing desk, placing weights on each end of the rice paper. "I have only made a few changes," he said.

The emperor eagerly leaned forward to study the eminent scholar's corrections to the revised text for the Imperial Tomb Tablet, which would be carved into stone and placed in the imperial cemetery near the new city of Fengyang, along the south bank of the Huai River. It would replace the original text by a court historian, which the emperor had found insufficient.

The emperor pointed at the line in his revision about how the landlord shouted arrogantly over a burial place. "You do not think it too vulgar to use the phrase 'ang-ang'?" he asked.

Song Lian shook his head. "It seems correct to me because it makes the landlord sound petty."

"He was more than petty."

"He was," Song Lian agreed.

The chancellor noted some minor corrections here and there and the emperor nodded his head in agreement with each.

The emperor pointed to circles next to the phrase about parting from his second brother after the plague deaths, "Under the bright sun in Heaven our sorrow rent our hearts. Elder and younger, we took separate paths, with even distant Heaven moved by our sorrow."

"Is it a correction?" the emperor asked.

"No, your majesty," Song Lian replied. "I marked that phrase because I found it so moving."

"Thank you," said the emperor, his voice softening. "Do you know – that was the last time I ever saw that brother."

Song Lian waited, quiet but attentive, as the emperor stared out the window latticework. After a few moments, the emperor turned back and continued.

"And do you know that the Imperial Tomb Tablet will be erected before the burial site for my parents and oldest brother and nephew, next to a matching tablet that will be just as large and just as majestic, but with no text cut into it? It will be called the Wordless Tablet to express the idea that no mere words can fully convey my gratitude to my parents."

"Your majesty, the revisions have changed the original text into the words of a filial son," Song Lian said, but then he hesitated. "However..."

The emperor leaned toward him with an expression of concern.

"Yes?"

"You said it was almost finished," Song Lian noted, looking confused. "But you have not said anything yet about the founding of the dynasty."

The emperor smiled and waved his hand in a dismissive

gesture.

"I will add a few more lines about all that," he said. "I will mention my brave generals — Xu Da and Harmony Tang — and my wise strategists, including you. But that is the easy part. The spirits of my family will not want to have me going on and on about my accomplishments."

The emperor gazed back at the scroll and sighed, his expression once again turning pensive. He reached across the table to select another sheet of paper, which contained only a few lines. The calligraphy on this sheet was uneven, as if his brush had wavered.

"It is the conclusion," the emperor said. "After I finish the part about the founding, I will end with this. You are the first to read it."

Song Lian scanned the text to the end. He stepped back from the table and clasped his hands, raising his eyes to meet the emperor's glance.

"Your majesty, it is worthy."

The emperor took a deep breath, and then read the short passage aloud in his famously rich and measured voice, flavored with the accent of the Huai River Valley:

Thinking of my parents' hardships I know I can never repay their limitless kindness.
If the generations of this dynasty are ordained by Heaven,
they will be righteous and endure.
With tears falling on my brush,
I relate my difficulties and instruct my heirs to nurture prosperity.
I bow down, and bow down again,
desiring to offer up this text for time everlasting.

The two stood in silence, side by side, for several moments after the recitation ended. The scholar contemplated the lines of calligraphy, while the emperor absently reached for the talisman around his neck. Then he laughed.

"It's an old habit," he said.

"What is, your majesty?"

"Reaching for my talisman when I think about my family," the emperor replied. "But it's long gone. When I established my capital city here, right before the founding of the dynasty, I found a place for it. I found a place my grandfather would approve of, a safe resting place."

The emperor noticed a blank look on Song Lian's face.

"Chancellor Song, surely you know about my talisman?"

"Your majesty, you are speaking of your Grandfather Chen, the Posthumous Lord of Yang?"

"Yes, of course. You helped me select his posthumous title and write his epitaph."

"Your majesty, I have heard mention of your necklace, but I have never seen it and I have never heard where you placed it –"

The emperor laughed and patted Song Lian's arm, indicating that it was time for them to leave.

"That was all before I met you," he said. "The story of where I put my talisman is a good one. But it's a story for another day."

APPENDIX

The Imperial Tomb Tablet of the Great Ming
大明皇陵之碑

The Imperial Tomb Tablet of the Great Ming is encased in glass and covered by a pagoda, but the weather-beaten stele still stands, borne on the back of a stone turtle. And, as was indicated in the Prologue and Epilogue, the surviving text is the emperor's personal revision of an epitaph composed by the scholar and historian Wei Su 危素 (1303-72). The emperor explained in his introduction, "the original text for the Imperial Tomb Tablet had been embellished by the Confucian ministers to the point that I feared it would not sufficiently admonish later generations and descendants."

You can visit the tablet at a park southwest of the town of Fengyang 鳳陽 in northern Anhui Province, at the Ming Huangling 明皇陵, or the imperial tomb for the Ming founder's family.

Dating to the 11ᵗʰ year of the Hongwu Era, or 1378, the emperor's text contains five lines of introduction followed by 96 rhymed lines of text.

The first 53 rhymed lines provide the framework for this story:

昔我父皇寓居是方

In former times, my imperial father lived in this place;

農業艱辛朝夕彷徨

He endured the hardships of agriculture, working day and night, always worrying.

俄爾天災流行眷屬罹殃

All at once, calamities gripped the land and my family met with disaster.

皇考終於六十有四皇妣五十有九而亡

My imperial father had reached the age of 64, and my imperial mother 59, when they perished;

孟兄先死合家守喪

My eldest brother was keeping vigil with the family before he died.

田主德不我顧呼叱昂昂

Our landlord would not attend to our needs, carrying on with his arrogant shouting;

既不與地鄰里惆悵

Our neighbors were saddened that we had not been offered a burial plot.

忽伊兄之慷慨惠此黃壤

To our surprise, the landlord's elder brother was generous to us, and kindly offered some yellow earth.

殯無棺槨被體惡裳

Carried to the grave with no coffins, the bodies were shrouded only in rags;

浮掩三尺奠何殽漿

They float concealed three feet under, how could there be proper food and drink offerings?

既葬之後家道惶惶

After the burial, the path before us was fraught with suffering and worries.

仲兄少弱生計不張

My second brother was young and frail, with no livelihood to depend on.

孟嫂携幼東歸故鄉

Eldest sister-in-law had taken her children in hand and headed east to return to her own village.

值天無雨遺蝗騰翔

Heaven offered no rain, allowing the locusts to rise and circle in the air.

里人缺食草木為糧

In my village, food was scarce, with grasses and bark serving as nourishment.

予亦何有心驚若狂

As for myself, what did I have but fear to the point of madness?

乃與兄計如何是常

Therefore I made plans with my second brother about what would make sense.

兄云去此各度凶荒

He said he would leave, so that we each could find a place to endure the fearsome drought.

兄為我哭我為兄傷

My brother wept for me, and I grieved for my brother,

皇天白日泣斷心腸

Under the bright sun in Heaven our sorrow rent our hearts.

兄弟異路哀動遙蒼

Elder and younger, we took separate paths, with even distant Heaven moved by our sorrow.

汪氏老母為我籌量

Old Mother Wang helped me prepare a temple offering,

遣子相送備醴馨香

She sent her son to accompany me, laden with sweet wine and incense.

空門禮佛出入僧房

I underwent the Buddhist rites and entered the monk's world.

居未兩月寺主封倉

I had not lived at the temple for even two months when the abbot had to close the empty granary.

眾各為計雲水飄颺

Everyone made their own plans and the wandering monks drifted apart.

我何作為百無所長

As for me, what was I to do? I had no skills.

依親自辱仰天茫茫

Turning to my relatives would have been shameful, so I could only raise my face to boundless Heaven.

既非可倚侶影相將

With nothing to rely on, my shadow became my companion.

突朝煙而急進幕投古寺以趨蹌

In the mornings I would make my way through the mist, while in the evenings I would seek an old temple for lodging.

仰穹崖崔嵬而倚碧聽猿啼夜月而淒涼

Facing a lofty precipice, I would rest on the green moss; listening to the night calls of the monkeys, I felt cold and desolate.

魂悠悠而覓父母無有志落魄而倘佯

My spirit fretted and sought out my father and mother, but to no avail; my will ebbed and I wandered aimlessly.

西風鶴唳俄淅瀝以飛霜

The west wind carries the crane's cry and suddenly a bird appears flying through the frosty air;

身如蓬逐風而不止心滾滾乎沸湯

Like tumbleweed, I followed the wind and could not stop; my heart churned like boiling water.

一浮雲乎三載年方二十而強

Three years passed like floating clouds, until I was just over 20 years old.

時乃長淮盜起民生攘攘

At that time, bandits arose along the Yangtze and the Huai rivers, and the lives of the people became chaotic.

於是思親之心昭著日遙眄乎家邦

My thoughts turned toward my father and all became clear as I glanced with anticipation toward my distant home.

已而既歸仍復業於於皇

Thus I returned to my native place to resume my role at Tiger Empress Temple.

住方三載而又雄者跳梁

I spent three years at the temple, a time when strongmen were once again stirring things up;

初起汝穎次及鳳陽之南廂

They rose from Ru and Ying and then reached the southern gate of Fengyang.

未幾陷城深高城隍

The city was taken by only a few who surmounted the walls and moats;

拒守不去號令彰彰

They encountered no defenders and took clear control.

友人寄書云及趨降

A friend sent me a letter saying that I should hasten to submit;

既憂且懼無可籌詳

But I was too worried and afraid to make any plans.

傍有覺者將欲聲揚

Others were aware of the letter and wanted to reveal its contents.

當此之際逼迫而無已試與知者相商

At this point I was compelled to make a decision, so I consulted the one who was knowledgeable.

乃告之曰果束手以待罪亦奮臂而相戕

I said to this person, "I can either have my hands bound like a criminal, or raise my arms in resistance and end up killed!"

知者為我畫計且禱陰以默相

The knowledgeable one made plans for me, and advised that I pray in secret and think it over.

如其言往卜去守之何祥

Following this advice, I went to divine whether fleeing or guarding the temple was the most auspicious choice.

神乃陰陰乎有警其氣郁郁乎洋洋

The divinity answered with a yin-yin reply as a warning, the clouds of incense billowing.

卜逃卜守則不吉將就凶而不妨

Escaping or guarding, both were inauspicious; then I understood and did not try to interfere.

即起趨降而附城幾被無知而創

I hastened to the city gates to pledge allegiance, but some of the gate guards did not know who I was and harmed me.

少頃獲釋身體安康

After some time, I was released and ready, my health restored.

The remaining 43 lines will be the basis for future volumes in this story.

AUTHOR'S NOTES

PLACES

Besides the imperial tomb for the Ming founder's family, here is more information about other locations featured in this story, in order of appearance:

- Yashan (also sometimes spelled Yaishan) 崖山, the location of the last stand of the Song Dynasty navy, is commemorated at a tourist zone in Jiangmen's Xinhui District 江門市新會區, Guangdong Province.
- Chive Mountain 韭山, which is spelled Jiushan in Chinese pinyin, is located south of Fengyang and is known for its limestone caves and namesake greens.
- Chanku Temple 禅窟寺, is near Chive Mountain and contains the enchanting "wolf-path gorge 狼巷迷谷."
- Tiger Empress Temple 於皇寺 took its name from an old Chu word for tigers, 於菟 (pronounced Wutu). I am indebted to Xia Yurun for the stories about its origins. Nothing remains of it today beyond some broken stones and an ancient well that villagers say marks the place where the Ming founder served as a novice.
- Spirit Mountain Temple 靈山寺 (Lingshan Si) is located near the city of Xinyang 信陽 in Henan Province. Several stories are still told about Zhu Yuanzhang being sheltered at this temple during his rise to power.
- The Gaocheng Astronomical Observatory, also known

as the Dengfeng Observatory 登封觀星台, is a UNESCO World Heritage site and lies in Gaocheng Township 告成鎮, southeast of Dengfeng City in Henan Province. It was built by the Yuan astronomer Guo Shoujing 郭守敬 in 1279.

- Central Peak Temple 中嶽廟 (Zhongyue Miao), to the east of Dengfeng, is a Daoist temple located in the Songshan 嵩山 range, one of the five sacred mountains of Daoism.

Sources:

Zhu Yuanzhang's revision of the Imperial Tomb Tablet is the main source for my story. In translating and understanding this important text, I relied on the Tomb Tablet annotations by the Fengyang local historian Wang Jianying, and also on Wu Han's seminal 1949 biography of the Ming founder. Romeyn Taylor's article, "Ming T'ai-Tsu's Story of a Dream" provides a full translation and annotation of another key text by Zhu Yuanzhang, in which the Ming founder more fully describes his fateful decision prayer – when the divination shell stood erect and convinced him to join the Red Turbans. But readers of this important article will then want to consult Hoklam Chan's work, which stresses the role of mythology in presenting the stories of dynastic founders, even when it is the founder himself who is telling the story.

The early life of the Ming founder is replete with famous stories that were not documented in the official histories or writings by Zhu Yuanzhang. I have included a few in my tale that I consider revealing about Zhu Yuanzhang's place in Chinese history – including his pockmarked face, his instigating a pack of herders to eat a calf, and his beating of the temple god during his novitiate.

Zhu Yuanzhang has mentioned in his writings that, during

his wandering years, he encountered people caught up in the rebellions of the late Yuan. However, he did not specifically cite the monk Peng Yingyu 彭瑩玉, who is referred to in this story and who led an unsuccessful rebellion in Jiangxi Province in 1338 before escaping north to the Huai river region.

All family members who appear in this story are listed in Zhu genealogies, though for most not much is known beyond their names (the biography for Grandfather Chen in the official history of the Ming states that he was a fortune teller and fought for the Song at Yashan). Other historical figures, in order of appearance and with dates if known, include:

- The Song Dynasty General Yue Fei 岳飛 (1103-1142)
- Old Mother Wang 汪氏老母 and her sons
- Tang He 湯和 (1326-95, called Harmony in this story) and Xu Da 徐達 (1332-85), who became leading Ming generals
- The evil landlord Liu De 劉德 (called Squire Lin in this story), and the much kinder Liu Jizu 劉繼祖 (called Lin Ji here). After becoming emperor, Zhu Yuanzhang granted Liu Jizu the title of Yihui Marquis and wrote an edict saying, "At the time when I was struggling over my parents' corpses, finding a place for them was difficult, and you exhibited a heart of great kindness and benevolence, offering your fertile soil. To see such benevolence, how could I forget it?"
- Tiger Empress Abbot Dezhu 得祝 and Head Monk Gaobin 高斌 (who are referred to here as Prayerful Virtue and Exalted Balance)
- Red Turban leaders in Hao, Guo Zixing 郭子興 (1303-55) and Sun Deyai 孫德崖
- Hanling Academy Chancellor Song Lian 宋濂 (1310-81)

AUTHOR'S NOTES

For those who wish to read more about the facts, fictions and literature of Zhu Yuanzhang's China, here are key sources for this book:

1. Works in Chinese.

Wang Jianying 王劍英. *Ming Zhongdu Yanjiu* 明中都研究 (A study of the Ming central capital). Beijing: Zhongguo Qingnian Chuban She, 2005.

Wu Han 吳晗. *Zhu Yuanzhang Zhuan* 朱元璋傳 (Biography of Zhu Yuanzhang). Shanghai: Sanlian, 1949.

Xia Yurun 夏玉潤. *Zhu Yuanzhang yu Fengyang* 朱元璋與鳳陽 (Zhu Yuanzhang and Fengyang). Hefei: Huangshan Shushe, 2003.

2. Works in English.

Chan, Hok-lam and Laurie Dennis. "Frenzied Fictions: Popular Beliefs and Political Propaganda in the Written History of Ming Taizu." In *Long Live the Emperor! Uses of the Ming Founder across Six Centuries of East Asian History*, edited by Sarah Schneewind, pages 15-36. Minneapolis: Society for Ming Studies, 2008.

Davis, Richard L. *Wind Against the Mountain: The Crisis of Politics and Culture in Thirteenth-century China*. Cambridge: Harvard University Press, 1996.

Dennis, Laurie. *The Imperial Tomb Tablet of the Great Ming, with translation into English, annotations and commentary*. October 2017. Monograph is available for download as a PDF from the website: lauriedennis.com

Goodrich, L. Carrington, and Chaoying Fang, eds. *Dictionary of Ming Biography*. New York: Columbia University Press, 1976.

Little, Stephen, with Shawn Eichman, eds. *Taoism and the Arts of China*. Chicago: The Art Institute of Chicago in association with University of California Press, 2000.

Low, C.C., ed. *Yue Fei: Pictorial stories of the Great Chinese National Hero in English & Chinese*. Singapore: Canfonian, 1991. In three volumes.

Minford, John, and Joseph S.M. Lau, eds. *Classical Chinese Literature: An Anthology of Translations*. New York and Hong Kong: Columbia University Press and the Chinese University of Hong Kong Press, 2000.

Needham, Joseph, and Colin A. Ronan. *The Shorter Science and Civilisation in China: an Abridgement of Joseph Needham's Original Text, Volume* 2. Cambridge: Cambridge University Press, 1981. (See especially Chapter Two on astronomy.)

Needham, Joseph, and Francesca Bray. *Science and Civilisation in China, Volume 6, Part 2: Agriculture*. Cambridge: Cambridge University Press, 1986.

Overmyer, Daniel L. *Folk Buddhist Religion: Dissenting Sects in Late Traditional China*. Cambridge: Harvard University Press, 1976.

Prip-Møller, Johannes. *Chinese Buddhist Monasteries: Their Plan and Its Function as a Setting for Buddhist Monastic Life*. Hong Kong: Hong Kong University Press, 2d edition, 1967.

Schafer, Edward H. *Pacing the Void: T'ang Approaches to the Stars*. Berkeley: University of California Press, 1977.

Stephenson, Richard F., ed. *Oriental Astronomy: From Guo Shoujing to King Sejong*. Seoul: Yonsei University Press, 1997.

Taylor, Romeyn, "Ming T'ai-Tsu's Story of a Dream," *Monumenta Serica*, Vol 32, 1976, pages 1-20.

Ter Haar, Barend J. *The White Lotus Teachings in Chinese Religious History*. Leiden: E.J. Brill, 1992.

Welch, Holmes. *The Practice of Chinese Buddhism, 1900-1950*. Cambridge: Harvard University Press, 1967.

AUTHOR'S NOTES

3. Poems and songs quoted in the text, in whole or in part:
Chapter One: "South Sea" 南海 by Wen Tianxiang 文天祥 (1236-1283).
Chapter Two: To the Tune "The Charms of Niannu" 念奴嬌, 赤壁懷古 by Su Shi 蘇軾 (1037-1101).
Chapter Four: "Poem in Seven Paces" 七步詩 by Cao Zhi 曹植 (192-232).
Chapter Six: "Seven Songs Written during the Qianyuan Era while staying at Tonggu County" 乾元中寓居同谷縣作歌七首 #4 by Du Fu 杜甫 (712-770). "Bidding Elder Brother Goodbye" 送兄 by Qi Sui Nu 七歲女 (700s).
Chapter Seven: To the Tune "The River Runs Red" 滿江紅 by Yue Fei 岳飛 (1103-1142). To the Tune "Beautiful Lady Yu" 虞美人 by Li Yu 李煜 (937-978).
Chapter Eight: "Thinking of My Brothers on a Moonlit Night," 月夜憶舍弟, by Du Fu (cited above).
Chapter Eleven: *Book of Poetry* 詩經 #34 (earliest anthology of Chinese poetry, 12th to 7th century BCE).
Chapter Twelve: "Three Hundred Three Poems" 詩三百三首 #28 by Cold Mountain Master 寒山 (627-650).
Chapter Fifteen: "Yellow Crane Tower" 黃鶴樓 by Cui Hao 崔顥 (704-754). To the tune "Drunk in an Age of Peace" 醉太平 by Anonymous (my melody is a condensed and modified version of this popular Yuan Dynasty song). To the Tune "Crow Calls at Night" 烏夜啼 by Li Yu (cited above).
Chapter Sixteen: Quote from the Heart Sutra is based on the translation by the 14th Dalai Lama.

ACKNOWLEDGEMENTS

MANY PEOPLE have helped me in the writing of this book. Brave readers of early drafts included: Bob Anholt, Shireen Campbell, Bonnie Cronin, Lori Davis, Mark Dennis, Ted and Judy Farmer, Randy Harris, Gill Holland, Joanna Kakissis, Dawn Kotva, Valerie and Jerome Kyllo, Dave Porter, Richard Robinson, Sarah Schneewind, Kelli Schuster and Betty Ann Zeoli.

I am indebted to the many scholars of China who patiently answered all my questions, including Professors Fuji Lozada, Hun Lye and Shao Ping at Davidson College; Chen Huairen and Xia Yurun in Fengyang, Anhui Province; and the Ming triumvirate of Edward Farmer, the late Romeyn Taylor, and Ann Waltner at the University of Minnesota. It was my honor to be included in the 2006 conference, "Ming Taizu and his Times," held at the Chinese University of Hong Kong, where I served on a panel with one of the great scholars of the early Ming, the late Hoklam Chan, and benefitted from an extraordinary gathering of scholarship on Zhu Yuanzhang, all organized brilliantly by Professor Hung-lam Chu.

I also benefited immensely from my writer groups – starting with Kevin Bell, Lisa Schwartz Jewel and Vivian Shen in Davidson, N.C., and ending with Charity Eleson, William E. Lewis, and Paul Waldhart in Madison, Wisconsin. The annual UW-Madison Writers' Institute, and in particular Laurie Scheer, helped me understand how to think of my book as something that could be published. Author Jerry Shine in Somerville gave me sagely advice on pacing, while Selina Min Chen helped with the book title.

I would like to express appreciation for the following coffee shops: Someday Café in Somerville's Davis Square, Summit Coffee in Davidson, and Amélie's *French Bakery & Café in* Charlotte. Thanks also to the following libraries: Boston Public Library (and its splendid Bates Reading Room, where this book was launched), the Harvard Yenching Library, Davidson College's E.H. Little Library, Madison Public Library's Sequoya Branch, and UW-Madison's Memorial Library.

If not for Harry Miller, I would not have found my publisher, and without Graham Earnshaw of Earnshaw Books, my lifelong dream of publishing a novel would never have come true.

My children grew up with this book, and because it took so long to finish, they were able to help with production – Christina as a final reader and Kerry as a cover illustrator. My old friend, Donna Kelly – who was a classmate in my first Chinese class with Margaret Wong at Minneapolis Central High – came through as my photographer. Above all, two people were key to this project, from start to finish: my mother, Martha Harris (to whom this volume is dedicated), and my husband, Joe Dennis (my own personal and always amazing Ming scholar, and the creator of the Huai River Valley map), who never doubted my abilities and yet always voiced their honest opinions.

THE LACQUERED TALISMAN

About The Author

Laurie Dennis grew up in Illinois and Minnesota and has been studying Chinese since she was a high school freshman in Minneapolis. She has worked as a journalist in the U.S. and in Beijing, China, and she has traveled widely across China, including a research trip to Fengyang, Anhui Province, the birthplace of the founder of the Ming Dynasty. She currently resides in Madison, Wisconsin, where she lives with her husband and works on China programs for her alma mater, the University of Wisconsin-Madison. This is her first novel.